David Compton

# CLAXTON HALL

10-Digit ISBN 1-59113-849-3
13-Digit ISBN 978-1-59113-849-5



Printed in the United States of America.

The characters and events in this book are fictitious. Any similarity to real persons, living or dead, is coincidental and not intended by the author.

Booklocker.com, Inc.
2005

*for Carol, a teacher in her own right*

# Claxton Hall Heads of School

Obidiah Rue 1793-1795

Elijah Coombs 1795 (interim)

Matthew Caul 1795-1796

(school closed 1797-1798)

William Harrington 1798-1808

Howard Shackleton 1808-1826

(school closed 1826-1861)

Daniel Peabody 1861-1867 (military academy)

Horatio Worthington Bradley 1867-1871 (military academy)

Alonzo Record 1872-1900

Jeremiah Osgood Tremaine 1900-1906

Randall Franklin Butler 1906-1919

Samuel Forest 1919-1930

Marshall Thompson 1930-1951

Roger S. Nielsen 1951

Oliver Lawgood 1951-1952 (interim)

Everett Record 1952-1974

Robert Bosworth 1974-1980 (alumnus)

Elrond Young 1980-1988

James Thatcher 1988-1999

Elaine Brownsmith 1999-

# CLAXTON HALL

## Part I: 1791–1867

Claxton Hall is in Connecticut. Claxton Hall has always been in Connecticut, the wishes of its founders notwithstanding.

In 1791, the Rev. Obadiah Rue, perhaps alarmed by the recent turn of events in France, and perhaps fearing a spread of the general malaise across the Channel to his homeland, decided to decamp from his native England and seek his fortune in the former colonies. There are those who believe the move motivated by the purest of reasons: a desire to bring salvation to the heathen, who, it was said, peopled those verdant shores most densely. Other tongues, more scurrilous, attributed his hasty departure to other motives, less pure; pecuniary, perhaps, or even of a more intimate, personal nature. The Rev. Rue himself seems to have said that the opportunities offered by the emerging nation were simply not to be passed over lightly, and that a man could still procure himself "a bit of coin" without too much effort. History, unhappily, has not recorded the real reason.

Upon his arrival in Boston, however, the Rev. Mr. Rue found no streets paved in gold, nor, indeed, anyone in a great hurry to press a bag of such riches into his hand. He therefore betook himself westward, and a little south, not being of a mind to remain by the sea which had offered him not a little discomfort on the voyage over.

Whatever the circumstances, it chanced that the worthy Rev. Rue found himself in a fair spot, located somewhere near the confluence of the Connecticut and Farmington rivers. He could not find employment in this picturesque area, however, no church being of a mind to take him into their employ, for reasons again unknown. At this point, the Rev. Mr. Rue, finding himself bereft of financial means (those same evil-wagging tongues would have him prey to the Demon Gambling), he decided to undertake an enterprise of his own making, to wit: to found, among the maples lining the banks of the aforesaid rivers, an Academy, or, to be more precise, an Institution of Learning for Young Gentlemen, he having found prospective pupils among the local populace; young rascals, it would seem, in sore need of discipline and learning, for America was still a rough, young country, and many of its first generation settlers yearned for the comforts and advantages of a society they had left behind in His Majesty's care.

In its first year of existence, 1793, there were but four students at the Rue Literary Institute, only one of whom was a boarder, a gangly lad of some sixteen years who took up residence in the Rev. Rue's parlor, on a sofa. For this privilege, he paid the princely sum of four pounds six per term, meals and instruction included.

The Rev. Rue served as the entire staff of the Institute in its first years: headmaster, teacher, cook. The curriculum was founded upon Latin, Greek and Rhetoric, subjects in which the principal felt fairly well-versed. He also endeavored to impart such knowledge of Elementary Mathematics as he himself possessed, and some rudiments of Spelling, which was not entirely successful, the Rev. Rue being himself an indifferent speller. As to Science or History, he had not a whit of either; neither, therefore, had his students.

Lessons were conducted in the Rev. Mr. Rue's house, in that selfsame parlor which served his boarder so elegantly as dormitory. There were no textbooks, these being beyond the Reverend's limited means, but the pupils did have copybooks, into which they wrote laboriously, setting down the lectures. The lectures, themselves, alas, varied neither in substance nor in style, being, as it may be guessed, made up, for the most part, of the Rev. Mr. Rue's former sermons, which made up in length what they lacked in matter. The teacher himself had but a scrap of slate onto which to copy those points he felt especially relevant.

For whatever reason, the Institute flourished, and the number of enrolled students doubled the second year, making the house entirely unsuitable, due to lack of space. The Rev. Mr. Rue therefore rented an old house, not too well kept up, from the heirs of Mr. James Claxton, recently deceased. While this provided him with the needed space, it did not come equipped with the amenities of the former school building, lacking in such niceties as a complete roof over the upstairs. Much of what the Rev. Mr. Rue would normally have regarded as profit that winter literally went up in smoke, the amount of wood consumed by the small stove which served as furnace for the chamber being prodigious. It is said that, towards the end of the winter term, wood being in scant supply, a couple of the more enterprising pupils remedied the situation by supplying their small stove with copious fuel in the form of bundles of the Rev. Rue's sermons, which he had left thoughtlessly lying about.

It was perhaps these conditions which led to his untimely demise in the winter of 1795, due, according to the local physician, to consumption, but attributed (at least in part, and only by some locals) to an over-familiarity with the Demon Rum.

Elijah Coombs, father of one of the late Rev. Mr. Rue's pupils, took upon himself the task of continuing the boys' education, perhaps seeing some small merit in what his predecessor had been trying to accomplish. Though hardly prosperous, he had some small amount of wealth—a few guineas brought over from his former homeland—and he was able to execute some small repairs to the school building, making it tolerable, if not comfortable, for the remainder of the winter. He had, as it turned out, no objection to the boys' continuing to use the late Mr. Rue's manuscripts as fuel, a selfless act for which history may be profoundly grateful to him. In the meantime, a call went out for a new schoolmaster.

It was answered (providentially, according to some) by Matthew Caul, an individual of sober dress and severe mien. Indeed, while history has not seen fit to provide us with any likeness whatsoever of the late lamented Rev. Obadiah Rue, we do have one of Mr. Caul, a period *eau-forte* discovered some years back in the basement of the local library. It is yellowed and stained, and the features somewhat blurred, but it does depict an individual of rather severe aspect, an untidy shock of hair and piercing gaze, a portrait which would seem to penetrate to one's very soul, there to ferret out any misdeeds or peccadilloes one might have carefully hidden away in one's youth. Mr. Caul, according to reports, was tall and angular, awkward in gesture and hesitant in speech. He was, nevertheless, the only one applying for the position, and thus the maintenance of Claxton Hall (as the school building had come to be known) and its charges were entrusted to his care.

Mr. Caul was headmaster (indeed, the only member of the faculty) for about a year and a half. During the first part of his tenure, the institution and its twelve young men seemed to do quite well: he induced the father of one of his students, Jakob Huis, to donate to the school the magnificent sum of one hundred pounds, with which Mr. Caul purchased about a dozen volumes, the beginnings of a modest library, and began to effect some much needed repairs on the building itself, beginning with the addition of a fireplace to the main room. At the same time, he removed himself to a stone cottage a little ways distant, so that the boarding students, now four in number, might have his old room, which was converted into a sort of dormitory. He also brought some modifications to the curriculum, suppressing Rhetoric in favor of Declamation, and adding a course which he called Natural Science, though most of the material seemed to be drawn rather freely from the Book of Genesis. He also raised the tuition to eight pounds, six shillings, an increase which caused two families to promptly withdraw their sons.

During the winter of 1796, however, some other families began publicly to express some grave concerns about the school in general and Mr. Caul in particular. Their sons were returning home in the gray of a winter's eve, blue with cold and bearing marks upon their heads and hands. It was known that Mr. Caul made rather free use of his wooden ruler upon recalcitrant students, a fact to which not many parents would normally object, but at least two families, the Holloways and the Phersons, thought that this treatment went well beyond the bounds or normal punishment. If their sons needed whipping, so be it, but the schoolmaster should have at least used a willow switch on those parts of the anatomy not normally in public view, and not belabor them about the head and shoulders in a manner dangerous to life and limb. In addition, the same boys (and one or two others, as it later turned out) complained that all they had to eat for the noon-time meal was a bit of watery gruel, and none too warm at that, while the schoolmaster partook of roast chicken and kidney pie, washed down with a good measure of ale, or, if the weather were particularly bad, a draught of port. He occupied the armchair by the fire, while the boys were huddled together in the coldest part of the room, squabbling over a crust of bread. The interns, as the boys called the boarders, looked in even worse shape.

For a while, their remarks were laid to adolescent complaining, for it is a fact that some boys, having everything, will complain of everything, while others, having naught, have nothing to complain of. But the complaints became more numerous and more vociferous and the charges attached to Mr. Caul more serious, to the point where the two aforementioned families thought they must lay these charges before the vicar, who, in the absence of sheriff or constable, acted as judge in some local matters. The vicar, the Rev. John Goodman, took it under advisement, and, after a period of due deliberation said that they might confront Mr. Caul with the accusations and at least demand some sort of explanation, if not a reckoning.

It was thus that a small committee consisting of the vicar and the two fathers in question presented themselves at the stone cottage on the evening of 31 December 1796. They were most surprised and chagrined to find the house empty and cold, deserted apparently at least a day before, all belongings having departed with the previous tenant. Of the remainder of the hundred pounds, some eighty-six by the reckoning of Miller Trelaine, not a single penny remained, nor was any trace ever found of a bit of that tidy sum, vanished as it was in the wake of Matthew Caul. The school was promptly closed and its pupils reabsorbed into the life of the community.

In the spring of 1797, however, that same community was granted a charter and started a new existence under the name of Upper Granby Lake, which name, if we can believe accounts of that period, was a sort of compromise arrived at after a frenzied period of town meetings and not a few heated arguments among the supporters of Lakeville (already claimed, alas), the proponents of New Granby and those who wished (and lobbied) for Upper York (the appellation New York sounding, apparently, rather frivolous). In any case, the newly formed Baptist Church, having gotten a bit carried away on the idea of incorporation, proposed to reopen the school, incorporating it under the direction of a board of governors, drawn, not surprisingly, from its own leaders. The idea was approved because only those who had proposed it in the first place were permitted to vote thereupon.

Exactly why the wooden building housing the former school should choose that moment to burn down will probably never be determined to anyone's satisfaction. One faction contended that it was the poor design of the fireplace Mr. Caul had had installed: he had undoubtedly used cheap materials and cheaper labor and the whole installation was flawed to begin with; another maintained that one of the former pupils, having suffered ill at the hands of the same Mr. Caul, and being afeared of more of the same treatment should the school reopen, had decided to dispatch the whole matter by the most expedient means available.

Nevertheless, the deacons of the Baptist Church, having gotten the notion into their heads, were not about to be gainsaid by such a small trifle as the lack of a proper edifice in which to house what they perceived to be a real strength for their nascent community; they proposed, therefore, to replace the structure by one of sound stone, much in the manner of their local jail, of which they were (it must be said) inordinately proud. It was in the spring of 1798, therefore, that Claxton Hall opened its doors once again. The old name had been retained, in spite of some strenuous objections, for two reasons. First, no one could recall what it might have been called originally, and second, each of its founding fathers seemed to think it should be named after himself. It was a spirit of compromise which finally decided the issue. The deacons, in their infinite wisdom, had also decided that they were the best equipped to teach whatever young minds might venture through its portals and named themselves its faculty.

This arrangement was evidently satisfactory for the next few years. The good name of the Church attracted likely candidates to the doors of the school, and enrollment swelled (along with tuition) until it had reached nearly thirty youths, many of whom were lodged with local families. The curriculum remained much the same, with the addition of Scripture and French, the latter of which could be had for an additional £1 per year. Some concession was also made to the physical side of the boys' conditioning; one of the local gentlemen offering boxing lessons in the afternoon.

Sometime around 1807, however (the date is inexact, many records having been lost in the Baptist Church fire of 1809), the deacons decided to divest themselves of much of their interest in the school, the maintenance and support of which had become, to their minds, entirely too time-consuming and much too worldly. Retaining only a grasp on the spiritual aspect of Claxton Hall, the Church body put the entire institution up for sale, such institution at that period consisting of the stone building (Claxton Hall proper) housing the classroom, a master's residence and an office; a barn and stable; and divers outbuildings. It was purchased, after a suitable period of negotiations, by one Mr. Howard Shackleton, a business man out of New York, who saw in it perhaps an opportunity to advance his own theories of education—based firmly in the principles of Rousseau—or perhaps an occasion to turn a profit.

Now Mr. Rousseau himself, for all of his fine philosophy, admitted that his carefully contrived system of education, based upon the one-pupil, one-tutor model, was, at best, idealistic, and that whoever tried to actually rear a child under such conditions would be a foolish man indeed. (The French author, in spite of his seeming vehemence on the subject of education and the rearing of children in general, is known to have farmed his own out to other houses, to have them brought up there.) This seems to be the one part of Rousseau's philosophy with which the esteemed Mr. Shackleton was unfamiliar.

In spite of Mr. Shackleton, Claxton Hall limped along for nearly a score of years, sometimes prospering, sometimes declining. Its enrollment varied between twenty and fifty students, but, even raising tuition again, Mr. Shackleton found it a poor business venture withal and lost money almost every year. It is to his credit that he did put up two new buildings, one a combination kitchen/refectory and dormitory, the other to house faculty, whose number also varied between three and eight.

In 1826, however, Claxton Hall received a blow which sent it reeling and which was to lead to its demise. In May of that year a Mr. Eleazer Claxton, claiming to be the grand-nephew of James Claxton, presented himself to the selectman of Upper Granby Lake. He bore what purported to be a deed to the property on which the school sat and challenged the town or Mr.

Shackleton to produce a bill of sale giving them title to that property. In fact, should they be unable to do so, he proposed to charge them a rather exorbitant rent for the period in which they had made so free with the use of his land. Whether Mr. Claxton, nephew, knew of the fire which had destroyed most of the town's records in 1809 or not is a moot point and which has no real bearing upon the subsequent events. Mr. Shackleton hired a lawyer, Mr. Claxton hired one also and there ensued one of those legal wrangles in which the newspapers take great delight for a week or so, the matter quickly fading from the realm of public interest after that. In short, Mr. Shackleton could not prove ownership of the land, but, while Mr. Claxton did indeed seem to hold title to the property, the judge ruled that the Claxtons had been absentee landlords for a period greatly exceeding the statute of limitations and had therefore relinquished all claim to the said property, any documents notwithstanding. Since it could be established, as a matter of public record, that the property and buildings had once belonged to the Baptist Church and since laws enforcing the division of Church and State were well established and need not be discussed at this juncture, the judge ruled that neither Mr. Claxton nor Mr. Shackleton had any legal claim to Claxton Hall and that it must therefore revert to the Church, who would recompense Mr. Shackleton for improvements made to the property during the period of his tenure.

Alas, the Church did not have the requisite resources, and Mr. Shackleton, having exhausted most of his personal fortune on Claxton Hall and on the lawyers he had hired to retain it, declared himself bankrupt and withdrew from the scene, washing his hands of the matter. The Church had no further interest in Claxton Hall and promptly closed it again.

Except for pigeons and other small animals, the buildings sat empty until 1861, passing rather quickly from a state of neglect to a state of disrepair. At various times proposals were advanced for their use, but all were seen as costing too much for negligible benefits. Small boys used the remaining panes of glass as targets for stones and the school building, being thus exposed to the elements, suffered the ravages of rain and snow as well as the ignominy of serving as a roosting and nesting places for birds and their rodent counterparts.

In April of that year, an event transpiring far to the south was to change yet again the fortunes of Claxton Hall. A fort in Charleston Harbor came under attack by military forces of South Carolina, recently seceded from the Union. This precipitated not only a war which was to last four years, but also a frenzy of patriotic fervor on both sides, the South believing it had any number of grievances to be redressed and the North unwilling to let the rebels have their way. The South was quick to assemble its troops, convinced that any conflict would be resolved in a matter of weeks, at the outside, and that any Confederate gentleman worth his salt could easily whip twice his weight in Yankees. The North may have been a bit slower to mobilize, but it had the weight of an industrial society behind it, and the eventual result, many historians would maintain, was a foregone conclusion.

In the meantime, however, the call to arms reached every village and hamlet in the North as well as the South, penetrating eventually even unto Upper Granby Lake. That community was expected to supply, as were its neighbors, a quota of men to fill the newly formed 51st Connecticut Rifles, each contingent to be trained and equipped (for those men not being able to afford their own arms) by its respective community. Arms were not much of a problem, each family possessing at least one rifle, ranging in vintage from breech-loaders to squirrel guns, and the women were more than willing to sew uniforms of a sort for their brave boys in blue, but training facilities posed more of a problem. Daniel Peabody had served in the War of 1812 and, though getting on in years, avowed himself capable and willing to take the training of the young men in hand, to be assisted by some of the more able townsmen. As to facilities, someone realized that they, too, were close to hand, if enough volunteers could be found to renovate the buildings which formerly comprised Claxton Hall.

Those too old to bear arms and some too young to be seriously considered enlistees fell to with a will and within a week underbrush had been cleared, the roof repaired, the inside of the Hall itself repainted and plastered, the floors refinished. The athletic field, where students formerly played ball or practiced their newly-acquired skills in fisticuffs, while small, would serve as a parade ground and training field.

Many of those who availed themselves of the facilities were not, alas, to return, losing their lives in places with strange-sounding names like Manassas and Antietam, but the War between the States, while undoubtedly the greatest tragedy to befall the young nation, assured the future of Claxton Hall as an institution. It continued into 1867 as a military training school, a bulwark against a possible resurgence of hostilities.

It was a gentleman by the name of Horatio Worthington Bradley, a former captain in the Union Army, who took the reins of Claxton Hall in hand in August of 1867, having envisioned for the school possibilities which would move it to the forefront of education, or so he believed. In his youth, Captain Bradley had toured Europe with his parents and was much impressed with what he saw there, believing that the Europeans, and more specifically the French, had the right idea concerning the formation of their youth and that America would do well to follow her lead, with certain personal modifications he intended to introduce.

# ZACHARY REKKORD (1793)

20th Oct$^{r}$ 1793

My Dear Sister:

I am but recently arrived here, in this Village they call Farming Towne, which is naught but a small settlement of rudely built Farms & to my mind, at least, offers nothing of the Beauty of our native Mass$^{cts}$. As to the School, it is none, & to call it an Institute of Learning would be like calling our Barn a Manor. The sole Building is a ramshackle House, nor is there any Evidence of the Room I was promised in the Correspondence which our Grandfather held with the Rector, R$^{ev}$ Obadiah Rue. Indeed, for Bed I have naught but a Sofa, infested, I believe, with all manner of Vermin. Although the Nights are already turning cool, the R$^{ev}$ does not seem inclined to make a Fire. The Victuals are poor & not of copious Quantity. The R$^{ev}$ has no Servants, nor even a Housekeeper & does the Cooking by his own Hand, an Art which he has not master'd.

Indeed, I feel that our Grandfather has shewn me no great Kindnesse in sending me to this forlorn Spot, but that it is rather in a Spirit of Revenge, in spite of what he may have told you. You know that he speaks of our Father—may God have Mercy on his Soul—only grudgingly, & of my Mother, not at all. I fear that he has not forgiven our Father for his first Marriage, & that he continues to think ill of me, for all that the Fault is not mine. He thinks it a Sin against the Almighty, nor have I been able to dissuade him. Before I left, he spoke to me thus: "Perhaps the Air of a Good Christian Community & the Ministrations of a R$^{ev}$ Man of God can wash the Heathen Taint from your Immortal Soul, should you have one." I found them harsh Words indeed, nor has the Spot in which I now find myself done anything to alleviate their Sting.

There are three other Boys in the School, all coming from the Neighborhood, that is to say, they live with their families, attending Lectures during the Day but returning to the Warmth & Comfort of their own Hearthe by Night. Thus it is that they have to suffer only one of the R$^{ev}$ Rue's meals per day, whilst I must break my Fast & sup with him, too. Todd Cutter is the eldest & the biggest; already at least six Foot & somewhat of a Bully, I fear, slow as he is of Wit & Reply. In front of the R$^{ev}$ Rue, he appears most gracious & co-operative, but mocks him behind his Backe. When the $R^{ev}$ is absent, Master Cutter makes it known that it is his Orders we are to follow, &, should we be slow to respond, he enforces his Law by boxing Eares. Earl Smallfellow is another of our Groupe, & well he lives up to his Name, being quite short of Stature for 14 $yr^{s}$. What little Food he has at Noon is oftimes snatched away by Master Cutter. Jonathan Wright is also large for his Age, though not as big as Master Cutter. I have never seen Handes so large on a Boy of 15. Master Wright is much given to Introspection & Daydreaming. As a Consequence, the Wrath of our Schoolmaster oftimes falls upon his Shoulders.

I write this early in the a.m. by the feeble Light of one small Candle, the only one such, I think, in the House. The Rector is not yet risen, & it is my Task to see that the Fire is started before he does, so I must end this now.

Yr. Respectful Bro.
*Zachary*

$12^{th}$ $Nov^{r}$ 1793

Dearest Sister,

You ask for Particulars concerning the Falling out with our Grandfather, & Details which I am loathe to impart. I had assum'd that he might have given you such Information, as inclined as he seems to spread such Tidings abroad. But as you are now 12 yrs., dearest Charity, I will tell you the Story, though Grandfather would be angry, should he know. It is best, therefore, that you destroy the present Missive once you have committed its sad News to Memory.

You know that, whilst we share a common Father, I am a Child of my Father's first Marriage, while you are a Daughter of the second. You will therefore not have known my Mother, God rest her Soul, dead now these ten yrs. Indeed, it seems I can scarce remember her myself, though Grandfather says her evil Taint is still within me. Here is the terrible Secret he keeps from you: my Mother was a Senequa, that is to say, an Indian. To Grandfather, she was an evil Savage, a red-skinned Heathen. I do not know how she & my Father met, but Grandfather cursed their Union & the Fruit of it. Indeed, I have heard him refer to me as an Imp of Satan & a Devil, though not when he thought I might hear him. He was scarce mollified upon her death by Drowning (it is supposed) or by my Father's subsequent Remarriage to your Mother, Faith Hapgood, the following yr, for I still remained as a Remembrance of what he regarded as my Father's Sinne.

I fear me that he may be correct in some of that, for I resemble my Father very little, having taken, it would seem, most of my Features from my Mother. They caused me no little Grief when I was growing up, & will continue to plague me even to-day. But with those Details I shall not trouble you.

It was thus that, our Parents, the one & the other having been taken by the Pox very nearly at the same time, we fell to our Grandfather's Care, having no other Relatives. Upon this unhappy Occasion, Grandfather determin'd to send me away, that I should trouble his View no further, while giving out the Excuse that he, being a Widower, was ill-equipt to raise me & that I had sore Need of Christian upbringing, to "cleanse my Soule."

I misdoubt that I will receive either an Education or a Christian Upbringing in this Spot, however, for Conditions are frightful. But I have no wish to burthen you with my troubles, as I count you my only living Relation, dear Sister, & thus will close as

Yr loving, humble & obed$^{nt}$ Bro.
*Zachary*

25$^{th}$ Nov$^{r}$ 1793

My Dearest Sister:

I would that you not press me for such News, dear Sister, for it can do naught but add to your own Distress. Still, if it be your Will, & as it serves as some Solace to me to speak of them, I shall.

I do not know if our Grandfather communicated Details of my Heritage to the R$^{ev}$ Rue or not, but it does not matter, as the Outcome has been as if he had. I am little better thought of here than I was under our Roof & am constantly tormented & teased, esp. by Master Cutter who has decided that I am a "pagan Red Man" with no Soule. The R$^{ev}$ Rue, who is present at some of this Tormenting, has done nothing to stop it & indeed, by his lack of Action, seems to encourage it. At the noon Meal yesterday M$^{r}$ Cutter took my Fork & Spoone & hid them, saying "Heathens do not use such Implements." If I were not to go hungry, I must needs eat my Victuals with my Handes, to the great Delight of all present. This is but the merest of the Incidents & I will not trouble you with the more Awful.

What distresses me most, Dear Sister, is that, with the Continuance of these Incidents, I feel closer than ever to my sainted Mother. I was but 6 yrs when she died, but I feel that she is more responsible for whatever Education & Formation I may have received than any Teacher afterwards. She had, I think, but little in the way of formal Schooling, yet she always seemed to me the wisest of Persons. It is not true that she was a Heathen, for our Father insisted that she receive the Baptism of Our Lord, which she did, taking the name of Elizabeth. It may be, however, that the Change was external only, & that her Soule (for I do believe the red Man to be possessed of one indeed) remained that of her People, the Senequa. I suspect that, in my Heart, I may resemble her more than mere external Features might suggest. This is a dangerous Secret I entrust you with, dearest Sister, & should our Grandfather learn of what I have just imparted to you, his Wrath would scarce be contain'd. I implore you, destroy this present Letter once you have read it.

I have been accounted by some the best Hunter & Trapper in our Community. If this be so, it is my Mother's Doing, for it was she who took me on long Walks in the Woods & shewed me how to read the Signs of Animals & Birds. To this day, I would rather sleep under the Stars than on the softest of Beds, though Need drives me indoors at this Season, not having the proper Clothing to endure the Outside. I often wonder exactly where I belong.

It is Time now for Lessons, so I must close. Pray forgive the Manner in which this is written, but I had no writing Paper save this Scrap torn from my Copy Booke, & should the R^ev^ discover its Absence, he will be wroth.

Yrs in Secrecy
*Zachary Rekkord*

29^th^ Nov^r^ 1793

Dearest Charity:

I account this somewhat of a Holiday, for the following Reasons: Firstly, my chief Tormentor, Master Cutter, has been absent most of the Weeke, taken with some Sicknesse. Without his Leadership, the other Boys have left me alone, thank God. Secondly, the R^ev^ Rue is also afflict'd & keeps to his Bed, though I do not believe for the same Reason. Yestere'en he complained of feeling poorly & took to his Bed. At his Bidding, I fetched him a Bowl of Brothe from the Kettle & brought it to his Room. As he keeps little Light there, it was difficult to see, & I stubbed my Toe on an Object which I later found to be an empty Bottle of Rhum. If indeed he is given to Drink, it would explain some of his Behavior, which does not suit a Man of God.

Although it is Time for Lessons, the R$^{ev}$ is not risen, nor do I expect him to, given over as he is to great Snorings at the present Moment. I have sent the other Boyes home, telling them the Rector is in-disposed & to return on the Morrow. So I have a Holiday & may do what I please. I shall take the Opportunitie to give you some of the Particulars of my Life here.

The R$^{ev}$ Mr. Rue, for all he may be a Godly Man (& here you will permit me to voice several Doubts), is no Teacher. I have gleaned divers Rumors from the Folk in this Village which say, to wit: that he is a Man giv'n to strong Spirits & can oftimes be found in a Publik House when I am abed. He is also said to visit Women of loose Morals, but I can give no credence to these Rumors, as I do not believe him as debauched as all that, nor fallen so far from Grace. Others claim he started the Institute as a Means of turning a Profit, in which Hope he has been severely disappointed. He wishes (so I have heard it said) that he had started the Enterprise in England where People can appreciate the Value of an Education as those here cannot.

As to the Education or Training, I feel it is sadly wanting. Our Classes are mostly in the form of Lectures, derived from his Sermons, of which the R$^{ev}$ has an enormous Supplie. Thence he endeavors to impart to us Greek & Latin & some Cyphering, the latter being the Part I enjoy most. Supplies of all Kindes are wanting, as we have neither Textes nor Bookes & must needs copy everything he says into Copy Bookes, having only the Stump of a Pencil for this Work. Each Night we must memorize what we have written & on the Morrow does he question us thereupon, wrong answers being punished by a severe Looke, a sharp Reprimand or a Blow from the Hickorie Switch. I have, I believe, rec'd more than my share of the Latter, tho' my Answers are surely no worse than those of M$^{rs}$ Cutter, Smallfellow & Wright. As I am the sole Intern, or Boarder, it falls to me to clean the R$^{ev}$'s House & to prepare his Breakfaste & Supper. This last is no great Chore, as the R$^{ev}$ is very frugal & keeps little in the way of Victuals on hand. He is extremely parsimonious in other Wise, also, as there is never more than one Candle lighted & the Fire (when lit) is very small.

For my Part, I see little use in Latin nor Greek, tho' I can recite the necessary Formes, but the R$^{ev}$ says it is necessary in Matters of Rhetorik, a Subject he promises we shall shortly take up.

It is necessary that I leave this for the Moment, as my Hande has become too cold to permit me to continue.

*[a part of the MS, a page or more, is missing at this point]*

...especial Treatment.

"What," says he, "and you would not be saved?" I must confess, dear Sister, that I do believe at this Moment the Devil himself got aholt of my Tongue, for I heard myself reply "For what?" I do not know what possessed my to utter such a Thing, except that it was perhaps foremost in my Mind at the Moment. I have never seen a Man go so white & then red all within the Space of a single Second. I still bear the Weltes I received from the Beating he then administered. At the Time, I thought I deserved it, for saying such terrible Words, but as I think me on it further, I realize that such is not the Case.

Now I will tell you why, Sister, but again, it is a deep & awful Secret, & should it be known, the Weight of Excommunication would surely fall upon me. For myself, I do not care, but to Society it would matter greatly & would surely lose me what few Friends I have. I beseech you, therefore, as before, to destroy this Letter when you have read it, nor speak of its Contents to anyone. Should you find this too much, I implore you, stop reading at this Point.

I have no Thing against the Christian God nor His Son; indeed I find Their Teachings to be enlightened & beneficial. Yet I cannot feel that He is next to me, nor, indeed that He answers many Prayers. While Memories of my Mother are dimm'd with Time, I do remember long Walks we took together in the Woods & what she endeavored to teach me there. Everything has a Spirit, each Rock & Tree, each Rabbit & Bird. They are giv'n by the Creator, & each has its Purpose, even Things Venomous. This is why, when the Indian kills an Animal for food (& never for Sport, as some of the Village seem to be wont to do), he always gives Thanks to the Spirit of the Beaste which has giv'n up its Life that the Hunter may eat or be warm. Is this a Religion? I know not, dear Sister, but I do confess that it makes more Sense to me sometimes than the Sermons of the R$^{ev}$ Rue. If we live & we be Part of Nature, is not Nature alive also? Betimes I must needs lie awake at Night thinking upon such Matters.

But it is not for me to trouble you with such Things, which even a Woman should not listen to, & you still so young. The Sun is now setting, but the R$^{ev}$ not yet risen; I believe he plans to keep his Bed all the Day. I know where he has the Carcasse of a Turkey outdoors, wrapp'd & preserv'd against the Cold, & some Turnip & I will make me a fine Stew for Supper. I hope that I shall perhaps be permitted to return Home for Christmas, but that is Grandfather's Choice to make.

Yr loving Bro
*Zachary*

2$^{nd}$ Dec. 1793

My Loving Sister,

(Please forgive the Condition of the present Paper; there being no foolscap nor any other scrap to be found, I have taken a Page of one of the R$^{ev}$ Rue's Lectures, scarce chang'd, I doubt not, from a sermon he deliver'd one Sunday; a Thinge of tremendous Weight, but little Substance, at least to my mind. There being no other Material available, I am endeavoring to write on the reverse & there in the Margines where his own Scribblings have left a bit of blank Parch$^{t}$.)

If you have believed Halve of what I have already written you, you would scarce credit the Facte that Conditions at the Schoole (& here I do it a Kindnesse) could have become worse. The R$^{ev}$ Rue has scarce left his Bedde these last few Dayes; indeed, he may be truly ill, though I suspect his Afflicktion may be more an Effect of what he has inflicted on himselfe than any external Factors. These, however, cannot be discounted, as the Weather has turn'd most unbearably cold, & the Winde enters the House unopposed thru large Crackes in the Walls and Chinks in the stone workes.

Perhaps because of the Weather, the other Pupils come now infrequently. I do not, however, find the absence of Master Cutter onerous, and, whilst he is absent, neither Master Smallfellow nor Master Wright seem inclined to mete out their customary Punishm$^{t}$. I am thus left to fend for myselfe; it is betimes difficult to find enough in the way of Victuals to sustain myself, the R$^{ev}$ Rue eating but little, tho' his breath bespeaks strong Spirits. I am fortunate, however, in that some Folk of the surrounding Area seek to pay at least a Portion of their Fees in Food stuffs & labour. Thus it is that a Hamme, a Chicken & some Veg. have been recently left. I was able to make a passable Stew, which has sustained me for these sev'ral Days.

I perceive, however, that I cannot write more, being at a loss for Paper. I bethought me again of tearing a Leafe from the Copy Booke which the R$^{ev}$

Mr Rue has procured from the Goodnesse of his Heart & at great Expens, if he may be believed, but, should its absence be discover'd, it would go ill with me. I must needs therefore, dear Sister, leave until another Tyme the Subjt I had intended to write upon. I trust you are well.

Yrs in haste,
*Brother Zachary*

19 Decr 1793

Dear Charity,

You might wonder at my Silence during the past Fortnight. I would have written but for two Factors. First, as I told you, I lacked any Paper but that which was in my Copybook & which I dare not use. It was not until the Arrival of Yrs. of the 13th inst. that I found myselfe with the Wherewithal to write again. I must thank you, dear Sister, for penning such a long Missive & beg your forgivenesse for using the Reverse to answ'r. You must have wondered, should you have seen only the Obverse upon breaking the Seale, how your Letter came to be returned to you!

The secd reason of my long Absence in Correspondence is due to Events which have transpired here over which I have had little Control. The Weather here has turn'd somewhat milder. This has the Advantage of using less Firewood (which I am responsible for supplying, the Rev having planned poorly for the Coming of Winter & having laid in a Supplie of only about a Cord, long since exhausted) but having also the Disadvant. of making a great Quantitie of Mudd, the Frost being temply alleviated. Master Cutter has found a new Amusemt of tripping me & causing me to fall, with the result that I have at the present inst. Clothes neither clean nor dry. In such Effort he is sometimes aided by Jon. Wright, who positions himself in such wise that, when Master Cutter pushes me, I fall over Master Wright who has taken up a Station behind me. Tho' they have done this sev'ral Times, they do not tire of the Sport which always produces great Laughter. The Rev seems to get the same Enjoymt & indeed seems to encourage their Behavior. I will try to make the Reasons clear to you.

It was about a Weeke ago when we gathered for our Holy Services (the Rev prefers to hold them of a Monday, as the other Boyes are not present of a Sunday & as of late he desires to keep to his Bedde as late as possible on the Sabbath, not even going into Farming Towne to Church) that the Rev brought with him a great Bible, such as I had not seen on the Premises before. I do not know how he came by it, nor where, but that is of little Import and does not bear upon this Storie.

The Bible had many wonderful Illustrations, but we were not permitted to see but one, it being an Image of the Creation of Man. The $R^{ev}$ took his Texte from the first Book, that is Genesis, & read how Man was created in the Image of God. He took Pains to shew that Adam was white, and therefore God must also be white. (I do not think it shews aught, dear Sister, but the Fact that perhaps the Artist was white.) "Therefore," he said, "he who is not white is not in the Image of God," & hereupon he looked directly at me. I do not like to think of the mien of Master Cutter at this Point, but I can assure you it was not pleasant to look upon. Then he asked, "And what color is Satan?" Now Master Cutter was quick to reply, still looking upon me, "Red."

Now the $R^{ev}$ spoke of the Christian Dutie of each of us (tho' he did not look at me) to bring the Red Man around to "our" Waye of Thinking, and how it is right & correct, &c. "For tho' the Heathen have not Soules, yet may they be led unto the Light, & tho' theirs will never be the Kingdome of Heaven, yet may it be granted to them to see some of the Light from afar, to be converted to Right Thinking, should they follow the White Man."

I found the whole very distasteful, but it seemed to please $Mess^{rs}$ Cutter, Smallfellow and Wright, who wore evil smiles upon their Visages, most unsettling to behold.

"And what if the Savage refuse to follow the Pathe to Right Thinking?" asked Master Cutter.

"If it is the Wille of God, he may have to be led to the Light of Conversion," said the $R^{ev}$ Rue, with a goode Deal of Conviction.

Thus far, dear Sister, I have managed to absent myself from the Presence of Master Cutter save another be present. I do not believe the other Boyes have the Courage to 'lead' me unless Master Cutter be present. I cannot depend on any Aid from the $R^{ev}$ Rue nor from any other Source, I fear me I have no more Tyme & must close to attend to my divers Duties.

Yr loving bro.
*Zachary*

24$^{th}$ December 1793

Dearest Sister,

I have bethought me that, in spite of the length of my latest Missive, I had not touched upon the Subj. about which you had earlier inquir'd, to wit, my Mother, God rest her Soule. I am pleased that you take an Interest, & will endeavor to satisfy your Curiosity, I having the Tyme at present, as the R$^{ev}$ has declared a three Dayes Holiday. The other Boyes being gone, I have the House to myselfe. The Rev has absented himselfe on Business of his own & which he has not communicated to me. It is a delightful Tyme, tho' I was not, as I had hoped, vouchsafed an Invitation from Grand-father to come Home for the Holiday; nevertheless, I have Food aplenty & may build the Fyre as high as I wish, there being none here to deny me.

Alas, I know little more than I have already told you. She was a Senequa Indian. Our Father Simon met her, according to what he has told me, in the year 1773, whilst he was at a Trading Post. She was very young, barely 13 yr$^{s}$. and quite beautiful. Her Name was Sings A Dawn Song, if we translate the Indian Tongue to English, tho' Father called her Dawn Song. It seems that the Red Man names his children for Events or for Thynges he sees which may be Omens & cares little for Family Names as the Whites do. If I understand aright, he bought her from her Familie, tho' he spoke of the Transaction as a Bride Price. To me, Dear Sister, it seems a bit too much like Slaverie.

The Marriage, however, made him an Outcaste among his own People & he was mistrusted by some Indians, also. As I have related, I was verie close to her and was Grief-stricken when she was taken by her Creator. Upon her Deathe, Grandfather decree'd that her Name should not be spoken more and that her Possessions be burned & forgotten. It seem'd to me at the Tyme that he wished to count me among them, tho' perhaps I judge him too harshly.

The Light grows dimme & the R$^{ev}$ has left me no Candle, so I must close. As always

Yr most loving brot$^{r}$
*Zachary R.*

Farming Towne
Jany 2, 1794

Oh my Dear Sister,

This may be the last Letter you shall receive of me, tho' I pray it shall not be so. You will note that I am in Farming Towne, tho' I may not reveal exactly where. The Reason I will make clear to you.

O my Dear Sister, the Marke of Cain is upon me, & I am surely damn'd for Eternitie. I must now believe that Grandfather was correct & that the Sinne of my Father (if indeed such it be) is upon my Heade and shall follow me as God pursued Abel's Brother. And yet I cannot believe that it be all my Fault & Blame, for I was defending myselfe. Still, I doubt the Law would see it in this Wise.

I will tell you that I am hiding in a Bldg. in this same Farmingtown, but that when you receive this Missive, I shall have been departed some Tyme ago. Circumstances have forced me to become a Thiefe as well as a Murderer, tho' to this point I have stol'n but Food & Shelter & the wherewithal to write you the present inst. Yet my Candle is now but a Stubbe & the Cellar in which I presently crouch is dank & damp, so I must needs tell you what Awful Thyng has transpired.

As I wrote, the Rev Rue gave us a Holiday to celebrate the Coming of the New Yeare and the other Boyes went to their divers Dwellings. Upon their Return, they told me—more to torture me with their good Fortune, I suspect, than to share with me any Joyes of the Season—how they had eaten & what Gifts they had received, &c. Master Cutter had gotten a great Knive for Hunting, an Instrument in whose display he delighted, waving it about in the Air & describing what he planned to do with it.

It was two Dayes after their return when it became obvious that we would have no Classes that Daye, the Rev Rue being indisposed. In Truth, his Indisposition, to my Mind, resulted from his own Conduct & not from any other Cause. He returned the e'en before, unsteady in his Gait and glazed of Eye. The other Boyes had departed for the Daye & there was none but I to observe him. He smelled—I do not tell you this, Dear Sister with the Intention of offending your Sensibilities, but only to shew you how grave the Case was—he smelled, I say, like a Back House into which someone had poured a great Deal of Scent, such as Women far gone in Harlotry may use, according to what I have heard, for I have never encountered such a Creature myselfe.

I put him thus into his Bedde, tho' I found touching his Person distasteful.

He not being risen the next morning at the accustomed Tyme, I determined that he should probably not rise before Noon and resolved to send the other Boyes home again, as soon as they should arrive. But as I imparted the Tidings to Master Cutter, he seemed pleased, and such a Smile crossed his Visage that I should hope never to see again. He drew forth that great Blade which he now always kept upon his person and asked if I knew what the Savages did to White Men with their Knives. I replied that I did not. They scalp them, he replied. I have heard that this was so, tho' I had also heard that the White Man saw fit to do the same to the Indian.

I saw what was in his Minde, and being of no Minde to let him accomplish his Deed, I backed from him, until I fetched up against a Wall, near the Stove, and could go no further, whereupon, commanding Messrs Wright and Smallfellow to hold my arms that I might not escape, he advanced upon me once again.

I thought he was merely trying to frighten me & I suspect the other Boyes did also, the whole being a rather unpleasant Prank. But he put the Knive to my Forehead and drew the Blade along it, not such a deep Cut, but painful nonetheless. Master Wright gave a Gasp & loos'd his Grippe somewhat, enabling me to shake him from me. My free Hande then found a Sticke of Woode near the Stove, a Billet which I swung with all my Force at Master Cutter's Heade, e'en as he approached once more. The Appearance of his Countenance gave me to think that he intended to finish the Job he had begun.

I swung, I say, with all my Strength & felt the Blow strike home & watched Master Cutter's Bodie drop to the Floor. Master Smallfellow shouted that I had surely killed him & he would fetch the Constable & I would be hanged & burn in Hell for my Deed. I suspect that all Reason left me at that point, Dear Sister, for I bent and took up the Dagger which Master Cutter had dropp'd & replied that I should surely do the same to them, should they stand in my way. They fled then, nor did I try to pursue or e'en determine if Master Cutter were really dead. I knew only that I must get away quicklie & ran away to Farmingtowne where a poorly latch'd Doore admitted me to the Shoppe where I now hide.

I shall endeavor to post this Letter to you, Dearest Sister, so that you may know the Fate of your Brother and not forget

*Zachary Rekkord*

5$^{th}$ Apr. 1794
Concord, New Hamps$^{re}$.

Dearest Charity,

You shall be happy, I trust, that your bro. is still of this Earth, and of reasonably good Healthe. I have made my Waye Northwards to the State of New Hampshire. Should you desire to contact me, Dear Sister, you may do so under the Name of Geo. Tinker at General Delivery, as I have, for the Moment, at least, tho't it prudent to leave the Name of Z.R. in Conn$^{t}$. There have been, however, no Signes of Pursuit, and those Questions which are put to me concerning my Past I have been able to respond to with convincing Lies, tho' it pains me to do so. Nor have I any news concerning the State of Healthe of Master Cutter. be he alive (as I hope) or no, there has appeared no Newes in any of the Journals I have been able to procure.

I will tell you that I have procured Employment as an Apprentice at a Print Shoppe here, tho' I shall for the present keep its Name to myselfe, lest this Missive fall into the Handes of Grandfather. To that end, Dear Sister, I pray you burn the pres$^{t}$ when you have read it. I have at present little Coin, nor do I ask you to send me aught, my present Employ giving me little more than Bedde & Boarde. Nonetheless, when I shall have put aside a sufficient Summe, I shall make my Waye ever northwards again, until I be at such a Distance so that even Grandfather may renounce pursuing me further. Perhaps I shall go e'en as far as Canada, where the Laws of Conn$^{t}$ can not reach me & where those of Indian Blood may be better treated.

It now being Dawn, I must build up the Fyre, for my Master will arrive soon to begin the Daye's Work. It is in any Case an honest Profession, tho' bringing but scant Remuneration, nevertheless it shall provide me the Opportunitie to make my own way in this World.

Do not forget me, Dearest Sister, & if God wills it, you shall hear from me again.

Yr. loving & obed$^{t}$ bro.
*Z. R.*

(*a portion of the final letter is missing, and one may only conjecture when and where it was written.*)

…Forsythe, a goodly Man & one well thought of in the Community. He is a Purveyor of Gen'l Merchandise; indeed, his is the only such Establishment for at least a League in any Direction. It may be understood, therefore, that he does a good Business in all Seasons and makes a good Living for himselfe and his Familie.

But it is not for this Reason that I pursu'd my Suit for the Hande of Abigail. Tho' you might count her young, she is nineteen, & certainly of a marriageable Age. She is well skill'd in all Matters touching the managm$^{t}$ of a Household, having been well school'd by her Mother. The Familie knows me as George Tinker, & it seems to me wise t…

# THOMAS WHITCOMBE (1794)

The November rain beat against the glass, blurring it even further. Occasionally, a bit of sleet would mix in, as though the rain were becoming more earnest in seeking an entry. Not that it needed to try that hard, Thomas Whitcombe told himself. There were certainly more than ample openings in the roof and walls. He moved slightly to the right to escape another drip, this one seeking to enter via his coat collar, pulled up against the chill, and run in an icy stream down his back. The noise of the rain, for all of its glacial intent, was almost soothing and almost masked the hesitant voice behind him.

"*Gaium, filius mea in…*"

Whitcombe swung around to face the offender.

"No, you great lout! Listen to what you're saying. In the first place, 'my son' is in apposition. If 'Gaium' is in the accusative case, then 'filius' must be also. Furthermore, my young illiterate, you've made Gaius a girl, which will most certainly come as a great shock to his poor parents. Good Lord, lad, at your age, Caesar spoke perfect Latin, and he was a foreigner!"

*Let him chew on that a while.*

Earl Smallfellow looked appropriately baffled and stood with his mouth partially opened, unsure how to reply. It gave Whitcombe a chance to look once again over his class of eight, wondering where the next generation was going.

As always, Todd Cutter, that great oaf, wore a smirk upon his face with its crooked nose. He looked as if he knew more than you did or was privy to some dark secret he wouldn't share. Either that, or he was troubled by flatulence. He had some intelligence—that could not be denied—but chose not to use it except in nefarious ways. He seemed to think himself too good for the school, too smart for the schoolmaster, and certainly far superior to any other biped who had ever trod the surface of God's green earth.

"*Gaium, filium meus in ager video*," Smallfellow offered uncertainly.

Whitcombe sighed loudly and clasped his hands behind his back, that he might not be tempted to seize an inkpot and hurl it as the student who seemed determined to make sure that the Roman Empire, once fallen, should not rise again. Smallfellow's diminutive stature seemed to equal his paucity of intelligence.

"Sit down, Master Smallfellow. I hope your parents entertain no thoughts of having you prepared for the priesthood."

The offending pupil sank back upon his bench. "Yes, Schoolmaster. I mean no, Schoolmaster."

John Aaron squinted nearsightedly at the piece of slate on which Whitcombe had written "I see my son Gaius in the field," as if there might be some deep, hidden message which had escaped the others.

"Master Aaron, would you care to attempt this? No? Master Cutter?"

Cutter's eyes lost their glazed look for just a moment. "Well, since I don't have a son named Gaius, Schoolmaster, I couldn't see him in the field, could I?" He smirked in triumph. The others tittered, save Peter Tuttle, who merely looked confused, and Joshua Coombs, the youngest, who seemed to be trying to decide whether Cutter was jesting or not.

Whitcombe repressed a sigh. He was repressing many of late, it seemed. Perhaps he should abandon his personal ideas on discipline; they were considered too radical in any case. He looked with a sort of longing at the willow switch standing in the corner. He'd placed it there in plain sight on the first day of classes, and although he'd picked it up several times, he had never applied it. He had determined, upon leaving Dartmouth, that pupils could be reasoned with and that trying to beat knowledge into their heads was, for the most part, a waste of time and promoted only resentment. Still, he was beginning to wonder if he shouldn't rethink his philosophy. Many teachers—including those he'd had—believed that discipline was the soul of teaching and that books and beatings were equally important in the instruction of a young mind. He believed that the discipline should be mental, not physical. Cutter was forcing him to re-evaluate his position.

"'Tis near noon," he said at last, breaking a weighty silence. "You may as well go eat. Arithmetic in one hour."

They shuffled off, some to recover lunches left near their coats, a few to the kitchen.

A good part of the problem, Whitcombe thought, was his own age. He thought himself a mature nineteen, nearly twenty, but this put him only a few years senior to the older boys. And only two separated him from Cutter. Whether Cutter knew or sensed this, Whitcombe didn't know. But it made no difference. He realized that he was, in a sense, being bullied by Cutter, just as Cutter bullied some of the younger boys when no adults were present. He wondered how much of the story about Cutter and "the Indian boy" was true. There were many conflicting versions. The one Cutter adhered to had him nearly scalping a half-crazed savage who attacked him with a war club.

Adding to the problem of his age was undoubtedly that of his size and physical presence. At somewhat less than five and a half feet, he hardly towered over his charges. And his smooth cheeks did not bespeak great wisdom, especially not on a pale, rather thin face. Nor was his clothing markedly different from that of his pupils. His coat, indeed, was somewhat threadbare and hardly any protection against the chill in the room. He pulled it somewhat more tightly around his spare frame.

*And how can one teach effectively under such conditions?* He looked around the room in which he stood, blinking instinctively as a drop of water from the leaking ceiling narrowly missed his eye.

He understood that the Reverend Rue had rented this dwelling because he needed more room for his "Institute" and because the rent was so reasonable. It was easy to understand the latter reason. The upstairs had but half a roof, and the remainder was in poor repair. Such containers as could be spared or scavenged were placed at strategic spots on the floor, presumably to catch the water dripping from the floor above. But there were not nearly enough containers, and some leaked as badly as the roof. Still others, neglected, overflowed, adding their contents to the already sodden pine floorboards. And at least once a day, one of the boys, usually Cutter or Wright, managed to "forget" that the jars were there and "tripped" over one or more, trying to get their profuse apologies out around a mouthful of giggles.

The Hall—for so the Reverend insisted on calling it—was barely fifty years old, but had been in a state of disrepair and neglect for at least forty of that period. The plaster originally covering the walls had long since parted company with them, and no wall, in any case, seemed to run true. Few doors fit their frames and few windows could be opened fully, and, if one actually succeed in doing so, the perpetrator found that the window steadfastly refused to close again. Whitcombe doubted there was a level floor in the structure. The ceiling plaster, where it was present at all, was water-stained or soaked or hung down in great leprous scabs.

Two rooms, a parlor and a dining room, led off from either side of a small, rather plain and windowless entry hall, the middle of which was occupied by a set of stairs with an ornate banister. The parlor was currently using for storage, mostly incomplete pieces of furniture which seemed to have come with the house. As a window was missing in this room, its contents had suffered greatly. The dining room, by contrast, was largely intact and leaked less than the other rooms. The fireplace worked, to a degree, though the chimney was poorly constructed and inclined to send the smoke back into the room at odd moments. In addition, there was a small and quite inefficient stove, which, although it emitted less smoke, gave little in the way of real warmth. It was this space that was given over to a classroom.

Past the dining room was a large kitchen with two ovens, one functioning, the chimney of the other blocked. Here the meals—such as they were—were prepared and the boys ate. This was a favorite room, as it was the warmest in the house. A pantry and a room for a servant completed this wing. The "servant" was a Negro woman called "Miss Lispeth" by all, students and adults alike; if she had another name, no one knew it. She prepared meals for the boarders from the roughest and most meager of ingredients, all the Reverend allowed her. Her role went far beyond that of cook or mere domestic, however, as she also knew various medicines—folk remedies, Whitcombe was sure—guaranteed efficacious against stomach disorders, earache, coughs and sore throats. To some of the younger students, she may have been more of a mother than they had at home. Even Cutter, who held little sacred, had a good deal of respect for her and would not risk an encounter with the iron spider she brandished when angry.

In the other wing, past the ruined parlor, was yet another water-damaged room which might have been a sitting room or even a library at one point. No furniture remained, and all of the shelves were empty. But there were traces of paper, or perhaps paint upon some of the surfaces which suggested that the room might have been quite elegant at some point.

Two of the upstairs rooms were inhabitable; the great oak tree which had fallen on the house in its first decade of life and which had broken the roof had rendered the others unfit to live in. The tree had long since been cut up and carted away, but Mr. James Claxton, owner of the house, had lacked the initiative or the necessary funds, or both, to make the needed repairs and had abandoned the Hall. For the next forty years, it had been open to the weather and the nearby rodent population.

The larger of the two bedrooms was that of the Head of the Institute, the Reverend Obadiah Rue. In fact, the Rev. Rue rarely left the room now, or at least was rarely seen by other members of the community. He received parcels at regular intervals, had meals delivered and the slop pot emptied by Miss Lispeth. Once in a while, the boys would hear him moving about upstairs, apparently in deep conversation with himself, and on occasion, especially of a Sunday, he might come clumping downstairs and disappear for the day. He usually smelled of strong spirits and looked unkempt.

The smaller of the bedrooms actually had a better fireplace and was the second-best room in the house, or would have been, if the supply of firewood had been adequate to heat it. It had been fitted with rough bunks for the three "boarders," Coombs, Tuttle and Aaron, though they used the room only for sleeping, doing their evening studies in the cheerier atmosphere of the kitchen, where Miss Lispeth sometimes had hot tea for them or showed them how to find the answer to a problem in arithmetic, for though she could not read, she kept what records the Institute maintained and knew to the last penny how much remained in her weekly food budget. Whitcombe, in fact, admired her head for figures.

As for Thomas Whitcombe, he took his lodging with a neighboring family, that of Seth Cubbins. The Rev. Rue had procured this for him and grudgingly paid his room and board, telling Whitcombe that this was the major part of the generous stipend he would award him for teaching at the Institute. Rev. Rue insisted that he was getting too old to keep up with the coming generation, and that he was presently occupied with more important tasks, such as the writing of his memoirs and a treatise on Modern Education. The latter, he expected, would bring him a great deal of renown and not a little coin. He had told Whitcombe, upon engaging the younger man for the teaching position, that, in his capacity of expert on the aforementioned Modern Education, would undoubtedly be called upon to lecture at many great universities and could therefore be expected to spend much time traveling.

Whitcombe had yet to see much more than a shilling a week as his salary, but there were other recompenses, the chief of which was Sarah Cubbins, the fifteen year-old daughter of his host. She intruded far too often upon Whitcombe's thoughts. He was especially troubled by the memory of her offering him a sweet upon his arrival and the fact that he had stared down the front of her dress at her bosom as she bent toward him with the tray. His face flushed every time he recalled the incident. Surely the thoughts that came with the memory were unwholesome, if not unholy. He had tried to remain at a discreet distance from her since that time, but she seemed not to notice, one way or the other.

What he *was* certain of was that his education at a prestigious university had in no wise prepared him for life beyond that idyllic period and that the theory which he had so assiduously endeavored to master during his tenure there was of absolutely no use in his present situation. The students categorically refused to be classified as any of the types upon which his professors had expounded at length, nor did they respond to any of the methods of education which were all but guaranteed to instill in them a life-long love of learning and a deep appreciation for the finer things of life. Whitcombe had supposed that, even taking into account their tender years, they had some degree of intelligence and could be reasoned with. Once they saw the error of their ways, they would surely mend their conduct. But they could not see the error of their ways, no matter how often Whitcombe had tried to point it out to them. Indeed, it seemed to him that he spent more time doing that than any actual teaching.

During his first weeks at the Institute, he had planned his lessons with the utmost diligence, writing detailed outlines and notes, preparing questions that were at the same time penetrating and elucidating, searching for recitations that were sure to pique their curiosity. He had abandoned this practice shortly thereafter; not only—given the pupils he had to work with—did he find himself incapable of sticking to his prepared plans, but he had discovered also, much to his chagrin, that their level of intelligence was too low to allow them to appreciate any but the simplest of concepts and that the breadth of their experience lessened the effectiveness of any methods he might try or examples he might suggest.

The worst, however, was the joy they seemed to take in their own ignorance. They could not see the utility of anything Whitcombe essayed to teach them, save a bit of ciphering. Latin and Greek would certainly play no part in their lives and they needed to know just enough writing to sign their names and just enough reading to understand the Bible.

The weather throughout the remainder of November was somewhat drier, for which Whitcombe was extremely grateful—the constant dampness was hard on his bones—but overly cool during that same period. The Institute was using firewood at an alarming rate, and, as most of the supply had to be used in the kitchen, what remained was insufficient to heat the rest of the house.

December, however, brought relief of an unexpected sort. Reverend Rue had granted the students several days' reprieve in the form of a holiday around the time of the winter solstice, and, at the end of the period, master Cutter failed to return to school. Whitcombe subsequently learned from Miss Lispeth that the Reverend Rue had received a communication from the father of the aforementioned scholar that he was withdrawing his son from the Institute "because it should be obvious to the veriest Idiot (of which the School undoubtedly had a copious supply) that his son was learning nothing, due, no doubt, to the fact that the School had no teachers worthy of the name, nor anything worthwhile to impart to his son, who, already precocious, was showing signs of true genius in several areas," and would the Reverend be good enough to refund that part of the tuition, paid in advance, which his son would not be using.

The departure was a mixed blessing in the end. True, Whitcombe, freed from his chief tormentor, was able to teach somewhat more effectively, and even Wright was very much subdued in the absence of his mentor. On the other hand, Reverend Rue became even stingier, saying that it was undoubtedly Whitcombe's fault that they had lost "such a promising student," and fearing that the loss of revenue would have to be made up for "in some fashion," viz., a reduction in Whitcombe's "generous stipend."

The strong cold continued through the month of December and threatened January as well. Shortly after the New Year, the supply of firewood was exhausted. Whitcombe, entering the classroom on a Monday morning, found there a notice in the hand of Reverend Rue stating that as "certain persons" had been too "liberal in their use of firewood," he was constrained to save what was left for cooking purposes and for heating his own quarters so that he might continue his most important work. There would be no heat in the classroom from this point forward, though the students might sleep on straw pallets in the kitchen, if they so chose.

Whitcombe was incensed. The school, after all, should be run for the students, and not as a whim of the Head. He suspected that the Reverend did very little writing in his room and precious little thinking. Whitcombe didn't know (though he suspected Miss Lispeth did) how, when and where the students' tuition money went, but surely Reverend Rue would have allotted enough for fuel. It was also evident that the students could not learn under the present conditions. A body shivering to keep warm has difficulty holding a pen or a piece of chalk and it was difficult, even for Whitcombe, to remain focused enough for any meaningful exchange of knowledge to take place.

He was therefore somewhat surprised, upon entering the classroom about a week after what the students were calling "the Edict," to find the room, if not comfortable, at least tolerable. The stove was working, though not at full output, and the students, still swaddled in blankets, were huddled around it.

"I see the Reverend Rue has decided to provide some fuel," Whitcombe remarked dryly.

The students looked at each other in a manner Whitcombe would later remember as odd. It also would strike him later that there was no wood in evidence.

"Oh, yes, indeed, Schoolmaster," Smallfellow answered. "Indeed he has."

The room nevertheless, became cooler as the morning wore on; it was not until after the noon recess, after the boys had returned from lunch, that it was warmer again. Whitcombe supposed that the stove had been stoked in his absence.

It was several days later, on the 14th day of January to be precise, that Whitcombe was awakened by a scratching and an insistent rapping at his door. The room was very cold and very dark; Whitcombe could not guess at the hour, save that it must be quite early, still well before sunrise.

"Yes, yes, just a moment." Whitcombe, still groggy, fumbled to get his candle alight. His heavy coat was thrown across the bed in the guise of another blanket, and he shrugged it across his shoulders. He almost winced from the shock of the cold boards as he put his feet on the floor.

The voice beyond the door was muffled, but urgent, as though the person who stood there had a message of great importance, but feared to wake the rest of the household. It sounded like it might be Sarah Cubbins.

Indeed it was, but Whitcombe had no time to admire her in her dressing gown. She held a candle aloft and spoke in a rapid whisper.

"It's the Negro woman from the school, Mister Whitcombe. She's downstairs. She says it's a matter of great urgency and that you should come immediately, sir."

"What…?"

"No, Mister Whitcombe, I have no further details. But she said you must hurry."

With that she turned and fled down the stairs. Whitcombe listened to her bare feet until they were silenced by the carpet in the hall, then returned to his room where he began to pull on his clothes. His mind, however, worked faster that his cold fingers. Had there been a fire at the school? Had one of the boys injured himself? He wished Miss Lispeth had been a bit freer with details.

It was normally a quarter-hour walk to the Institute, but Whitcombe made it in ten minutes, despite the slippery conditions and an inch or so of new snow. To his surprise, no window in the Hall showed any light, nor was it until he had got the front door open did he see the glow from the kitchen. Miss Lispeth was there, raking coals in the fireplace and throwing in a bit more wood. One of the boys—muffled as the figure was, Whitcombe could not determine which—was evidently asleep on a pallet under the table, wrapped in a blanket and a winter coat. Miss Lispeth made a hushing motion with her finger, pointed to the sleeping figure and motioned Whitcombe toward the rear door of the kitchen. There was a small alcove there, normally used for the storage of firewood, where they could speak without disturbing the kitchen's other inhabitant.

"I think he's dead, Mister Whitcombe. I seen dead people before, an' there's precious little doubt, but I reckon you'd better check for yourself." Her hoarse whisper was equal parts desperation and resignation.

"Who, for God's sake? One of the boys? What happened?"

"No, I checked all o' the boys, and they're all fine, thank the Lord. No, Mr. Whitcombe, it's the Reverend. I don't know what done him in, whether it was the drinkin' or the cold, but he's dead."

"Miss Lispeth, could I enjoin you to begin at the beginning?" Whitcombe was beginning to shiver again—the fireplace heat didn't reach this area—and he had no wish to drag this out.

She took a deep breath and let it out—Whitcombe watched it steam in the frosty air—and began again. "I'm in the habit o' taking him his evenin' tea 'long about ten o'clock. I knock at his door, as always, but he don't answer—probably busy writin'. So I set the tray on the floor and come back down. I helped young master Coombs make his bed up under the table an' sat down to have a cup o' tea myself. But suddenly, there's this great thump from above, as though somethin' heavy fell on the floor. I went up to see if the boys was all right, but they were all sleepin'. So it had to come from the Reverend's room. The tray was still on the floor. He don't keep the door locked, so I peeked in. Well, Lord, there he is lyin' on the floor near his desk, just like he'd fell off o' his chair. And, Mister Whitcombe, there's a empty bottle on the floor beside him and he's smellin' powerful o' drink.

"Well, I don't want to wake the boys an' frighten them, an' I can't think o' what else to do, so I close the door again and come to fetch you. I figure you'll know what to do, Mister Whitcombe." Her eyes bored into his own, seeking affirmation.

Whitcombe didn't have the slightest idea what he should do, but he sensed that this was not the moment to make that fact known.

"I think we ought to confirm the fact that the Reverend is…deceased," Whitcombe began, "and then—" he licked his lips, not really knowing, but not wishing to appear indecisive—"and then inform…the magistrate." *Whoever that might be.*

Miss Lispeth looked uncertain. "I ain't sure we got a magistrate, but there's a judge, or a notary, leastways: Mr. Cavanaugh."

Whitcombe nodded. “Be good enough to fetch him, Miss Lispeth. I’ll see to the…Reverend.”

The woman gave him a tight nod and drew her shawl more closely around her shoulders. She shuffled away.

Now it was Whitcombe’s turn to take a deep breath. He took a candle from the kitchen and made his way to the stairs. The Hall seemed preternaturally silent, holding its breath. Every creak of a floorboard or a stair tread sounded like a pistol shot in Whitcombe’s ear. The air was glacial.

The tea tray was still on the floor near the door. Whitcombe rapped softly, tentatively, hoping that perhaps Miss Lispeth had been mistaken and that the resident therein was merely in a drunken sleep, after all.

Whitcombe entered cautiously, the candle held aloft. He noted that his hand trembled only slightly, perhaps from the cold. The Reverend lay on the floor, partly curled, his back to the door. Whitcombe circled the figure on the floor and knelt near the head, approaching the candle slowly. Rue’s eyes were open, staring, his jaw clenched.

How does one check a body? Whitcombe wondered. He extended a hand, not really wanting to touch a dead person. Whitcombe reached out, recoiled, steeled himself and tried again. Rue’s skin was cold. Whitcombe prodded him gently, not really expecting a response. Then, remembering the time when he’d watched a small boy’s drowned body fished from a river, he rolled Rue onto his back and, holding his own breath, put his ear to Rue’s chest. There was neither sound nor movement nor warmth.

Can you close a dead man’s eyes? Whitcombe asked himself. I suppose I ought to try. Averting his own eyes to avoid the corpse’s gaze, Whitcombe pulled the eyelids down. He was relieved to note that his efforts had been successful. Whitcombe guessed he ought to cover the body; he could think of nothing else to do. He removed the coverlet from the bed and spread it over the recumbent figure. His own hands felt numb, though whether from the cold—the fire had evidently gone out some time ago, he noted—or from emotion, he could not say.

Suddenly, it became impossible for him to remain in the room. The presence of the dead man was too much. Forcing himself to walk rather than run, he exited, shut the door carefully and quietly and descended to the kitchen. He was wondering if Miss Lispeth had anything stronger than tea hidden somewhere when the rear door opened, admitting the cook and the worthy Mr. Cavanaugh.

The magistrate was taller than Whitcombe, bright of eye and quick of movement. He always wore a look of mild astonishment on his smooth face with its pointed, dimpled chin. He had dressed—at least partly—but had not put on his wig and wisps of white hair escaped from under his three-cornered hat. He nodded to Whitcombe, shrugged off his heavy cloak and rubbed his hands in front of the fire before speaking.

"Have the boys been told, then?"

Whitcombe waited just a moment before shaking his head. He realized that he had assumed Miss Lispeth would take charge and had been waiting for her to reply. Obviously, the others thought he was in control of the situation and would be issuing orders. Whitcombe felt very inadequate.

Cavanaugh nodded again, looking into the fire. "It's just as well. There'll be time enough for that later." Then he turned to Whitcombe. "Have you checked the body, Mr. Whitcombe?"

Whitcombe tried to speak, but found his mouth dry. He swallowed and tried again. "Yes, magistrate. I…I believe he's dead." It sounded inane, but it seemed to be the response Cavanaugh expected.

"I'll just go up and make it official, then," he said. "I'll get a couple of lads to remove the body tomorrow. Could you get the boys out of the house for a bit at that time?"

Whitcombe was suddenly inspired. "Yes, sir. I can organize a bit of an expedition to gather some firewood. We're a bit short."

A final nod from Cavanaugh, who took a candle and made his way to the stairs.

Miss Lispeth looked hard at Whitcombe. "You're a mite pale, Mr. Whitcombe. I suspect I could find a little of the Reverend's port, if you'd like a drop."

"Yes, thank you, Miss Lispeth. Perhaps you'd take a glass as well?"

She looked surprised, but pleased. She fetched the bottle and poured a small amount into three mugs which they warmed a bit at the hearth. When Cavanaugh returned, he accepted one wordlessly. His lips were compressed into a hard line.

"I can't be certain, but I saw several empty jugs and there was a strong smell of spirits…" He didn't finish the sentence, but buried his nose in his mug. Then he looked up again at Whitcombe. "You'll make a thorough inventory of his effects, of course."

Whitcombe was caught a bit off-guard. "I…certainly, magistrate. If that's what must be done."

"Good then. Well, I must be off." Cavanaugh drained his mug, draped his cloak around his shoulders and was gone, leaving Whitcombe and Miss Lispeth staring at each other.

"What's happened?" inquired a sleepy voice from under the table. They had completely forgotten about Coombs.

Whitcombe opened his mouth to reply, then realized he didn't know what to say. Once again, Miss Lispeth took matters into her own hands.

"Hush, child, an' go back to sleep. The Reverend's leavin' on a long speakin' trip, an' we're just gettin' his trunks and boxes ready to load on the wagon. They'll be bringin' them down shortly. A long trip, child, an' we don't know just when he might return."

This satisfied the boy, who acknowledged with a sleepy sigh and was soon asleep again. Whitcombe could not help but admire the ease with which Miss Lispeth had handled the situation.

It being near four in the morning, Whitcombe saw little point in trying to get more sleep. He walked slowly back to his own cold lodgings and finished dressing, reviewing in his mind how he might spend the day with the students. They'd have to be kept away, that much was sure, and an expedition to gather wood did seem like an excellent idea. He borrowed a hatchet from Mr. Cubbins and located a somewhat dull axe and a rusty saw at the Hall. It looked as if the latter tools had done as little work as some of his pupils and were just as dull.

The boys were gathered in the classroom when he arrived; he noted that the chamber seemed somewhat warmer again, though the fireplace showed no signs of recent use, and that the boys wore guilty looks. He was suddenly suspicious.

"I didn't realize we had any more fuel for the fireplace," he remarked off-handedly. "I wonder where the Reverend keeps his wood." He crossed to the stove and peered in. There were a few scraps of charred paper. He decided the youngest of the students might be the least inclined to lie.

"Master Coombs, what have you been burning in here?"

Master Coombs looked as if he might burst into tears. Peter Tuttle seemed to take pity on him suddenly. "It's this, Schoolmaster," he said, moving the coat which he had thrown over a large sheaf of papers on the floor. Whitcombe moved to snatch them up, words of rebuke already forming in his mind. How dare they burn such an expensive commodity? On looking at the top sheet, however, he quickly determined that what he held was a stack of the late Reverend's sermons and lectures, written in a cramped hand and decorated with ample margin notes. He leafed quickly through the papers to determine that they were all the same sort of thing.

His eyes swept over the assembly. "Do these provide any warmth?" he asked mildly.

Tuttle seemed somewhat bolder now. "Not enough, Schoolmaster, but it's better than nothing." He was quite astonished when Whitcombe handed the papers back.

*He never managed to inflame the soul, but perhaps he can warm the body a bit.*

The foray to gather wood was a success, though some of the stumps would seem to suggest that the trees had been beaten into submission, rather than cut cleanly. Whitcombe was amazed at his students' cooperation. Did they sense that something important had happened. Why had none of them spoken of Rue?

The smaller boys gathered what dead wood they could carry in their arms and made trips back and forth to the house while the older ones tried their skill with the tools Whitcombe had found. For a wonder, there were no injuries. Even Smallfellow seemed pleasant and cooperative.

Whitcombe had expected to resume some of the school's normal routine when he brought the boys back for some soup at noon, and, indeed, the next couple of days passed in that fashion. The students seemed more responsive and less recalcitrant at recitations and there were fewer complaints when they were required to perform some task. They also maintained, to Whitcombe's surprise, an utter silence regarding the late Head of School. Whitcombe could not fathom if somehow they had learned the truth and chose not to speak of the dead, or if, on the contrary, young master Coombs had related to them what Miss Lispeth had said in the kitchen, and that was an end to the matter. For fear of provoking questions he could not answer, Whitcombe remained mute on the topic, also.

On the third day, however, Whitcombe found Elijah Coombs, father of Joshua, awaiting him in the kitchen when he arrived at the school. Whitcombe imagined that the news of Rue's demise had reached Mr. Coombs and that the latter had come with the purpose of withdrawing his son from the school.

As it turned out, the first part of Whitcombe's surmise was correct, but not the second.

Elijah Coombs was seated on a kitchen bench, his back to the table, on which one elbow leaned. He was round and ruddy of face, looking every inch the prosperous farmer. One hand held a mug of tea which Miss Lispeth had prepared.

"Ah, Mister Whitcombe," effused Coombs. "Please sit down and join me. We have matters of grave import to discuss."

Whitcombe accepted a second mug from Miss Lispeth, who then withdrew to another part of the kitchen, but made no secret of the fact that she planned to listen and judge what she heard. Whitcombe sat on a stool facing Coombs, forgetting to remove his coat. He felt not a little apprehensive. He'd met Coombs only once, when the man had delivered his son to the school. He knew little of the farmer, save that he was a man of some means and considerable influence.

Coombs took a sip of tea and smacked his lips before speaking. "I'm told, Mister Whitcombe, that you acted quite creditably during the recent…crisis, keeping a cool head and assuming command in a rather delicate situation. All in all, you conducted yourself quite well and with a good deal of wisdom."

Whitcombe couldn't imagine where Coombs had gotten such a notion. "Mr. Coombs, with all due respect…"

But Coombs held up a hand, forestalling any objections. "Please, Mr. Whitcombe, hear me out." It was evident that Coombs was not a man accustomed to being interrupted or contradicted. Whitcomb fell silent.

"What we need now is a course of action and a capable individual to see it through. Either the school must close or a qualified Head must be found immediately. I will tell you, sir, that I have been in communication with one or two of the other parents regarding the former points as well as the necessity of acting quickly."

Whitcombe couldn't disagree with any of the points Coombs was making, but he didn't see exactly were the conversation was leading. Everything the man had said thus far was obvious. Why did it need to be stated?

"In short, then, we'd like you to take on the position."

Whitcombe gaped at the man for a moment before he could find voice to reply.

"As…as Head, you mean? But I'm not…"

Again the raised hand. "Qualified? Possibly not yet. But it's something you can learn as you go. You're the only Schoolmaster, the only one possibly qualified. Oh, it's true we might find someone eventually—from Boston, perhaps. But that would take too much time. No, we need someone who knows the school, the boys and what needs to be done." He rose. "I expect you'll need some time to think about it, of course. I'll return in two days for your answer." He took his hat from the table, nodded to Miss Lispeth and shook Whitcombe's hand. "We're counting on you, Mister Whitcombe." Then he was gone.

Whitcombe, somewhat stunned, looked to Miss Lispeth for moral support. "Rather…direct gentleman, isn't he?" He was annoyed to note that his voice squeaked at the end.

Miss Lispeth nodded. "But knows his own mind, anyways. I think you should listen to him, Mister Whitcombe."

Whitcombe could not have said how he got through the remainder of the day. He undoubtedly spent it in the classroom, but he couldn't remember what he had taught. The students probably learned nothing. Following lessons, he sequestered himself in the Reverend's room, after building a fire there. He intended to inventory the Reverend's possessions, as the magistrate had requested, but found himself sitting for long moments with some item of the recently deceased's in his hand, his mind far removed from his task.

It certainly was a heady thought. He, Thomas Whitcombe, Head of School at twenty-four! Think what he might accomplish. Why, he could choose his own students, set his own curriculum and bring some modern ideas into a staid and strait-laced profession. He could see the school becoming a grand success, the parents chanting its merits and singing his own praises. He might well be held up as a model for other schools to emulate. He could charge what he wished—though he wouldn't want to price himself out of the market. Could he do it all himself? Or would he be forced to hire another instructor? Instructors, he corrected himself. With the reforms he had in mind, he'd surely need more than one.

Other benefits were evident: he'd grant himself a decent stipend, certainly, be able to afford more of the things he'd doubtless need: clothes, a horse, a servant or two, better quarters…

This last rumination led him naturally to think of Sarah Cubbins. With his new station in life, he would most certainly be in a position to approach Mr. Cubbins and win his approval to court his daughter. And this thought led to others which he quickly repressed, ashamed of himself.

Now he was assailed by doubt. He was surely far too young and too inexperienced to accept such a position. He'd spend most of his time, surely, justifying himself and his methods to parents and have little time left for his own agenda. And the school was in such dire need of repairs that any funds which came in and which were not strictly needed to feed the students and to purchase essential supplies would be quickly swallowed up by the needs of the crumbling building.

What opportunities for advancement were there? He'd essentially be starting at the top; where could he go from there? Mr. Cubbins would certainly not be anxious to have his daughter courted by a man too young for his responsibilities, with little experience and few prospects for the future.

His short tenure in the classroom had already proved to him that there was little chance that he could light a love for learning under his students—not this particular group, anyway. Perhaps he was not meant to be a teacher.

Whitcombe arose, threw another log on the fire, and resumed his inventory.

# HANNAH SMITH (1796)

I wish to make it known at the outset of this Record that I am a sober, God-fearing woman and that calumny is the furthest thing from my mind. But I cannot, in all good conscience, keep silent about these events for the rest of my life, lest the good People of the town, to say nothing of my Family, think me in some measure responsible for them, or an accomplice thereto, by my very silence. I shall therefore endeavor, to the best of my ability, to set forth the events exactly as they transpired. Where I do not have first-hand knowledge of such Events, I have reconstructed them to fit all the known and salient Facts; nor do I believe that any will find evidence to gainsay them.

I have no personal knowledge of what transpired prior to my arrival at the School in the Fall of the year 1795. I will relate what I was told, however, so as to establish a background for the Events that occurred later.

Upon the death of the Reverend Obadiah Rue, founder and first Head of the School, the position was evidently offered to the Teacher, a Mister Whitcombe. He refused it, however, and for the remainder of the academic year, the position was filled by the father of one of the students, a Mr. Coombs. Mr. Whitcombe resigned his position in the spring and subsequently left the area.

As Mr. Coombs already had heavy responsibilities and as his Farm work did not permit extended absences, he engaged, for the Fall of 1795, Mister Matthew Caul to oversee the School. Some say that Mr. Coombs was fortunate to find so capable an individual on such short notice; such was his enthusiasm for Mister Caul, however, that Mr. Coombs appears to have accepted Mister Caul at his Word on all matters & made no inquiries as to his previous employment, not did he request any references. In the light of subsequent events, it would seem that Mr. Caul, if he did not actually falsify some Records and wholly fabricate others, was at the very least prone to Exaggeration and Hyperbole of the worst sort.

It would appear—according to sources, as I did not see the documents myself—that Mister Caul presented to Mr. Coombs ample evidence of his matriculation at and subsequent graduation from, with honors, a prestigious university in Mass^ts^. I did see a Diploma hung in his study, but did not take the trouble to read it, though I will confess that my Latin is not as strong as it perhaps should be.

Lest it be thought that the observations herein set forth are those of someone unfit to judge what she saw and inexperienced in the ways of Education, let me state that I was trained as a Teacher and that I received a strict & solid Normal School education in England. My Father's position, however, required a move to America and thus we settled in this area. I have found no great Call for women as teachers and was on the point of hiring myself out as a housekeeper when I heard of a Position at a literary Institute, one which would require, in addition to the duties of supervising a gentleman's Household, supervision of several young children, perhaps as a governess. I therefore wrote to Mr. Caul and secured the position, no interview or further Letters being necessary, to my surprise. Perhaps if I had inquired more closely, I might have refused.

It wasn't until my arrival in October of the previous year that I learned the full scope of my Duties & even then some of the tasks which Mr. Caul would require of me were not made plain until even later. Of those I will not speak, save in allusion, for fear of offending sensibilities. I will only say at this point that I refused on every count.

It was Mr. Caul's intent to hire me as a Preceptress, not a Teacher, for then he would have to pay me more, but as someone who would act as a surrogate mother and tutor to three children, aged three to five, who were judged too young to attend classes with the others—twelve in number. These were not the Children of Mr. Caul, but had been left at the School by their parents. The reasons for this were never entirely clear.

Mr. Caul was initially known as a great Benefactor, and with good reason. He became Head of an Institute which was a school in name only. The previous Head had died under rather mysterious circumstances, I gather, for it was not a ready topic of conversation. The Hall itself was in very poor repair, a good part of the structure being unusable. Mr. Caul contributed some of his own Fortune towards its restoration, and several Parents of the Scholars contributed likewise. There was one large gift of one hundred pounds, which permitted the completion of most of the repairs to the structure itself, the purchase of enough Books to start a small Library for the use of the Students and enabled masons to begin repairs to the fireplaces and chimneys. The latter constituted a real danger of fire, I am told.

Mr. Caul also purchased a small cottage at not too great a distance from the School, in which he would reside. The upstairs bedroom thus became sleeping quarters for the four Boys who lived too far to return home at night. The old sleeping quarters became a nursery of sorts for the younger children, and I had my bed in the former servant's quarters.

Several months into the School Term, however, Mr. Caul found himself short of funds and abruptly raised the Tuition, causing two families to withdraw their Sons, and thus instead of generating extra revenue, Mr. Caul actually found himself with a bit less than before.

Mr. Caul, I can say without fear of contradiction, was never pleasant to look upon. The engraving of his visage, which he placed on prominent Display in the Library, will bear this out, though in my Opinion, the portrait flatters him too much. The defeat of his project to raise additional money for the school seems to have soured his disposition and rendered his features even more disagreeable, however. At present, I can wonder if he indeed ever had the best interests of the School in mind; at that time, however, I attributed the change in his Personality to the fact that he was unable to carry out the good works he had planned for the School.

He did make some modifications to the Course of Study, in the interest, perhaps, of modernizing it, or perhaps of making it less English. To my mind, however, he has merely given new names to old Subjects. Nevertheless, I suppose that it is not my place to judge such matters.

I thought his methods of Correction somewhat excessive. There was, apparently, before the arrival of Mister Caul, a young Schoolmaster who did not believe that sparing the rod would spoil the Child, and consequently never lifted a finger against them. I understand further that the students took advantage of this Fact and held this particular individual in very little respect, forcing him—if one is to believe what one hears—to withdraw early, renouncing the teaching Profession. Such Persons, whatever their Intent, make poor Schoolmasters, for the undisciplined Body houses and undisciplined Mind.

That being said, I found Mr. Caul's methods too severe for the offense. Many Masters will keep a Stick or Switch within easy reach, and its very presence may dissuade some younger minds from thoughts of Evil. Mr. Caul, however, carried one whenever he was in the classroom, and used it rather freely. I myself did not witness these Acts, but the cries of the Students were certainly plain to anyone in the House, and the results of such treatment were readily visible to all, *viz.* Welts and Marks upon the Body. On one occasion he was said to have used an iron ruler or perhaps an instrument such as a poker on the Head of one of his charges. I do not affirm that this was so, for I did not observe it. I know that my assistance was required to staunch a great flow of Blood and that the services of a Surgeon were necessary to apply several Stitches of thread to the area. Mr. Caul insisted that the Boy, Jeremiah Fisher by name, had fallen and stuck his head upon the stove. Master Fisher would neither affirm nor deny this.

The Negro woman who prepared meals showed, when she felt she was not being observed, some little Sympathy for the Plight of the Scholars and I have seen her slip them bits of food or Sweetmeats. The Boys seem to hold her in high regard. I endeavored several times to engage her in conversation, but she was always polite and distant. I believe that she thought me in League with Mr. Caul, for I was always essaying to question her regarding the Quality and Quantity of Victuals which she prepared. It seemed to me very poor Fare indeed. I noted that Mr. Caul seemed to dine very well, and that there appeared to be no shortage of Funds when it came to purchasing the Meats for his meals. The Pupils, however, were fortunate to get leftovers; mostly it was only cooked grains and a bit of bread. The Cook (I believe her name was Elizabeth) was always careful, however, to set aside a plentiful amount of good food for the three young children in my care. I suspect she could do this because they did not take their meals in the Presence of Mr. Caul. Nevertheless, I feel that she feared I might tell him and that his wrath might fall upon her.

It was a day in November, as I recall, when, finding we were short on some Necessaries for the School, I put the small children into Elizabeth's care and went into the village of Farmington for paper & pens. I was in Mr. Brooke's shop where Mr. Brooke was waiting on other customers. Either they did not know I was there, or, more likely, they did not know who I was (in truth, I rarely left the confines of the School grounds), for they spoke freely of the conditions at the School, saying much the same thing as I have related above.

I did not know the persons speaking; they might have been Parents or Guardians of some of the Students, or they might simply have been repeating Gossip they had heard elsewhere. In any event, I gathered from the Conversation that there was some little Disappointment with the way Mr. Caul was handling Matters, and most especially the Discipline. How they came by this information, I know not, but it was none of my doing. I did feel enough Loyalty to my Employer (I see now that it was misplaced, and it may be that he misunderstood my Concerns as a Sympathy or as a desire to become his Benefactor), enough Loyalty, I say, to inform him, being careful to give no clue as to the speakers' identities, of what I had overheard.

He betrayed no emotion, neither Anger nor Shock nor Regret, but rather dismissed the remarks as idle gossip, not meriting his attention. He made it plain that Students will complain about something, no matter what the circumstances; if they find the Victuals sufficient, they are apt to complain about the Schoolmaster; if the Schoolmaster cannot be faulted, then the Instruction is wanting in Quality, &c. In brief, then, the opinions of others were of little import to him.

It was shortly after this Incident (and perhaps in part because of it) that occurred the *contretemps* of which I am loathe to give details. I speak of it only to show that Mr. Caul and I were not of the same mind. I mentioned to him at one point that the Weather was certainly colder than one might expect for this time of year; an idle remark so that we did not sit together at the table in silence. He replied that it was indeed, and that, should I find my own quarters too cold, I might come and share his.

I was, you will appreciate, taken aback by his remark and feigned not to understand his meaning, replying that I might, after all, keep the door to my little room ajar, thus permitting more of the heat from the kitchen to enter. He said that yes, that was one way to keep warm at night, but there were others. At this Juncture, I informed him that my Duties necessitated my presence elsewhere, wished him a good day, and left.

I wish to make known that he did not repeat his offer in so many Words, and that I always sought to have one of the Students or Elizabeth present when I thought I might encounter Mr. Caul, nor did I sleep, as I had proposed, with my door open to the kitchen. You will appreciate the reason why, and I shall not need to state it.

It was not until afterwards that I learned that the Persons I had heard conversing in Mr. Brooke's shop did not represent a small body of Malcontents, but, indeed, represented but a fraction of a number of People who were not pleased with the turn matters were taking at the School. I suspect there may have been other Incidents of which I was unaware at the time and about which I remain ignorant even to this day.

It was upon the last night of the old Year that I was awakened by an insistent rapping upon the kitchen door. We were having a three-day Holiday, and I was alone in the Hall. Elizabeth had banked the fires and had gone, I suppose, to stay with relatives or visit friends. My first thought was that it might be Mr. Caul, so I did not draw the bolt immediately, but instead looked out of the window which adjoins the door. To my surprise, I perceived a small group of People waiting without. I unbolted the door and bade them enter.

I knew the vicar, of course, the Rev. Goodman, and recognized one or two of the others. They would not sit nor tarry, but inquired as to the whereabouts of Mr. Caul. I responded that I thought him home. Mr. Goodman said they had tried with no success to rouse someone at the cottage and might I have a key?

I did not, but I knew that Mr. Caul had another hung in the shed which adjoins the cottage; if they would wait while I dressed and fetched a lantern, I would accompany them and find the key. To this they agreed.

I have no wish to draw this narrative out unnecessarily. Suffice it to say that upon our arrival, we found the cottage cold, dark and deserted. It did not appear that a fire had been made for at least two days. Of Mr. Caul and his belongings there was no sign, though the furniture was left.

These are the ensuing events: the school was closed by order of the vicar, and I found myself without employ, as did Elizabeth. The interns were returned to their families, and, I assume found other schools or gainful Employment. No trace was ever found, to my knowledge, of Mr. Caul, nor of any Money belonging to the School. I will not speculate, though I may be permitted my suspicions.

I hope I have established by this admittedly lengthy Letter that I had no knowledge of Mr. Caul's Intentions, nor did I aid him by any Means, save in the fulfillment of my Duties.

*(The document is signed by the hand of Hannah Smith and by a notary whose signature is illegible. It is dated 15$^{th}$ January 1797)*

# THE GRANBY *REGISTER*, May 12, 1797

## Great Conflagration.

One of our town's landmark buildings was lost in a Fire two days ago. The Rue Literary Institute, also called Claxton Hall, was completely destroyed by a great Blaze that all but leveled the structure. This Edifice had until recently housed a School and about a dozen young Pupils, as well as their Teacher and various other Workers. We are happy to report, however, that there was no concurrent loss of Life, as the Building had been deserted since the first of this Year.

Ten or twelve of our stalwart Townsfolk, either upon sighting the Fire or perhaps hearing the Commotion generated by its discovery, attempted in vain to quench the fire by bringing buckets of water from nearby wells. The Fire, however, had already gained an advance which could not be stemmed and the Building was a total loss.

The Cause of the Fire is unknown, as there have been no fires kindled there (it is presumed) since the School was closed earlier & was uninhabited. It is speculated that an Itinerant, seeking shelter from the chill, might have entered and essayed to warm himself by burning some logs in a Fireplace. The other Proposal is somewhat more sinister, and is not espoused by many: that the Fire might have been deliberately set by an as-yet-unknown Criminal Element.

It will be remembered that, upon incorporation of our town as Upper Granby Lake last Month, the Baptist Fathers announced their intention to acquire the property from the heir or heirs of John Claxton, could they be located, and to reopen the School under their Guidance. It is possible, though admittedly unlikely, that some Individual opposed to this Project might have seen fit to stop it early, to strangle it in its cradle, so to speak. We may dismiss one claim that it was one of the former Pupils of Matthew Caul seeking revenge for the wrongs done him, as there is no evidence to support this Theory.

If any of our Readers have any further Knowledge of this Event, we pray them to communicate the same to the Offices of this Newspaper. Such new Developments as may come to light will be published in the next number of this Journal.

# CHARTER OF THE CLAXTON HALL SCHOOL, 1798

Statement of purpose: To provide a Christian learning experience for young men of this community and for those not of this community whom the Board of Governors or Deacons may suggest or recommend. To encourage said Pupils to live Godly, upright lives and to train them to find gainful employment by which they may bring betterment to the Community.

Administration: The Officers of the Covenant Church of Upper Granby Lake shall serve as Trustees and Board of Governors and the Head of School shall be one of their number, appointed by them. The Faculty to be made up of those church-going men as the Officers shall see fit to appoint to the various posts.

Curriculum: While it is recognized that the needs of those students to be educated at the Hall may change from time to time, the curriculum shall nevertheless be firmly rooted in the classic studies of Latin and Greek. Additional training will be offered in Scripture, English Composition and Declamation, Mathematics and Economics. Once a year the Officers of the Church shall review the Curriculum and make thereto such modifications as they may deem appropriate.

Financial: The Officers shall appoint an Overseer whose task it shall be to maintain the financial soundness of the Institution. He will set Tuition and Fees yearly in an amount sufficient to ensure that the Hall remains financially independent, even though it not show a Profit. The Overseer shall also seek new sources of revenue to maintain the Buildings and Grounds.

Given unto our hand and seal this 2nd day of January 1798

*Matthew Bishop*
*Jon. Hamilton*
*Azariah Collins*
*Jos. Collins*
*Wm. L. Harrington*

# WILLIAM HARRINGTON (1798)

17th Jan^y 1798

My Very Dear Sirs:

It is with an admixture of Pride and a deep and respectful sense of Resolute Purpose that I reply to yours of the 16th inst. That you see fit to endow me with this Responsibility bespeaks a Trust that of which I will do my utmost to be worthy. I pledge to you to carry out the Task of Head of the School to the best of my Ability, bearing in mind at all times the Sacred Mission of the Church and the teachings of Our Lord.

I will remove to the stone cottage, which was the Residence of the previous Head, Mr. Caul, as soon as it be convenient and shall use that Edifice as Dwelling and Office until the construction of the new Building be complete. In all things, I shall work closely with Mr. Thackery, whom you have wisely appointed Overseer to the School.

I am pleased to learn that you have generously offered the use of the Church until such time as the new Facility is available.

Yours in Christ,

*Wm. L. Harrington*

5th March 1798

My Dear Mr. Bishop,

I was most gratified to receive your Draft in the amount of £50 this morning. From that amount I shall take my salary for three months, as you so kindly suggest, and use the rest to purchase Supplies for the School. If you have any idea of how many Pupils we might expect upon the opening, I would appreciate hearing at your earliest convenience, as there is still the matter of procuring an adequate Staff for the Institute.

In the matter of Curriculum, I would like to advance one or two Suggestions, which I hope will meet with the Board's approval. Chief among these is the addition of French to the Curriculum. I need not remind you that, in the recent unpleasantness with England, the French proved to be a staunch Ally and that their Language, melodious in the extreme, is the preferred speech of many of Europe's courts, to say nothing of the Imperial Court of Russia. Surely the language of Voltaire deserves a place in our Course of Studies.

I note with interest the progress on the Schoolhouse. The foundation has been laid, along with several courses of stone. There shall be a commodious Schoolroom, a Refectory and kitchen, a Pantry and Storage for divers Supplies. It is my understanding that students who board at the School shall be housed with families in the Community. I should offer a space in my own stone cottage, but it is, alas, entirely too small.

To that end, I wonder if the Board might see its way clear, should there be Material remaining from the Construction of the Schoolhouse, to allowing me to use such Surplus in the construction of an Addition to that Structure.

I anticipate eagerly your reply to the above matters.

Your obt. servant.
*Wm. L. Harrington*

22nd July 1798

My Dearest Mother,

It is very warm today, but this is normal for the Clime, I have learned. At least my little cottage is cool, but it is also dark and for that reason I have brought my desk near the window from where I can watch the masons at work.

We have dismissed School for a time, the weather being unsuited to Learning. The stone cutters, masons and carpenters continue their labours, however; I suppose they are accustomed to such conditions. It is marvelous to watch the Schoolhouse rise; already they are above the first floor and soon the rafter timbers must be lifted into place. Although the Deacons believe the construction seems to drag at a snail's pace, (they are, after all, paying for it) it could really advance no faster. We shall, I estimate, be able to occupy the Premises this Fall. We have twelve Pupils enrolled at the present time, and I have engaged the services of one other Teacher. I am teaching Scripture and Grammar; Mr. Collins instructs the Students in Composition and Mathematics. The Board of Governors would have other Subjects offered, but our financial state, alas, does not allow this at the present Time. Nevertheless, the Church has been unstinting, and has allowed me to purchase such Supplies as I feel we need. I should not wish it communicated with the Board, however, that I have taken some Monies from my own Pocket rather than petition them for a few Pence. I feel that the Stipend they allot me is adequate, if not generous, nor would I wish them to believe I was mis-spending their funds.

The News of the School and of my Situation, however, is but a Pretext, dear Mother, for the Tidings of the present Missive and will explain the Enclosure to this letter, which you will have already noted. I trust it shall come as an agreeable Surprise to you, dear Mother, to learn that I am engaged to be wed.

Mistress Sarah Cubbins is a young Woman well thought of in the Community. She is nineteen years of age and quite pleasing to the eye. Her Father is a fairly prosperous Landowner and offered no Objections when I asked him if I might call upon his daughter. You might wonder that such a woman is as yet unmarried; indeed, she did not lack for Suitors, but found none who pleased her. I have known who she was for some little Time, but did not think to speak to her—nay, even to think of her—until such time as I might look to support a wife and family. Such an Opportunity presented itself when I was offered the position of Head of School. I held out no great Expectations, but was delighted by her Consent to see me.

Well, I shall not go into greater Detail at this point, but shall recount all when I see you. Hence the ticket, dear Mother. We are to be wed in October, just at the start of the new Term, and I very much hope you can attend. I shall procure you a Lodging at the best Inn in Town, as the cottage could not house us all. I have no Doubts but that you will find Mistress Sarah to be even more attractive and charming than I could tell you here.

I remain, in the hope of a favorable response,

Yr. loving son,
*William*

21st June 1799

To the Board of Governors
Claxton Hall School
Upper Granby Lake Connt

Gentlemen:

It is with a deep Sense of Pride and thanksgiving that I report to you upon what I regard to be a most successful Year in the School. It is with

God's Help and yours that we have overcome many of the Difficulties with which any new Enterprize is beset.

I applaud your decision to offer no Summer Term this Year and to delay the Opening of School until the Fall so that we may accomplish some much needed Tasks. I am further most grateful for your permitting me to wed and have found much delight in the company of Mistress Cubbins, now Mrs. William Harrington. The Stone that remained from the building of the Schoolhouse is being put to good use, I may assure you, and it is my hope that the Renovations & Addition to my Dwelling may be completed by the time School opens again. Be assured, however, that I shall not stint in my Labours for the School, and that the Construction on the Cottage shall in no wise interfere with the Fulfillment of my Duties.

A Summary of the Year's Events follows:

1° - We had enrolled some twelve Youths, though the Number varied somewhat throughout the Year. Of these, four were Boarders, coming from Mass$^{ts}$ and in one case, as far as N. Hampshire. We must look into the possibility of constructing a Dormitory, for if, as I hope, the enrollment should increase, there will not be sufficient Families in the Community willing or able to host all of those who wish to attend in the capacity of Boarder. In that case also, it must be clear, better Kitchen and Dining Facilities must be provided. Eight Boys are already enrolled for the Fall Term.

2° - I would suggest to the Overseer that we consider increasing the Tuition that we may begin to lay aside Monies for the Projects mentioned above.

3° - I have engaged a Teacher of English Grammar and Composition for the Fall Term. I myself will lecture in Declamation, Scripture and Mathematics. We have as yet found no Teacher for Economics, though I have found a Gentleman willing to impart to our Pupils some Knowledge of Husbandry. I have urged him to communicate with you as I cannot judge if such a Subject might have a place in our Curriculum. I am attempting, at the present time, to engage a Teacher of French and have written to a Gentleman in Canada, whose Name was given to me, but I have received no Answer as yet.

4° - We must find some Method of occupying our Boarders in the after noon hours. If we were to clear one of the adjoining Fields of Brush, &c, perhaps the Boys could amuse themselves with a Ball for some hours.

5° - In regard to 1°, above: I would beg the Board to consider some of the other Needs with which we may be beset in the Future and to move to forestall Difficulties which might arise should we tarry too long in the execution of some of these projects, to wit: engagement of a Cook who may prepare healthful Meals for the Pupils. For the Boarders, Missus Harrington prepares a Porridge in order that they might break their Fast, and at the Noon meal there is usually some remaining meat of a Joint we have dined on the previous evening, but she finds it difficult to prepare an evening Repast for the Pupils whilst tending to her own Duties at home. My Resources do not permit me to engage a Domestic at the present time.

Respectfully submitted,
*William Harrington*

1st September 1799

To the Board of Governors
Claxton Hall School
Upper Granby Lake Connt

Gentlemen:

I am pleased to report a successful Conclusion to the Negotiations re: engaging an Instructor in the French Language.

Mr Jean Chardin, of the Province of Quebec, has consented, pursuant to agreement of Salary, to serve as Instructor at the Hall, provided some Lodging may be found for him in Town. I pray you look into this Matter, as I am at present far too preoccupied with the Opening of School to do so.

I expect Mr Chardin to arrive sometime in the first Week of October.

I am further pleased to report that I have retained the Services of M[r] Matthew Brandeis, a resident of Upper Granby Lake, who has Knowledge and Skill in the art of Fisticuffs and who will instruct such Boys as wish to learn the Art of Self Defense Wednesday and Friday afternoons at the School.

I remain,

Yr. respectful & obt. servant,
*William Harrington*

**personal journal**

Oct. 23, 1799

We are occupying the new Schoolhouse at this time, and my next Report to the Board will undoubtedly be optimistic. We have enrolled eighteen Boys and there is a Prospect of one or two more. Our Reputation and the high Moral Standards set by the School are undoubtedly attracting attention, for there have been no fewer than six Inquiries this month.

The Teacher of French arrived as scheduled and has begun his Duties. He is somewhat younger than I had expected, but seems nonetheless competent. As of yet, he knows few People in the Community, and, although he is comfortably lodged in the Village, he spends considerable time at our House, being present for Dinner three or four times a week, it seems.

Nov[r] 12, 1799

At their last meeting, the Board approved several of my Requests, to my great delight. We have engaged a Cook to prepare one or two Meals a day for the Boys: one, if they take their Dinner at home, two if they do not. I have found it necessary to charge twenty-five cents per meal, else I could not cover Costs of the Victuals nor the Salary of the Cook. I was relieved that the Parents seemed to find this Fee reasonable, and most who wish their Son to dine here pay it weekly, without question. Indeed, they seem thankful. To my mind, however, the Kitchen and Dining Facilities are still inadequate.

The Boys have begun to clear the field of brush and trees. This Activity has proven very beneficial as it warms them on cool afternoons, provides healthful Exercise and is giving us a Supply of Firewood against the coming Winter. I venture to say that we shall be able to use the space for sports and games once the warmer weather returns.

M^r^ Chardin continues his frequent visits. Sarah has told me that, as her Household Duties do not require her full Attention, she is desirous of taking French Lessons and has requested that Jean, as she calls him, be permitted to come twice a week for that purpose. I have agreed, albeit somewhat reluctantly, as it appears that M^r^ Chardin will be at my Home when my duties would keep me at the School. Nevertheless, it is my greatest Desire to please Sarah, as to see her happy is a great sort of Contentment to me. It is also gratifying to see a Woman who wishes to develop her Intelligence, though I confess that I do not see to what use she might put it.

14^th^ Dec. 1799

Have I taken a Viper into my Bosom?

I was drafting a Report to the Board yesterday when I realized that I had left some necessary Notes I had been making upon my Desk at Home. I tried to recall their Contents, but could not do so successfully; thus I felt it necessary to return to get them. It is not my Wont to return during the day, as the Events which I am about to relate will show:

The front door of my cottage opens directly to the Staircase, yet one may see the Dining Room to the left, and the Parlor to the right, immediately upon entering. In the Parlor I perceived my Wife, seated on a Divan, and M^r^ Chardin opposite, upon a Chair, drawn up quite close to the Divan, their knees almost touching. I supposed that my Wife was being tutored in French, yet the look upon her Face, indeed, her entire Demeanor, gave me pause, and, though, my foot was raised to place it upon the Step, yet did I withdraw it and proceed instead into the Parlor. My Wife, it may be supposed, looked somewhat surprised to see me, as did M^r^ Chardin. I was, however, immediately concerned for Sarah, for I perceived that her bodice was partially unlaced and that she appeared flushed, and breathing with some difficulty. Upon seeing me, the Pair drew apart, and M^r^ Chardin rose, his Consternation apparent. He said that he was glad that I had come, for my Wife had been taken with a brief spell of Vertigo, had felt warm and faint and was even just now recovering.

—Shall I send for a surgeon, I inquired.

—No, she said quickly, for the crisis is past.

I looked then upon our Guest and inquired if he had Medical Training.

—No, said he, but it was evident that her Breathing was constricted, I did but essay to ease it.

—I thank you, *monsieur*, for your thoughtfulness, I told him, but as I am now returned Home, I shall see to the comfort of my Wife.

I thereupon bid him good-day, though I fear my tone was rather brusque. At that moment, I could not have said if it were because of a Concern for Sarah's Welfare, or from some dark Suspicion I could not name, and which, indeed, I should have denied vehemently should someone have suggested it.

21$^{st}$ Dec$^{r}$ 1799

The first Snow of the season has fallen, not a great amount, to be sure, but sufficient to keep the Boys indoors during afternoon Recreation. In the classroom, we have pushed the benches & Tables to one side, clearing a sufficient Space for our Boxing Lessons, which most of the Boys delight in. M$^{r}$ Matthew Brandeis certainly fits the role well, for he is a large Specimen of a Man, but very patient for all of that, & he takes considerable Pains to ensure that every Boy is included, but that none are injured.

I have almost decided that the unpleasant Incident of a week ago was perhaps more innocent than I perceived it at the time & that I perhaps over-reacted. In any case, I note that Sarah has been very loving & caring, nor have I found the Frenchman at my House again.

In another few days, we begin not only a new Year, but a new Century. May it be a prosperous and joyous one for all of us!

4$^{th}$ Jan$^{y}$ 1800

We have begun a new Term with four more Pupils, though one of our older Boys did not return, and I suspect he will not. I have written the Board to see if they might find Funds to engage another Instructor, as, given the Differences in Age among the Boys, it is difficult for one Teacher to successfully instruct all of the Boys at different Levels at the same time. It may be that we shall also need to seek an additional Classroom.

11$^{th}$ Febr$^{y}$ 1800

O, I have been shamed, betrayed & cuckolded!

There can be no Doubt of the Matter, for I have a Confirmation from her own perfidious Lips!

I was to have a Meeting late this morning with the Board, to give a Report on the Progress of divers Matters &c. However, I chanced to spill some Ink upon my weskit, which necessitated a return Home to change it. No sooner had I opened the door, when I heard a Commotion upstairs, like a great Shuffling of feet & Banging. I thought perhaps my Wife was moving some Articles of Furniture about, or perhaps that some Object had fallen & was rolling about the floor.

Upon arrival in our Bedchamber, I perceived the Casement open, the Bed in a state of disarray & my Wife hastily knotting the sash of a Dressing Gown. I crossed to the window to look into the Court, thinking that I might have surprised a Thief in the Act of a Crime & that he had escaped thereby. Indeed, I caught but a Glimpse of some Person exiting our Gate, but I could see naught but the legs.

I was suddenly taken with a terrible Suspicion, which was partly confirmed when I placed my Hand upon the Bedclothes & found them warm. I then turned to speak to my Wife and knew that she was endeavoring to hide her Nakedness under that thin Gown, whose weight was entirely unsuited to the season.

—Woman, I demanded, have you taken that Frenchman to our Bed?

If I expected her to be shocked by the Question, I was disappointed, for she gazed upon me coolly and retorted that this was no kind of Question to put to one of her Station, and, if I did so, then I were no Gentleman.

I raged at her: —You are a shameless Harlot, an abominable Adulteress!

Never had I spoken thus to a Woman, and never with such vehemence. I can not say what Reaction I expected; had she denied the Act, or wept, or begged my Forgiveness, none of these would have surprised me. Yet the words appeared to have little Effect on one who had just committed a heinous Crime and who had defiled the Sanctity of the Marriage Bed, setting aside, by this same Action, God's Commandment.

Her Voice remained calm, and even (unless I am very mistaken), defiant: —So you have named me, Husband, and, therefore, so will I comport myself.

I believe I might have struck her at that point, nor is there any Court that would condemn me, but I am neither a large nor a violent Man and thus did naught but raise my Arm & then let it fall again. It emboldened her to see me thus, and she spoke again: —Therefore I pray you, Husband, to set me aside and I will go. I shall leave with Jean and you shall be rid of us both; we shall trouble you no more.

I was on the point of acceding to her Request; indeed, I had already opened my Mouth to order her out, when a Thought stuck me, and I answered instead: —No, Madam, that I will not do, for that is what you want, to run away with that Scoundrel, and it were no Punishment if I were to allow it. Therefore, you shall continue to reside in this House, and I shall permit no further Contact with that Man: you shall neither speak to or of him again, nor shall you ever see him more. Moreover, I shall make your grievous Fault known to all, I shall shame you publickly, and your Whoring shall be the topic of every Conversation in every Alehouse. You, Madam, will have to live with your Sin, and in full View of all. This is a fitting Chastisement, I believe.

Again, I was disappointed in her Reaction, for she neither showed Remorse, nor recanted her Act. Instead, she said:

—Should you do that, Husband, then I would swear before a Magistrate that I caught you disporting yourself with the bakery Girl.

I was so astounded that for a Moment I could not answer. At length I found my Wits & my Voice once again, and said: —That is the purest Perjury and Slander! There are none who would believe such Lies and Falsehoods!

At these Words, she cast down her Eyes, and I thought for a Moment that Reason had convinced her of the Wrongness of her Course and that she was reconsidering her Conduct and would soon realize her Error. Again, I was grievously mistaken an once more her Response took me off-guard:

—It may be as you say, Husband, and none may give my Reports any Credence, save my Father. For look you, if I go to my Father, and tell him of your Debauchery and your attempts to lead me into the paths of Evil and Perverseness, should he not believe me? Would he not listen to the Tears of his Daughter? And is he not one of the most powerful and influential Men of our Community? He would, I think, send stout Men with great Cudgels in pursuit, and I cannot say that you would be much alive after meeting them.

I could hardly credit what I was hearing. O vile Woman, has there ever been a creature so deceitful and base? For she said all with a Tone so honey-sweet that she might have been talking to a Lover. I could not believe her so unrepentant.

I could find no other Words, save to tell her that I would sleep elsewhere, perhaps in the Kitchen, and that I had no Desire to touch the Bed nor any of the Bedclothes ever again.

—I shall put your Clothes in the Hall, that you may never have Cause to enter again, she assured me.

At first light tomorrow, I shall go into the Village and instruct the Smith to fasten a Hasp and Lock to the Window of the Bedchamber.

I am Prey to the blackest Despair ever experienced by Man.

Feb. 12

I have taken up Residence in the Parlor; it is not comfortable, but it cannot, at least, be used for other Purposes.

Upon my return from the Blacksmith, I found a letter from Mistress Cubbins (is she still my Wife? How many other Men have taken her to Wife?) stating that neither shall I seek any Vengeance upon Jean Chardin, or she will make good upon her Threat to denounce me to her Father. I am to do Nothing which might indicate that there has been Anything amiss with the School, nor in my Household.

Why am I being so tested, O Lord?

8th March 1800

It is warmer to-day. In one sense, then, the coldest part of the Winter is past, though it continues in my Soul. If I were asked how the School fares, I could not answer with Certainty, for I have been absent in Spirit, if not Body.

Of Sarah I see little. I suspect she emerges from her Room when I am absent, but has a Care to keep from my Sight when I return, tho' I can upon occasion hear her moving about upstairs. Whether she still receives Chardin, I do not know, nor do I care overly. It seems as though that part of my Life is over, and I must put it behind me. The most difficult part is seeing Chardin each day. He is evidently well-acquainted (I know not how) with what transpired between Sarah and myself; he also suspects that I have no real Proof of his Guilt (for I cannot swear with Certainty that it was he whom I saw disappearing out of the Gate that day) and therefore has adapted a superior Air, tinged with Arrogance and wreathed in a sort of Smirk, as he knows he is beyond my Reach, protected by my Wife. I am sure they are still wallowing in their Sin, else why would he still be here?

I have engaged a Domestic (which I can ill afford), since Sarah no longer prepares Meals nor tends the House. I have not questioned her concerning Sarah's Behavior: I do not wish to know.

How many others are aware of her Transgressions and laugh at me behind my back?

Apr. 19, 1800

If what I did today was a Sin, O Lord, I accept willingly whatever Consequences You may seek to visit upon me, but I cannot believe that You would deny me a Vengeance which is so richly deserved.

After several weeks of living in what I considered to be my Exile, I conceived a Plan which today came to Fruition. Things came about in this Way:

Last week I sought out Matthew Brandeis in the Village. I did not give him the full Particulars of my Situation (in point of Fact, I mentioned my Wife not at all), but concocted a Tale that intrigued him sufficiently that he agreed, for the sum of five Dollars, to do what I requested. Given the Circumstances, he said, it would give him some Pleasure to help me.

It has become somewhat of a Custom for those who do not have other Duties to attend our afternoon Boxing sessions. It is not unusual to see several Villagers there (for they enjoy the Spectacle), nor even, from time to time, *monsieur* Chardin. It was perhaps on the third Occasion after I reached an Accord with Mr Brandeis that the Frenchman made an Appearance at one of our Sessions. After a lengthy Talk and Demonstration of some Technique, Mr Brandeis feigned to notice Chardin among the Onlookers and addressed him thus:

—Come, sir, let us spar a bit, for I hear that you Canadians are hearty Souls indeed, and the least of you can endure a Blow as easily as he endures the cold Wind of the North.

—Nay, replied the other, for I am no Fighter, sir, and you would easily best me.

—Not so, for this is but a Sport. We do but demonstrate, and I am sure the Boys would enjoy seeing me receive a sound Thumping. Right, lads?

Of course, the Pupils responded that they would very much like to witness such a Bout. Chardin realized that he could not, in good Conscience, refuse further, for if he did so, he would be showing Weakness and Reluctance to answer what was merely a sporting Challenge. He therefore acquiesced with as much Grace as he could muster, removed his coat and took up a Stance in the center of the room. Either because he had some Knowledge of the Sport or because he had been observing Mr Brandeis, he held himself in the proper Positions, insofar as I could determine.

Mr Brandeis allowed Chardin to essay several Blows, neatly avoiding each, before he himself attempted one. It was not so hard as might have felled an Ox, but solid nonetheless, and it sent Chardin reeling backwards. He might have fetched up against a table had he not been caught by several of the Boys. I saw the astonished Look on his Visage and noted a Trickle of Blood from his Nose. Yet he seemed more surprised than injured. Mr Brandeis moved quickly to succor him and said:

—O, I am sorry, sir, for I did not think it such a great Blow, and I regret the Effect it has had. I apologize, for I see that I was much misinformed as regards your Countrymen. We shall shake Hands, and that shall be an end to the Matter.

I was greatly chagrined to think I had got so little for my five Dollars, but I did not at that point appreciate Mr Brandeis's Stratagem.

Chardin had put his Hand to his Face and was staring at the Blood on his Palm, but he pushed Mr Brandeis away and said:

—You did but catch me by Surprise, sir, but now I am ready and I will show you that what you have heard about Canadians was not exaggerated, but rather understated.

They took again their Places in the Center of the room.

I had never, up to this Point in Time, considered Boxing to be anything but a Sport, at most, or at least a Pass-time. I can appreciate now the Art & Skill required, for I watched Mr Brandeis work with all of the Precision of a Surgeon. At no time did Chardin land a Blow, for Mr Brandeis always seemed to recognize the Frenchman's Intentions, and always moved his Body from harm's Way, in such a manner that the Frenchman became enraged and began to swing somewhat wildly. Every so often, one of Mr Brandeis' Fists would pass the Frenchman's guard and land a telling Blow, not hard, for I could see that Mr Brandeis wished to draw out the Contest as long as possible. First one of the Frenchman's Eyes was blackened and closed, then the other. The Boys had fallen mostly silent now, whether in Awe of Mr Brandeis' Skill, or in Fear for Chardin's Life, I could not say. But Frustration and Anger were plain on the Frenchman's Face.

Now Chardin's Mouth was bruised and bleeding, but still he would not yield. I admit to a grudging Admiration for a Man who could tolerate so much Punishment and still remain upon his Feet. But any Skill he might have demonstrated earlier had deserted him long ago, and he now moved forward against his Foe, his Arms swinging in wide Arcs, but bootlessly. Mr Brandeis kept backing away, not allowing the Frenchman to approach closely enough to land a Blow. Then, of a sudden, Mr Brandeis stepped toward the Frenchman, and, eschewing another Punch to the damaged Face, struck him with such force in the Stomach that Chardin sat immediately, his Eyes bulging, all the Breath gone out of him. The Look upon his Face at this point was unmistakably Fright.

The Boys seemed to come to Life again, calling to me to end the Fight, entreating me to save Chardin. I saw that I must, or possibly be seen as an Accomplice. I therefore stepped forward, between the two, and announced that the Demonstration and Lesson were at an end, that the Boys should now disperse.

I moved to help Chardin to his Feet, for Mr Brandeis had moved to a Corner, where he was pulling on his Shirt.

—We must get you to a Physician, sir, I told him.

He could scarcely breathe, but managed to gasp that he needed no doctor, that his Wounds were but superficial and that he had had much worse and needed but to return to his Lodging to clean up and change his Clothing. I suggested that, as M^r Brandeis was return to the Village, they could perhaps accompany each other, but Chardin refused this Suggestion and staggered out of the Room.

I thanked M^r Brandeis for his Lesson. He replied that he hoped it had been a good one.

Apr. 23

I have not seen the Frenchman since that Day, nor do I think to see him again. I received a Letter from him to-day, delivered by Messenger. It contained his Resignation, for reasons of Health, and stated that he would be returning to Canada as soon as he could put his affairs in order and that if he were still due some Salary, I could send it him at his home.

April 24, 1800

I suspect that the Frenchman has got Word somehow to Sarah, for Rachel (our Domestic) reports that she is very morose.

For my part, I can feel no Remorse for what I have done. It is a beautiful Spring Day.

May the First, 1800

With the Departure of Chardin, I thought to have won the War of the Strumpet, as I was calling it privately, but from what followed, I see that it was but a Skirmish and that my Opponent is diabolically clever.

Upon my return this Evening, Rachel told me that her Mistress had now refused all Victuals for the third day, and would take only a little Water and was looking poorly. Thereupon I mounted to the Bedchamber (I no longer call it "ours" and knocked until, at length, the Creature condescended to open it, more from a Desire to silence the Racket, I daresay, that from any Wish to confront me. She was, as Rachel had said, looking pale and wan, her Eyes lusterless. Her Cheeks were begrimed with Tears.

—Madam, I told her, it is of little Consequence to me whether you die of old Age in this Room or of Hunger, so if your Fasting is some Artifice to win my Sympathy and give you your Freedom, you should rethink your Strategy, for it will not work on me.

She remained, however, as defiant as ever, and told me: —But should it get out, Husband, that you are keeping me confined to the room, with only a bit of water, I daresay it would go hard with you.

I was tired of her Threats.

—-Should you attempt that, Madam, I know a Physician who will write a Document saying that you have the Consumption; indeed, that such is the Explanation of your Appearance, and that you should avoid all Intercourse with others and that is the Reason why you are herein confined. (In Truth, I knew no such Physician, but she could not know that.)

She stared at me for a Moment, her Eyes as hard as Granite. Then she told me: —Then I must die.—and closed the door. I did not derive as much Satisfaction from this Interview as I thought I might.

15th of May

Have we found a Solution? I cannot be sure, but I pray it be so.

Time may dull even the most grievous Pain, and I found myself growing weary of the Battle. I even felt the first faint Stirrings of Pity and resolved to do something to end the Confrontation which has—in more than one sense—divided our House for so long. With my Idea, I visited a Notary of my Acquaintance and, upon returning to my Dwelling, sought Audience with my Wife.

I had not set Eyes upon her for a ten-day, and I am certain that the Shock was plain upon my Countenance when I beheld her. She was thin unto the point of Emaciation, and her Eyes rimmed with dark Circles; they seemed to stare sightlessly into Space, her Pallor was extreme and she moved listlessly. This Sight hardened my Resolve to bring this Matter to a swift Conclusion.

—You have won, I told her, for I cannot bear to see you in this State. I give you your Freedom, and I will not contest it.

Her Eyes, if it were possible, widened even more, and for the space of a Moment, there shone a Spark of Life within. She asked what Price I attached to this Freedom.

—Just this, Madam, I replied. Upon her dressing Table I placed the Document which I had brought from the Notary.

—In this Paper, I said, you do confess to certain Offenses against me, which Crimes are unspecified. You do further state that at no Time did I mistreat you in any Wise, nor raise a Hand against you, nor force you into Confinement. For my part, I state that I release you unconditionally from your marriage Vows, nor do I make any Accusations against you, provided you leave my House with all possible Dispatch, taking only those Goods which you brought with you and any I may see fit to give you. Should any Ill befall me, Madam (and hereupon I gazed at her with such Intensity that I am sure she caught my full Intent), any Violence, I say, then this Document shall be made publick and published in a Journal. Upon my natural Death, or yours, this Document will be destroyed without opening it, nor disclosing its contents in any Way.

She looked uncomprehending for a Moment, then asked:

—And if I sign this Paper, Husband, I am free to leave?

—Immediately, Madam. Upon our return from the Notary, in whose Presence we shall both affix Signatures and in whose Charge it shall be placed, Rachel will help you to pack your Affairs and make ready your Baggage. I will assist, if you so desire, and you may be quit of this House today, to go where you will.

She licked her dry Lips then said: —I accept. Let us go immediately.

I had hoped for such an Outcome and the Carriage I had hired was still outside. We signed before the Notary who read the Document carefully, sprinkled Sand upon our Signatures and added his own. Then he folded the Paper and placed it within a metal Box, securing it with a small Lock. The Box itself he placed within a stout Drawer and, producing a second Key which he wore around his Neck, he then locked the Drawer also and returned the Key to his person. It was done.

May $17^{th}$, 1800

Sarah is gone, taking Rachel with her. I do not know at this Point if a great Weight has lifted from me or yet if another, heavier than the first, has settled about my Shoulders. I know that I must put my House to rights (I shall sell the Bed and purchase another, or I may indeed transform the Parlor into a Bedchamber) and then turn my attention to the School, which I fear I have badly neglected these past Months.

# DECLAMATION DAY ADDRESS
# 20TH OF JUNE, 1800
## THE REMARKS OF WM. HARRINGTON TO THE STUDENTS

Members of the Board of Deacons, Honored Guests, Teachers, Students, and well-wishers, it is my Pleasure to greet you to-day on this, the final Meeting of the Term, to celebrate the Accomplishments of our Pupils, and to wish them Luck and God-speed in the days ahead.

The past year has brought us Trials and Triumphs. But we must not, at this point, look into the Past, except for the Lessons it may yet teach us, but rather into the Future, into a new Century. We have been a free and independent Country for a quarter of a Century. While other States still struggle with the very Concept of Freedom, we have realized it. Under Napoleon, Europe is again at War, while we are at Peace. Yes, we know the Blessings of Peace, but, in another Sense, the Revolution continues, and it is a good Revolution.

None can know what that Future will bring. But look what has been accomplished in just the past few years: Mr Jenner has developed a method for preventing Disease which may revolutionize Medicine. Furthermore, a method has been developed whereby Foods which would otherwise spoil quickly, can be preserved in glass Containers, perhaps indefinitely. This may well revolutionize what we eat, for we may now eat that which has been prepared in another part of the Country and safely transported to us.

Lads, you who are Students of Claxton Hall, and those about to leave us, you are part of that great and continuing Revolution. And, like its Soldiers, you will march forth from these Grounds to accomplish great things. You may become Generals, or Inventors, or Explorers. You may become Merchants or Writers or Teachers. You may travel to Parts of the World heretofore unknown to Man.

The Portal is open, and a Light shines through. The Light is that of the Future. To those who have finished their Course of Studies and who are leaving us, you stand upon the Threshold. None can say with Certainty what lies beyond, but the Promise is great, and it is you who are a part of that Promise. Now pass through that Portal and follow the Light with Conviction, for you are an integral Part of it, and it shall be this Light which the rest of the World shall follow.

Go, lads, with our best Wishes, and with the Knowledge, the Courage and the Wisdom to perform great Deeds.

# GEORGE TINKER (1803)

It had rained in earnest the night before, as it had for several days preceding. The earth was saturated and could not absorb all of the water; the ditches, too, were having a hard time coping with the runoff. As a consequence, the road to Upper Granby, never too carefully maintained at the best of times, was now truly a hazard. Several sections were washed away entirely; the rest rutted and, in spots, soft enough to mire a wagon wheel to half its diameter. The condition of this thoroughfare necessitated that the wagon make several detours, sometimes through fields, once through the woods, where the driver could find a path only with great difficulty and on at least two occasions it had been necessary to turn the wagon and backtrack until a suitable alternate route could be found.

*April in Connecticut*, thought the driver, *is more or less a wasted month. It is too late for sugaring or lumbering, too early for plowing or planting. Unless one lay planks from the house to the barn, one may lose a boot or two to the mire, or even a small child,* he thought with a grin.

With that thought, he glanced at his wife beside him, stoically enduring the jostling and the swaying, narrowly avoiding being pitched off when a wheel hit a rock under the surface of the mud. His son, Jonathan, sat on some bedding in the wagon bed and gripped the sideboard firmly, poking up his head from time to time, when he thought he might do so without being thrown out. Jonathan was some three years and eight months and curious about everything, as children of that age often are. Even though he had already bumped his nose two or three times on the rough wood, he could not bear the thought that a part of the world might be passing or something transpiring without his seeing it.

The woman at the driver's side was Abigail Forsythe Tinker (or that was, at least, the name she gave out). She was, he thought, undeniably pretty, though some might find her a bit short or perhaps a bit plump, but she was—normally—of an extremely pleasant and cheerful disposition, inclined to talk but not to idle gossip. There was little she could not do, once she put her mind to the task, and that included such things as putting the harness correctly on the horse and hitching him to the wagon (or even a plow), if need be, or walking four or five miles (carrying her son part of the way) to do some trading or to visit their closest neighbor.

The driver, calling himself George Tinker, was a printer by trade. He had completed an apprenticeship in New Hampshire, and, the town in which he apprenticed not being large enough to accommodate two printers, he had gone south to seek a larger community, there to set himself up in business, build a house and raise his family. He loved his wife and son very much. She had endured the ride without complaint, though he had not really revealed to her why this detour to a small community was so important.

He had often thought she might be capable of reading his thoughts, and she now confirmed it by turning and asking, “The road might be easier, my dear husband, if I knew why it were necessary to endure it. Perhaps you thought to shorten our time in Purgatory?” She tried to sound severe, but there was a trace of laughter in her tone and in her eyes and she could not completely repress a smile.

He pulled the horse to a slow walk, so that they might talk more comfortably. “I can tell you no more than I did before, Abigail. I have to see a man about some unfinished business.”

She looked at him shrewdly. Trying to conceal something from her was like trying to hide a bucket under a chicken. “Is there a debt to be paid then, one way or the other?”

He had to look away then. She could see entirely too much on his face, even if she could not read his mind. He merely nodded and flicked the reins so that the horse resumed his former pace. He watched her from the corner of his eye, though, and was surprised to see her nod also, as if the lack of an answer on his part had confirmed something she was already thinking.

There was an inn in Upper Granby, as he had hoped there might be. He procured a room and then took the horse and wagon to the livery stable. The horse had been limping a bit for an hour or so and he wanted to have its hooves checked. He was sure the beast would be glad of a dry stall and some feed that wasn’t moldy, too. Unless things went badly, he planned to stay here for a day, perhaps two. They needed the rest.

As he removed the harness, he made idle talk with the proprietor of the stable, a middle-aged man with a limp, a squint and a grizzled beard.

“The Cutters still live in the area?”

“Yep.”

“They had a son…Todd, I think.”

“Yep.”

“Any idea where I might find him?”

“Yep.”

“And where might that be, sir?”

The older man pointed with his chin. “Yonder. Crowder’s Mercantile. But he don’t work this late. Be there t’morrow.”

Tinker thanked him and returned to the inn. He was betting on the fact that the fellow's reluctance to part with information would ensure that he wouldn't get word to the Cutters that someone had inquired about Todd.

The following day dawned clear and bright, with the sun promising some warmth. Perhaps it had decided that the sodden earth could tolerate no more rain for the moment and that it would consider actually starting spring. After breakfast, George Tinker left his wife and son at the inn and walked to the mercantile. Todd Cutter was sweeping the porch and seemed quite intent on his work. Tinker stopped and watched him, curious.

Cutter looked a bit larger than he had remembered, but different, somehow. There was a slowness, a deliberateness to his movements that hadn't been there before. The broom moved carefully around the crates and barrels stacked on the board floor and Cutter swept under the chair without bothering to move it. He accumulated a pile of dust in a series of short, deliberate movements and swept it to the edge of the stoop and into the street. At that moment he looked up and saw Tinker.

George Tinker waited for a flash of recognition, a glimmer of surprise or a sneer of remembrance. But there was nothing. The eyes appeared empty. Then Cutter turned away and began to assemble another pile of dust. He didn't turn when Tinker stepped onto the porch and entered the store.

The storekeeper turned at the sound of the door and nodded at Tinker, wishing him "good morning" and asking how he might be of service. Tinker glanced back over his shoulder before replying.

"Uh…that fellow on the porch…"

Crowder—if indeed it was he—chuckled a bit. "Oh, y'mean Todd? Big, ain't he? But don't worry, he's harmless, for all o' his size. If he gets in th' way, just ask him t' move aside. He's kinda slow."

"Kind of slow?"

Crowder nodded. "Yup. Got throwed by a horse some years back. Hit his head on a post, he did. Never been quite right afterwards. Not much for rememberin'. Simple soul. But y' can set him a task, an' he'll do it. Work all day, he will. Now, what can I do for you?"

But Tinker had turned and was watching his former nemesis through the glass. It was another moment before Crowder's words sank in and he turned back once more.

"I…well, I just came in for directions, actually. What's the best road to Hartford?"

Crowder chuckled again as he arranged some merchandise on the counter. "Just passin' through, huh?"

"Uh…yes. I figured there'd be a better chance of some employment in a larger town."

Crowder was interested. "Y' don't say? What kind o' work you seekin' mister?"

"I'm a printer by trade."

Crowder stopped wiping the counter and repeated, "Y' don't say. Well now, that's somethin'." He looked more intently at the man who called himself Tinker. "We used t' have a newspaper in this town. The *Register*. But ol' man Sorenson died a couple o' years back, an' there weren't nobody t' continue. So the shop's just set there, idle-like. Presses an' everythin', just waiting for a someone t' take it over."

Crowder took Tinker's silence for indecision rather than for the astonishment it was. So he pressed his case:

"Bank 'ud lend y' money, an' I'm sure we could find some folks t' help clean up th' place an' get everythin' workin'. I know they'd like t' have a paper again." Then he thought of another argument: "An' if y' got a boy o' school age, why there's a good school not too far. Claxton Hall. Run by a fellow name o' Harrington. Doin' a good job, he is. Wife left him a couple years back, so he throwed all o' his time an' energy into that school. Good place t' raise a family this is." Crowder nodded at the wisdom of his own words, though he continued to watch Tinker closely. He thought he might risk one final question:

"What'd y' say your name was, mister?"

Crowder was surprised at the time it took the stranger to answer. He appeared to have been considering something. But at length he said:

"It's Rekkord. Zachary Rekkord."

# JONATHAN REKORD (1817)

There was a rooster, of course, but Jonathan Rekord always awoke before that bird bestirred himself.

He hesitated only a moment before throwing back the covers, appreciating once more the warmth of his mother's quilt—really, the only thing he had left of hers. His trousers hung on the chair beside his bed, and he fumbled for them in the dark, pulling them half-way on before he shed his nightshirt. That way, not all of him was exposed to the chill October morning at the same time. His shirt should be dry, hanging before the fire downstairs, so all he needed were his boots, into which he now slipped his feet. In another few weeks, he'd leave them downstairs, too, so they wouldn't be icy cold in the morning. He'd repeated these actions so many times that he had no need of a candle, nor any light as he descended the ladder from his garret room.

He liked this hour of the morning. No one else was yet astir; he was—for a few minutes at least—master of the house. The banked fire gave hardly any light, but he raked the coals into a thin layer and threw on some wood while he finished dressing. He pushed the spider closer to the fire so that the thin porridge would be hot by the time he finished chores. He added some water to the kettle and pushed that closer to the coals as well.

Yellow Fellow raised his head as Jon exited the house, but didn't bark; he was used to the routine, too. He made a sound that sounded like a cross between a sneeze and a snort and laid his head back on his paws. Jon lit the lantern hanging on a post by the front door and made two stops on his way to the barn: the outhouse and the well, where he splashed cold water on his face. At least there wasn't ice in the bucket this morning. He filled another to take into the barn for the stock.

The lantern didn't light the entire barn, but it gave enough light for him to mount to the mow and throw down a couple of forkfuls of hay for Amy and Beth. He fetched the milk pail, stool and damp rag to wipe the bags before he started milking. This was another moment he enjoyed; no matter how cool the weather, it was always warm and almost comfortable when you pushed your head into the cow's side. Milking was almost mechanical, and you could think of almost anything as the milk squirted into the pail.

As they often did, however, Jon's thoughts turned to his parents and his present situation.

He wondered where his father was, or if he were even still alive. Zachary Record had left home, son and wife six years previously. He had talked vaguely of "Indian trouble" and how he was not going to let the white man push them off of lands guaranteed to them by treaty. There had been talk of "Tippecanoe" and "Tecumseh," but Jonathan had understood little of it. He knew vaguely that his father was related somehow to some Indians, but he had never understood how deeply his father felt that relationship or how much he felt the need to help them. Zachary had sold his printing business and had left all of the money with Abigail, promising to return "in a few months at most." There had been one letter, soon after his departure, then nothing. Then news had come about a place called Prophetstown, and there had been no word from his father after that. Abigail and Jon had kept their hopes alive until the war started five years ago, then by mutual but tacit consent, they spoke no more of Zachary.

Amy shifted her weight and Jon realized she'd given about all she was going to. He stripped the last of the milk from the teats, poured the pail into the milk can and moved his stool to Beth's side. She was less tractable than Amy, and Jon would have to watch her tail and feet while he milked.

He and his mother had moved to the Charles Merrill farm, where old Charles and his aging wife were glad of the help, in exchange for room and board. Abigail didn't want to live alone and didn't know how long their money might last. She had been losing strength lately and coughing up blood, but she had carefully concealed the fact from her son.

Abigail Rekkord died of what the physician called "consumption" in the late fall of 1812. Jonathan was, as far as he knew, an orphan.

"Well, you haven't got a fortune, Jon," Faith Merrill had told him, "but you've enough 'til you come of age, if you have a care how you spend it. Now, Mr. Merrill and I, we feel you should spend it on your education. There's a good school real near to here, Claxton Hall, with real nice teachers, but it costs some to go there. You can live here and take your meals with us, in return for taking over some of the chores. We can't do everything any more, you see. But it's up to you, boy, how you want to spend your money. It's all here, any time you want it."

The smoke-gray cat entered the tie-up at this moment, blinking a little in the light. He stretched fore and aft, yawned and sat, front paws carefully aligned, waiting expectantly. Normally, one didn't name barn cats. They were tough to keep track of, anyway. But Jonathan called this one Graymalkin, because they were reading *Macbeth* at school. Jon took careful aim with a teat and sent a stream of milk at the cat's muzzle. Graymalkin got a mouthful, then another. When it became evident no more would be forthcoming, he began to wash himself vigorously.

*Macbeth* was interesting. Jon also liked history and Latin. He found the Greek alphabet difficult however, and was doing less well in that subject. But he didn't think he was getting as much from the Shakespeare play as he should have been. He had little to compare his experience with, but he wasn't sure the teacher was going about it the right way. Mr. Cullen was nice enough, but he didn't really *teach*, if you got right down to it. He just sat—or stood—there and waited for you to ask questions. Then he'd answer, sometimes at great length. But you never knew if you were right or not.

"All viewpoints are valid," he'd insist, "as long as you are able to defend them successfully."

Jonathan couldn't imagine when he'd ever have to defend his views on *Macbeth.*

Mr. Batterson was even more frustrating. Jon couldn't even be sure what subject the master was supposed to be teaching. Most of his classes seemed to consist of accompanying his students for walks in the woods. If the students said nothing, he'd remain silent, also. Then, when some student became bored, he'd ask a question such as, "Sir, what wood is best for firewood?" At that point, most of the boys would stifle giggles, for this was an easy question, one which any lad of six or seven should be able to answer competently.

But the master would stroke his chin, look up at the trees, and, after a few moments' consideration, respond with something that amounted to a dissertation on the relative merits of birch, pine and popple (not recommended) versus ash, oak and apple (preferred). At the end of one of these sessions, none of the students could say for certain what knowledge had been gained, if, indeed, anything at all had been learned. To other questions ("If a person were all alone, sir, since he was a babe, and never had anyone to talk to, why, what language would he speak?"), Mr. Batterson was liable to offer a serious, albeit completely absurd answer ("Hebrew, of course, my boy. It's the language of the Bible. It's what God taught Adam and Eve to speak."). It was therefore difficult to determine, Jonathan decided, if the answers the teacher gave contained any truth at all, or if, indeed, they were inventions of the moment.

It was at this moment that Jonathan decided that he could do a better job, were he ever a teacher.

In the evening, after chores and supper, Ma Merrill cleared the table and set a lantern on it. That, with the light from the nearby fireplace, gave

Jonathan enough light to do his lessons. There were only two books: the *New England Primer* and the Bible. Most of the teachers didn't give homework, but one or two demanded that a verse or two be learned by heart each night or that certain letters be copied on a slate until perfect or that the multiplication tables be recited and written until a student knew them flawlessly, and that required practice.

Jonathan opened the former tome, skipping past the alphabet, the "easy" words of two, three and four syllables. The first part of his task was to copy the first five five-syllable words onto his slate, erase them and recopy them until he could write them from memory and without error. Tomorrow they would find out what they meant and tomorrow's assignment would undoubtedly be to use them correctly in an original sentence, which might have to be transcribed in front of the class.

That chore accomplished, Jonathan skipped past the simple alphabet verses, having long ago learned that "In Adam's fall/We sinned all" and not really caring that "The idle Fool/Is whipt at school." The catechism part didn't interest him either, but there were other verses to be memorized, as well as the Shakespeare passage that he'd written into his copybook, tasks that would keep him busy for the next half hour or so. Ma Merrill sewed by firelight, humming softly to herself, and Pa Merrill whittled a new tine for a hay rake. He inspected it by candlelight, then turned to Jon.

"So, you're what, sixteen? seventeen? 'Bout time to be giving some thought to your future, ain't it? Can't stay in school forever."

Faith Merrill gave her husband a warning look, but if he saw it, he chose to ignore it.

Charles Merrill pressed ahead: "'Less you plan to be a preacher or a lawyer or a doctor, you've probably got all the book learning you'll need, ain't you? I mean, if a man can read some and sign his name and do some ciphering, why, he's as educated as he needs, seems like."

Jonathan pretended to consider for a moment, rolling his pencil between his fingers and looking at the fire. Then he met Charles's eyes. "I want to be a teacher."

Charles was a bit taken aback. "A teacher? What'd you want to do that for? Now, a preacher, I can understand. If you like schooling so much, there's a seminary up north, I b'lieve, somewheres in Massachusetts. I guess you take classes in sermon-writing and what not. Or you could be a soldier, Johnny, maybe even an officer, 'cause you're so bright and always reading."

"I'm going to be a teacher."

"Well, now, look." Charles's tone of voice said he was trying to be reasonable. "I don't expect you're going to settle here and take the farm after I'm gone; I know you've got bigger plans than that. Never expected it. But see, there ain't no normal school around here, and ain't likely to be one anytime soon. So if you're a teacher, why, you have to go to a college, at least some, and I don't know of no colleges that'll let you study for nothing. You've got enough for maybe one more year at that Claxton school, and then what? How're you fixing to get money to go to some college, Jon?"

"I don't know."

Charles shrugged. "'Course I suppose you could always try your hand at the printing business, like your daddy, but that tends to tie a fellow down in one place. Not that that's a bad thing," he added after a short pause. "Fellow could do worse than learn himself an honest trade."

"A teacher, is it?" Mr. Hawl's voice was carefully non-committal. "There's a lot more to it than reading to the pupils, answering their questions and chastising those who don't measure up."

"Yes, sir, but I…"

"Sit down and listen, lad. If Charles Merrill couldn't discourage you, maybe I can."

They were in one of the three drafty rooms in the Hall that served as classrooms. There was a fire in the hearth, but it was a very warm afternoon for late November, and the autumn sun, low on the horizon, but still bright, did its best to add its warmth, filtered through panes of wavy glass in need of a substantial cleaning. A persistent fly made half-hearted attempts to escape through the window, making soft bumping noises with each effort.

Of the three full-time instructors at Claxton, Eli Hawl was the only one Jon really trusted and respected. Like the other teachers, he taught several disciplines: scripture, English composition, spelling and geography. He was also willing to impart information and not wait for students to extract it from him by questions, the Head's educational theories notwithstanding.

Hawl kept a clay pipe on the mantle and he began stuffing it with tobacco taken from a jar on his desk as he continued.

"All right, let's say you've a class of, oh, ten boys in… What subjects are you planning to teach, by the way?"

"Well, uh, English of course…"

Hawl nodded vigorously through a cloud of smoke which seemed to be trying to envelop his head. "Good choice. Now, you've a class of ten, as I say. How many lessons have you prepared for that class today?"

"Uh…one, I suppose."

The teacher was trying to relight his pipe, but this time he was shaking his head sternly. "Wrong. Ten." He puffed furiously.

"I'm afraid I don't understand, sir."

Hawl took the pipe from his mouth long enough to shake the stem at Jon, in the manner of a cautionary finger. "Are they all the same age? Have they all equal intelligence? Do they all learn in the same fashion? At the same pace? Look you, lad…"

Now the pipe stem began to wave about as if Hawl might be herding geese as he paced about. "Look you, one might be slow at reading but good at remembering what you say. Maybe one can't write so well, but he can follow perfectly what you put on the board. One memorizes easily, another has trouble remembering his own name. One gets so embarrassed when you call on him that he's tongue-tied, but writes the most beautiful prose you've ever read." Now he turned to face Jon. "You've got ten individuals there in front of you, lad. If you were one of them, would you like to be treated just like all the others?"

"No, I guess not."

"If you were the smartest one, would you like to be held to the speed of the slowest?"

"Well, no, sir."

"And if there were pupils brighter than you, would you want the teacher to teach them and ignore you because they could learn faster? No. So each lesson must be made to fit the talents and abilities of each student, if you want to be a real teacher."

"I didn't consider…"

The pipe stem was in his face again. "Not many do, lad, who're not teachers. And remember, the students aren't always your biggest problem."

"Then who…?"

"Administrators. Other teachers jealous of your success. And the parents. If they're paying for their son's education, why, you can be pretty damn sure they'll want a say in it. And you've got to balance all of this carefully. Show no favoritism."

"I didn't realize there was so much to it that wasn't really…teaching."

Hawl shrugged his shoulders to settle his coat. He seemed to have given up on keeping the pipe alight.

"Well, then, here's another question. Suppose you've assigned a passage to memorize for the morrow, and come the class, one of the boys doesn't know it. What do you do?"

"I suppose he must be punished."

"Perhaps. But you'd better be sure he deserves it, or you'll quickly lose him as a student. Is he merely lazy, or did something prevent him from doing his work? Is a family member ill? Was he ill? Was his help needed urgently? Did a mare foal last night? Did he forget to take his copybook home?"

"I…well, how do you know?"

Hawl made a final attempt on the pipe, but only managed to drop embers down the front of his coat. He brushed at them impatiently. "You don't. You've got to ask a question or two, make a guess. And it'd better be the right one, or you'll lose not only his respect and cooperation, but that of all the other boys, too."

Jon stared at the floor and let out a long sigh.

"Well," Hawl demanded, have I discouraged you?"

Jonathan looked up at the teacher for a long moment before replying. "No, sir, you haven't. I want to be a teacher like you."

Hawl snorted and shrugged. "More's the pity. Well, very well, then, we've got work to do. First, you've got to do a lot more reading, especially for English. Come here, boy."

From a shelf behind his table, the teacher took several books, stacking them into Jonathan's arms. "Here: Defoe. *Robinson Crusoe*. You'll like that one. I did, when I was your age. And here: *Gulliver's Travels*. Swift. It's a sort of fable and a satire. I'll expect a report. And here: fellow named Voltaire. Frenchman. Don't care much for the way he writes, but he's got some important things to say. *Candide*. When you finish those, I've got more." Then, noticing Jonathan was still standing there, somewhat dazed, Hawl waved him away. "Well, get you gone. You've work to do, I daresay." As Jonathan reached the door, Hawl called him back. "And, oh, yes, I'll expect a lesson plan on how to teach the first chapter of that Voltaire fellow by Tuesday next. You've a class of ten, remember."

Jonathan stumbled out, wondering if he'd made a mistake.

By his final year at Claxton, he was still wondering. He'd read every book on Mr. Hawl's shelves, finding some tolerable, and some, like *Pilgrim's Progress*, almost unbearable. A few he actually enjoyed.

In the fall of 1820, Ma Merrill suffered a stroke, paralyzing her and robbing her of speech. Charles and Jon tried caring for her, but it was obvious that she'd lost her will to live. She died shortly before Christmas. Charles didn't outlive her by more than a few months. They had no children, and Jon suddenly found himself owner of a farm he had no interest in. In March of 1821, he sold it to Alton Thurlow and all at once had sufficient funds to seriously consider college.

In the summers of 1821 and 1822, he worked in the tobacco fields to earn enough money to pay for a room in a boarding house, saving every dollar he could towards furthering his education. The rest of the year, he worked part-time for a farrier in town, but, when time allowed, returned to Claxton Hall where he observed the teachers at work in the classrooms, practiced making lesson plans and grading student themes and once in a great while stood before a class himself, under the close supervision of Eli Hawl.

He also developed a taste for poetry and an eye for the daughter of Micah Corey. Patience Corey had a brilliant smile that befuddled his brain and weakened his resolve not to be married until he should be well established as a teacher. They were married in June of 1821. Their son, Alonzo, was born the following year. Jonathan was quite happy, but realized that his hopes of attending a college and teaching was becoming a bit more remote. He seemed to be tying himself down more and more.

Then in 1823, a new school, Washington College, opened in Hartford. Realizing that this might be his last chance, especially as Patience was now expecting their second child, Jonathan determined to go. He remained there only one year, but felt that he now had a solid enough base from which to launch a teaching career. He applied for a position at Claxton Hall, hoping to fill that just created by the retirement of his mentor. Largely on the basis of Eli Hawl's recommendation, Jonathan secured the post.

He would teach Composition, Grammar and Rhetoric and Declamation. He already had plans to try to modify the curriculum somewhat, to include more modern works: Taylor, Wordsworth, and perhaps even the woman novelist, Austen, whose recent work was quite promising. He drew up an outline for the entire term, noting briefly what he wished to cover in each area each day. He planned—in some detail—how he would introduce himself and the course material. He gave a good deal of thought of what he could reasonably expect from the students. Hawl's numerous counsels were never far from his thoughts. He was, in fact, well prepared for everything except the students.

The first one through the classroom door was nothing if not self-assured, but his pinched mouth and furrowed brow suggested he might have breakfasted on lemons.

"I'm Holling Charles Baxter," he announced without preamble, "and my father is a person of some considerable importance." His look defied the teacher to challenge that.

"I'm quite sure he is, *Master* Baxter. However, to the best of my knowledge, you are *not*. Nor are you likely to be unless you apply yourself in this class. Take a seat, please."

It was in the back of Jonathan's mind, all during that first class, if perhaps he'd been a bit precipitous in his response. Therefore, the first class didn't go quite as smoothly as his plans called for, but it appeared afterwards that Master Baxter's bluster was just that, and there were no consequences.

Still, he'd been told that the students would test him immediately, to see just how far he could be pushed before they got into trouble, and just how many lies he'd swallow.

"We didn't have to do that last year, schoolmaster."

"I don't have time to memorize all that, schoolmaster."

"We should have a recess now, schoolmaster."

"I've hurt my hand and can't write."

"Book? Which book is that, schoolmaster?"

By December, however, things were going better. Since the students had been unable to get him to back down on any of his demands, they had decided it was less trouble to do the work than to complain about it. Some actually began to enjoy it, and by the end of the spring term, 1825, Jonathan Record was sure he'd found his calling. There had even been a few small gifts from grateful parents: a small snuff box (not anything he'd ever use), a pen-knife with a mother-of-pearl handle, an attractive inkwell of cut glass.

Patience kept a comfortable, if modest, home, producing quite palatable meals with the little money he was able to give her. She seemed—and indeed, said she was—quite content taking care of Alonzo and Charity and seemed to be looking forward to the birth of their third child.

Of course, there was no stipend paid during the summer months if school was not in session, but Jonathan returned to work in the tobacco fields and for the farrier when the weather was not conducive to outdoor work. All in all, he thought, not a bad existence.

The second year went even more smoothly than the first, and Jonathan was beginning to develop a real bond with some of the students, as well as some affection. He found he particularly enjoyed working with those who seemed to be a bit brighter than the norm, or whose talents showed exceptional promise in one area or another. These boys received a bit of extra praise, along with a bit of extra work, and even put on a passable little play, derived from *Julius Caesar*, toward the end of the winter term. By the spring of 1826, Jonathan had truly settled into a comfortable existence and had convinced himself that he had, indeed, found his life's calling.

Then Mr. Shackleton summoned all of the teachers to his office.

"It's a rum business, no doubt. I'm sure we can resolve it to everyone's satisfaction, but our situation is a bit doubtful at the moment, gentlemen."

"Sir," one of them wanted to know, "can this gentleman *prove* he's descended from James Claxton? I mean, a document's all very well, but documents can be forged, and for all we know, it's not the same family at all, merely a coincidence in names."

"He can't really force us out, can he?" asked another.

Shackelton's sigh was one of deep resignation. "It's too early to tell, I'm afraid. He says he's descended from the original family and that he's in possession of a deed to the property, which we are occupying illegally. If we cannot produce a bill of sale showing the land and buildings are ours, why…" he shrugged his shoulders "…why, it could get…unpleasant, I suppose. At any rate, he's engaged the services of an attorney, and I suppose we must do the same."

"But there must be *some* record…"

"Unfortunately, that's not true. As far as I can recall, the church purchased the property some fifteen or twenty years ago, so they would have kept all of the records of the sale." Another sigh and shrug. "I fear they would have been lost in the fire of '09."

His next words were a bit more positive. "But all of this is just speculation at this point, gentlemen, and I daresay we'll get the matter resolved in due course. In the meantime, return to your duties, and I'll keep you posted on events."

They returned uncertainly to their students, resolving, by mutual consent, to say nothing that might alarm the boys until the matter was decided one way or another.

On Friday, May 12$^{th}$, 1826, Judge William Tyler ruled that, as neither party could produce a satisfactory and uncontested title deed to the Claxton Hall property, said property should revert to the Church. The Church, however, did not want it, as it could no longer afford the taxes, and it would just as soon continue to rent it to Mr. Shackleton.

Regretfully, Mr. Shackleton had for his part exhausted his resources and could afford neither rent nor upkeep for the property or buildings. He announced that the school would close immediately.

Jonathan watched in silence as the draymen removed the last of the furnishings from the Hall. They would be sold at public auction, the proceeds going to pay creditors. If any funds remained, they would be distributed among the teachers, but Jonathan was not expecting anything.

*What shall I do now? I suppose I shall be obliged to take up farming or be apprenticed full-time to the farrier. My father was one of the first students here, and I had hoped to carry on the tradition. It appears rather that I shall be the last, and that no Rekord will ever enter Claxton Hall again.*

# JONAS BURKE (1862)

*The manuscript which follows was in a tin box, sealed with wax, found in the wall of the building known as the Atlee Barracks when that wooden structure was demolished in 1923. The document was signed, but undated. We conjecture that it was written at some time between 1861, which, according to town historical records, was when the Barracks was built, as quarters for soldiers, and 1865, when the need for the Underground Railroad was past.*

I pray that these documents shall never be needed, but I wish to state at the outset that I acted of my own volition, according to the dictates of my conscience, and that the Claxton Hall Institute (also known as Fort Peabody) is to be held entirely blameless, as no one connected with it had, to the best of my knowledge, any suspicion of the events which I had set in motion there. Indeed, I would not have the Facility calumnied in any wise, as I hold it in high esteem and have especial regard for M$^{r}$ Daniel Peabody, its Provost.

To understand the facts of the matter, as well as my motivation for my actions, I think it best that the narrative be told in its entirety. To begin with, and in the case that the present document not come to light until after my death, my name is Jonas Burke. I was born in 1820, in Talcott, Mass$^{cts}$, to Elias Burke and Martha Linscott. My Father was a dealer in textiles and a speculator in cotton. From the time I was old enough to have some understanding of his affairs, it was assumed that I would become a partner in his Enterprise, and ultimately its proprietor, upon his demise.

In July of 1844, I accompanied my Father on a buying trip to Charleston, South Carolina. It was there I first saw Negro slaves. I had, of course, seen the occasional Negro in the North, especially when Father's business took him to Boston, but I had never seen them in such numbers, nor under such conditions. You will suppose my education and experience to be lacking, nor can I offer any defense of my ignorance, save that I was not exposed to Negroes in servitude in Talcott, or, if such there were, they were paid domestics, be it only in room & board, &c. But come face to face with those in Charleston, I found their condition to be abhorrent in the extreme. I was assured, when I dared speak of the matter, that they were content, had gainful employment and enough to eat. "Why," I was told, "they even sing as they toil in the fields. They are a simple people, and by supplying their wants, we have given them a purpose in life."

Happy they might be, knowing no other life, but the notion that one man might possess another, and dispose of that man's life and family as he saw fit, revolted me. I could not conceive of a God who would create one race to be the servants of another. Were the Hebrews born to be slaves in the land of Egypt? Were they happy in their labours? Did they, too, sing in the mudpits of Pharaoh? It cannot be so, nor will any argument convince me to alter my opinion.

Two things happened upon our return to Mass. that were to change my life, tho' I could not know it at the time. Firstly, I was so incensed by what I had seen in the South (tho' I must confess, lest I put blame where it is not due, that I never witnessed any mistreatment of Negroes) that I felt compelled to express my feelings, and this I did, somewhat too frequently, it seems, and in somewhat too publick a manner. It was my custom to visit (I do not say frequent, because it was no more than twice a week) an alehouse after the close of my work for the day and before returning for supper. There I would discuss my views with any who would listen, tho' it is now a certainty that some were listening whom I did not know at that time. The consequences of this action will become clear anon.

Secondly, I incurred a serious injury during the course of my work, catching my right hand in a gin and severely mangling it, losing two fingers and so crippling the member that it was all but useless for many tasks. In no wise do I relate that to gain any Sympathy for those who may condemn my actions, but rather as an Explanation as to why I should not be in Military service at this time. When Mr. Lincoln called for volunteers in the present conflict, I presented myself for Duty, but was declared unfit, for the reason I have just given. This will explain my continued presence at the Hall, whilst so many good lads have gone to War.

It was a month or so following the declarations of hostilities that I was approached by a gentleman of military bearing, tho' he wore no uniform. Yet he carried himself like a soldier. He asked if he had the pleasure of addressing Jonas Burke, and, when I confirmed this, he introduced himself as Daniel Peabody.

(I was not mistaken in my first estimation, for I learned subsequently that M$^{r}$ Peabody had served in the military forces during the Black Creek War in 1832 and had also seen service in Texas, pursuing the bandit Santa Anna. He had retired subsequent to that campaign, aged 44, with the rank of colonel. I will not describe him, as good likenesses of the Colonel abound.)

He then surprised me by telling me that he had heard I had a good head for ciphering. I will say with no false modesty that it was perhaps my strongest trait, tho' I did not impart this immediately to Col. Peabody. During my trips with my Father, I discovered I could do sums accurately and more rapidly in my head than most men could accomplish with pencil and paper. I said rather that I reckoned I could hold my own. The Colonel further surprised me by informing me that he would like to engage my services as a teacher. I shall herewith endeavor to reproduce the ensuing conversation with as much exactitude as is possible:

"You are no doubt aware, M^r^ Burke, that the Union is in need of soldiers and men to train them. It is therefore my intent to establish necessary training facilities here in Upper Granby Lake, using the buildings and grounds of what was once the school here—Claxton Hall, I believe it was called. The Government has asked me to use my expertise and experience to ready our troops for conflict with the rebels. Obviously, some construction will be needed, and I have already seen to that, though we can use tents in the interim."

I replied, "I understand the need, sir, & you are to be commended for taking on such as task, but I fail to grasp what help I might be. I grant that you need instructors, & quite quickly, but I cannot fathom why you would need someone good at accounting. Surely the common soldier has no need of arithmetic other than the ability to do a few simple sums, and even had he gone no further in school than age seven, he would already have acquired that skill."

"That is true," he concurred, "and were it a matter of the infantry soldier, I should not have approached you, sir. But you shall not be instructing foot soldiers, but artillery troops. You do, I presume, have a knowledge of geometry and other higher forms of mathematics?"

I began to see what he was driving at. An officer of artillery—if not the gun crews themselves—would need some knowledge of Geometry to calculate the angles of elevation necessary to hit a target at a certain distance, &c. "Indeed, sir," I told him, "for such a skill is useful in calculating the area of a field and such. I have done some surveying and am not unfamiliar with the instruments used, nor even with a sextant."

This seemed to please him, and he replied almost jovially, "Excellent! I can see you are the very man I am seeking. Would you consider serving your country as an instructor, then? You would have the rank of captain with the pay and privileges accruing thereto."

It was thus that I became an instructor at Fort Peabody, which was but a short remove from my lodgings in the village. I was given a house a little distance away from Claxton Hall itself (I mean, of course, the large stone building which, I am told, used to house the school). It is here that I would teach my classes. Two wooden barracks buildings, named Atlee and Patterson, were already being constructed. (I was never able to determine who these individuals might be, nor did I wish to expose my ignorance by asking. I supposed them to be military figures of some note.) Behind the dwelling was a small carriage house, which I was to use as a stable, or I might leave there the old wagon that presently occupied it. Temporary stables were also being erected on what the Colonel was calling the "parade ground," tho' it was so overgrown at this point that its clearing required a good two days' labour of plow and harrow. Such were the facilities upon my arrival. The troops themselves would occupy the barracks, once they were completed, while the officers (all married, save me) remained in town or on their farms with their families.

The second gentleman who was to change my life I met several months after I had commenced employment at the Fort. It was late of an October evening, and I was on the point of extinguishing my lamps and retiring when I heard a knock at the door. It was beyond a doubt a strange hour to come calling, nor was there a great deal of urgency in the summons, but it rather seemed as tho' the caller did not wish to call attention to himself, should anyone be passing by, unlikely at that hour.

I do not, as a practice, dislike anyone on first sight, but there was something about the fellow on the doorstep that made me wary, and I nearly closed the door in his face, but he held up his hand, begged my pardon, assured me he was unarmed and no highwayman, and begged leave to come in and speak with me a moment. I hesitated, then stepped back and bade him enter.

My second impression did little to allay my fears, & I wondered if I had erred in judgment in permitting him to enter. He was a small man, unshaven and creased of face. His age I could not tell. He wore what is, I believe, known as a forage cap, and an old frock coat, threadbare and many sizes to big for him; in fact the garment hung almost to his ankles. I do not believe that his skin had known soap for perhaps a fortnight, and the stains around his mouth bespoke the use of tobacco, or perhaps snuff. His eyes darted about the room, as though he might be seeking someone I had hidden in the shadows.

I asked him to be seated, but he waved off my suggestion and remained standing by the door. He gave his name as “Atticus,” and would give no other, saying the less I knew about him, the better. (To this day, I know no more about him than I learned that first evening, save by inference.) In spite of myself, I began to get intrigued; even taking into account my injury, I believe I could have, in case of need, wrestled the fellow to the ground, but he made no hostile moves.

Again, I will attempt to reproduce our Conversation as exactly as possible. It was, in fact, so extraordinary that I do not believe I will ever forget a word of it.

“I heard ye talkin’ down to th’ inn,” he said. “Are ye a abolitionist?”

“Well, no, not formally, I guess, though my sympathies lie in that direction.”

He nodded, apparently satisfied. “Good.” Then he fixed me with a gaze which might have transfixed a sparrow in flight. “But ye would like t’ help some?”

I nodded in my turn, uncertain where this conversation was leading.

“D’ ye know aught o’ what they calls th’ ‘underground railroad’?”

I confessed I did not.

Again he nodded slowly. “P’raps I’d better take that chair, atter all. This could take a bit o’ time.” When he was seated, he continued: “They’s those who’d help the slaves escape. Not stealin’ ’em from their masters, mind ye, but helpin’ ’em as they makes their way north t’ freedom. Now th’ underground railroad isn’t what ye’d call a real railroad, y’unnerstan’. We got no trains, no tracks. What we *do* got is stations and them we calls ‘conductors’ an’ station masters. The conductors, they’s the ones that takes them slaves from station t’ station, or at least points ’em the right way. The station masters, they takes care o’ the passengers—hides ’em and feeds ’em and passes ’em off to th’ next conductor, or gives ’em instructions on where th’ next station be.”

I was fascinated by Atticus and his tale. I found myself asking if he’d like something to refresh himself. For the first time, I thought I discerned a slight smile. “Well, now,” he answered, “that’s right neighborly, M$^{r}$ Burke. If ye’ve a sip, I wouldn’t refuse.”

I had a couple of jugs of cider working in the cellar, and I fetched him a mug. He smacked his lips over it and settled himself more comfortably. But I was bursting with questions.

“But how do they get free? And how do they travel?”

He spoke slowly, considering how much it might be safe to impart, I suppose. "Well, as to th' first, I dunno exactly. An' I don' wanna know. Ye'll see: th' less ye knows, th' less ye can tell." He paused for another sip. "Mostly they walks. Sometimes they gets th' loan o' a wagon, or mebbe a mule fer a bit, but 'tis mostly on foot they comes."

I was incredulous. "They walk all the way here? To Connecticut?"

His smile was a bit broader this time, and there was a little cackle of laughter. "T' Connecticut? Ha! Fer many o' 'em, 'tis only 'bout halfway. Many goes on t' Canada. They may be free o' their masters, but there's still th' Fugitive Slave Act." He watched me over the rim of his mug.

In my excitement, I had forgotten this for the moment. My consternation showed.

"Yep. 'Tis a dangerous business, make no mistake. 'Specially after that there compromise a few years back. Makes things even tougher. 'Specially as there're them what would seek t' profit from it." He watched me carefully.

I thought about his words. I tried to recall what I knew about this law, wishing that I had paid more attention to its provisions. It was, after all, an old one, but I did remember reading of its being strengthened some ten or so years ago. I knew that it granted slave owners the right to attempt to recover what they considered their property, even in the North. I suppose that it required citizens, if not to actually aid the owners in the recovery of their slaves, at least not to abet the slaves' escape. I knew further that owners often offered rewards for the return of their property, and that these rewards were enough to entice those who either supported the Southern cause or whose desire for money overrode any consideration of humanitarianism. I do confess that I had not paid as much attention to these matters as I ought, having contented myself with voicing opinions and never considering any actions. The fact that our Country was now split asunder, with hundreds dying daily, did make me a bit ashamed of my inaction. It might well seem to the observer that, having filled the air with protests against injustices I had never witnessed, and sundry imprecations, I then retreated to an academic donjon and bolted the door with my own arrogance and ignorance.

"Well," I said slowly, "let us suppose for a moment that I would like to help. What would I be expected to do? Given my job, I'm not often free to travel great distances."

Atticus drained his mug. "Oh, we're aware o' that, M^r^ Burke. 'Tis rather a station master's job we're considerin'."

I wondered briefly just how much he knew of me and my habits. It occurred to me that Atticus and his group (he had, after all, spoken in the plural), had been observing me for some little time, to ascertain if I might be trusted.

Atticus peered into his empty mug and glanced up at me. I took it and descended the stairs into the cellar again to refill it, all the while thinking what sort of a refuge I might offer to Negroes making their way North. The cellar, wherein I presently found myself, was dank, dark and smelled of earth. I could not imagine anyone staying here for several hours, to say nothing of a more extended period. I returned to the parlor and passed the mug to Atticus.

"How many would I be required to…host, and for how long?" I asked.

Atticus smacked his lips in appreciation. "Depends. They generally travels in small groups, o' course. Too many at once'd attract attention. Sometimes there're singles, sometimes two, mebbe three. They stays one night, two at th' most. Keep 'em movin'. Don't want 'em attractin' attention." He peered at me over the rim of the cup. "How many could ye take?"

I spread my hands in a gesture of indecision. "I don't know at this point. I…I've got to consider some alternatives." Then I thought of some other questions. "How would I know when to expect them? Would I have to go fetch them? Would they leave on their own or would I take them somewhere?"

Atticus swallowed the rest of the cider at a gulp and rose to go. "Each one's different," he informed me. "Some'll be escorted by a conductor, some'll find their own way. Some'll be picked up here, some'll know where t' go atter they's rested. Only thing what's sure is that it'll be at night. They most always comes and goes at night an' stay hid durin' the day." He shrugged to settle that long coat about his shoulders (he had removed neither that nor his hat). "I've stayed o'er long already, M^r Burke, so here's what we'll do. If ye decides ye can help, then ye places an order for…oh, molasses…at th' mercantile. One pint means ye can take one, two means two, an' so forth. When ye've a space prepared, ye hangs a bucket on the pump. Then ye wait." He touched the brim of his hat briefly, nodded and was gone. I thereupon fetched myself a cup of spirits (I keep some in the house for medicinal purposes and for the rare social caller) and sat down to reflect on all I'd heard.

Now the house I inhabit is comfortable, if somewhat old. There are two bedrooms (I, of course, occupy one), and the parlor could serve as sleeping quarters also, but these chambers would hardly be the place to conceal people who are, after all, criminals in the eyes of the Law (I mean here the laws of Man, not the Law of God, for Slavery is surely an abomination in the sight of God). I had already decided that the cellar would not serve, and the carriage house would require an inordinate amount of labor to prepare. Then, too, were I to use that spot, I could be seen by anyone passing by, and they could easily speculate on the reason why I might be so industriously engaged, since I had no need of the space. Anyone entering or leaving that facility could easily be seen by any soldiers who might happen to be about, and I fully expected pickets and watchmen to patrol the area which was a military post, after all. No, it had to be some place over which I had absolute control and which I could oversee at any hour of the day. I decided to sleep upon it and hope that I might be vouchsafed an inspiration.

Nor was I disappointed. I awoke with a plan in mind and was so eager to commence its execution that I was in a state of feverish excitement all day. After my lectures, I returned home and set about work at a frantic pace and thus continued until I fell into bed, exhausted, sometime after midnight.

My lodging is, as I said, old, and somewhat queerly designed, at least to my mind. This fact may be due, upon reflection, to the house's undergoing a number of Renovations under its successive owners. It may well be that each proprietor, having a different plan for the place, modified it to suit his own Whims, leaving in place other parts which did not trouble him. However that may be, there was, extending from the kitchen, a very narrow room, almost like a hallway, but leading nowhere (at least not at the present time). At present, I was using the space as a pantry, though if this be its original intent, I could not say. It was not well suited to the task, being too long and somewhat narrow, and I did not use the greater part of it, which consisted, as you may imagine, of numerous shelves built against the wall. At the end was a small, high window.

It had occurred to me that one might erect a sort of false wall, sealing a good three-quarters of the space off from the remaining quarter, which would still be largely sufficient for my needs. The larger space, that with the window, might serve as an overnight refuge for one or two persons. Then it further struck me that, if I were to remove the shelving from one wall, the available space would be greatly increased. In addition, I thought with mounting excitement, every other shelf from the opposite wall could be removed, thus providing sleeping spaces, albeit somewhat narrow ones, for three persons, or four if they be small. The shelves wanted but a piece of ticking or perhaps a straw pallet to become cots, one above another.

You may wonder that a man with but one good hand could successfully realize such a project, yet it takes but one hand to manage a hammer or saw, provided the piece be well secured. I was ripping out the shelving along one wall when another serendipitous thought presented itself, to wit: the unpainted boards I was removing were the same color as those making up the walls, they having been in place the same amount of time. I could therefore construct my false wall from this same shelving, and it would be virtually undetectable. It also meant that I could do most of the work indoors, far from curious stares wondering what sort of repairs I might be effecting within my Dwelling. I would not have to purchase planks from the mill, nor even transport them from the outside into the kitchen.

When finished and set into place, the wall was indistinguishable from its neighbors. I may be pardoned, I hope, for the sin of Pride, for I was well satisfied with my work. I even made short shelves for the new wall, and the effect was as if the shelves on each side simply continued around the rear wall.

I thought of putting hinges on my new wall, so that it might swing in the manner of a true door, but decided against it. I did not believe I could be clever enough to accomplish a task of this nature one-handed, and in a manner whereby the hinges would not be visible. I therefore contented myself with being able to lift it by one of its shelves to be set aside when access was desired, tho' I did install a pair of handles and a latch on the other side that it might be fitted into place and secured against intrusion by a potential occupant.

Several nights later, I visited the Mercantile at Granby Lake and, among other things, asked the clerk for three pints of molasses. I had thought that I could put up three refugees—for that is how I had come to think of them—in reasonable comfort. Whilst I was waiting for my order to be filled, I idly inspected the wares displayed on the shelves and watched the other customers. I was a bit surprised to find three of them watching me. One fellow I knew to be Ethan Furman. He was not well thought of in the village. He was of medium height and build, distinguished only—may I be forgiven for saying so—by his expression, which seemed to be twisted into a perpetual snarl. He liked no one, and those with whom he came into contact reciprocated this sentiment. He thought ill of everything, and, it was said, would stoop to any sort of malfeasance. His two companions resembled him in manner, if not appearance. I do not know why it made me uneasy to see them so. Surely I had done nothing to offend them; indeed, I had not so much exchanged a word with M^r^ Furman on any occasion I could recall. Be that as it may, he was regarding me with some suspicion and an equal amount of antipathy. I chose to ignore them and, having collected and paid for my purchases, I left without looking again in their direction, but I could feel their eyes upon me. Upon my return home, I hung a bucket on the pump.

It was in the second or third week of November, on one of those queer balmy nights we sometimes get just before a freeze, when there was a gentle but insistent tapping on the front door, just as I was lighting candles and preparing my usual evening meal of corn meal cakes and beans. I opened the door to find Atticus—I had not seen him since that first evening—accompanied by a tall Negro, his coat collar drawn up, tho' not against the weather. Neither of my visitors spoke, but rather Atticus drew his companion inside and motioned that I should shut the door. The two then remained standing there until I had drawn the drapes over the windows, that none should see whom I had received at this hour.

My visitors appeared to be a bit out of breath, which gave me leisure to study the black man. He was, as I have said, of above average height, and of regular features. His eyes, however, darted here and there as though he might be searching the shadows for enemies hidden there. He wore a short coat, which he held closed, and breeches whose previous owner had obviously been shorter and stouter than their present one. They were secured with a bit of rope. The Negro's feet and head were bare, even in this weather. In one hand he clutched a knotted kerchief; I surmised it contained his worldly possessions.

Atticus jerked a thumb at him. "Name's 'Burlevin,' near's I can make out. Put him up fer two nights, will ye? Someone'll come fer him day atter to-morrow. G'night t' ye." And he slipped out of the door and was gone before I had a chance to say a word.

I looked back at Burlevin and found him watching me intently. What must he think, I wondered, to be deposited at another white man's house every day or so? He must be confused, if not frightened. I tried to smile and reassure him. I told him I had been about to prepare a meal and inquired if he might like to join me. The idea of sitting at a table with a white man seemed to frighten him. He spoke for the first time.

"Well, boss, if you've got some t' spare, I wouldn' mind none."

I showed him his quarters and how to move and secure the wall. I told him where the back house was, but cautioned him about using it except at night. I had put a slop pail under one of what I had come to think of as "sleeping berths" and told Burlevin that he'd better use that during the day and empty it at night. He nodded vigorously at all I said as though he were eager to please.

I sat him at the table while I fed some wood into the stove, heated the beans and made the cornbread. As it was, to my mind, a rather special occasion, I decided to fry some eggs and ham, also. I went to the cellar to fetch some from the cold stores. I brought up some milk as long as I was down there and poured a mug for him. Burlevin watched me closely. It seemed to me that he looked uncomfortable and I realized that he had probably never had a white man cook for him. I handed him a knife and asked him to slice the bacon. Given something to do, he seemed happier.

During the course of the meal, I endeavored to engage him in conversation. I began by asking him about his name: what nationality was it? He laughed at this and his eyes sparkled. As fully as I can remember them, his words went like this: "Well, boss, t'ain't a proper name a'tall, but I can' remember my own. You see, boss, I was took from my mammy an' pappy when I was but a young'un. Lesse'n two year, near as I can figure. Me an' my sister was sold separate from them. I guess them that bought my folks didn' want no children hangin' 'round. They was fifteen of us children, all tol'. We was bought by this white gemmun to work at his farm. I was number 'leven. That's what they tol' me. I couldn' say it right, so I was just 'Burlevin.' At firs', my job was bringin' water t' the field hands, then when I was mo' able, they tol' me 'drive the wagon'. Finally I was growed enough to pick cotton. Didn' see my sister much; she workin' at th' big house. Then, one day, she jus' not there. She done been sold," Burlevin told me bitterly, "an' ain't no one told me nothin'. None o' th' others knew nothin' an' we don' ask the master. We wasn' bad treated. I mean, we wasn' beaten unless we done somethin' really bad, but all th' same…." He shook his head.

I attempted to find out more concerning his past, but it seemed as though he still didn't trust me fully, or perhaps he had been instructed not to reveal too much about where he had come from nor what his ultimate destination might be, in order to protect those who might still be there. I gave him a candle and told him to be sure the window was shuttered before he lit it. He went to the privy and then I helped him seal himself in for the night. I then retired in my turn, in a very pensive mood, nor did I sleep overmuch that night.

I must nevertheless have dozed off, because I remember being awakened sometime just before sunrise by a soft, dragging sound from somewhere downstairs. It was a slow, regular sound which I couldn't place. I surmised that Burlevin might be up and about, but I couldn't fathom what sort of activity might be occupying him. I put on some shoes and wrapped myself in a blanket before descending to the kitchen. There was a little light from a small fire; a kettle, steaming gently, sat on the hearth. If my nose didn't deceive me, cornmeal mush was simmering in a spider. Burlevin was sweeping the floor.

"Burlevin, what in God's name are you doing at this hour?"

He gave me a sheepish grin. "Sorry, boss, didn' mean t' wake you. I can' sit around bein' idle. Gotta keep busy. I knowed you wouldn' want me goin' outside t' chop wood, so I looked for somethin' t' do in here. 'Fraid I ain't much of a hand for housework, boss. I fixed you some vittles," he finished, almost apologetically. "I seen it done enough, but this be th' firs' time I tried."

I assured him that it smelled fine and had a mug of tea while he made cakes of the mush and fried them in last night's bacon grease. I told him that I much appreciated his help, that I had to absent myself for a time, being required to instruct at the Fort that day and that he should not venture outdoors, nor even quit his hiding space unless he hear two knocks, followed by another pair, then a single rap. I was surprised, as I departed for my employment, just how much I enjoyed his company (I had, after all, lived quite alone for much of the thirty years of my life) and how much I might miss that company when he departed on the morrow.

I pleasured myself that evening by reading to Burlevin, at first from Fenimore Cooper, a favorite of mine. But after a while he became restless (I have noted that this restlessness is a rather common affliction among certain individuals upon first exposure to Cooper's style) and asked me to read from what he called the "Jesus Book." I understood that he meant the Bible and read first from the Gospels, then from Exodus. He seemed to find the latter intriguing and asked me to read it again. I suspect that the depth of his understanding (judging by the rapt look upon his countenance) is far greater that that normally attributed to "darkies." Whence, I wonder, comes the strange notion that the color of the skin is a key to its owner's intelligence?

Our third evening was, to my mind, all too short. We had dined elegantly on salt cod, potatoes and turnip and I had found a book of Wordsworth, a modern poet. Whether Burlevin grasped the meaning of the words, I cannot say, but he found the rhythm almost hypnotic, and, observing him carefully, I could see that he was anticipating the rhyme. He had instinctively understood the concept of meter, something which escapes—truth be told—many poets. I had almost decided that he had a lyrical bent when I heard someone mount the stairs and knock softly. It was, as I had suspected, Atticus, and in a moment, I was alone in the house once again. It is strange, but I felt much more alone at that moment than before Burlevin's arrival. I did not fully understand why.

The following evening I visited what I had come to think of as the "secret room" with a view towards putting it to rights before the next "visitor" should arrive. Burlevin had removed all traces of his presence (indeed, this would be an easy task, as he had arrived with next to nothing). But upon the shelf which, I suppose, he had used for his bed, I found a curious object. I took it into the kitchen where I might inspect it in better light. It proved to be a wood carving, but so wonderfully and ingeniously crafted that I studied it for some moments. It had evidently been carved from a stick of firewood of some one and one half inches in diameter and about four inches in length. There was a sort of rectangular cage at the one end, in which a wooden ball rolled freely. It was obvious that in no wise could the ball have been inserted, as it was too large to pass between the bars, yet it was a separate piece and an almost perfect sphere. A bit of reflection showed that it must have been carved inside of its prison, yet I could not fathom how this might be accomplished, save, perhaps, by a craftsman of extraordinary skill. The other sections of the work were links of chain, interlocked as are real links, yet free to move independently. These links were attached to the wooden cage by a loop—again, of wood—carved into the bottom of the cage. My first thought was to show the piece to those in the village who might appreciate such a Wonder, but, alas, I could not. I would naturally be questioned on how I came to be in possession of such a thing, and, of course, I could not truthfully answer such inquiries. I have the piece still, nor shall I ever willingly part from it. It may be that Burlevin overlooked it in his hasty departure, but I, in my arrogance, choose to believe that he left it in token of thanks for my poor hospitality.

Over the course of the next year or so, I hosted others, yet none remain etched in my memory as firmly as Burlevin. They came sometimes escorted, sometimes alone. Some were evidently strangers to each other, others were members of a family. If they came alone, some brought written instructions (which they could not read) of their further disposition. Sometimes I was to take them to the next station, sometimes only part way, and sometimes they would be called for by the next "conductor." If escorted, it might be by Atticus, or by someone unknown to me. None, I am sure, gave their correct names. If unescorted, they might tell me they were sent by Atticus, or they might say nothing at all. One couple—two older men, as I recall—said they had been sent by "Moses." I knew this to be a *nom-de-plume*, as it were, but I never discovered who this "Moses" might be.

My tenure as "station-master" lasted a little more than a year. My last guests arrived early one January evening, during one of those mild periods which we sometimes see about the third week of that month. Indeed, for several days the temperature had fallen below freezing only at night, so that the roads were muddy and rutted during the greater part of the day, and some in the village had already begun to speak—albeit not seriously—of preparing their sap-buckets. Atticus arrived with two women—or rather, a woman and a half-grown girl. Their escort stayed but a moment, time enough to introduce them as "Margaret" (the mother) and Sarah; then he was gone. Both seemed very frightened. The woman clutched a piece of paper in her hand and passed it quickly to me, as though it might be poisonous, or a burden she could no longer carry. Having had experience in this sort of thing by now, I knew it to be instructions on how I was to "pass them along."

I endeavored to smile in a reassuring fashion and showed them to the secret room. I gave my usual instructions as to the window, the privy, and such, and Margaret nodded curtly at each, showing that she understood, but she spoke not at all, nor would questions evoke any response. She was a comely Negress of above-average height, but quite thin. Her eyes were lively, but the remainder of her countenance betrayed no emotion. I wondered how many homes she had stayed in, with none to call her own. Her clothes were old and faded, but nonetheless clean. She carried a small traveling bag, the first I had seen one of my "visitors" possess. It occurred to me that some kindly soul along the way had seen to it that her dress was clean and that she had something to carry her meager belongings in. The child, Sarah, spoke no more than her mother, but clung to her skirts and attempted to remain somewhat out of sight. That is to say, each time Margaret moved, the child would reposition herself to put as much of her mother's skirt between us as possible, while not losing sight of me. It was not in the least astonishing that she were affrighted upon seeing me; she had no time, poor thing, to become accustomed to one strange visage before she was confronted with yet another. Her young world must have been a most confusing place.

I told Margaret I had some salt-back and white beans remaining from my supper, and that I would be pleased to fry some left-over potatoes as well. At this point she did smile, and nodded her acceptance. She put the child to bed whilst I prepared the victuals. As I was setting the table, however, I was interrupted (I say interrupted, for I stopped my task to listen) by perhaps the most Angelic voice I have yet heard, or that I may ever hear this side of Heaven. It was an unwavering, sweet soprano, soft, yet most powerful, and quite compelling. There was a yearning there, and a Hope, and other elements I can not name, for they were felt, almost experienced, rather than absorbed directly by the ears. How poor and unworthy that sense seemed at that moment! I remained transfixed, the plate still suspended over the table until the lullaby ceased, or rather, trailed off, and I found myself released from the charm of that siren-like song. It seemed to me that, at the moment when I listened to her, my very blood had ceased to circulate in my veins, so that the noise of its passage might not interfere with the beauty of her song.

She ate slowly, glancing at me between forkfuls, but the haunted look was gone from her eye. The note she had given me revealed that she was to be with me but a single night and day and that at dusk the following day I was to escort her and Sarah to a crossroads a few miles north, where she would be met and taken on the next leg of their journey.

My duties, unfortunately, kept me absent all of the next day, and it was fast nearing sundown when I returned home. I had already determined that I would hitch my horse to the wagon in the shed and allow Margaret and Sarah to ride, for the weather was cold and the mother without shoes. Margaret had prepared corn-meal cakes for their journey, but she had kept several warm for me and I ate them quickly with a little syrup, anxious to see them safely on their way. I had known them but a short time, nor had I heard the child speak a single word, but I knew I should never forget them.

Preparations were quickly made, and the pair seated in the wagon bed when I threw open the doors and prepared to drive out. The horse had barely cleared the shed when a lantern was abruptly unshuttered and I saw three men blocking our way. As the lantern was raised, I recognized the surly visage of Ethan Furman. Another lantern shone forth and I saw also his two cronies, looking no more hospitable than their leader. Furman carried a musket, held in a rather negligent fashion under one arm. One of his friends was likewise armed, his rifle thrown over his shoulder, his finger on its trigger. The pistol of the third, though holstered, was very much in evidence.

Once again, in the interest of historical accuracy, I shall attempt to render the conversations verbatim. Ethan Furman began:

"Well, now, and just where might you be goin' with them darkies?"

I am not usually at a loss for words, but my vocal cords seemed momentarily paralyzed, and the best response I could muster was something like "Get out of my way."

The rifle came up a bit and he said, "I can't do that. You've got runaway slaves there, seems like."

At last my brain seemed to be functioning again, and I was able to reply with a bit more confidence: "These are my mother's new domestics. I am delivering them to her in Hartford."

Furman looked at his associates. Although the light was poor, I was sure I could see them grinning at each other. Then he spoke again. "Sure seems like a strange time o' day t' be startin' such a long ride, M$^r$ Burke." I replied that since I worked during the day, I could only do this at night. I did not suppose that the reasoning would satisfy him, as indeed it did not. I suspected that reason would be lost upon him, in any case. He spat tobacco at the horse's feet before speaking again. He had an irritating, slow drawl.

"Maybe so, maybe not. Don't matter. Unless they got papers showin' they ain't slaves, why, I guess maybe you goin' against th' law, Burke. It's my job t' collect 'em an' take 'em back. An' I never goes against no law." This last pronouncement brought laughter from the other two. Furman grinned at his own witticism and looked at the other rascals for their approbation.

I managed to draw myself up a little taller, though I do not fancy they could see me. I responded: "And how would they have such papers, sir, seeing they were never slaves, but free people?"

Again, the logic of this argument failed to make any impression. One of Furman's friends moved to take the bridle. I fancied I could hear Sarah whimper a bit. Furman chuckled a bit before answering. Then he said, "Well, then, if what you says is true, then I reckon I'd be satisfied seein' their work contract, or even a letter from your ma, sayin' they got work there." He grinned up at me expectantly while the other of his gang went around to the wagon bed. "Hell," he continued, "I'd even settle for seein' a coach ticket for these here darkies, so's I'd know they come here legal-like."

I flicked the reins and the horse started forward, but the bridle was still firmly held, and we advanced not at all. "I might have something in the house that would satisfy you," I told him (naturally I did not), "but I have no time to search for such things now. If I am to return in time for my work tomorrow, I must leave without further delay." It will be appreciated from the speciousness of this last argument that I was getting desperate. It was only a matter of moments, I feared, before the women were taken from the wagon and marched off at gunpoint.

I stated earlier that Margaret's voice was perhaps the sweetest I shall ever hear, nor will I retract that statement. But at that moment there came, out of the darkness, the most welcome voice I have ever known, nor can I imagine another being so timely.

"What's going on here?" it boomed from the shadows. In a moment, the figure of Colonel Peabody emerged. In the light of the lanterns, his visage looked unhappy indeed. He looked not at me, but at the three blocking our way, first at one, holding the man's gaze for an instant before moving to the next. His hands were balled into fists and rested upon his hips. His right hand was not so far removed from the Army pistol stuck into his belt. He still wore his uniform, I noted, tho' the tunic was partly unbuttoned. Perhaps he had been preparing to retire.

Furman recovered his composure quickly, however, and addressed my employer. "Why, good evenin' Colonel," he said, making a slight bow. "We was just about t' take some fugitive slaves into custody. Nothin' for you t' worry about, sir."

"Fugitives? What in thunderation are you talking about, sir?" His voice was belligerent, and Furman stepped back a pace, involuntarily. I should tell you—I had forgotten that the reader of this narrative may be somewhat removed in time and place from the events I am describing—that Colonel Peabody was quite well-thought of in our community, and commanded not a little respect, not only from the officers and men under his command, but equally from the citizens of Upper Granby Lake.

Furman's voice, when he spoke again, sounded a bit less sure. "Why, Colonel, this man's been helpin' slaves escape for 'most a year now. We been keepin' an eye on him, sir, an' we seen him. This is th' first time we caught him in th' act, though. Why, just you have a look in that wagon bed, Colonel. You'll see what we mean." He nodded at the spot, and the one standing there stepped back.

But Colonel Peabody moved not an inch. "Of course he's got darkies in there, you damned fool. I know that."

Furman's mouth dropped open. All he could manage was a strangled, "But…"

"You should get your facts straight, sir, before you go accusing one of my employees. He told you they were hired domestics, and so they are. I'll vouch for him and for them. I myself fetched them from the stage last night in Southwick. There were no connections 'til this evening, so I told him to take them to Hartford tonight. Now do you doubt my word, sir? Perhaps you'd like to go to Southwick yourself and verify the truth of what I'm telling you?" With these words, he took another step towards Furman, his hands still upon his hips, and Furman was forced to recoil a pace.

"Well, no, sir, o' course not," Furman managed to say. "O' course, if what you say is true..."

He was unable to finish his sentence, because the Colonel, whose nose was now only inches from Furman's, fairly bellowed, "'*If*'? Did you say 'if,' boy?"

I don't know if Furman fully appreciated the new appellation, but he retreated several more steps. Both of the others stepped away as well, leaving the way free.

But the Colonel wasn't finished yet. "You men are trespassers on United States Government property," he informed them, "and liable to prosecution if you're still here ten seconds from now." He glared at them. The trio hesitated but two of those seconds before moving quickly away, first at a rapid walk, then at a run, if I might judge by the sounds of the footsteps.

The Colonel looked up at me for a moment, then gestured me forward. "Get along," he said, in a quieter voice. "You still have to report for work tomorrow, M^r^ Burke. See that you're not tardy." I attempted to reply, but found that my mouth was too dry to allow the passage of anything which might be considered intelligible, so I merely nodded and flicked the reins once again. We started with a jolt.

We none of us spoke on the journey north to Two-Mile Bridge, where I was to entrust the care of my guests to others. I doubt that I could have formulated a coherent thought in any case, my mind being overwhelmed by the events of the evening. Indeed, I can say little regarding the trip, nor yet about the return to my own house, for I remember none of it.

It was not until the following morning that I could think clearly again, and I presented myself in the Colonel's office at the first opportunity. But though he received me immediately, he gave me no chance to speak, not did he even look at me while he worked on the papers before him.

"If you've come upon military business, M^r^ Burke, I'll have to request you make an appointment for a more opportune moment. As you can see, I'm extremely occupied at this moment." Now he did set down his pen and look at me. "And if your visit is regarding any other matter, then I can really devote no time to it at present. What a man does in his spare time, M^r^ Burke, and whatever views he may hold, are strictly his own. But I could not approve of any employee of the United States willfully contravening any of its Laws. Should I hear of such a thing, I would be forced to take action, even should my own opinions be in accordance with his. Do I make my meaning clear, sir?"

"You do, sir. Thank you, sir."

He held my eyes for a moment longer before acknowledging with a grunt, then returned to his work. How long, I wondered, had he been aware of my actions? I never found out, for I never broached the subject with him again.

This narrative is nearly at an end. It remains only to say that I never saw or heard from Atticus again, nor did I host any more refugees. Furman and his cronies give me a wide berth when they see me in town, but their looks are no less hostile.

Shall history vindicate or condemn me? I cannot believe that Involuntary Servitude be the Natural Order of things, yet you will find those who point to the Bible as proof. If that be true, then I alone am guilty of my acts, and, should the Truth be discovered, I accept full and total responsibility for them. In no wise should this Institution, nor its Provost, nor any of the Faculty, nor yet any other connected thereto be held liable. I have done what I believe to be the right and just thing, and if there be consequences, then let them fall entirely upon me. If, however, as I believe, history will show that it was right to stand up against the Institution of Slavery, then I have acted according to the dictates of God's own Law, and need answer to no man.

Even so, it is better that this document be laid away against a time of need. Should it become public knowledge, I might be judged harshly for my actions, however warranted they may have been. History will judge. May God have mercy upon our Souls and may this War Between Brothers come to a swift conclusion, with a lasting Peace for all men.

## PART II: 1867–2000

Mr. Bradley continued to lead Claxton Hall more or less well for the next several years. He was, however, a military man at heart, and this stood somewhat at odds with the reforms he had intended to introduce. His curriculum continued to follow the classic model, although he now admitted "modern" languages and biology. He was a bit troubled by the latter, as certain aspects of the course, recently changed after Mr. Darwin's work published a few years previously, seemed in direct contradiction with his admittedly fundamentalist upbringing. Nevertheless, he felt, one must keep up with the times. Parents would certainly not seriously consider sending their sons to an institution which might appear to resist progress and new trends in education. Organized athletics were suppressed in favor of military training, and boys were expected to spend at least an hour a day (unless confined to the infirmary) on the parade ground. He even made an abortive attempt to have these exercises conducted in Latin, feeling that his charges would appreciate Caesar all the more.

But history moved beyond Horatio Bradley, and by 1871, the world, or in any case the community of Upper Granby Lake, was no longer interested in matters military, at least insofar as such matters pertained to the education of its sons. Somewhat discouraged, Bradley relinquished the academic throne to Alonzo Record, who was to guide the institution into the next century.

Claxton Hall remained somewhat aloof from the travails of a country struggling to reunite itself, isolated at it was from the major metropolitan areas. Although what historians would later term "the industrial revolution" did not leave the town untouched, the major industry of the region at this time was tobacco growing, labor intensive, but not lending itself to mechanization to any great extent. The leaves still had to be harvested by hand, bundled and hung in barns to cure.

Mr. Record, a descendant of one of the first students at the school, was content to maintain a status quo. Military training was, however, eliminated; football and baseball were substituted. Several years before the end of his tenure, he added basketball in the winter, the sport having been recently developed in Springfield, Massachusetts, just a bit to the north. Other than replacing the stables with a more modern building, Mr. Record added little to the physical plant.

Over the course of the next quarter century, however, Claxton Hall would see the beginnings of a growth which continue into the present day, though progress was not steady. There were periods in which the school appeared to leap forward, with buildings either under construction or in the planning stage at any given moment. There were also periods of decline; indeed, some despaired of the school's survival.

At the turn of the century (1900), the village of Upper Granby Lake was still in large part agricultural. The school was bounded on the north by the farms of Alton Thurlow and Harlan Drummond. Indeed, certain boys who had the inclination and who could find a few free moments could earn a bit of pocket money by doing chores there. One or two even hired themselves out for the summer months, when work was plentiful. It was good, honest work, and they could almost cover the cost of their tuition (several hundred dollars per year at this point) with what they earned.

In 1920, the last of the Hammond family died, and the School purchased the land, with an eye toward expansion. Many buildings, especially those built as "temporary" structures when the institution was a military base, were showing their age. Two new dormitories, Preble Hall and Wannamaker House, were added during the first quarter of the twentieth century. This period also saw the construction of the classroom building which still stands today, and the gymnasium, the first structure built solely for that purpose. The old barn burned and the refectory was torn down.

It is perhaps well that this first building phase was completed before the stock market crash in 1929, for money for further expansion was scarce for a while. In point of fact, there were no new buildings until 1948. At the best of times, the School's endowment was unimpressive. Conversely, because the school had relatively little money (as compared, for instance, to Deerfield or Exeter), it had relatively little to invest, and therefore suffered less in the way of losses.

Samuel Forest took over as headmaster in 1919 and held the post until 1930, taking the school from the difficult period following World War I to the difficult period after the beginning of the Depression. While the School did not prosper during this period, neither did it suffer. The reasons for his rather sudden resignation have never been made public, and, at this point in time, are a matter for conjecture. The more benign rumors have him resigning "for reasons of health." Other rumors, less favorable, suggest that the health problem was syphilis, and that he had contracted the disease through an "affair" with another employee of the School. It has even been proposed that the other party was not an employee, but rather the daughter of a faculty member, but this can be given little credence, as a check of the available records reveals that the oldest faculty daughter at this time was a mere fourteen years old. Nevertheless, his portrait, which hangs today in Rector Hall, shows a face either in pain or torment.

The Great Depression and the years immediately following marked one of the low points of the school's existence. It will be readily appreciated that there was little money at the beginning of the Depression for such luxuries as a private boarding school, and attendance fell precipitously. At one point, the school's entire enrollment was but 38 students, and it seemed that it must surely founder at any moment.

Although he holds no prominent place in the school's history, Marshall Thompson, Head from 1930 to 1951, must be accounted one of its foremost headmasters. As has been mentioned, little or no building was accomplished during this period, an era of almost negative growth, save at the end. Yet Thompson would not allow the school to close, nor even approach bankruptcy. He had no grandiose vision for the institution, no master plan. He was brought in by the Board of Trustees solely on his business credentials.

Marshall Thompson held the post of vice president of the First National Bank of Hartford for approximately twelve years. He counted Chief Loan Officer among his duties, and his business acumen quickly established him—in the eyes of the bank president, at any rate—as a financial genius. The loans he approved always turned out to be excellent risks, while those he did not recommend never prospered. It seemed to the Trustees of Claxton Hall that this was the ideal person to lead the School though a time of financial uncertainty.

Thompson's solutions to the institution's pecuniary difficulties were makeshift, and more patches than long-term answers. He cut the curriculum drastically, so that he could make do with four or five teachers, each teaching six periods a day, often four or five subjects. While no teachers would accept this kind of workload today, it must be remembered that during this period jobs were extremely scarce, and those looking for jobs did not feel they could dictate the terms of their employment. Many of Thompson's employees were reluctant to talk about their life at Claxton Hall, but one may infer that they were, in some rare instances, treated little better than slaves, working ten to twelve hours a day at a minimum and subsisting on the most meager of rations.

Even in the worst of economic times, however, there will still be families wealthy enough to send their sons to boarding schools. Claxton Hall was ideally situated in this regard, being located in a state considered wealthy, and neighboring two others, Massachusetts and New York, also generally well-to-do. Thompson was evidently willing to sacrifice quality for quantity, and his main objective in the early '30s was to "fill the beds."

He made several other temporary changes, some of which lasted into the war years. As there was a dearth of young men to fill the available slots, because families could not afford to send their sons, Thompson began accepting young women, though not as full partners in the enterprise. There were no facilities for female boarding students, so all of the girls were local, and returned to their homes at night. Thompson also discovered he could cut costs by having the girls work in the kitchen and dining room to reduce their tuition. This left them less time for classes, of course, so many enrolled for just two or three, which meant that they couldn't graduate in the usual four years, meaning that Thompson would have their services all the longer. Surprisingly, the system worked, after a fashion, though by 1942, these early "co-eds" had all but disappeared from the campus.

As women went to work to fill the jobs their sons, husbands and brothers had been forced to leave when they joined the military at the outbreak of the Second World War, they sometimes left their younger children in the care of older women, those too advanced in age to work in defense industries and whose own children had long since left home. It occurred to Thompson that the school, having much unused space at this time, could rent out some of that space for "nurseries" (now called "day care"). He would hire some of the older women—at minimal wage, of course—and offer child care services to the community. This scheme was not a great financial boost to the school, but it did serve to enhance its reputation.

Women also served as instructors (Thompson refused to refer to them as "teachers") for a time, when male instructors were scarce. The Headmaster hired them to teach subjects such as penmanship and spelling, or perhaps French, but there is no record of their teaching "serious" subjects such as mathematics or science.

By 1951, however, both the school's resources—already tightly stretched—and Thompson's strength were at an end. Marshall Thompson had held the school together for twenty-one years, but in the June of that year, when the Trustees announced that Claxton had sufficient funds to operate only through November, Thompson resigned.

The Board scrambled to find a replacement before the opening of school. As interim, they named one of their number, Roger Nielson, to fill the void.

At 53, Nielson was still young enough to develop a long-range plan for the school and carry it out. He was experienced enough to know what would work and what would probably fail. As President of the prestigious financial consulting firm of Shawmut and Noyes in Hartford, he also had a firm grasp of the economics necessary to revive and restore the ailing school. After a bit of initial hesitation, Nielson agreed to accept the position and threw himself into his new job with a will that astonished even those who knew him well.

On August 1, 1951, Roger Nielson was found dead at his desk in Bassett House, victim of a massive coronary. The Board met in emergency session on August 8, with the intention of closing the school. Trustee Everett Record made an impassioned plea to keep the school open, saying that he had been in communication with the firm of Collins, Shepard and Robestelli, investment brokers. His conversations with them had convinced him that, with the right man at the helm, Claxton could survive the current crisis. A member of that firm, Oliver Lawgood, had tentatively agreed to take the position of headmaster for one year, until a permanent Head could be found. He brought a strong business sense and many years of experience as an administrator to the task. The Board agreed, albeit somewhat reluctantly. Lawgood would be given free rein to attempt to save the school.

Lawgood's program was one of austerity. He immediately fired the kitchen staff and brought in a catering firm, one which, coincidentally, he owned. He saved an enormous amount of money by reducing food purchases and the amount served at meals. A typical lunch might consist of clear broth and a limp sandwich. Lawgood was unconcerned about complaints relating to the diet, for, he said, "They're going to complain about something. Let them complain about the food. It takes their mind from other areas needing attention." To make up for the meager fare, the service offered a once-a-month "theme banquet." Hawaiian night turned out to be ham with a pineapple slice, a couple of overweight staffers in grass skirts over their whites and some records of Hawaiian music. Students and faculty stayed away in droves.

In April, Lawgood told the Board that the school needed infusions of cash and talent, and that he could see no readily tapped source for either at the present time.

At this point, Everett Record stepped forward. He was independently wealthy, an avid sportsman, patron of the arts and a firm believer in private education in general, and particularly in the promise and potential in Claxton Hall. He used his own money to get the school back on its feet and instilled in it a new sense of pride. He had a vision and the wherewithal to realize it. A charismatic leader, he was able to attract quality faculty. The fact that Claxton was suddenly offering competitive salaries also drew talented teachers who might have been seriously considering other offers. Financial aid was increased, and enrollment began to climb. Recruiting trips for the admissions staff became possible, and Claxton began to pull in better students from greater distances.

Carter Hall, a facility to house a dining room, the kitchens and the student union, was built almost immediately. Farnsworth Health Center, a converted residence, was opened in 1955. Lowe Library was erected in 1967 and Cooper House, the first of the girls' dormitories, in 1971. Extensive renovations were accomplished on most of the other buildings, and other facilities were modernized. Many alumni speak of the Record years as the golden years of Claxton Hall.

Record's successor, Robert Bosworth, had a different agenda. In retrospect, it seems that Bosworth was more interested in show than substance, but he did leave behind the legacy of a modern Claxton campus, with excellent facilities, and a firmly-entrenched co-educational curriculum. His sudden departure, however, left many with unanswered questions.

The Board of Trustees was very careful in choosing its next Head. The members seemed to feel that Claxton had strayed too far from their concept of the ideal prep school. Elrond Young was to be, in effect, their instrument, one who would carry out their policies with little action or thought needed on his part. He was to attempt to alleviate the bad taste left in some mouths by Bosworth's hasty exit. If anything, Young was worse than Bosworth in some ways. He was in some respects a martinet, but one who always performed as he thought the Board would want him to. He made few friends, and few respected him. However, it took the Board nearly eight years to discover that he was an ineffectual leader. To Young's credit, he put into motion the plan which resulted in Claxton's upgrading its athletic facilities, which became the envy of many nearby schools.

James Thatcher followed Young as Head. His priority was to modernize and revitalize the curriculum, an area neglected by both Bosworth and Young. He encouraged more seminars and honors courses, cross-curriculum and team teaching, peer teaching under teacher supervision, projects both large and small for all classes, and insisted that some teachers, who had been depending far too heavily on video in their classrooms, get back to basics. "The teacher is the greatest resource any classroom has," he insisted. He encouraged students to bring computers and started a fund drive to get the entire campus wired for internet access. He encouraged the library to get rid of books which hadn't been checked out in five years or more and start buying new ones. He started the Parents' Association, a sort of pep group for parents which was also a fund-raising organization. The school began to throw off the shadows of the previous administrations.

By the close of the 20th century, Claxton Hall had moved into a position of some prominence. While still not considered a "top tier" school, it was nevertheless fairly highly regarded. It still kept and cherished many of its old traditions, though the only original building still remaining was the Cottage. In a rather bold move, Claxton Hall found itself, for the beginning of the 1999-2000 school year, with a female Head, the first school of its type to dare such a thing. History will judge the wisdom of the Board's decision in this regard.

# COLLY WRIGHT (1872)

She decided that she didn't much care for the man seated behind the desk, but she was determined to see this through. She was just as qualified as any other teacher, and she had to make him understand that. At first glance, however, it didn't appear that it would be an easy task. He looked as starched as that collar he wore—and that included his face and his manner, she decided. He also seemed to have used an inordinate amount of wax on his mustache and oil on his hair. She wondered briefly—as he continued to read the papers before him—what the results might be should he get too close to an open flame.

Alonzo Record, newly-appointed Head of Claxton Hall cleared his throat (*he sounds as if he were trying to dislodge a peach pit*) and looked up at the woman.

"You understand, Mrs. Wright, that I should not be offering you this position if there were any qualified gentlemen to fill it. However..." He paused and curled the end of his mustache a bit more. "...however, present circumstances require extraordinary measures. The war has evidently left us with a dearth of men, to say nothing of those qualified to teach mathematics. And those who might otherwise be qualified seem to be finding employment elsewhere." He looked at her again and seemed slightly surprised to see her still there. "Although your qualifications are...impressive, Mrs. Wright..." Another pause, during which he shuffled some papers. "...I cannot think that boys can learn effectively from a woman."

When she looked at him, her eyes widened slightly. When she spoke, her tone was that of a woman to whom a great truth had suddenly been revealed.

"Why, Mr. Record, if that be the case, then of what possible use are mothers?"

His own eyes widened at her impudence, and his mouth opened to speak. Then he thought better of it. He had better tread carefully here. School was due to open for the fall session in two days, and he had no instructor for mathematics. Still, perhaps he could make the job so unattractive that she would refuse. His wife wouldn't let him forget that a few years ago, the Anthony woman and another whose name he couldn't recall, had started that confounded suffrage movement, to accord equal rights to women, of all things. It *had* to be counter to the natural, God-given order, he was sure, but Roselyn Record was not a woman to be crossed...

"I should prefer a married woman...that is to say, with a husband."

She drew herself up a bit taller. "I should too, Mr. Record, but my husband was at Andersonville and did not return."

He forced himself to mumble, "My condolences, Mrs. Wright." The horrors of the Confederate prison camp there were well known and he had no wish to get into that topic. "Well, we are fairly strict with our faculty here at Claxton Hall, Mrs. Wright. They are, after all, models for our young people to emulate. We insist, for example, that they lead moral, upright lives. We expect to see them at church and prayer meetings regularly, engaged in charitable works if they find they have free time which they wish to use constructively, and so forth."

"That is not a problem, Mr. Record."

"No, I did not expect it to be. You would be expected to fulfill all of the duties of a teacher. In addition, you may not receive gentleman callers except on Sunday, you will not frequent certain public areas and you will refrain from reading certain books, notably popular fiction, which has no literary or social value. Do I make myself clear?"

"I understand you perfectly, sir." *You are a self-centered prig, at the very least.*

"And you still wish this job?"

"I do."

Record reflected a moment, but he could come up with no more objections. There was therefore an obvious reluctance in his voice when he said, "Very well, Mrs. Wright. I shall engage you until a permanent teacher can be found. Mrs. Hampton, whose office adjoins mine, will have you sign a standard contract."

"I am to be hired as a substitute, then?"

He shrugged. "It is the best I can do under the present circumstances, Mrs. Wright. If that's not sufficient…"

Colly took a deep breath. It wasn't what she'd been hoping for, but she needed an income. She couldn't raise the twins on promises. "Very well. I shall take the job until someone more qualified is hired." She laid special emphasis on the last six words. She wasn't about to back down.

She was a bit taken aback by the sum noted on her contract. To be sure, it wasn't a salary, but a *per diem* payment for services rendered. And not a very large one at that. She hesitated a moment before putting pen to paper. The stipend would barely cover her room at Mrs. Pickens' and what she paid Susan Langdon to look after Dora and Daniel when they weren't in school. There would be precious little for such niceties as clothes or even soap. Still, perhaps she could take some of her meals, at least, at the school, and even bring some home to the children. She needed *some* sort of income, and this was evidently the best to be had in Upper Granby Lake. She couldn't think of moving the children yet again.

She sighed and signed her name. There was one advantage, at least: there was no notice to give if she wished to leave.

There were six classrooms in the Hall, a workroom for the teachers, a coatroom and a small office. The classrooms were arranged so that the stoves which warmed them might share a chimney; the building boasted three. The room assigned to Colly was neither the biggest, nor the warmest. The stove, however, did seem to draw fairly well. She assumed one of the boys would be assigned to bring in wood each day and keep a water bucket more or less full. There were no accommodations for women, of course; she'd have to make sure one of the outhouse doors could be firmly secured from the inside. The desks were well-worn but serviceable, each designed for two students. The blackboard, like the desks, wore the ghosts of marks and grime which wouldn't come out. The stacks of books on the teacher's table looked fairly new. There seemed to be an ample supply of pencils as well, though not sharpened. She supposed most of the boys would carry penknives for that purpose. She took one of the books with her so she might prepare some sort of lesson plans for arithmetic and algebra. Perhaps some of the boys had advanced to geometry. She'd have to find out.

It was nearly dark when she arrived at Mrs. Pickens' boarding house. Susan had already fed the children and put them down for the night, though both were still awake. She talked quietly to them as she moved about their room, folding clothes and putting things to rights. They were asleep before she blew out the lamp.

She took time the next day to familiarize herself with the campus before reporting to the faculty meeting in the Hall. It was wedged between two farms to the north and the fairgrounds to the south, with the Head's residence on the west side of the road and the other buildings on the east. Most of the activity which concerned her would take place either in the Hall itself or the refectory. The other two buildings were wooden barracks, fairly new, which had housed the troops training here during the War. She hadn't learned their names yet. She supposed the boys would also work in the barns or stables and exercise on the parade ground. They probably attended services in the Covenant Church just down the road. Alonzo Record hadn't been overly generous with details of what was expected of her.

*I trust he doesn't expect me to cook, clean or wash dishes. He said 'all the duties of a teacher'. I wonder what that entails.*

Now she was late. Hiking her skirts just a bit, she walked quickly to the workroom in the Hall. It had an enormous table, seating at least twenty, and this is where Mr. Record presided at weekly meetings.

Her entrance was ill-timed. She coughed once as she opened the door, as the air was thick with cigar smoke. Evidently Mr. Record was an extremely punctual man or he tended to begin his meetings a bit early, a fact which everyone save herself seemed to know. A dozen heads turned to look as she entered. Several of the faces wore frowns if not silent condemnation. She had evidently interrupted Mr. Record, a fact which seemed to classify her, in the eyes of some of these gentlemen, at any rate, as something between an annoyance and a boor. A few looked genuinely surprised. Apparently they hadn't heard that a woman was to join their august ranks this year.

"Ah." Record spoke as though a small fact, which he'd not considered important enough to make public, had just thrust itself on his consciousness. "Ah, gentlemen. Mrs. Wright. She will be helping us out in mathematics. Mrs. Wright, if you would be good enough to find a chair…" He gestured vaguely towards the opposite end of the table, disturbing a layer of smoke, which whirled momentarily around his hand. "We had already begun."

She looked. There were no empty chairs at the table, nor did anyone rise to offer her one. There were a few against the wall, and Colly moved tentatively toward one, expecting one of the teachers to at least move a bit and make a place where she might put a chair. No one did. Some of the disapproving looks had changed to curiosity, but other heads had turned back to face Record, apparently not thinking her worth further attention.

She refused to be cowed. She set her bag at her feet and took out a pencil and notebook. Record resumed speaking. He seemed to be emphasizing once again the importance of the teacher's role in the formation of young minds, the nobleness of the profession, and so forth. Colly had the impression that he gave the same speech at each year's opening meeting. As a mother, she felt she probably knew more about the subject than most of the men and her attention began to wander.

The room was paneled; in oak or another wood, she could not be certain. Years of smoke and dust and neglect had certainly darkened it considerably. Portraits were hung at regular intervals, but they, too, had been there too long without cleaning and were now tones of brown, tan and black. She supposed they must be important figures in the history of the school. There were, of course, no women.

Record moved on to a new subject, and Colly began listening again.

"There are no funds available to engage masters for the express purpose of leading the boys in some form of physical exercise in the afternoons, so you shall all be required to contribute in this area." He gave Colly a hard look, then turned to each man in turn. One would help with football, another with horsemanship, a third proposed marching and calisthenics, and so on around the table. All eyes then came to rest on Colly.

She tightened her lips to avoid showing a smile. *He thinks to catch me on this, does he? Well, I'm not so easily caught, you old hypocrite.*

"Why, archery, of course." The tone of slight surprise in her voice suggested that she'd already told him and was amazed to find he'd forgotten so quickly. "I'm sure you must have the necessary tackle and targets." *Did I put too much sweetness and innocence into that last?*

Her first class was 3rd form arithmetic. The students seemed to vary widely—or wildly—in ability. Some, even equipped with paper and pencil, seemed unable to add two single-digit numbers without recourse to their fingers. Others flew through a series of three-digit additions and subtractions as fast as Colly could write them on the board. She considered this, her tongue pushing out her left cheek as it always did when she was deep in thought.

When the class entered the following day, the pupils saw no books on the table. She had stored them out of sight. Nor were any writing materials in evidence.

She clapped her hands to bring the class to order. "All right. Three digit additions for everyone." She waited for the groans and little exclamations of surprise to subside.

The students looked at each other, bemused. *The same problems for everyone? That isn't the way it's done.*

Turning to the board, she pushed her right sleeve up a bit, took the chalk and wrote

198
201
555

and put a line under the column. Then she crossed her arms and waited, looking expectant.

It was a full eight seconds before Ethan Young raised a hesitant hand.

"Excuse me, miss. May we have paper and pencil, please?"

She shook her head slowly. "You don't need them for such a simple problem, Ethan. Look at the first number. It's almost what?"

"Two hundred, miss."

"Correct. And the second?"

"Well, that's almost the same."

"Right again. So we have almost…?"

"Four hundred."

"Um-hm. And if we add five to four?"

"Nine. Or in this case, nine-hundred fifty five, Mrs. Wright." Ethan's mind had skipped ahead.

*The boy's bright enough. He knows where we're going.*

"Ah. So all we have to do is…?"

Another hand went up. After glancing at her seating plan, she called on Matthew.

"Subtract one, 'cause the first two numbers make one less than four hundred, so the answer is nine hundred fifty-four." He looked quite smug.

She picked up the chalk again and pretended to do the sum on the board, quite laboriously. Then she feigned surprise at the answer.

"Why, I do believe you're right, Mr. Loring. However did you do that so quickly, and with no pencil or paper?"

John Peterson's hand shot up. "Please, miss, could we do another?"

After several problems she began keeping score, putting the student's name on the board and adding a little star each time a boy solved a problem correctly. After a furious forty minutes, she tried to explain that there were other ways, all coming down to simple one- or two-digit addition, which anyone should be able to do in one's head. They actually seemed pleased with themselves when the hour came to an end.

"Well, miss, I guess we shan't need books, shall we?" Colin Masters smiled up at her as he left.

"Oh, yes, as we get to harder material," she assured him.

During her free periods, she discovered, she was expected to supervise groups of boys as they did their work in an unoccupied classroom. This did not prove to be an undue hardship, however, though she did not get as much of her own work done as she might have wished. She spent a good portion of the hour reprimanding one boy or another for misconduct, trying to get them all focused on a certain task or helping yet another with schoolwork. Once, she even found herself dealing with a homesickness issue. Perhaps she would become a sort of surrogate mother to some of the younger boys, she mused.

However, the real benefit was not having to go to the workroom where the teachers congregated in their free periods to smoke, talk and even correct a theme or two. It was obvious she wasn't welcome there, her two or three abortive entrances having been met with cold silences and stony stares. Most men didn't seem ready to admit women as teachers at any level higher than elementary education. She certainly wasn't about to tell them that she had a degree from a normal school and another from a university.

*Let's not roil the waters. This job hangs by a rather slender thread as it is.*

The final straw had come when she collided with a teacher—Mr. Silas, it was—as he backed out of the room, still speaking to someone inside, and she had been passing, her arms laden with textbooks she intended to store until she felt the students needed them. She hadn't fallen, but several books had. Silas had looked at her with what she could only interpret as disdain and said icily, "Madam, have a care where you're walking, if you please." There had been no apology, no effort to help her gather up the fallen books.

Colly went through several appropriate epithets in her mind, discarding "blackguard" as too mild and finally settling on "whoreson" as strong enough, if perhaps not entirely appropriate. She bit her lip to keep from saying it aloud.

"Here."

Startled, she turned to find the man behind her holding two of the fallen books.

A bit astonished at the fact that one of these misogynists should choose to help her, she didn't move for a second, and he finally put the two volumes on top of the stack she was carrying.

The man smiled. "Don't mind Silas. He's a bit of a curmudgeon and is rarely polite to anyone. His bark is much worse than his bite."

She continued to stare, trying to determine if he were serious. After all of the hostility she'd been met with, this little kindness was a bit…unnerving. The man who had helped her was perhaps a bit thin, with a neatly trimmed mustache. Both the mustache and the dark hair were lightly flecked with gray, somewhat lighter than the shade of his eyes.

She finally found her voice. "Thank…thank you, Mr. … I'm sorry, sir, I don't know your name. I've heard others call you 'Jeremiah," but I don't know your family name, I'm afraid."

He smiled again. "'Jeremiah'" will be fine."

She tried to get a hand free so she could shake his. "And I'm…"

He took the offered hand. "Mrs. Colly Wright. Yes, everyone knows you, even if you don't know everyone quite yet. You've already made quite an impression on some people, you know." He smiled once more, nodded, turned and disappeared into the workroom.

*Now what did he mean by that?*

On a fine fall day not too long after that incident, she decided it was time to begin archery. She had no class during the final hour, and a respite from the study room, as well. She returned to the boarding house and told Susan to take the children out to the parade ground for some fresh air and exercise. From under her bed she took a long, slender, cloth-wrapped object. She unwrapped the bow and ran her hands over the polished surface. It had been quite a while since she'd practiced. Her father had had it made—so he said—by an Abenaki skilled in such things. It was of lemonwood, save for the grip. That was oak or perhaps ash; she couldn't remember. Of the dozen arrows she'd received at the same time, only three remained. Over the course of the years, some had been lost or broken. One or two had run off into the woods in the bodies of animals she'd hit, but not killed. That meant fetching her father or brother and starting a long tracking expedition.

She examined the feathers on the remaining shafts: two white-striped brown and one white at the end of each. They looked to be still serviceable. Bracing one end of the bow on the floor against a foot, she bent the bow with one hand and, sliding the other along the arc, moved the string into the notches at the upper end. She tugged at the cord tentatively. Everything seemed in order.

Groups of boys were already assembling on the parade ground when she arrived. She saw Dora and Daniel playing tag with another child she didn't recognize—perhaps the daughter of one of the teachers. The four boys who had indicated some interest in "shooting things with a bow" were assembled near the gazebo. Two had produced child-sized bows and arrows from somewhere; she guessed they'd just have to take turns.

"Well, we'll need something for a target."

"You could use my brother, miss," one suggested brightly.

She tried to scowl to hide a smile. "No, I'm afraid not. Timothy…it *is* 'Timothy,' isn't it? Timothy, do you think you could find an empty feed sack in the barn? And stuff it with as much hay as you can? Really tightly?"

He nodded and ran off, taking another boy with him.

"I'll need a stake and some twine."

"I know where I can find those, Mrs. Wright." It was the tallest and perhaps the oldest who volunteered.

"Good. Then we can make a proper target."

It wasn't much when it was assembled: a sack of hay tied to a stake driven into the ground, but it was a start. She moved her group back twenty or twenty-five yards. After putting on a leather arm guard, she handed two arrows to one of the boys, then prepared to shoot, explaining all the while how to stand, how to set the nock of the arrow to the string, making sure the feathers were in the right position, how to draw and release. She drew the string back smoothly, locked her hand against her jaw, found a point of aim and released. It wasn't the best shot she'd made, but it did hit the sack, a bit high and left. She have to move her aiming point for the next shot. The second shot was dead center, the final only a bit high and right.

"Not bad shooting," came a voice from behind her. She almost expected it to add, "For a woman."

The short man with the slightly *démodé* muttonchop whiskers was scowling a reluctant approval. His name was…Potter, or something like that, if she recalled correctly. She forced herself to say "Thank you," though her teeth wanted to clench.

The man—short and red-faced—stepped closer. He seemed to swagger a bit. "Yes, well, I was considered a pretty decent shot in my youth, you know."

"I'm sure you were, sir."

One of the boys came running back with Colly's arrows and handed them to her. She prepared to shoot again, this time explaining *why* she was doing things in such-and-such a manner.

"Mmm. I wonder if I still have the touch."

She sighed—not too loudly. If she didn't let him have a go, he'd tell all of his colleagues how uncooperative and unfriendly the Wright woman was. If she did…well, perhaps it might make some of the men a bit less hostile.

"Would you care to have a try, sir?" She tried to keep her voice polite. *If you break this bow, I swear I'll tan your hide for a quiver.*

"Well, maybe just one or two." He took the bow and arrows from her and pulled the cord experimentally. "Not too tight, is it?"

"It's a forty-pound draw, sir. About right for a woman, but I expect you're accustomed to much more powerful bows."

"Yes, yes, of course. But I'll make do." He dropped two of the arrows and nocked the other.

She bit her tongue. He'd nocked it incorrectly, with the cock feather against the bow. That was a good way to strip the fletching. Now he was drawing it back, holding the arrow between thumb and bent forefinger. Definitely not the best way. Even before he released—jerkily—she knew the shaft would go high.

"Hey, have a care, there!" one of the footballers yelled as the arrow buried itself in the earth only a yard or two from his foot.

"Yes, sorry!" he waved cheerfully back at them. Then he turned to Colly. "I'm not used to this light bow, you see."

She nodded, tight-lipped.

"Well, let's try again."

His best attempt came within ten yards of the sack. He handed the bow back. "Not very accurate, is it?"

Without waiting for an answer, he turned and stomped off.

"No laughing," she admonished the boys. Their number seemed to have grown by two or three. "I'm sure he's a fine shot with his own bow. Now watch once more, and then we'll all try."

She was a bit surprised to find Jeremiah waiting for her after church that Sunday. She realized that she'd been too busy even to inquire about his last name.

"May I walk you home, Mrs. Wright?"

"Why, yes, thank you." To her surprise he offered his hand to Dora, who took it, looked up at him, and asked "Who are you?" Eight year-olds have little sense of propriety, Colly thought.

Jeremiah took no offense. "I'm Jeremiah Record," he answered off-handedly, but his eyes were on Colly.

She stiffened a bit. She knew that the Head had a son who taught here, but she'd never thought to ask…

She could think of nothing to say, but Jeremiah chatted brightly with the children until they reached the boarding house. Then she managed to stammer, "Would…would you come to tea this afternoon?" She had to find some way to thank him, after all. "Mrs. Pickens serves at half-past three in the parlor."

"Why, yes, that would be most pleasant, thank you, Mrs. Wright. I'll see you then." He touched his hat and was gone. She stared after him for a long moment, wishing she hadn't been so tongue-tied.

By three she'd put on her best dress, the one reserved for very special occasions, brushed her hair until it shone and tried to put Dora and Daniel down for a nap. They were having none of it, protesting they were far too old and besides, they were *always* allowed a cake from the tray before retiring upstairs.

Colly wondered briefly why she was going to so much trouble. William had been gone nearly eight years, true, but she should be well past the age where she wanted to impress a man. Shouldn't she? Well, she was just 28, after all, and perhaps not *too* plain looking, but she'd determined long ago that William would be the only man in her life, and that she would be tempted by no other.

*So there.*

The hour passed pleasantly enough. Colly learned that Jeremiah had seen action only briefly in the War, his unit having been sent to Virginia barely before the cessation of hostilities. Most of the time he'd spent at Camp Chase in Massachusetts, where he'd been a quartermaster. He'd never married, had worked as a baker and then as a journalist before the War and had taken a position teaching English "for just so long as it takes me to make up my mind what I really want to do. Father was in a bit of a bind, so I offered to help him out."

He brushed some crumbs off his lap. "No, I realize he's not the easiest person in the world to get along with, but really, Mrs. Wright…"

"Please call me Colly."

"…Colly, we're not all like that. You've got to realize that private education has been a male-dominated bastion for so long that it may take some time to change the way people think."

"There are several good schools for young ladies," she countered.

"Yes, I believe they're called 'finishing schools'. Not quite the same thing, perhaps."

"Well, I don't want to teach in a finishing school. I want to make a difference here."

Jeremiah considered her from over the rim of his cup. "Believe me, Colly, you already have."

Her third formers were having trouble with multiplication.

"Look, boys, we can't start algebra until you can do some of these facts in your head. I mean, you're going to encounter expressions such as this…" She turned and wrote on the board. "…and you'll have to know how to find the product of '2' and '$x$' without counting on your fingers. Suppose $x$ is a number like 12? You're going to run out of fingers very quickly."

"But ma'am, those multiplication tables are awfully hard to learn. Do we have to memorize all that?"

She thought for a moment, than said, firmly, "No. We're not going to use multiplication tables. Not in this class. You can just forget about them."

The chorus of sighs was quite audible.

"We'll just use counting and adding. You can all do additions in your heads now. Can you count by twos?"

Matthew Fletcher began to count without raising his hand. "Two, four, six, eight…"

Colly stopped him with a raised palm. "Good. What about by fives?"

Several voices answered in a sing-song cadence: "Five, ten, fifteen, twenty…"

"And by tens?"

She let them get up to one hundred before stopping them. "More difficult: by threes?"

The answer was slower in coming, but Arnold was fairly sure of himself: "Three, six, nine, twelve…"

"Thank you Arnold. Now, I want everyone to count together, but here's what we're going to do. Hold your hands over your desks, not too high, like this. Every time you count, touch one finger to the desk, like this." She demonstrated: "Three, six, nine, twelve, fifteen, eighteen…. Now, how many fingers are touching the desk?"

Josiah, seated in the front row, craned his neck to see. "Six, teacher."

"And we're counting by…?"

"Three."

"So six threes are…?"

"You were at eighteen when you stopped."

"So six threes are eighteen?"

Several boys opened their eyes in astonishment. "Ohhhhh…."

She folded her arms. "And how many threes in twenty-seven?"

They got to work. By the end of the hour, she had to urge them to leave.

As Christmas neared, Colly decided she was fairly happy at Claxton. The students were responding well, her own children seemed content with their new school and had made new friends, and the attitude of the other teachers toward her wasn't quite as frosty. In addition, she had been seeing quite a bit of Jeremiah, and that was always pleasant. Still, she reminded herself—more and more frequently, it seemed—that her work and the welfare of the children came first. Jeremiah was, after all, only a bit of a Sunday diversion—at church and tea...and perhaps other times, as well.

He'd taken to calling for her and walking her to church, then accompanying her back home afterwards. He was normally present at Sunday tea, even inviting her once to the Head's home where his mother served once a month. There had been one or two church suppers, a carriage ride or two, but always in daylight, and usually around town where everyone could keep an eye on them. In early October, they'd gone to the county fair, held on the parade ground and the adjoining fields. They'd admired the quilts and handcrafts, the preserves, produce and pies. Jeremiah had wasted ten cents trying to throw hoops over stakes and another fifty cents at the race track. Afterwards, he admitted ruefully that he should have listened to Colly and bet on the mare named Ruby Rose. Everything was perfectly proper.

*Well, except for that one time when he stopped the horse by the brook. I mean, he caught me completely by surprise and I certainly didn't kiss him back. Well, not very long, anyway. After that, I told him to behave himself. And he had the nerve just to smile and flick the reins along the horse's back.*

*He gave up far too easily.*

She was reliving this pleasant little daydream when she was brought up short by the Head's voice calling to her as she passed the Hall.

"Mrs. Wright, would you be good enough to step in here a moment?"

The air suddenly seemed more chilly, but she went in. His office door stood open. As she entered, another man rose from the chair facing Record's desk. He was of average height and build, but his complexion was quite florid, as though he might have spent too much time in a stiff, cold wind. His smile was genuine enough, though.

Rector smiled, too. "Mrs. Wright, I have some good news for you." He gestured at his visitor. "This gentleman is Mr. Robert Williams, and he will be taking over your duties as instructor in mathematics directly after Christmas. I know that you will be most pleased to get back to your many responsibilities as a mother."

Once, as a child, Colly had run full-tilt into a wheelbarrow and had had the wind knocked out of her for a full minute. She remembered that feeling now, finding herself unable to speak, even to breathe. Her hand, extended toward Mr. Williams, remained stiffly outstretched in the air.

Rector's smile seemed mocking now. He stuck his thumbs into his waistband and patted himself impatiently on the hips. "Well, we shan't keep you longer, Mrs. Wright. I'm sure you have students waiting. We'll be in touch. Good day."

Then she was back on the street, still dazed, having no memory of leaving Rector's office. His words clouded her head like a fog.

Fortunately, her 5th formers had a test and she didn't have to teach. She couldn't have in any case. She started blankly out over the rows of bowed heads and tried to sort things out. She felt hollow inside.

*Oh, Lord, I'm going to have to move again. Some place where I can find work. But where? I can't move without work and I can't work without moving. Whatever shall I do for funds? There's nothing I can sell. The school still owes me a little money, but it won't last more than a week. Wherever shall we live?*

When she returned home, she sat in her room, staring at the stack of tests she had to correct, but unable to start the task. *What's the use?*

A knock on the door snapped her attention back to the real world. "Mrs. Wright?" It was Mrs. Pickens' voice. "You have a visitor in the parlor."

She wiped her eyes. *Oh, please, let it be Jeremiah. Oh, please.* She was about to ask, but Mrs. Pickens' footsteps were already descending the stairs.

It was Jeremiah. Without waiting for him to speak, she poured out the whole story, her own doubts and fears. He listened, hands clasped, bent forward to catch every word.

He listened in silence, but she could see his teeth worrying his lower lip. It was a moment or two before he spoke, but his tone held traces of doubt, also.

"Well, Colly, as it so happens, I *do* know of a full time position available." He paused, as if considering whether to continue. "You're ideally suited for it, but there are some disadvantages."

She was ready to consider anything. "What?"

"Well, you'd have to move again, though not very far. And I'm afraid you wouldn't be earning as much as you are here. You'd also have a broader range of responsibilities."

She had to force herself to listen to her head, not her heart. "But the advantages…?"

He sat up a little straighter. "Well, your quarters would be larger and somewhat more…comfortable than what you have now. Your children would be well-cared for, that I can guarantee. You'd have no financial worries and a lot of job security. You'd certainly have more of a say in your day-to-day affairs."

Colly had to wait a bit for her heart to quiet before she asked the next question, the one she was afraid to ask, but had to. She forced herself to look Jeremiah squarely in his gray eyes.

"And…and does this position come with some sort of…job title?"

He nodded slowly. "Yes, yes it does." He returned her look. "Mrs. Jeremiah Record."

## BENJAMIN SUTTER (1897)

8TH September 1897

Dear Mother,

You will see from the post mark that I am safely arrived at the school, though the trip was long and excessively fatiguing. In fact, I had to wait four hours for the coach to Granby, and did not arrive until after nine o'clock. I had to make my way to the school in the dark, on foot, there being no way to contact them. I had to leave my baggage (save for one small handbag) at the station, but it was locked safely away until I should claim it tomorrow. There is talk of bringing the railroad into town, but I cannot count on that anytime in the near future.

I do not require any additional funds at this time. I shall surely be able to subsist on what you have so generously given me and on what I am able to earn here.

I am housed in the Patterson Barracks, along with twenty-two other boys. It is an older wooden structure, recently divided into rooms of four boys each, though there is an empty bunk in mine, at least for the time being. There are but two stoves to heat this large building, so the sleeping rooms do not get much heat, but the common room is comfortable enough, and I suspect it is here I shall do most of my studying.

As the hour is late, I shall wait until I again have a chance to write to tell you of my courses and the school.

Your loving son,
*Benjamin*

20th September 1897

Dearest Mother,

There are six forms at the school. The first-formers are 12 and 13 years of age, and so on up to the sixth formers, boys of 17 and 18. I am therefore a fifth-former, and while I must respect and obey the seniors, I might lord it over the younger boys, as some do, but I derive little pleasure from it.

My course of studies is as follows: English Grammar and Composition with Mr. Reeves three times a week, English Literature with Mr. Thomas once per week and Spelling with Mr. Hayes once (Mr. Hayes also teaches Speech and Drama, but these are not courses I am enrolled for). I have French with Mr. Cochran and Latin with Mr. Williams, both twice a week. Algebra and Geometry are taught by Mr. McLeod. History is with Mr. Trotter. Afternoons are given over to Physical Training, but we also have Sacred Studies, conducted by the Rev. Lachaise before dinner. Study hours are from seven thirty o'clock until quarter of ten, by which time we must be abed. It makes for a very full day.

To-day, as it rained, we did not have Physical Training outdoors, though there was a half-hour of Exercise in the barn, so I have some free time to write.

I have indicated my willingness to perform chores to several of my teachers, and I hope that I shall find some sort of employ, though I confess I do not know where I might find the time.

I still have fourteen sentences to translate from Latin to English, so I must return to my books. I hope that you are well.

Your son,
*Benjamin*

4th October 1897

Dear Mother,

It has turned quite chilly, with frosts the past two evenings. If you should find my woolen coat in the trunk in my old room, I would appreciate your sending it, as it appears I shall have need of it sooner than I expected.

As a consequence, the stoves have been started in all of the buildings, and Headmaster Record himself has given me $1 to split and stack a half-cord of wood for his house. He has also suggested I might do the same for my dormitory and that the school would pay me at the rate of $1.50 per cord to do this. Thus I hope to be able to defray all of my expenses. I shall give you herewith an accounting of my budget since my arrival:

DEBIT:

| | |
|---|---|
| Transfer of baggage to school | $0.10 |
| Books, supplies and materials | $4.13 |
| Laundry | $0.15 |
| one meal in the Village | $0.25 |
| soap and towel | $0.32 |

(my soap was quite used up and my towel could not dry in this weather)

picture show in the village ........................................................ $0.10

TOTAL: ..................................................................................... $5.05

CREDIT:

for splitting & stacking wood .................................................... $1.00

BALANCE (as I started with $7.00) ............................................ $2.95

Thus I have nearly $3.00 until the end of term, when I shall see you again. It is unlikely that I shall require more funds at that time, if I can continue to find work here.

I had intended to give you a fuller description of the school, but I find that time does not permit. Nevertheless, I was able to send you a postal from the village which depicts the main school building. If you have received it, you will have some idea, and I will give you a fuller description in my next letter.

Your son,
*Benjamin*

19th October 1897

Dearest Mother,

I received your parcel today, and was very thankful for it. The coat will be most welcome and I was delighted to find the scarf from Caroline. You did not say if she had knit it herself, but it is very fine. The biscuits were somewhat broken, but quite tasty nonetheless. I shared them with my room-mates, who found them every bit as delicious as I did, and they also send their thanks and tell me that, should you decide to bake more, they will be pleased to offer their services as "consumers." I shall tell you more of them in a future letter.

The color on the trees is quite beautiful, and the nights are becoming rather chilly (I will now sleep with my coat on the bed, as well), but the days continue warm. Some of the boys have been collecting apples from the near-by farms, though I don't suppose this action was in response to an invitation from the farmer.

It had been my intention to tell you something of how the school is laid out, but the press of other matters has delayed that until now.

I told you that I reside in a dormitory called Patterson. There is a second, quite close and nearly identical, called Atlee. I am told they are about 25 years old, and they are showing their age somewhat. The wind enters freely through some cracks, though my own quarters, I will say, are among the most comfortable, having few openings by which cold air might enter. In any case, most of the boys hang blankets (if they have sufficient) or coats upon the wall to block drafts.

The farms which I mentioned—one belonging to Alton Thurlow and the other to Mr. Drummond—lie directly across and to our right. Some of the boys object to the smell, but as I am used to it, I don't notice it. A few are also distressed by the crowing of the cocks or the barking of dogs. Again, these are of no consequence to me. The orchards of these gentlemen are the source of the fruit I mentioned earlier.

To our left lies the school building, nearly 100 years old. Being stone, it is in somewhat better condition than some of the other structures, though it tends to be somewhat dank and clammy. Directly behind that is a barn in which not much is stored. We are therefore able to use it for exercise when the weather is poor. Recently we have been learning the sport of basket-ball, a relatively new game, and quite amusing. It certainly furnishes all of the exercise and physical training one could wish! And it is all played indoors.

A little behind a barn sits the refectory and kitchen building. It is here that we take our meals, as you might guess. There are many things at Claxton which are to my liking, but, dear Mother, I cannot list food among them. Many of the dishes are rather tasteless, though the quantity is usually sufficient. But I could wish for more fruit (other than apples, which seem to be plenteous!) and vegetables from our own garden. I much prefer the meals you prepare at home, but I suppose there is no way to preserve chicken and dumplings that it might travel safely to me!

Then to the east of all of this one finds the old parade ground, which we use now for Physical Training outdoors. If we do not play foot-ball, then we run. One of the boys has heard that we might soon get some archery equipment and be instructed in that sport, as well. I would just as soon take a cane and a bit of line and indulge myself in the "sport" of fishing, but that does not seem to be on the school's curriculum!

Well, next time I shall give you a further accounting and tell you what we are studying in my classes.

Give my love and thanks to Caroline.

Your son,
*Benjamin*

30th October 1897

Dearest Mother,

Well, there is some excitement to-day! First, your letter arrived with the \$1. Although I had told you that I should not require any more funds, I shall not return it, for the reason I shall tell you presently. To begin with, here is the accounting I promised you:

| | |
|---|---|
| BEG. BALANCE | \$2.95 |
| CREDIT ½ cord wood split & stacked | \$0.75 |
| \$1 rec'd from you | \$1.00 |
| DEBIT: | |
| 2 new pencils | \$0.04 |
| buttons and sewing kit | \$0.10 |
| deposit on new suit | \$3.00 |
| END BALANCE | \$1.56 |

So you see, had you not sent me the funds, I would currently have but 56¢ and lack the wherewithal to finish paying for my suit (on which I still owe \$2). However, since I have two further orders for wood and the promise of remuneration for other chores, I should have no monetary worries at this time.

You are undoubtedly wondering why I need a new suit, as I arrived at school with a perfectly serviceable one, albeit rather old and somewhat small. Well, that is the other part of the news. Today the Headmaster announced that we (that is to say, the fourth-, fifth- and sixth-formers) would have a "social" with the young ladies of Miss Fremont's School the second week in November. It is to be a "tea dance," which, I take it, is not so grand as a cotillion, nor a ball, since it takes place in the afternoon. Well, it has caused quite a stir among the boys here. Everyone wants to know about the girls there, does anyone have a sister? etc.

I did not think my old suit would be quite good enough for such a grand occasion, and thus I ordered the new one. If I can earn extra money, perhaps I can have a photograph taken and send it to you.

Well, I must return to my studies, as Mr. Williams has given us quite a bit of translation to do. He says we shall all sit for the State Latin Examination in late February and that we should carry top honors, if we apply ourselves. For my own part, I cannot see the usefulness of being a top Latin student. If one has a good reading knowledge of the language, that should suffice.

Your son,
*Benjamin*

18th Nov. 1897

Dear Mother and Caroline,

There were a few flakes of snow in the air this morning! Except for the oaks and beeches, the trees are bare, and only the winter birds remain, though we can still occasionally see geese flying south.

Most of us agree that the "social" was a great success! My suit fit very well and looked good, if I may believe the remarks directed at me. Of course, most of them were from teachers, but I was nevertheless satisfied.

The young ladies arrived by coach just after 2 o'clock and we met them in the Assembly Room of the school, where most of the tables and desks had been removed to one wall. The remaining tables were covered with white cloths and set with a tea service and punch bowl. For dancing, there was a fiddler and a man who played the coronet and another at the piano. I do not believe that they could have practiced together for any great length of time.

I did not dance at first, for I lacked the courage to ask a young lady, but after a while I saw a very pretty one sitting with some of her friends and I decided to ask her. Her name is Jenny and she dances far better than I, but I found her a charming companion. I managed three dances with her that afternoon, but she seemed popular and danced with other boys, also. Before she departed, however, I asked her if I might be permitted to correspond with her, and was delighted when she said that I might.

It is almost time for study hours, but I find myself unable to concentrate very well.

Your loving son,
*Benjamin*

19th December 1897

My Dearest Family,

It seems hardly possible, but in just a few short days, I will see you again and be able to spend the Holiday with you! I am fortunate to live close enough to make the journey possible, but there are several boys who must remain at the school, either because there is not enough time for them to make a longer trip or because conditions do not permit them to join their families at this time. I therefore count myself especially fortunate.

I have received three letters from Jenny since I told you about her and have written three in return. I shall look forward to telling you about her, but shall wait until I see you, inasmuch as I suspect you will be reading this aloud to Caroline, if she is not reading it herself!

Until I see you, I remain

Your loving son,
*Benjamin*

3rd Jan. 1898

Dearest Mother,

My joy at seeing you is somewhat tinged with sorrow at having had such a short visit and now being returned to school, though, truth to tell, I like it here well enough. I was also chagrined to see father in such poor health, and while I do appreciate the fact that you did not tell me of this in your letters, for fear of worrying me, part of me wishes that I had known, though I do not believe I could have made matters any better, and, indeed, I might have left school and returned home to give you some help with the chores at least. But, as you say, Tad is much grown now and is able to do a good portion of a man's work, so I shall do your bidding and remain at Claxton as long as I may.

I have become somewhat concerned about one of my room-mates, Calder Thorsson, whom I told you about over the Holiday. He has never shown much inclination to be a serious student, and now shows even less, spending study hours reading dime novels or writing things in his copybook which he shows to no-one. He is a decent sort nonetheless, and I would not like to think he might be expelled, though his marks are certainly suffering. I do not know if it be my place or not to speak to him, and I thought I might ask your advice on this matter.

Upon my return to school, I was delighted to find another letter from Jenny and a small parcel containing a fine pair of gloves she had knit for me. Of course I wrote her immediately to thank her, but I find myself unable to think of something I might send her in return and will once again appreciate any advice you can give me on this topic, dear Mother.

I have another piece of good news, also. I have been asked to supply firewood for the school building as well as several homes. I have hired one of the other boys to help me, so that I might accomplish twice as much in the same period and thus lose no time from my books. And so I shall earn a bit more money than before with little more work and be more financially stable.

I shall have more news soon.

Your loving son,
*Benjamin*

10th January 1898

Dear Mother,

It has been quite cold here for several days and I am glad of the extra clothes.

Well, we have finished Silas Marner in English, and although Mr. Thomas assures us it is a classic piece of literature, I found it rather ponderous and slow-moving. I guess my tastes runs more to Conan Doyle. His stories are very popular among the boys here. I was surprised to learn that the author of Silas Marner is a woman. Next we shall begin Henry V by Shakespeare. Mr. Thomas seems quite enthusiastic about the play, though I have heard from a couple of the sixth-formers (who read it last year) that, except for a couple of battle scenes, it is a real yawner. I also hear that we shall be forced to memorize and present to the class some of Mr. Thomas's favorite scenes. I was told that, were I smart, I should start to memorize "Once more unto the breach, dear friends" forthwith. Thus far, I have been able to contain my own enthusiasm for the project.

Calder Thorsson, it seems, has ceased any pretense of work and has even absented himself from several lectures. I fear that he may not finish out the year.

I have had no further letters from Jenny, but please thank Caroline for her note.

Your son,
*Benjamin*
P.S. I got a Mention in assembly to-day for having solved a problem in Arithmetic faster than anyone in my form!

P.P.S. My accounting for mid-December to mid-January:

| | |
|---|---|
| BEG. BALANCE | $4.51 |
| DEBIT: | |
| cap with ear flaps | $0.35 |
| new copybook | $0.10 |
| Shakespeare book | $0.20 |
| dinner in village | $0.50 |
| picture show | $0.10 |
| paying helper | $0.70 |
| CREDIT: | |
| 3 half-cords @ $1.50 per cord | $2.25 |
| cleaning stove & hauling & spreading ashes | $0.25 |
| END BALANCE | $5.06 |

P.P.P.S. One of the shops in the village is having electric lights installed!

21st January 1898

Dear Mother and Caroline,

I am pleased to know that the doctor thinks Father is somewhat better, though I would caution Father not to overexert himself, especially in consideration of the very cold weather we have been experiencing. It makes arising very difficult in the morning and the boys all rush to dress in front of the stove. The advantage, I suppose, to the cold spell is that more wood is needed, and thus I and Peter (the boy helping me) are kept quite busy. But for all of that, I have not let my schoolwork suffer, for Mr. Record has said that I need not attend Physical Training in the afternoon, as I probably get more exercise than many of the other boys and do the school a service at the same time!

I received a letter from Jenny yesterday, which made me quite happy.

I continue to be concerned about Calder. He has taken to borrowing my copybook so that he may copy notes from class. I do not know why he does not take better notes himself, unless it be that he is too lazy or inattentive. I am afraid that if he comes to depend on me, he will see no reason to depend upon himself. And yet, it seems like such a small request, that I am loathe to refuse.

From your son,
*Benjamin*

2nd February 1898

Dearest Mother,

You know that I have often asked for your advice and that I have always followed it. Now I am in sore need of counsel and I urgently request that you answer this letter at the first possible opportunity. Here is what has transpired:

I have told you that Calder (my room-mate) has taken the habit of borrowing my copybook, even if I am not in the room. Yesterday evening, I needed it for study hours, as I had written in it ten algebra problems we were to solve, as well as some sentences to put into Latin and a list of Spelling words to master. The copybook, however, was not among my things on the table, so I supposed it must be with Calder's. But going through his stack of books and papers, I came across one titled thus: STATE LATIN EXAMINATION. STATE OF CONNECTICUT, 1898. TEACHER'S ANSWER KEY.

How Calder came by this, I do not know. But my concern is rather what my course of action should be. I immediately returned the booklet to its place in the stack, for, in my state of shock, I could think of nothing else to do.

Now I face a real dilemma, and it is for this reason that I most urgently solicit your advice.

I could say nothing to anyone, but my conscience will not permit me this alternative.

I could confront Calder, but I do not believe he will repent, return the book and offer himself up for discipline. It is more likely he will tell me it is none of my business, in which case I become an accomplice, or threaten me (I am stronger than he, and not particularly frightened of this), in which case we shall be forced to fight, and this will surely be known, sooner or later, by the Masters, in which case we shall both be disciplined, and the story is liable to come out in any case.

I could tell one of the Masters, in which case I would become known as a snitch, not something I particularly relish. Or I might write an anonymous note—but to whom? It is certain that my hand would be recognized, for it is somewhat distinctive.

Please tell me what course I am to follow.

In haste,
*Benjamin*

11th Feb. 1898

Dear Mother,

Thank you for your prompt reply to my urgent letter. Your advice—that I seek aid from Father Lachaise—was, as always, sound, but even before receiving it, I thought of another solution to the problem. Not wishing to delay, I put my plan into motion, and I think it may have worked. It avoids embarrassment to all parties and distances me (I hope) from the affair.

This afternoon, I took advantage of the fact that all, save me, were at Physical Training. I had even sent Peter away, that I might be unobserved. It was an easy task to find the stolen booklet once again among Calder's things and hide the item inside of my own copy book. I carried the copybook and another volume or two (so it should look as if I were headed for a class or a study session with a Master). I entered the school building where Headmaster Record has a small office and slipped the booklet under his door. Then I returned to my room.

Calder did not notice its absence until study hours this evening. He spent some little time searching his belongings and under the bed, etc. At length he asked me if I might have seen a thin blue booklet, his "Latin study guide." I said I had not, and Tucker Phillips, our other roommate, also answered in the negative. Naturally, Calder could not pursue such a discussion further without revealing much more than he cared to. I was pleased to see that he gave up the search after a while and, with a great sigh, opened his Latin book and set about studying. I doubt very much that he will pursue his search any further.

Perhaps the matter is successfully resolved. Let us hope so.

No further letter from Jenny.

Your loving son,
*Benjamin*

# JOHANN EISENSCHMIDT (1915)

Through no fault of his own, John Ironsmith arrived a day or two late at Claxton; all of the other New Boys had been there for several days, and even the Old Boys had returned and settled in.

The card on the door was written in a feminine hand. There were two names on it:

*Christopher Hawley*
*John Ironsmith*

John didn't knock; after all, it *was* his room, but he opened the door tentatively.

"Hullo," he said to the boy sitting on the bed. "I guess we're to be roommates, then."

"I'm Hawley," the youth on the bed announced. "I was here last year."

Had John Ironsmith been a bit more perceptive, he might have noted the belligerence in the other's voice, but he was too busy taking in his new surroundings. The room had obviously not been designed with the comfort of its occupants uppermost in the planner's mind. The walls were plaster, but it had evidently been some time since they'd felt any soap or sponge. Even from the doorway, John could see penciled scrawls on the wall, though he was too far away to read any. The floor was plain pine boards which had once enjoyed a coat of paint—gray at one point—but only traces remained where years of feet hadn't quite worn it away. The remaining iron cot looked as if it might have been a hospital cast-off and its dusty mattress sagged badly. The earlier arrival had obviously appropriated the best furniture.

The desk and chair, at least, looked serviceable, if worn. The rest of the furnishings consisted of an armoire with two drawers but no clothes hangers. There was also a battered waste-can, evidently to be shared.

"Well," Christopher Hawley repeated, "are you Ironsmith or not?"

John thought the question a bit absurd, given that his name was on the door and that he had announced himself as Hawley's roommate.

"Yes, I'm John." He didn't know what else to say.

"You'll call me 'Muggins'," Hawley told him. John waited for an explanation of the nickname, but his roommate didn't seem anxious to volunteer the information. "What kind of a name is Ironsmith, anyway? Where did you get that? It's very odd."

John studied the other boy, trying to determine if his question were serious or not. He was perhaps five foot six, maybe three inches taller than John. His black hair was carefully parted in the middle and slicked down with some sort of oil. He had a short, pug nose and his eyes appeared to be in a perpetual squint, as though he might be peering as something slightly distasteful. His freckles did nothing to soften his expression.

John decided the other boy was serious.

"It's my parents' name, of course. It's an American name." John hadn't meant to sound quite so defensive.

"No, it's not. It's a queer name. Why do you have it?"

John certainly didn't wish to antagonize his new roommate—not right away, at any rate. He explained as though he might be speaking to a small child. "It used to be German: Eisenschmidt. That's what it would be in German. That's where my parents were born. But when they came to America, they changed it. And when I was born, it was Ironsmith. It means someone who works with iron, the metal, you know. Like a blacksmith," he added, hoping this would clarify the matter and satisfy Hawley's curiosity.

Hawley's eyes seemed to narrow even more. "So you're a Jerry, then?"

John didn't understand the question. "No, I said my name's Johnny. I'm in the fourth form," he continued, hoping this might confirm his identity.

Hawley appeared to loose interest. "Everybody in Atlee's either in third or fourth." His tone suggested that even the veriest idiot should know this. He returned to the book he'd been reading. He didn't offer to help John with his bags.

**John Ironsmith to Anna Ironsmith, September 11, 1915.**

Dear Mum,

This can't be a long letter, as I'm a little behind in what I must do to prepare for classes, which begin tomorrow. Nonetheless, I wanted to let you know that I arrived safely. The train got into Hartford on time, and someone from the school was there to meet me. We traveled to Claxton Hall in a motor-car! I had expected a buggy. There are more motor-cars in the city than I could count. The roads don't seem made for such traffic, however, and the trip to the school took several hours.

I haven't met all of the boys yet, of course. But some seem very nice, others less so, including the fellow I'm sharing a room with, I'm sorry to say. Well, perhaps we shall get along better as we come to know each other.

The room is not like mine at home and seems rather bare and cold. I suppose we can put up pictures and the like, but there's been no time for that. The rooms aren't heated (we don't need it yet, in any case), but there's a coal stove in the Main Room which I expect we'll use for studying when the weather gets cooler. I haven't had a chance to see much of the other buildings, tho' I have been to the Hall to draw my books and supplies. That is where I'll have my classes. It's a very old building; I guess it's where the school started.

Here's what I'm taking: English (of course), 5 days, History and Geography (4 days), Spelling (1 day), Algebra (3 days), French (2 days), Latin (3 days), Singing (2 days) and Physical Training and Games every afternoon. For this latter, there are several options, and I don't yet know which I'll select.

The bell has rung for Vespers and I must close.

Love from
*Johnny*

***

There is a hierarchy which exists in prep schools, a hierarchy every bit as important as any tradition and as rigorously adhered to. It's not mentioned in the guides or brochures, yet it is better known than any of the school rules, and most certainly more stringently followed. Any boy who seeks to step out of line or circumvent this pecking order is quickly—sometimes forcibly—reminded of his place in school society. The caste systems of India might seem pale compared to the complexity of the prep school Order of Battle.

Freshmen (3rd formers) are automatically on the lowest rung. Any one of that class who is undersized or underdeveloped moves to the bottom of the food chain. When and if that individual displays some talent in some area, whether it's in sports or the arts or perhaps even a flair in one subject (and a corresponding willingness to help an upperclassman), he may advance to the bottom rung of the ladder. If he is wise, however, he will not boast of his accomplishments, nor seek to lord it over his less fortunate peers, for then he will set every boy against him.

Sophomores (4th formers) might be sergeants compared with the younger boys, who are only privates. However, a strict division exists here, also. Old Boys are higher than New Boys. New Boys must prove themselves worthy, and should do so quickly. In some cases, this may involve showing a willingness to contravene the rules a bit, to show a bit of daring and bravado. In any case, sophomores, as their name suggests, must give the impression that they know everything, and it is only their age which prevents them from being the equals of juniors or seniors, an attitude which is quickly quashed by the members of those two exalted classes. Boys who show some aptitude for leadership—even if the faculty perceives them to be leading in the wrong direction—may move another rung up the ladder. Those boys with some potential are beginning to manifest it now.

Juniors ($5^{th}$ formers) are the lower class of upperclassmen, though not all seniors will allow this. Again, New Boys are not ranked as high as the returnees, though the division is not quite as sharp, for at the age of sixteen or seventeen, many of these youths are almost men, and their judgment is apt to be a bit more mature. Juniors are a bit more tolerant, but, by now, each should have an enviable talent which sets him apart from his peers. Juniors speak knowingly of women and snicker at the misconceptions of the younger boys. By now, they have "the system" completely mapped out and know numerous ways to circumvent the rules. The faculty allows them to continue in this misapprehension, since it's always better to allow your adversary to underestimate you. Juniors cannot conceive of ever being so young as to have been sophomores, nor will they ever admit to such a shortcoming.

Seniors ($6^{th}$ formers) consider themselves only slightly less exalted than faculty, and standing very nearly on the same level with God. Some of the underclassmen allow them to believe this, wishing to occupy the same position when they are elevated, somewhat in the manner of a rapture, a year or so in the future. From this class are drawn the Proctors and Monitors, responsible individuals to whom the faculty may delegate some supervisory duties. These individuals, the archangels of the prep school hierarchy, are allowed to mete out some punishments, though not of the corporal variety.

In addition to the New Boys (very few in number) and the Old Boys, there is another category, the post-graduate. These boys have already completed high school and have, in fact, a diploma. They are at Claxton for a "finishing" year before they attend a prestigious university. They should then be, by rights, superior to even the eldest senior. In point of fact, their position is somewhat equivocal, as they occupy a sort of academic and social limbo. They are unproven at Claxton; their past at other institutions having no validity here. They will normally succeed, because they are apt to excel at something, either sports or arts.

For most seniors, freshman are about on a par with the amoeba, with the amoeba having perhaps a slight edge, as it has mastered the idea and process of reproduction, albeit asexual.

John Ironsmith, when all of the factors were taken into consideration, was the lowest form of sophomore life. He was apt to be wrong, no matter what he did or however hard he tried.

***

Having arrived on campus late, John Ironsmith spent the better part of the first week trying to catch up. One of the first things he discovered was that he was lacking some paperwork, specifically a Certificate of Physical Examination, required of all students so that they could participate in Physical Training and Games in the afternoons. John would have been content to let things ride, being in no particular hurry to get onto a playing field and expose himself to almost certain ridicule and possible injury. But the School was most insistent on this matter, and ultimately John had to get an examination from Doctor Willins, in the town of Upper Granby Lake itself, the bill for said service being sent to his parents. In the meantime, he was assigned to an afternoon work detail, under the supervision of an indifferent faculty member and with two or three other boys in like circumstances, who evidenced a strong desire to be almost anywhere else. They were assigned the task of dismantling a stage set in the barn, which was used as a theater a couple of times a year. The stage set resembled the deck of a ship. John wondered what the play had been.

**John Ironsmith to Anna Ironsmith, October 9, 1915.**

Dear Mum,

Thanks for sending the sweater. The evenings are getting a bit cooler, and, while it's not cold enough yet to move our Study Hour to the common room, where there's a stove, it can get a bit chilly in the room.

The food's all right, I guess, but it can't compare to yours or Mavis's.

I've been on the junior Football Team for four days now. I'm trying not to get hurt, but there seem to be a couple of boys who think that's the purpose of football and who chase me around just so they can knock me down. I'm wearing enough padding so that it really doesn't hurt that much. The Coach doesn't seem to notice. But today one of the boys in the backfield—he's really big—told the others to stop it and play the game like it is supposed to be played. That stopped them for now.

I've joined the Chapel Choir. It's no big honor, for they will accept anyone. But it does get me out of some of Study Hour. I usually have all of my work done, anyway, and it's nice to get out of the dormitory to some place where it's well-lit and a bit warmer.

We shall have a holiday on Thanksgiving, but I don't suppose I'll be able to see you until Christmas. I very much look forward to that.

Love from

*Johnny*

***

Abbott "Froggy" Reynolds, English teacher and Atlee Housemaster, found John Ironsmith crying quietly in his room when he made a pre-Study Hour pass through the hall in mid-October.

Reynolds derived his nickname (which the students supposed—erroneously—that he was ignorant of) neither from his nationality nor from any physical resemblance to that amphibian, but rather from a quick and acid tongue which could lash out at an offending student and effectively silence him just as easily as a frog's tongue might snare a fly which had strayed too close. In fact, the nickname had been given out of respect; no student wished to feel Mr. Reynolds' displeasure. His temperament was quite at odds with his appearance: he was slight of build and rather unremarkable, save for a wild and bristly mustache which rejected all attempts to tame it. He was known among his students for using "big words" which he never bothered to explain. Some of the more diligent among his pupils looked them up, memorized them, and tried to use them. Coincidentally, these were some of Reynolds' best students.

Reynolds came in and sat on John's bed without asking permission. He waited until John's sniffles subsided, pretending not to notice, looking instead around the room, as if he were seeing it for the first time.

John finally gave a last, deep, sniff and wiped his nose on his sleeve. Only then did the Housemaster look at him. He decided to start with questions to which he already knew the answer.

"So, John, settling in, are we? How are you getting on with Master Hawley?"

John shook his head slowly.

Reynolds nodded sagely, as though John had just given a lengthy and in-depth account of his status at the School. "Hmm, yes. I see." He crossed his legs and laced his fingers around the upraised knee. "It's not always easy trying to fit in and live by rules that others set, is it?"

John shook his head again.

"Hmm." Reynolds' look was fixed on the wall opposite. He avoided looking at the student. "How's the football then? I gather it's not your favorite way of passing a pleasant afternoon."

Now John lifted moist eyes to the Housemaster. "No, sir."

"Anything in particular you don't care for? The game itself? The boys?"

"The boys, sir."

"Oh?" Reynolds allowed his eyes to open a bit wider, but did not otherwise alter his position. "Why's that, lad?" Reynolds already knew why. Charles Greeley, who taught mathematics and coached the younger boys in football, had recounted the incident over dinner.

"Well, this afternoon, one of them pushed me down, and then Hawley called me a dirty Hun."

Now Reynolds looked at the boy. "A Hun? Why would he do that? Do you know what that means, John?"

"Yes, sir. It's a German, sir. He called me that because I'm German, I guess. That is, my parents are. I was born here. In New York, I mean. Then he told me I should have been on that ship. I don't know what he meant, sir, I really don't."

Reynolds allowed the silence to build a bit and began rocking gently, back and forth on the foot that was still on the floor. He was trying to give the impression that he was thinking and was also attempting to put the boy at ease. In point of fact, he'd already rehearsed this scene in his mind several times since talking with Greeley.

"Well, Johnny, Master Hawley doesn't have his fact quite straight, does he? But I think I know why he's acting that way. Have you heard of the *Lusitania*?"

John look slightly puzzled. "Yes, sir. Wasn't that the ship that was torpedoed by the Germans last spring, sir?"

"That's right. Maybe you didn't know that Hawley's mother and sister were on that ship." Now Reynolds looked at John, a piercing gaze.

The boy looked back, his eyes open wide in shock. "You mean…you mean they were *killed*? His Mum and his sister?"

Reynolds nodded.

"But…but that's just *awful*, sir." John's thoughts seemed to have been diverted from his own troubles.

"Awful doesn't really begin to describe it, John. I just feel sick for him. I don't think any of us can really comprehend what he's going through. And while I certainly can't condone what he said to you, I think we can understand why he said it. I think we need to feel a bit of compassion for him, don't you?"

Now it was John's turn to nod. "Yes, sir. I guess I can understand, sir."

Reynolds put booth feet on the floor and looked intently at the student. "It doesn't excuse his bad manners, Johnny, and I intend to speak to master Hawley. That's a form of bullying, which I won't tolerate."

"Mr. Reynolds, perhaps it would be better..."

But Reynolds held up a hand. "I already knew about this, John. I'll make sure that master Hawley knows that I heard about this from another teacher, not from you. There'll be no more trouble."

John dried his eyes a final time. "Thank you, sir."

"Now..." Reynolds straightened the creases in his trousers. "I think we need to get you a bit more involved in the School, John. I've been giving the matter some thought, and I think you might like to try your hand at the Forensic Society."

"The Forensic Society, sir?"

"Mmm. Debating. "I've seen that in class that you've a good strong reading voice, John, and a bit of a flair for the dramatic. I think you'd do well. Come to a practice debate tomorrow night after dinner in my classroom. See what you think."

"Yes, sir. Thank you."

From that time, Hawley, while not overly civil to his roommate, was at least a bit more courteous, though he remained sullen and withdrawn except to a few of his cronies. John found that life went a bit more smoothly.

In the main, his studies went well, though he wasn't always convinced of their value. He saw little use for Latin, for example, until one day, when it struck him, as Caesar was conducting yet another campaign against some hapless foe, that the German word "Kaiser" and the Russian word "Czar" were both derived from the Latin "Caesar." Then the language seemed a bit more interesting.

Algebra frustrated him. He didn't have any trouble grasping the concept of an "unknown" number, nor of representing that number by a letter, but he couldn't fathom why it was always "x." Once you "solved for x," as Robert "Chalky" Gresham was always exhorting them to do, shouldn't "x" remain the same for the next problem? But it never did, and you were forever solving for *x*, a Sisyphian task which, John was beginning to suspect, was part of a plot involving all of the mathematics teachers in the United States.

He did enjoy English, and it was more from a desire to please his English teacher than from any real desire to find out what the Forensic Society was all about that caused him to take up Reynolds' invitation and stop in at the classroom the following evening. He stayed afterwards so that Reynolds could explain what had just transpired.

"A team consists of four members," Reynolds began, "two affirmative and two negative. They take turns arguing the opposite sides of a question. This year, it's 'Resolved: that the United States should remain neutral in the matter of the present conflict in Europe'. In other words, two will argue that we should remain neutral—that's the affirmative—and the others will take the opposing view: that we should in fact, become involved. We need a first negative for another team, and I thought it might appeal to you."

John wasn't sure. "Well, I'm not sure I'd agree to getting involved, sir, and I wouldn't know what to say in any case."

Reynolds passed him a booklet which had been lying on his desk. "The National Forensic Society puts this out each year, John. It's got outlines for arguments, some useful quotations from newspapers, magazines and public figures and some suggestions on where to look for other material. In short, everything you need to get started."

"But, sir, if everyone uses the same stuff, why, you know what everyone's going to say. What's the point?"

Reynolds smiled—a bit indulgently. "Well, that's when the real debating begins. First of all, with a topic like this, there's new material available each day. In the second place, it's not so much *what* you say sometimes, as how you say it. You've got to learn how to present your arguments in a more forceful fashion than the other fellow, even if you're saying about the same thing."

"But if I don't believe America should get involved in this war? I mean, President Wilson…"

"Do you know what a 'sophist' is, John?"

"No, sir."

"Well, I want you to look it up. Do you know that, in ancient Greece, there were men who earned a few coins for their ability to argue either side of an argument, sometimes switching sides in mid-stream? They were appreciated for their intelligence and quick wit. They didn't have to believe in something to argue successfully for it, John. They thought it developed the mind."

"Well…"

Reynolds passed him the booklet and gave him a pat on the shoulder. "Look it over, John. Try to draw up a case for America's joining the war. Bring it to me in a few days and I'll go over it with you."

John still looked dubious as he left the room, the rolled-up booklet in his right hand.

The peculiar thing was that, the more John Ironsmith argued the negative point of view, the more convinced he became that it might be the correct course of action. After a few debates, he stopped preparing his lengthy arguments beforehand, relying on his worthy affirmative opponents to slip up somewhere, either neglecting an important point, using outdated information, or specious reasoning which he could quickly punch holes in. He began to look forward to the practice sessions and even more to the inter-school debates.

In February of 1916, in a match against The Warden School, the Warden first affirmative, evidently desperate for a new reason to keep the United States neutral, stated, as a climax to his argument, something to the effect that "our mothers wouldn't want us to go to war." Incredulous, and unable to contain himself, John threw up his hands and used an expression he'd heard from his father in moments of exasperation: "*Du lieber Gott!*" which roughly translates as "Oh, my God!"

This brought a sharp rebuke from one of the judges. John, appalled at his outburst and quite embarrassed, subsided immediately and slouched in his chair. He was puzzled, however, at the slow smile from the timer, a Claxton senior who'd already debated and who'd been pressed into service in that capacity.

It's quite possible that the senior hadn't heard quite correctly or that John hadn't pronounced the words exactly, but by the third or fourth telling, *Du lieber Gott* had mutated into "Toliver got." Since this made little sense, the "got" was quickly abandoned, but the remainder was affixed permanently to John Ironsmith. John didn't appreciate the fact at the time, but he'd just been granted his nickname and was thereby accepted into Claxton society. By the end of the year, he'd be "Tolly" to all of the other students, some of whom, in succeeding years, wouldn't even know his real name.

**John Ironsmith to Anna Ironsmith, October 4, 1916**

Dear Mum,

Well, here's a surprise! We've just had the first Forensic Society meeting for the year, and I've been elected vice-president! It was the president who nominated me, a senior named Ben Morris. Usually, all of the officers are seniors, so I couldn't imagine why he'd do that. I have to make sure that everyone has the necessary materials and bring some of the new boys along. Mr. Reynolds says we'll even have a debate with a girls' school this year. I guess times change.

My roommate this year is Tad Olsen, a New Boy. He seems nice enough, but he's rather reserved. I wonder if I was like that last year. Classes are going pretty well; Geometry looks difficult, but English will be fun, anyway. I know we'll be reading *Othello* and Mr. Reynolds is quite keen on having students memorize Shakespeare and recite it at some school assemblies. There's a new penmanship and spelling teacher this year, a woman! She may take some getting used to.

The other good news is that I shan't have to play football this fall! Mr. Butler has said that the School needs some land cleared and to save money, he will use eight or ten boys to do some of the labor. In addition, we'll be laying by some firewood for use this winter or the next. I was one of the first to volunteer, so I was accepted.

**Excerpt from Second Negative speech, Claxton Hall vs. Willard Academy, December 12, 1916**

Madame Judge, honorable opponents, guests and friends, we have heard some very persuasive arguments advanced as to why the United States should revoke the recently enacted income tax, as this year's resolution proposes. It's been said that such a tax is unjust, as it takes from the American laborer what is rightfully his; that it is unfair, in that those who can least afford it bear the greatest burden and that there are so many exceptions and loopholes that many who should be sharing this burden are, in fact, paying nothing.

These arguments may be true, but our worthy opponents have advanced only opinions, unsubstantiated by facts. Any studies done are of necessity incomplete. The tax simply hasn't been in place long enough to permit us to judge any benefits or shortcomings. It is certainly unwise to abandon an unproven concept.

I believe, however, that it is not at the present we must look, but to the near future. It is, I fear, inevitable that the United States will be drawn into what we, in our short-sightedness, are calling "the European war." They are fighting against aggression over there, ladies and gentlemen, fighting for their lives and their homelands. If Europe should fall, where does that leave the United States? It is my firm belief that we must support them now, and our country in the near future.

And how should we do this? Some of our young men have already decided to join the fray, even if they fight under another flag. More will follow. Victory will come, sooner we pray, than later, but it is at the present hour that we must support their efforts. We must do so with money, for victory will not come cheaply.

Is it not, then, the duty of every American to contribute to victory? Fortunately, the mechanism to do so is already in place: the income tax. This is an equitable way for everyone to contribute to victory. We cannot abandon it now, any more than we would abandon those who are already fighting for us. It is more than simply the just and correct thing to do. It is no less than our patriotic duty…

***

John had been mildly surprised to see a girl on the Willard team, speaking as the first affirmative, the position usually given to the most junior member of a debating team. This person usually presented the stock arguments and laid the groundwork for what was to come. So he could pretty much ignore what she said and concentrate on her, instead.

Her name was Beth, and John thought she was pretty, despite the severely pulled-back hair and an effort to dress to pass unnoticed among her male peers. He didn't think she'd noticed him, so he was surprised again when she came up to him at the conclusion and spoke softly.

"Congratulations on getting 'best speaker,' Mr. Ironsmith. I thought you argued brilliantly. You didn't even use notes."

"I…uh…had enough material from what the others said. I did jot a few things down, but I guess I didn't need them," he finished lamely, aware that his face felt unusually warm.

She put out her hand. "I'm Elizabeth Warren." Her grip was firm and dry. His was moist and tentative.

"How did you know my name?" It sounded inane, but it was the only thing he could think to say.

She clasped her hands behind her and looked at the floor. "I asked."

"Oh." John couldn't seem to think of anything else to say.

Beth looked up. "There's lunch now," she said brightly. "We can eat together, if you like."

John nodded. His throat felt too constricted to utter any intelligible sound.

Lunch consisted of soup and some sort of bread and cheese. John had no idea what he was eating, nor even if he were eating anything at all. Beth held up both ends of the conversation. Near the end of the meal, when they were eating jelly squares, she said suddenly, "There's a Valentine's Tea Dance in February. Would you come?"

"Uh, well, I…"

"That's all right, John. It's all right if I call you John, isn't it? I realize you're very busy and I'm sure you have lots of invitations. But I'd be pleased if you'd accept."

John didn't know what to make of her. He'd never met any girl who was quite so forward. Not that he'd even met many girls, he reminded himself. But he didn't have anyone in his limited experience to compare her to.

"Here's my address." She wrote it on one of those cards debaters carry to make notes on. "Do let me know, won't you? Well, I've got another session in five minutes, so I must run. See you."

A bit of a wave—more a fluttering of fingers—another brilliant smile, and she was gone. John stared after her, his mouth agape. It remained so until Phil Frost dropped into the seat next to him and threw a comradely arm around John's shoulders.

"Well, well, Tolly, old chum. Fraternizing with the enemy, are we? Was she asking for debating pointers, hmm? Going to give some private lessons, are we?" The arm dropped from John's shoulders so that its elbow could dig into John's ribs.

"Shut up, Phil," John said absently.

Phil put up his hands in mock surrender. "Oh, of course, just two students talking about the finer points of the resolution. How *could* I have misconstrued such pure and honest intentions?"

"Phil, you really *are* full of bull."

Frost tried to look offended. "Well, now we know what my problem is, old man." He adopted a serious demeanor, stroking his chin as thought he were considering some deep, almost-insoluble problem. "But I suspect yours might be glandular. Now Doctor Phil can give you some advice on what to do."

John couldn't help but smile. "Go. To. Hell."

"Ah, well, now I'm deeply offended. No, mortally wounded. Cut to the quick. *Blessé à mort*. Are you going to write her?"

John flashed the card with Beth's address.

"Omigawd, he's done it. Overwhelmed the girl over lunch. Seduced her with the soup. Bewitched her with the bread. Charmed her o'er the cheese." He clapped John on the shoulder. "'You're a better man than I am, Gunga Din'."

John gave him a very sour look. He was happier than he'd ever been in his life.

# THE GRANBY *REGISTER*, April 21, 1917

## Claxton Speaker Wins State Forensic Tourney

HARTFORD, April 20—A debater from Claxton Hall walked off with top honors today from the annual tourney held this year at Wesleyan University.

Each year, debaters from some twelve colleges and high schools compete at several levels over the course of the two-day event. Each team debates six times. This year's topic (which is made known to the four-man teams only scant hours before the event begins) was, "Resolved: that the United States establish a military draft for men between the ages of 18 and 25."

John Ironsmith, vice-president of the Claxton Hall Forensic Society and arguing as the Second Affirmative in all matches, received five "Best Speaker" nominations out of six possible. No other nominee received more than three. In addition, Ironsmith's team won all six of its matches, as did Bates College of Lewiston, Maine.

Ironsmith, son of Henry and Anna Ironsmith of Collinsville, is a 5th former at the private school located in Upper Granby Lake.

The win entitles Claxton to send one four-man team to the national event in Washington, D.C. next month. The headmaster of Claxton, Mr. Butler, was unavailable for comment.

**Excerpt from the remarks of the Student Body President to the New Boys, September 5, 1917.**

Good morning, boys. Headmaster Butler will be here shortly to give you your official welcome to Claxton Hall, but, in the interim, he's asked me to say a few words.

My name is John Ironsmith, and I'm a 6$^{th}$ former and President of the Student Body, which means I'm also on the Student Council. In addition, I'm a classroom monitor and a proctor in Patterson, which, for those of you who are boarders, is the dorm right next to yours. So I guess you'll be seeing a lot of me, one way or another. Oh, by the way, my nickname is "Tolly," so if you hear people talking about "Tolly," you'll know whom they mean. A lot of people here have nicknames, and I guess that can be pretty confusing.

I remember when I first arrived here two years ago. Everything was very strange and I had a lot of questions. I guess I was also a little bit scared and maybe a little bit homesick. Well, if any of you are feeling that right now, don't worry. It's perfectly normal and it'll pass quickly. The Old Boys won't arrive until Sunday afternoon, so you've got the place to yourselves for a couple of days. By the time they arrive, you'll be old hands.

I know that you've studied the brochures and pamphlets of rules you received over the summer. Well, there's at least one change that even the Old Boys don't know about, and I think you'll like it:

"Coats and ties need not be worn on Saturdays and Sundays except for classes, chapel, meals and Sunday tea, if a student chooses to attend that function."

So the weekends will be a little more relaxed, and I know we'll all appreciate that. Whatever questions I can't answer, Headmaster Butler or one of the teachers can. All of the proctors and monitors are helpful, too. Most of the Old Boys will help you out, but don't go buying any late passes or lunch cuts; those are just pranks and are liable to get you into trouble if you do.

***

The door to the Reynolds' apartment in Atlee was open, but John Ironsmith rapped on the jamb anyway. A voice from within told him to enter.

Abbott Reynolds had shed his jacket but was still in weskit and tie. He had just set a plate on the small table before the hearth and straightened, dusting his hands, to face his visitor.

"Ah, John. Good of you to come." He gestured. "Please, sit. Coffee's almost ready and I see Mrs. Reynolds was kind enough to leave some freshly-baked sugar cookies." He motioned again.

The senior proctor grinned. "Well, sir, perhaps just one or two."

"Now," Reynolds began, settling in the chair opposite after he'd poured coffee, "being your advisor means I get to have first go at you at the beginning of your sixth form year, before you get corrupt and slovenly like the other members of your class."

"Yes, sir." John helped himself to sugar and another cookie.

Reynolds leaned back in his chair and reached for his pipe. He began stuffing it slowly. "It's really not too early to start thinking about next year, John. College, of course, but beyond that, too."

John watched his advisor over the rim of his cup.

"Now, I'm just going to throw out some thoughts." Reynolds had managed to get the pipe going and was waving away the smoke. "So you don't have to say anything. It's just something to think on.

"I really think you ought to consider some sort of public service, John."

"Sir? You mean like politics, sir?"

Reynolds nodded. "Yes, that's one possibility. You've got a lot of leadership potential, John. The School has certainly recognized it. I can't think when one boy has held so many positions simultaneously and still maintained the average you do. But beyond that, you're a first-class debater. There's no reason why you shouldn't take another first again this year. All of this bespeaks an almost certain success in whatever field you choose to enter."

The teacher's pipe had gone out and he fumbled for matches in his vest pocket while never taking his eyes from John.

"Now, I've taken the liberty of speaking to a friend of mine—Peter Littlefield, as it so happens—"

John's swallow of coffee very nearly went down the wrong way. He gasped and coughed to clear his throat. "Littlefield? The governor?"

Reynolds was pleased with John's reaction and smiled indulgently. "Yes, the same. We went to school, together, you know?" Reynolds leaned forward to deposit the match in an ashtray. "Well, it seems that from time to time he accepts especially promising young men to serve in his office as interns…"

John couldn't hide his astonishment. "An intern?" He was incredulous. "My God…oh, sorry sir. I mean, that's incredible."

"Well, it's not a paying position, you understand. But the experience is well worth the effort, I assure you. In any case, after I'd spoken to him, he was most eager to meet you."

John made several futile gestures, but couldn't seen to find the right words.

"If this seems like a good path to pursue, John, then I'd encourage you to apply at Harvard or Yale. Pre-law. You'll need a law degree to move up the political ladder."

John was having difficulty taking this in. "The…political…ladder, sir?

Reynolds set down his pipe and reached for his cup. "Mmm. Governor, senator, that sort of thing." He let the thought sink in for a moment before asking, "So, John, what do you think?"

John set down his cup. He laced his hands and stared at them for a long moment before lifting them.

"Well, sir, it's a great honor and all that. I mean. I'm really thankful for what you've done. But you see, sir… I mean, now there's the draft and all that. We're in this war now, sir, and we're in it for the duration. I…I guess I've decided to join the AEF, sir. If I'm not drafted before the end of the school year, I'm going to enlist."

**Announcement by Headmaster Randall Butler in School Chapel, Monday, September 9, 1918**

Please be seated.

It is my sad duty to announce to you that another of our lads has fallen in Europe. John Ironsmith was killed in combat in Belgium in July of this year.

You New Boys do not know him, but he was well known to all of the Old Boys and the faculty, all of whom respected him greatly. He had a bright future and shall be most grievously missed.

We shall observe a moment of silent prayer in his memory, then we shall rise and sing the first stanza of "A Mighty Fortress," number 56 in the hymnal.

# THE *CLAXTON FOLLIES* (1922)

*The following was found between the pages of a 1923* Herald, *the Claxton Hall yearbook. It is unfortunately incomplete, but one may suppose, based upon references to "Follies" in other yearbooks, that a play of this sort was a tradition at the school for some time. Other than the occasional reference in a yearbook, there is no indication of when the tradition of this type of "original" musical might have begun or ended. This gives rise to some speculation that the "Follies" might not have been sanctioned by the school.*

## Follies of 1922
## The Cast (in order of appearance).

Gary, the Senior........................................................ Mort Lancaster
Larry, a Freshman........................................................Oliver Peters
Barry, another Frosh.................................................. David McWilliams
Harry, yet another Frosh.......................................... Michael Leander Collins
The Headmaster...........................................................J. Clark Long
Gordon Gridiron ........................................................Ellsworth Masters
Peter Prep ...................................................................Tyler Morgan
Mr. Farnackle B. Unclesworth ........................................ Nate Gatesman
Mrs. Farnackle B. Unclesworth.....................................George Thackery
Mary Unclesworth, their Daughter..............................Peter M. Newmann

## Scene I.
## Enter Gary, followed by the three Frosh

**Gary:** Well, fellows, this is it, good old Claxton Hall, our Alma Mater! (**gestures**)

**Larry (looking around):** Gosh, it's big!

**Gary:** Golly, yes, there are almost a hundred boys here! It's like a small town.

**Barry (obviously awed):** Wow!

**Harry:** A fella could get lost here!

**Gary:** Naw, you'll get used to everything real quick. Do you all have your class schedules?

**Larry:** Yes, and they look swell! Are the courses hard? What about the profs?

**Gary:** They're all pretty good guys. Well, most of them, anyway.

**(They all laugh)**

**Gary:** Well, you're Claxton Hall men now. But remember, you're just third-formers, and you have to listen to the upperclassmen. You'll have a lot to learn!

**(Frosh Song.)**

Three little frosh at school are we,
Pert as a freshman well can be,
Filled to the brim with boyish glee,
Three little frosh at school!

**Barry.**
We may be new, but we're no fools. (*Chuckle*)

**Larry.**
We're far away from Daddy's rules! (*Chuckle*)

**Harry.**
We think we might just test the school's! (*Chuckle*)

**THE THREE.**
Three little frosh at school!
Three little frosh who, all unwary,
Just taking courses necessary,
One of our profs is large and hairy!
Three little frosh at school!
Three little frosh at school!

**Harry.**
One of the profs is a pip, it's Jerry.

**Barry.**
Two of our profs are really scary.

**Larry.**
Three of them are ordinary.

**THE THREE.**
Three little frosh at school!
Three little frosh at school!

**Harry.**
From near and far we've come today.

**Larry.**
Here at Claxton Hall to stay

**Barry.**
We'll be very glad, they say--

**THE THREE.**

Three little frosh at school!
Three little frosh at school!

**Gary**: Look, boys, here comes the Headmaster!

**Scene II.**
**Enter Headmaster**
**(song)**

**Headmaster**: I am the monarch of the school,
And with an iron hand I rule,
But thorny problems make me laugh!
**Students**: And so do the students and the teachers and the staff!
And so do the students and the teachers and the staff!
**Headmaster**. When I lecture or I speak,
It can take almost a week!
My secretary thinks I'm daft.
**Students**: But so do the students and the teachers and the staff!
But so do the students and the teachers and the staff!
**Headmaster**: And when I walk abroad,
All who see me, they are awed
And I'm more intelligent by half!
**Students**: But so are the students and the teachers and the staff!
But so are the students and the teachers and the staff!
His students and his teachers, (not the ministers or preachers), And his staff!

**Headmaster (seeing Students)**: Well, boys, welcome to Claxton Hall! Have you just arrived?

**Harry**: Yes, sir, and Gary was just showing us around.

**Headmaster**: That's dandy. Do you have any questions you'd like to ask me?

**Barry**: Well, yes, as a matter of fact. I know we're here to study hard and to get into a good college, sir, but gee, it all sounds like a lot of work. Don't you have any fun here?

**Headmaster (laughs)**: Why, of course we do! There are loads of sports and games and... Well, look! I see Gordon Gridiron over there! Let him tell you about our football team! Come over here, Gordy, and meet some new fellows!

## Scene III
## enter Gordon Gridiron

**Gordon**: Well, hello, chums! Welcome to Claxton Hall. Do you play football?

**Larry**: Yes, I do. Does Claxton have a good team?

**Gordon**: Yes, we do, but we can be even better with rugged fellows like yourself. If we stand together, we can defeat any foe!

**(song)**

**All**: Our Claxton Hall forever,
Strong and failing never
Where friendships strong
Last all life long
And bonds shall never sever.

We stand as one, united
And face the foe, unfrighted

*(The page is torn off at this point and the rest of the script is missing. This early school song, of which a fragment is reproduced above, was replaced about 1939, by something more "modern.")*

# SAMUEL FOREST (?) (1928?)

*Frances Ward Skillins (1838–1930) was the maternal grandmother of Samuel Forest, Headmaster of Claxton Hall from 1919 to 1930. At her death, there were no surviving children. A granddaughter, Ruth Moreno, was appointed executrix of Mrs. Skillins' will, as she lived fairly close to the Skillins' home and seemed to be the only surviving family member willing to take the responsibility. Mrs. Moreno sold most of Mrs. Skillins' effects, some to an antique dealer in Chicago, and other items at public auction.*

*Among the items sold at auction was one "steamer chest, leather, reinforced with copper bands, locked, no key, contents unknown." It was sold to a Mr. Ronald Harper. In the trunk, Mr. Harper found a canvas-bound volume labeled "Farm Record." Indeed, the first thirty or so pages contained records of sales of hay, eggs, milk and honey, and purchases of feed and veterinary expenses for the years 1897 and 1898. Following these ledger entries were several blank pages, then ten or twelve pages of what appeared to be a personal journal.*

*The individual who wrote the journal does not name himself (or herself), nor are there any dates or any but the most general indications of where the author wrote. It would seem, upon careful reading, that the journal is purposefully vague, as it hints at events which are generally not discussed in public. The only name mentioned is "Stella," but this is almost certainly a pseudonym, an attempt to hide the identity of this person who was obviously close (though in what way is some matter for speculation) to the author. No further details concerning this personage have ever surfaced.*

*We cannot be certain if Samuel Forest wrote this, or even if it might be an unfinished, unpublished work of fiction. Certainly the evidence is only circumstantial, and slim at best. Yet scholars who have studied this manuscript seem to think that Forest is the only one who would fit all of the facts (if indeed facts they are). It is true that the circumstances surrounding Mr. Forest's departure from Claxton are unclear, but the reader must judge for himself.*

If one may believe certain historians, Leonardo and Tchaikovsky were cursed with the same affliction. It is, however, no solace to share this sickness with the great and famous. It is a furious appetite which will not be denied, a ravenous hunger which cannot be long satisfied, and a shame and a fear which make the social pariahs of India pale in comparison.

All who are so cursed are damnèd hypocrites, living a lie at every moment, nor do they find any respite, only briefly. That they resolve to mend their ways matters not at all; they cannot. And yet we must live and breathe and move with the others of our race.

Oh, Stella, I would spare you the torment which I am experiencing, and yet, a part of me cannot but hope that you share my feelings and needs and suffer as I do. But—more's the pity—we cannot suffer together.

I am confident that I have hidden all symptoms of my affliction from those I work with on a daily basis; I have given them no reason to suspect any untoward behavior on my part, and I have taken great pains that all of my relations with my colleagues are carried out on a strictly professional basis. I have done nothing which could be considered "abnormal" or questionable, and though certain situations and crises might well call for quick, decisive action, I can make no move which might draw undue attention to myself. Nor have I seen any signs in the faces of those with whom I come into daily contact that they suspect aught is amiss.

It is at these moments that I am emboldened to push my luck a bit further. I write Stella and speak of my urgent need for a rendezvous, for I cannot deny my body's needs.

*The following is written in ink of a slightly different color and slightly darker.*

The beast was loosed for a while but is now back in chains. I do not know how long I can keep it under control, but I shall endeavor mightily not to put myself into the path of temptation, which means, for example, never venturing into the gymnasium.

I believe it is incumbent upon me, at this time, to be extremely prudent in the matter of finances, though there are members of the board who do not agree with my caution. They point out that the economy is currently flourishing and it is a time to think of growth and prosperity. I reply that I would like to wait a bit longer, as I sense currents in the air which, as an economist, I do not like. I would prefer to invest the institution's money in bonds and securities; although their return is often less, they suffer less from the vagaries of the stock market. I also point to the fact that three new buildings have been erected but recently, and that these structures have not been fully paid for, even given the generosity of some of the (*a word has been thoroughly scratched out here. Some scholars read it as "alumni," but no clear case for any word can be made*) donors.

*The following is written in pencil, rather hastily.*

Business calls me to New York next week. My sickness is stronger than I: I have sent Stella a train ticket, and an accompanying note giving the name of the hotel where I shall be staying.

*The following is in blue ink, but in a hand less firm than previously.*

Am I discovered? I know not, but the comportment of those who share my workplace betrays no hint of condemnation. If that be so, than it is clear God has given me a warning.

The first part of my sojourn in New York was bliss itself. I am ashamed to admit that I released the beast fully, nor did I have any regrets until later. That night, my body fully sated for the first time in weeks, I slept soundly in Stella's arms. Upon awakening, I announced that we should breakfast together in the hotel dining room. It would be a leisurely meal, as my first appointment was not until ten. We were careful not to stand too near in the elevator, lest the operator read something in our faces, and entered the dining room as any normal couple might do. I was enjoying my coffee, eggs and muffin when I was horrified to see a member of the Board enter.

Upon later reflection, I see that there was no reason for panic: we could be simply two old friends, or colleagues, or even business associates dining together. But at that moment, I was paralyzed, incapable of rational thought. I finally dropped my napkin deliberately and spent some moments fumbling for it while the gentleman passed our table. When I straightened again, I begged my friend's forgiveness, saying that I was suddenly taken ill (nor was that wholly a lie) and I felt the need to return to the room and lie down.

Stella was solicitous and wished to accompany me, but I insisted that it was not worth the trouble, and that the delicious meal we had ordered should not go to waste. I said we should meet later for lunch, and, to my relief, my companion agreed.

I fled to the room, avoiding the elevator and using the stairs. I wrote a quick note to Stella and packed hastily, returning down the stairs and exiting via a rear door. I had fortunately paid the hotel bill upon renting the room, so I did not have to use the lobby. I found a taxi almost immediately, reached the station and was on a train within forty minutes of leaving the hotel.

*The final entry is in faded brown ink.*

The mark of Cain is upon me. I had thought, even hoped, that it might be leprosy, but a visit to a physician (I went to another town and used a false name) has confirmed my fears. I am punished for my wickedness, but unlike Job, I cannot rail against it, for it is merited.

For a time now lesions and ulcers have been appearing on my skin. They are directly attributable to my sin. I do not know if madness be the ultimate symptom of this malady, but I fear I shall go mad in any case.

I shall, of course, resign from my position as soon as possible, at least before there occur any visible signs of the disease.

Nor shall I see Stella again. Although a part of me would still desire it, there is little doubt but that therein lies the source of my current suffering. For how else could it come about? And yet, if it be so, then my dear friend must have contracted it elsewhere, meaning that I was not the only love of Stella's life. Thus am I betrayed, as well. My shame is complete.

I should destroy this record, but I cannot bring myself to do so, for in it I have recorded one of the happiest moments of my life, albeit one of the briefest. I shall carry its memory to the grave, which I fear may not be that far removed in time.

I shall therefore put this chronicle in the safest place I can think of. Perhaps, should I survive, I may one day return to claim it and resolve to destroy it, leaving little record of my passing.

*The entry ends near the bottom of a page, and the next page has been torn out.*

# THEODOR WEIZMANN (1938)

"Mordecai, we have to get him out."

He repressed a sigh and removed his gold-rimmed glasses to buy a little time. He cleaned them carefully on a handkerchief, but didn't replace them immediately. Instead, he massaged the bridge of his nose where the glasses had left two little pink indentations and smoothed his bristly salt-and-pepper mustache. He had been planning to shave it off, since it looked too much like the one that bastard calling himself "the Leader" wore. He folded the handkerchief carefully and tucked it into his vest pocket.

"Esther, I tell you, it was just an incident. Serious perhaps, but things will quiet down. After all, we've been through this before." He hoped his voice conveyed calm and patience. He also hoped he wasn't lying to himself. But his wife was not to be put off this time.

"An incident?" She looked to heaven for confirmation that her husband had lost touch with reality. "An incident, he calls it." Now she fixed him with a hard glare. "You didn't see it, stuck in that shop downstairs all day. So much glass there was that you had to walk in the middle of the street. All the windows on the street broken. Only those with shutters were spared. And the writing on the wall. Do you know what they're painting on the wall, Mordecai? Do you?"

"*Juden raus*," he said in a soft voice. "Yes, I've seen it. 'Jews get out'." He shifted in the wooden chair, the one that creaked. "Esther, listen…"

"Listen?" Her voice rose a decibel or two. She shook a finger in his face before returning a balled fist to her hip. "Listen? You're the one not listening, Mordecai Weizmann. You're the one blind to what's right under your nose."

"Keep your voice down," he told her firmly. He was, after all, master in his own house. Well, perhaps it *was* just a flat, and not very spacious at that. "You'll wake the boy."

She glanced at the closed door before continuing. Her voice wasn't quite as loud, but just as urgent: "It's going to be just like Danzig, you wait and see if it's not. Do you know what they're calling it, out there?" She gestured vaguely toward the street.

"Out where?"

"*Kristallnacht*," she told him, "Crystal Night, as God is my witness. 'The Night of Broken Glass,' as if it were a festival or some sort. Listen to me, Mordecai, for the love of God, it's only going to get worse."

"I don't think we should rush…"

"It's *not* going to get better," she insisted, anticipating his argument, "Don't fool yourself. It's a ghetto they have now in Danzig, and it will be like that here. It's like they're prisoners in their own city."

"We're more civilized. It can't happen here."

"*Mein Gott*, are you as hard in the head as you are of hearing? It *is* happening here; you just don't want to see it. The burnings? The book burnings, Mordecai? You call that civilized? You call that another incident? And just two streets over, last year: they burned the synagogue, Mordecai, the synagogue! They threw the Torah on the fire! And the *Feuerwehr*, what did they do? They are supposed to put out fire, no? But they let it burn! They just watched! Only if other buildings nearby were threatened would they do anything. You remember, Mordecai?"

He nodded. There was no point in arguing with Esther at times like this. It would only upset her more. She tended to overreact at times. True, there was some ill-feeling abroad. People whom he used to consider friends now refused even to acknowledge him, should they see him on the street. True, they'd had to leave their grand, big house on Schillerweg and take a tiny, dark flat in the alley behind the railroad station. True, business had dropped off considerably since he'd had to move the shop, but that was only because his customers didn't know where to find him. At least that's what he told himself. The economic times were bad, but certainly they'd improve soon. Everyone needed clothes, that was sure: new ones or repaired garments, it didn't matter. He was skilled at his craft, and much in demand. Well, he would be again, once the present troubles abated. How long could the German people continue to be duped by this megalomaniac, after all?

"*Nu*, and how should we get him out?" he asked, falling naturally into Yiddish. They allowed themselves to speak it when alone, never when others might overhear. "Where would he go?" He hoped the questions would show he was interested and paying attention, even if he didn't think things had reached a crisis point yet.

"New York," she replied immediately. Evidently she'd already given the matter a good deal of thought. "Your cousin Isaac would take him in."

He pretended to consider this while he stared at the overstuffed horsehair chair in the parlor, just in his line of vision. The antimacassars were getting shabby, he noted. He stroked his mustache again. "Yes, I suppose so. I'll write him tomorrow."

But Esther was not to be put off. "You'll do it now, Mordecai. While there's still time. Who knows how much longer they'll let us write?"

Mordecai sighed, got to his feet and shuffled to the work table. They'd had to sell their beautiful desk—and for such a pittance!—when they moved. He would write slowly, and she would get bored watching him and move off to some other chore.

To satisfy her, he actually finished the letter and mailed it the next day. There were more fascists on the street every day, he noted as he walked to the post office. They looked at everyone suspiciously, but especially those whom they didn't regard as "pure German."

*As if anyone's pure anything any more,* he thought, moving so as to attract as little attention as possible. That was the secret: remain unobserved, mind your own business, be polite, even obsequious if the need arose, and as soon as they saw you weren't any threat, they'd let you go about your own business and not disturb you further. He stepped into the street to let someone pass. They had cleaned up most of the glass—after all, cars still had to get through—but no effort had been made to clean the painted words from the walls. Nor did he think there would be any effort. He tugged his hat down a bit more. The weather was getting colder and the rising wind was bitter.

When he returned to his dingy shop, there was only one customer waiting, old Lev Baumgarten. He just needed a pair of trousers mended, and Mordecai assumed, correctly, as it turned out, that Lev would ask, "I need you should put it on account, Mordecai, just for a bit, you understand."

Mordecai tried to make polite conversation as he worked. "So, and the family, how is everyone?"

Lev sucked on his lower lip and shrugged. "As well as can be expected. But Abram…" He shook his head. "Not a word for a month." He bent forward and whispered. "I think they took him to a camp, Mordecai. To a camp."

Mordecai gave him a sharp look. It wasn't that he doubted the old man believed what he said, but this was a dangerous topic. If someone should overhear…

"Those are just rumors, Lev," he said emphatically. "Everything you hear, you shouldn't believe." *But there were too many rumors now to just deny…*

Lev compressed his lips into a tight line, as if he wanted to prevent other words from escaping, but, though he rocked his head from side to side, he said nothing.

"Good like new." Mordecai handed him the mended garment. Lev inspected it critically in the low light and nodded agreement. He got up to go, but left Mordecai with a final piece of advice: "You should get him out, you know. Theodor. While there's still time. *Sholem*."

For nearly a week there was no more bad news. Mordecai Weizmann had almost convinced himself that what he had told others was true: after a bit things would quiet down, begin to return to normal.

"Did you see it?" Esther demanded shrilly after he had climbed the stairs to their flat after a particularly depressing and unprofitable day in the shop below. He'd closed early because of the lack of customers and work and because it was Friday.

"See what? How can I see anything, when I barely leave the shop? Suppose a customer should come when I was out?"

"The notice. It's everywhere." Esther appeared to be working herself up to a real fit of hysteria. That was to be avoided, if at all possible.

"What notice, Esther?" He tried to keep his voice calm, patient.

She took a deep breath. "The notice that says that Jews may not attend school after today."

Mordecai went cold inside. *No, it couldn't be. They wouldn't dare...* All he could manage was a weak "But..."

"There's no more time, Mordecai," Esther's voice was quiet, insistent.

He nodded. He knew that all of the hopes he'd been harboring were false. He'd known it all along, but refused to admit the truth. Now, if he wished to keep his family safe, he'd have to act. Things were not going to get better soon. He tried to formulate some sort of a plan, but could devise nothing on the spur of the moment. So he suggested, "Maybe we should all go."

"Mordecai, listen." She drew him into the bedroom and shut the door. "We need permission even to leave the city. Do you think they would give us that?"

"Maybe they'd be glad to be rid of us."

"No, they want us here, where they can control us and keep an eye on us. Besides, there's not enough money for three. Only for one. A young boy, he will not attract much attention. People will want to help him." She worried her lip with her teeth. "We'll just have to send him. We can't wait for an answer from Isaac."

"How...?"

She waved him to silence. "I have to think. Theodor is in the kitchen. Go talk with him."

He nodded and shuffled into the alcove they called a kitchen, his mind working rapidly. There was barely enough room for the small table, a miniature sink and the enameled stove. The icebox sat on the balcony outside.

Theodor Weizmann, a serious youth of 13, sat at the table, a book propped open before him. The yarmulke was perched atop his tightly curled brown hair. He wore it only indoors, in his own apartment. His face strongly resembled that of Mordecai's departed mother, God rest her soul: open and frank, the eyes always slightly wide in astonishment, the mouth a bit feminine. Esther always described him as "a good boy."

"Theodor…" his father began, uncertain.

"I know Papa." Theodor's voice was somehow reassuring. "I saw the notices, too. That's why I'll study here, at home. I'll work very hard, and now I'll have time to help you in the shop, too."

Mordecai took a deep breath. "Theodor, we're sending you to my cousin Isaac, in New York. You can go to school in America. His son opened his mouth to speak, but Mordecai held up his hand. "It's decided. Your mother and I have talked." *God forgive me these little lies.* "Things are not going well here. There is not enough work in the shop to keep one person busy, to say nothing of two. You'll be much better off there, get a good education. They won't break windows and write things on walls."

The boy looked to be on the verge of tears. "But…but why can't you come, too?"

Mordecai took a chair. He was conscious of Esther leaning against the door frame. "We will, Theodor, but we want to get you settled first. I'll have to sell the business and the apartment, too. You'll be our advance party, so to speak."

Theodor's face cleared and he smiled. "I can do it, Papa. I am a man now, after all."

Mordecai looked at his son's hairless face. Not even a trace of downy beard yet. That might be best after all. As Esther said, a boy should attract little attention. His mind, no longer quite as numb as it had been earlier, began to suggest possibilities. "Good," he said finally. He stood and looked at his wife. "Esther, I have to go out for a bit. I'll be back for supper."

"It's Sabbath soon," she pointed out.

"God can wait an hour, Esther. This can't."

They waited until their son had gone to sleep before they resumed their conversation in the kitchen. It was about as far from that oversized closet where the boy slept as it was possible to get without leaving the apartment. They kept their voices muted.

Mordecai spread a newspaper on the table. "The steamship *Bremen* departs Bremerhaven for New York in eight days. The trick will be to get him there and on it. He should go by train, in small stages: from here to Hamburg, from Hamburg to Bremen, and from there to Bremerhaven. If it looks like he's just traveling to the next town, it shouldn't look suspicious." He dug into his inner coat pocket. "Here is a ticket to Hamburg. I also stopped at the post office and telephoned Mrs. Kravitz. She will meet him in there. He'll stay overnight there and buy a ticket for Bremen the next day. After that...," he shrugged, "he will be on his own, I'm afraid. But I think he should not have a suitcase, only his school book bag. He'll have to manage. But there are other problems..."

Esther looked at her husband with the same respect she'd had when they were first married. She'd thought him beaten down, defeated, but now she was seeing the old Mordecai, the one she loved.

She reached across the table to pat his hand. "While you were gone, I had some ideas, too. He still has a valid passport, *Gott sei dank*. You know, when he went to Sweden and Denmark last year, with the youth orchestra. I think he should take his violin, too. It makes him look like maybe he's going for a lesson. The problem...." She paused, considering. Her forehead furrowed and he could see her teeth worrying her lip again. "The problem, Mordecai, is that he has no travel document, no reason to be away from home."

The crisis seemed to have stimulated his brain, shaking it awake after a long somnolence. "Esther, what about the letter?"

She looked a bit confused. "The letter? What letter?"

"The one he used last year. The one saying that he had been selected for the orchestra, telling about the trip, the travel arrangements, all of that. Did we save it?"

"Of course," she said proudly. "It was a great honor. I was going to have it framed." She paused, then found an objection. "But, Mordecai, it will do no good. It has last year's date."

He sat up a bit straighter. "Those things can be altered, Esther."

"*Vos zogst du*?" She couldn't believe her ears.

"In my business, Esther, we meet all sorts of people. Some on the right side of the law, some not." He made a rocking motion with his hand.

"Tomorrow I will take the letter to a friend. Then we must think of how to get him a boat ticket and how he should carry money. Now we must sleep. We have much to do tomorrow, Esther."

Mordecai didn't open his shop the next day. Instead, he went to a small restaurant on a side street, and asked to see someone he knew by the name of Leo. There was a long conversation in a back room. Some documents and a good deal of money changed hands. A deal was reached, sealed with a handshake and a small glass of schnapps.

"I have decided he will take no clothes but what he wears," Esther informed him upon his return. "That way he shouldn't look like he's going on a trip. Just going for a violin lesson, or maybe to school. In his school bag he'll carry some lunch. The violin he'll take, too. Who knows? If he needs to, God forbid, he can sell it. But he'll need money, Mordecai."

He nodded. "I used some of what was hidden in the shop today. Paper money would be easiest to hide and carry, but worth nothing when he gets to America. Also, maybe some people won't take it. Better he should carry some gold coins, also. They should be accepted everywhere. I think we should hide them in the lining of the violin case. Who's going to look there?"

There were other problems to be solved, but these would need the assistance of others. Mordecai was going to call in every favor he was owed any probably spend most of their savings. It didn't matter. What he didn't spend, he was sure the Germans would get.

*Listen to me. I don't even think of myself as German anymore. But neither do they...*

"About the visa, I can do nothing," Leo told him a couple of days later. "When he gets to America, he can probably get a temporary permit or something. After that..." he shrugged, "it's up to God. But—" he held up a finger before Mordecai could interject "—but, I've arranged for someone to meet the boy in Bremerhaven. My cousin Sarah will meet him as he gets off the train. If he's carrying a book satchel and a violin case, he shouldn't be too hard to find. He stays overnight, she gives him a small suitcase with clothes. She'll have the boat ticket, also. Tourist class." He shrugged. "Costs more, but less risky. Shouldn't be a problem, if the money gets there in time."

For the next few days, they kept to their established routine. Mordecai opened the shop, served one or two customers during the day, went upstairs for lunch, returned downstairs until supper time. Esther fretted upstairs, trying to decide which foods might travel well, wondering if Theodor couldn't maybe wear two pairs of underwear, or at least two sweaters, thinking about sewing paper money into his clothes. Theodor tried to study, thought about taking some books with him, or maybe just a small one, to read during the trip, paced up and down and generally got in the way of his mother, who had forbidden him to go out.

Then it was time for him to leave. Esther had wanted to go with him to the train station; Mordecai had refused. "It'll just make it harder. Right there on the platform, you'll be crying and attracting attention. He's not a child. We'll let him go like a man, Esther."

She had finally acquiesced, seeing some logic in her husband's reasoning.

Theodor stood by the door for a long moment, overly warm in the winter coat his mother had insisted he wear, because the day was mild, especially for November. Everything had been checked and rechecked: travel documents, the money in his pockets, the money hidden in the instrument case, the bread, cheese and sausage in his satchel, the one extra pair of underwear and socks his mother had been adamant about his taking. He seemed to be debating what to say.

Finally he gave a weak smile. "Next year in Jerusalem, Papa, Mama." He turned and left. Unable to reply, they listened to him clumping down the stairs.

Esther looked slowly at her husband. "He knows, Papa, he knows."

Mordecai nodded slowly. "He's a bright boy, Mama. He'll do all right."

At first, he was a bit frightened. There seemed to be more brown-shirts on the streets, all wearing the armband with the *Hackenkreuz*. People seemed to be looking at him with suspicion. He hurried along, head bowed. Then he told himself that his fears were ridiculous. He would only attract more attention by acting in this manner. He had taken pains to dress exactly like any German boy of his age. There was nothing to give him away. He was a student going to a music lesson. He wouldn't be home for supper, which was why his was carrying food. He straightened up and walked more slowly. An old woman actually smiled and nodded to him.

A thin snow had started by the time he reached the station, and the streets were getting slippery. An automobile trundled by, belching exhaust and sliding a bit. It blew its horn and Theodor jumped. In the station, he waited until the train to Hamburg was called, then, following his father's advice, waited again until the press of passengers trying to push onto the platform seemed to be the heaviest. They wouldn't likely check documents for a local train, though the conductor might, when he came by collecting tickets.

He passed the locomotive, taking a moment to be awed by the huge driving wheels, almost as tall as he was and the steam and smoke that seemed to be coming from everywhere. The red trim did nothing, in his mind, to detract from the sinister, black appearance. He found a spot in a crowded second-class car and extracted a book and some cheese from his satchel. He looked at no one.

Anna Kravitz hustled him off the platform and into a waiting taxi when the train arrived in Hamburg a half-hour late. He had been forced to give up his seat to what he had assumed were soldiers, but he'd made no protest, and they had ignored him, too anxious to resume what seemed to be an interrupted game of cards.

Anna's apartment was small, hot and over-full of furniture. He'd been given a hot meal of what appeared to be mostly cabbage and bedded down on the couch. She listened to a muted radio and knitted under a dim light until he fell asleep. The following morning, she replenished his food supply and took him back to the station where she bought him a ticket to Bremen and then waited for the train. They didn't speak much, and when they did, it was always in German.

The trip to Bremen was mostly uneventful. This time, the conductor had demanded to know why he was going to Bremen, and Theodor had wordlessly handed him the doctored letter. The conductor scanned it, grunted and handed it back. Theodor found time to start a letter to his parents.

The next night was easy, too. Sarah Cohen was much more outgoing than Anna Kravitz, and fussed over him as his own mother might have. Did he have enough to eat? Did he have enough money? Was he excited to be going? She gave him a large meal and a soft bed with freshly laundered sheets.

She dropped him at the train station the next morning, outfitted with a suitcase and some clean clothes. He'd left his book satchel and violin with her; they would no longer fit his cover story once he reached Bremerhaven. He hoped she didn't open the violin case. She might wonder why the lining had been slit in several places. She'd made him a sandwich, which he stuffed into his pocket. He waited until almost departure time to buy a ticket to Bremerhaven; up until that moment, he would have told anyone who might ask that he was waiting for someone to pick him up. He fretted a bit, eager and a bit frightened at the same time.

At the train station, he had to ask where he might get a bus to the port area, but the porter didn't seem to find the question at all unusual. He did, however, ask Theodor if there were some other bags he could carry. Theodor, suddenly conscious that one didn't cross the ocean with just one small suitcase, reminded himself not to ask anyone "official" again.

Signs at the port directed him to the Columbus pier, where the North German Lloyd steamship *Bremen* was moored. In a stall in the men's room, he unwrapped the sandwich. From the folded paper he extracted his boat ticket. Suddenly ravenous, he took a bite before he rewrapped the sandwich.

The ship looked huge. He could see that it had two funnels, but it seemed to extend forever fore and aft. He had to remind himself not to gawk. He moved toward the boarding ramp, trying to stay in the crush of passengers.

He got in line, joining those shuffling slowly forward. He wasn't tall enough to see over those in front, but the line seemed to be moving fairly steadily; maybe they were just glancing at papers and tickets and waving everyone ahead. He had his passport and ticket ready.

The person who took his ticket wore a blue uniform, so he wasn't a soldier, anyway. There were some insignia, so Theodor assumed he was a ship's officer of some rank.

The officer took the documents and scanned them. He seemed to take too long looking at the passport. He pursed his lips. Theodor was sure he was frowning. Then he looked up and scanned the people still in line.

Theodor waited for him to hand back the passport. Instead, the officer motioned him to step aside. "So, *Junge*, wait there for a moment, will you?"

Theodor went cold inside and his mouth went dry at the same moment. He managed a nod and stepped aside, wondering if he should make a run for it. Why had he been stopped? Weren't his documents in order? Were they stopping all Jews? Had his parents changed their mind and notified the company not to let him board? Had someone told the police that he was trying to flee the country?

The officer, however, went back to checking tickets and travel papers. Theodor gnawed his lip until he could taste blood. He forced himself to calm, but his mind was furiously trying to concoct a plausible story and seek an escape route at the same time. Maybe he could run back to Sophie Cohen's house. Or maybe she was the one who'd turned him in…

Then the line was past and the uniformed man turned again to Theodor. "So, where is the rest of your family? Is no one traveling with you? I thought perhaps you'd become separated. No mother or father?"

Theodor's heart gave a great thump and started beating again. He hoped his voice was steady enough when he answered, drawing himself up a bit, "No, sir. I'm going on holiday. To visit my uncle in New York. My aunt dropped me off and said you'd take good care of me and I shouldn't worry."

The man in blue smiled broadly and clapped Theodor on the shoulder. "She's right, we will." He pointed up the gangway. "Up there, a steward will help you find your cabin. Have a good trip, young man." He returned the papers, smiled again and waved as Theodor started up the stairs, his knees only a bit wobbly.

**Theodor Weizmann to Mordecai and Esther Weizmann**
**on board the *Bremen***
**25 November, 1938**

Dear Mama and Papa,

They say I can mail letters on this ship, though I don't see how. I suppose they will post this when we reach New York and then perhaps it will return on the same ship!

This is a fine, fast ship, and everything is going well, so far. I am beginning to relax a bit and even enjoying the trip. A few of the passengers have been a bit seasick, but I have not been bothered, and anyway the steward told me that if I should feel queasy, to eat an apple with the skin on.

The food here is quite good, even though it's different from what I got at home, and there's plenty of it. I'm sure it's not so fine and fancy as the first-class passengers get, but very good, all the same. We cannot all eat at once. They have "seatings." In the evening, I have the first, at six.

I have been assigned to a small cabin with a gentleman about Papa's age, I guess. I think he's Polish. He doesn't speak either German or Yiddish, so we haven't much to say to each other. I think he spends much of his days playing cards in one of the lounges. He smells strongly of tobacco and snores loudly at night.

While I was on deck today (we had fine weather but for some clouds), I saw an airship overhead. It was too far away to see much, but it seemed to be headed for America, too. I watched it until it was hidden by clouds.

They're going to show a film tonight, so I won't want to miss that. I'll send you more news from the New World! We shall reach America the day after tomorrow.
Your
**Theodor**

He was on deck again when the ship entered New York harbor. He watched a small boat come alongside and a man climb a ladder up the side of the *Bremen*. He was anxious to see the statue of the lady with the torch. He decided it was an impressive sight, though perhaps not quite as awesome as the city skyline itself. He couldn't imagine a city so large. They passed another island with a ferry moored at a dock. One of the other passengers, leaning next to him at the rail, pointed at it and said something that sounded like "Ellis," but it meant nothing to Theodor.

There had been a bit of an anxious moment the evening before when the steward had come by collecting passports. Theodor's fears were allayed when the white-jacketed man had told him that he'd get it back the following day, as he disembarked. When they docked, someone from immigration would come aboard to check passports. It was faster that way.

It seemed to Theodor that the wait that morning was interminable. Every time he moved a step forward, he tried to see beyond those in front, to catch a glimpse of anything American. When it was finally his turn, the harried-looking individual sitting at the table with stacks of documents started to ask him questions he couldn't understand. Fortunately, one of the stewards, standing at the man's elbow, translated into German. Theodor told him that he was on holiday, visiting his uncle in New York. This seemed to satisfy the individual at the desk and he stamped something on Theodor's passport and handed it to him. The boy looked questioningly at the steward who took the passport and glanced at it.

"It's a tourist visa, good for one month." He passed the document back.

Theodor took it, took a deep breath and stepped out onto the gangway. How was he ever going to locate Mr. Feldman?

It was easy, after all. Someone in the crowd was holding up a sign with his name on it. Theodor pushed his way through the crowd. The man with the sign was a bit older than his father, he decided, though he had a bristly mustache, too. He looked pretty much like all of the other people around him, with a tweed overcoat and a hat.

"Are you Theodor?" he asked in Yiddish.

Theodor nodded.

Isaac Feldman smiled. His teeth were a bit crooked and stained, but the pleasure was genuine. "I was expecting a little boy. You're a young man." He threw an arm around his nephew's shoulder. "We'll get your luggage, then a cab."

"No luggage, Mr. Feldman."

Isaac looked hard at the boy, then nodded. "No, of course not. Well, take your bag and let's go. And call me 'uncle Isaac' or something. If you're going to stay with me, I can't be 'Mr. Feldman' all the time." He steered Theodor toward the street, where a line of yellow autos waited at the curb. In a moment, they were in one. Isaac said something to the driver.

*Of course, he's speaking English. I'll have to learn it. How will I ever get along here?* He was suddenly less sure of his future, of his abilities.

"Where are we going, uncle Isaac?"

"Lower east side," Isaac told him. It meant nothing to Theodor. Lower east side of what?

Isaac spoke during nearly the whole ride, apparently a sort of travelogue, to which Theodor listened only partially. He was trying to read the signs—there were so many!—and looking at the people, buildings and cars whenever they stopped. There was so much; he'd never be able to take it all in. He'd never fit here.

Then the cab turned a corner, and Theodor's mouth dropped open in amazement. There were signs on the shop windows he could read! There: an English word, but "Delicatessen" was printed clearly above it, in Hebrew characters. And there were others: a tailor's shop, a doctor's office. Theodor let out a breath he hadn't been aware of holding. Maybe it would be all right, after all.

"Where are we?" he finally managed to ask, but his eyes never left the window.

"Orchard Street. This is where you'll live." Isaac said something to the driver, who swung the vehicle in next to the curb and stopped.

**Theodor Weizmann to Mordecai and Esther Weizmann**
**New York**
**29 November, 1938**

Dear Mama and Papa,

New York is so big, that it seems it must be a country all by itself. It seems everyone must have a car, though uncle Isaac says no, because with the taxis, trolleybuses and the subway you shouldn't need one. I should never be able to find my way around, except that the streets are numbered (all except Broadway), so it isn't difficult.

I have a fine room to myself in the apartment over uncle Isaac's grocery store. Well, one of his grocery stores. It seems he has a wholesale business that supplies quite a number. They're popular in this neighborhood, because he has a reputation for selling quality kosher foods. Even some people who are not Jewish shop there.

In any case, he seems to be quite well off. He doesn't say he's rich, but "comfortable." As I said, I have my own room with a bed, chest of drawers, a closet and a writing desk. On a little table beside the bed I have my own radio. I use it to listen to music, because of course I can't understand what they're saying. There's also a phonograph in the parlor that he plays in the evenings.

There's a woman who comes in to cook and clean every day but Sabbath. I think she's Russian, but only uncle Isaac can understand her. She's short and rather plump, but always smiling and laughing at something. She tried to show me how to make latkes, but I don't know if she was happy at my efforts or laughing at my mistakes.

I asked uncle Isaac when I will begin school. He says first I must learn some English. He has found a school for me in a place called Connecticut. The name of the school is Claxton Hall. That's all I know about it for now, but it is supposed to be very good. I guess you have to pay to go there, but uncle Isaac says this is no problem and that he wants me to go to school in the country, not the city. He also says that since Hanukkah is coming and then the school has Christmas vacation, I will wait until January. In the meantime, I will help him in his business and study English. I will have a tutor three evenings a week, and he will help me during the day. He has bought me some books about a boy named Dick and a girl named Jane. They are not difficult, but I don't find them very interesting, either. Anyway, I have already noticed that some English words are like German, so maybe it won't be as difficult as I thought.

Now I have to take one of my books and read aloud to uncle Isaac, so I will close.

Your
**Theodor**

P.S. Uncle Isaac says he will get my tourist visa changed to a student visa, good for a year at a time.

**Theodor Weizmann to Mordecai and Esther Weizmann**
**Hartford, Connecticut**
**20 December, 1938**

Dear Mama and Papa,

We are spending the night in the capital city of Connecticut (you must look at a map of America to see where that is) after spending some hours at the school I will attend beginning next month. The boys were all away on Christmas vacation, so we were able to visit many places.

We took a train from New York to a place called New Haven, where we changed to go to Hartford. Then we changed again to go to a village called Upper Granby Lake. I don't think you will be able to find that on a map, though.

It is perhaps not as large as some of our high schools in Germany, but it occupies a larger area and also has fields for playing sports, and so forth. I found out that sports are part of the curriculum and that every boy participates every day. It's not a club activity, as it is back home.

Everyone seemed very nice, though I had difficulty understanding everything, of course. I was able to answer a few of the simpler questions they asked in English, especially if they spoke slowly, but uncle Isaac had to help me most of the time. The *Rektor* is Mr. Thompson. He told me (well, actually he spoke to uncle Isaac, who translated) that I shouldn't worry about not understanding too much yet. I shall have a reduced schedule of courses to begin with, and tutoring every day. English, of course, and mathematics, art and music. They think they can find a violin for me! Then in the fall, I shall start my 3rd form year, a year behind other boys of my age, but by then my English should be much improved and I will be able to study the same things as the others.

I will be staying in a dormitory with other boys, and that will help my English, too.

Well, we spent so much time there that it was too late to return to New York, so we are here in Hartford tonight. We will return to New York tomorrow. Before attending Claxton, I must have a physical examination and buy some more clothes.

Don't worry, I have been attending Temple every week.

Your
**Theodor**

*Theodor Weizmann wrote his parents once or twice a week for the next nine months, though he apparently received no responses. He continued to hope for word of his family until September 1, 1939, the day when Germany invaded Poland, plunging the world into war once again. At this point he realized that he would probably never hear from them again.*

## ADMISSIONS BROCHURE (1940)

**About Claxton Hall.**

Claxton Hall, located in the beautiful Connecticut River Valley, is a fully-accredited college preparatory school (grades 9–12). Graduates of the school attend some of the best colleges and attain positions of respect and responsibility in business and industry. Claxton counts among its alumni military leaders, two state senators, three presidents of nationally-recognized companies, many teachers and even some radio personalities.

Claxton Hall was founded in 1793 as the Rue Literary Institute, and is therefore one of the oldest schools of its type in New England. At the outset, the School had close ties with the Baptist Church and, while it is no longer associated with any particular church, it nevertheless has strong spiritual ties with the community. Claxton welcomes students of all faiths.

**Access to Claxton Hall.**

Ideally situated between Hartford, Connecticut and Springfield, Massachusetts, the School is readily accessible by car, motorcoach or train. The Hampton Bus Line serves the town from the east and west, and the New Haven Railroad operates three trains daily through the town of Upper Granby Lake. You may contact the School (VAlley 4-1182) for up-to-date schedules. Students arriving by bus or train will be met by a school car. Trunks and luggage may be shipped via Railway Express; the School will transport them to and from the station.

**Academics.**

Claxton is fully committed to a liberal arts education. To that end, our curriculum is designed with the classics in mind, though there is leeway for individual growth, also. We never lose sight of our goals: to prepare students to enter the most competitive colleges and to prepare them for life beyond college.

Claxton prides itself on its small classes, averaging 8–10 boys, its student-faculty ratio (7:1) and the individual attention each student receives. In addition, masters are always available to give extra help and encouragement.

**Course of Study.**

To receive a Claxton diploma, each graduate must have four credits in English, three in mathematics, three in language, two in science, two in history, one in art, one in music, one in religion. There is generally no problem in accepting equivalent courses from other schools, should a student enter after the 3rd form (Freshman) year. As a student will generally take five courses per year, it will be seen that there remain three credits which may be in any field the student desires. Half-credit courses may also be offered in typing, art appreciation, or other subjects, depending upon sign-up and instructor availability. Please consult the current catalog for an up-to-date listing of course offerings.

**Facilities.**

Claxton has fine, modern facilities. The gymnasium (1924) and the Bascomb Building (classrooms) are fairly recent additions to the campus. There are three dormitories, and meals are taken in Bassett House. In addition to the gymnasium, the athletic complex features tennis courts, an outdoor hockey rink and the football and soccer fields. The gym has a basketball court, an indoor elevated track and locker and shower rooms. The School uses the nearby Covenant Church for religious services.

**Dress code.**

Claxton Hall requires students to adhere to a code of dress. Please see the clothing list for particulars. In general, a boy should have at least one conservative suit and several sets of jackets and slacks. He should have at least seven dress shirts, a clean one to be worn each day. Laundry and dry cleaning services are available, at extra cost. Some students choose to send their laundry home, however. Details are available upon request.

**Claxton life.**

Claxton students and masters live in close proximity. Each boarding student will have a comfortable dormitory room, probably shared with another boy. Each dorm has a resident dorm master, to whom the students are encouraged to turn with questions or problems. Boarding students will be housed in Preble Hall, Wannamaker House or The Cottage.

The entire school community dines together family-style three times a day, and boys will share their tables with a faculty member. In this way, all students and faculty will get to know each other in short order. This makes for a very close-knit community.

**Athletics.**

Claxton Hall has a strong tradition of athletics and sports, having won several state championships in six sports over the course of the years. Each boy is expected to contribute to the athletic tradition in some manner, be it as a team member, a manager, or in some other capacity. Most sports field teams on at least two levels, and several sports are offered each season. In the fall, football, soccer (varsity and junior varsity) and fall tennis. In the winter, basketball (varsity and junior varsity), hockey and exercise. In the spring, baseball (varsity and junior varsity, numbers permitting), track and tennis.

Horseback riding may be offered in the fall and spring as an athletic option. There is an additional charge for this activity.

**Extra-curricular.**

The School offers a full range of extra-curricular activities and encourages all boys to become involved in at least one. Some of the options include drama, the *Trumpet* (school newspaper), the *Herald* (yearbook), chorus, radio club, Stamp and Coin Society, the Debating Club and the Literary Club. Other activities may be added as interest warrants.

**Fees and finances.**

The fee for a year at Claxton is individualized for each student. The basic charge ranges from $500 to $575, which includes tuition, room and board, but many students pay somewhat less or a bit more. The final fee depends upon the type of dormitory room chosen, scholarships, and so forth. Parents are encouraged to work with the admissions office to individualize a payment plan for their boy(s). Many options are available.

Books and activities fees may add $10 to $25 per year.

In addition, a boy will need a certain amount of spending money. A sum of fifty cents to $1 per week is suggested and should be adequate for a student's needs. Rather than give your son the entire sum at the beginning of the year, we suggest establishing an account at the school from which a boy can receive a weekly allowance and draw other needed funds.

**Health services.**

The School maintains a fully-equipped four-bed Infirmary in the original Claxton Hall building. Sick call is held daily from 7:30 to 8 a.m. A Registered Nurse is on duty from 7:30 a.m. to 8 p.m. daily and is on call throughout the night. A physician visits the School twice a week, and holds office hours at the Infirmary from 2 to 4 p.m. Tuesdays and Thursdays. The village of Upper Granby Lake has a fully-staffed clinic for emergencies. Students may be referred there as needed.

**Job program.**

Claxton Hall strives to keep its fees as low as possible, in order to put a quality education within reach of qualified students. At the same time, the School seeks to build a sense of responsibility and pride. To these ends, the Job Program at Claxton has proven of great worth.

Each boy is assigned an area of responsibility at the School. Normally, these jobs are performed once per day, sometimes less often. They include waiting on tables, washing dishes, cleaning classrooms or other areas of the School, assisting one period per day at the library or the gymnasium, etc. Upperclassmen who have proven themselves may become Supervisors. Proctors and Monitors have no additional duties in the job program.

**Town permissions.**

Relations between the School and the town of Upper Granby Lake have always been excellent. Students visiting the town are expected to comport themselves in a responsible and gentlemanly manner and should do nothing to bring discredit upon the school. Upon signing out, students may walk to the village on Wednesday and Saturday afternoons if they have no athletic commitment. The town offers a full range of services, including a barber shop and a movie theater. At other times, students are permitted in town only if accompanied by a faculty member. Hitchhiking is strictly forbidden.

**Honor Code.**

Claxton Hall has a strict honor code. Cheating, stealing, bullying and violations of major rules will not be tolerated, as such conduct undermines the entire community. All students are expected to participate in the enforcement of school rules and to report non-compliance to a master, supervisor, proctor or monitor. Failure to do so is often considered as serious as the violation itself and may be cause for convening a disciplinary hearing. Full details of the Honor Code are given in the Catalog.

# GILLES LETOURNEAU (1943)

Gilles Letourneau wasn't surprised to find the door to the gym unlocked again. It was supposed to be secured by the last coach to leave the building each evening, but, as a lot, he didn't find them terribly responsible. Perhaps they "forgot," or maybe each coach assumed he wasn't the last and that someone else would take care of it.

He was about to turn his master key and walk away when he thought that he might as well take one more walk-through. That really wasn't his job, either. The night watchman was supposed to patrol starting at nine, but that was still two hours away, and, if anything were broken in the interim, Gil Letourneau, head of Maintenance, would have to repair it.

Gil snorted, smiled, and shook his head at the thought. "Head of Maintenance," indeed. Except for one part-time employee, he was the entire maintenance staff. The war had taken away some of the other workers, and budget cuts had accounted for the rest. Like other war-time institutions, it seemed the school was operating on a war emergency basis only, when it came to repairs. Everything was "deferred." Only emergency patches were done, and even then, only the critical ones. He supposed he'd find many lights on inside, too, though the blackout curtains prevented any light from escaping.

There was indeed a light left on in the shower room, where water ran in a fast trickle from one of the defective shower heads. He turned off the light, but couldn't do anything about the water. Washer defective, probably. He added it to his mental list of things to repair.

He used his small pocket flashlight to scan the rest of the area. That way, he wouldn't have to walk back and forth across the rooms to turn lights on and off. The light switches weren't conveniently located, but, then again, the place was built in 1924, and the builders probably thought one switch per room quite sufficient.

He was a bit shocked, but not terribly surprised, to find that the athletic locker had been broken into again. The padlock, still locked, hung from its hasp, whose screws had been wrenched from the thin wood.

The athletic locker was really a small room where the equipment—balls, nets, uniforms, and the like—was stored. There was also normally a small amount of cash in the cigar box on a shelf beside the door. Students sometimes had to buy items like shoelaces or pay for towels they'd lost. Sometimes the locker was broken into by students who just wanted a basketball to play with. That item was normally left on the gym floor when they were done. Too much trouble to return it.

*God damn kids. Don't respect anything any more. God damn faculty. No sense of responsibility. Can't be bothered to do something simple like turn out a light or lock a door. What in hell is this world coming to?*

No, that wasn't fair. A good portion of the faculty had a sense of responsibility, as he did. He knew they put in ten, twelve, fifteen hour days on a regular basis. They weren't that well paid, and they didn't get overtime. Gil Letourneau was supposed to, but he rarely declared the extra hours. If he did, he'd be billing the school for at least sixty hours a week.

And there were some good kids, too, he reminded himself. There was that kid the first year he'd arrived. Steel…something. No, iron. That was it, Ironsmith. Really bright. What a waste. What a friggin' tragic waste.

Gil sighed. There wasn't any sense in checking the cigar box. He didn't know how much—if anything—had been in there. Nor did he know how many balls of various sizes, jerseys, flags or helmets there should be. Somewhere in the filing cabinet would be an inventory, he was sure. The locker was staffed by some of the team managers, in rotation. There was really no one, he guessed, who knew just what equipment—and how many of each item—was stored there at any given moment, what with some always signed out to various teams. So there wasn't any sense in checking that, either.

There was really nothing further he could do here this evening, unless he repaired the lock. What was the point? It was Saturday evening and the gym wasn't used on Sundays. What with the two required church services tomorrow, morning worship and vespers, the formal Sunday dinner and the popular Headmaster's Tea in the afternoon, the quiet hours and the study halls, there wouldn't be anyone using the facility until Monday. He could get to it first thing Monday morning.

He hesitated only for the space of a long breath. He'd need a screwdriver to remove the hasp and relocate it into new wood. The screwdrivers were in the maintenance shed, all the way across campus. It was a simple job—not that it would last very long, he told himself—but it would occupy the better part of a half hour. He could imagine Sylvia's reaction when he got home:

"Damn it, Gil, your dinner's gone cold again. They don't pay you for all those extra hours you put in. What's the point? Do you think they notice? You've got three months until retirement, just in case you've forgotten. Don't you think it's time you took it a little bit easy on yourself? Nobody's gonna know, Gil. They don't give a damn, anyway."

*No, nobody's gonna know. Nobody except me.*

Gil Letourneau took a deep breath and decided Sylvia was right. Then he left the gym and headed to the maintenance shop, where he'd get the tools necessary to fix the lock before he went home. He thought he'd better bring a couple of extra screws, too, in case the ones that has been pulled from the wood had gotten stripped or damaged.

He'd arrived at Claxton in 1915, already 40 years old. Well, hell, forty wasn't too old to begin another career. The wounds he'd received in the Spanish-American War precluded his joining the fighting in what they were now calling the First War. It looked as if the one they were in now would be the Second. He fervently hoped it would be the last.

Things had been different then. There had been a lot more respect. Sure he was "just" a maintenance man, but people had been a lot more polite when they asked for something. Now they just demanded; they expected. In the old days, he'd gone out of his way to help in areas which weren't really a part of his job description at all. Hell, he'd even helped a couple of those young squirts in arithmetic. Because it seemed he was always measuring something, he'd gotten so he could add, subtract and convert fractions in his head. He'd had to figure out how to do that on his own, since he had no formal schooling after the sixth grade. It hadn't seemed particularly difficult; maybe it was just a natural talent. But some of the younger boys seemed to think it bordered on witchcraft. When he showed them how to do it, they held him in some sort of awe. He smiled as he remembered that one of the mothers—back in '26, he thought—had even sent him some homemade cookies as a thank-you for helping her son in mathematics.

Now it was different. Just yesterday one of the faculty wives had sent him a note telling him a light bulb needed replacing in her kitchen. Things had come to a pretty pass when an adult couldn't even change a light bulb, for God's sake.

No respect from the students, either, nowadays. For some years now, they'd taken to calling the maintenance staff "our boys in blue," because of the denim work clothes they wore. But it was always said facetiously, never in respect, or so it seemed to Gil, at any rate.

*Well, I won't have to put up with their guff much longer. Just gotta make it until July 1st, then I'm free of this place. Too bad I couldn't leave something a bit more permanent behind, but all the repairs I make seem to last only a matter of days or weeks before they need fixing again. It's just not worth it.*

There had been the storm in '38 that had done quite a bit of damage. He and his crew had worked twelve-hour shifts to keep essential services running, even though many of the kids had gone home and there had been no classes for almost a week. Somewhere they'd found enough ice for the refrigerators and sufficient candles and lanterns so that everyone left had at least a little light. When they hadn't been chasing down supplies, they'd been manning the saws to clear away the fallen trees.

Two years after that had come the ice storm, and that was even worse. They'd had to close the school then. The boys had been sent home, but the faculty living in school housing hadn't had anywhere else to go. A few of those residences had working fireplaces, but most who tried to use them discovered just how inefficient a fireplace is at heating a room, to say nothing of a house. Besides, most of the wood available seemed to be a few white birch logs stacked in the fireplace "for show." White birch was far down the list of desirable fireplace fuels; it split hard when dry, burned quickly and gave off little heat. And the burning bark produced a black smoke that could coat anything with sooty dirt in short order.

So while the remaining faculty shivered in their homes, the maintenance staff worked flat-out to drain pipes before they froze, get rid of perishable food before it rotted and corner the local market on generators before they were sold out. Fortunately, Gil knew a contractor—an alumnus, as it turned out—who used them on his construction sites. He'd be happy to lend the school a couple. A gas station on another power grid was still pumping gas, if you didn't mind driving a half-hour each way and waiting another half-hour in line. It was a good thing, Gil reflected, that this had happened before rationing. There wouldn't be any gas available now, even for another such emergency.

*I suppose*, he reflected, *that I'm lucky to have this job*. Other schools had closed "for the duration." But Sylvia was right. It was time to retire. Once, he'd dreamed of changing the world. Later, he'd have been satisfied with just making a difference in a few people's lives. Now, he suspected, he'd be completely forgotten within a year of his departure. Initially, they'd regret his going, but, like ripples decreasing as they move from the point of the splash, he would vanish from their minds in short order.

Near the end of February the boiler went out again. It was in the furnace room, deep in the bowels of the gym. The gym building wasn't that old, but, to save funds in its construction, they'd purchased a used furnace, an old coal-burning monstrosity that had to be tended almost constantly. Normally, when school was in session during the heating season, a boy would come in every few hours and throw in a few shovelfuls.

Like many schools of its type, Claxton Hall kept costs down by assigning each of the boys to a cleaning or maintenance task at some point during the day. Some were considered "cushy" and much sought-after: manning the circulation desk at the library during a free period, or escorting prospective families around campus. This latter task even got the fortunate student out of class on occasion, if the visit happened to come at just the right time. Other jobs were less popular: waiting on tables, washing dishes, cleaning classrooms. In addition, each boy was responsible for keeping his own room in order. The faculty enforced this by periodic "surprise" inspections, usually carried out when the defenseless inhabitants were trapped in chapel or a school meeting. Boys whose rooms received lower than a grade of "A" found themselves rewarded with extra cleaning duties: a week of sweeping corridors or perhaps polishing the silver service used at Sunday afternoon teas.

In any case, Gil doubted that the furnace's problem was a lack of coal. It was probably rather a lack of maintenance or simple old age.

Because the boiler room had to be left unlocked for whoever came in to feed it, it was a popular out-of-the-way gathering spot for boys who would rather not have their activities observed. It was shunned during the day, of course—too much traffic—but at night, after the fire had been banked, it was probably safe enough unless the night was really cold and someone would have to add more coal periodically during the night. In that case, however, it was too cold for the boys to sneak out at night, anyway.

Gil was therefore surprised to find the room occupied by three boys, all with cigarettes hanging from their lips, playing cards. Card playing was discouraged, if not actually against the rules, but smoking, except in certain designated areas, and then only by seniors, was strictly against the rules and was, if repeated, an expulsion offense.

Two of the boys, Harry Whittier and Tom Michaels, were underclassmen. The third was Don Penley, a senior, proctor and captain of the basketball team. All three now wore a look of stunned disbelief.

Gilles looked slowly from one to the other. "Not a very good decision, fellows." It was a matter-of-fact statement. There was no accusatory tone.

Whittier was the first to recover from his shock. "Oh, my God," he whined, "I'm dead. My folks'll kill me." Now the tone became beseeching: "Jeez, Mr. L, you're not gonna turn us in, are you? I've already got two demerits this term; another and I'm outta here. You'll get me kicked out of school if you tell."

Penley gave the younger boy a disgusted look. "Shut up, Whitty. You are *such* an ass." He snubbed his cigarette out carefully on the cement floor.

"Are you really gonna report us?" Michaels' voice sounded incredulous, as if such a thing would never cross Gil's mind.

*I'm not a teacher, so I wouldn't turn him in?* Gil wondered. *Does he think I'm any less responsible because I'm not a teacher? What the hell does he expect me to do?*

He held Michaels' eyes for a long moment. When he spoke, it was slowly and deliberately, to make sure the boys understood.

"I'll give you a choice, Tom. Either you tell Mr. Thompson, or I will. It'd probably go easier on you if you get to him before I do. Now get out of here."

The two younger boys were on their feet and out of the door in a moment, leaving cards scattered on the floor behind them. To Gilles' surprise, Penley didn't move.

"How long do we have, Mr. L?"

"Hmm? Until what?"

Penley drew up his knees and encircled them with his arms. "Before you go to Mr. Thompson?"

Gil opened his mouth to give a quick answer, then realized there was more to the boy's question than he'd thought. He pondered an answer while he fetched a broken-down wooden chair from beside the boiler. Sometimes he had to spend almost an hour sitting with the temperamental thing before all of the gauges read what they should. He pulled the chair over beside the student. He didn't say anything until he'd sat down. When he did speak, it was in a conversational tone, almost friendly.

"When's the basketball tourney, Don?"

"Starts this weekend, Friday after classes. If we make it all the way, the finals are on Sunday."

"How do you rate your chances?"

Penley shrugged. "So-so. McEnroe Academy is pretty tough this year."

Gilles appeared to be digesting the information. In fact, he already knew what his next question was going to be.

"Going to college next year, are you?"

Penley didn't answer immediately. Then he said, "I've been accepted at a couple of places."

"That's a fairly evasive answer." After a moment, Gil realized what Penley was hiding and said, "You're not going to college, are you? You're going to enlist."

Penley looked at the floor and shuffled his feet a bit on the gritty surface. After a moment he looked up. "You won't tell my folks, will you? I mean…I'm legal age and all. But if there isn't already a letter waiting for me when I get home, yeah, I'll sign up the next day." A brief pause, then: "It's something I've gotta do, Mr. L."

Gil couldn't argue with that, so he just nodded slowly. *Who knows if this kid will even be alive a couple of months from now?* He thought briefly of Ironsmith. This whole graduating class probably didn't have much of a future. An illegal cigarette didn't seem to matter very much under those circumstances. But his conscience couldn't just dismiss it. And Penley wouldn't respect him very much if he did, Gil realized.

He rose from the dilapidated chair and dusted at his knees, though he hadn't gotten them dirty. "Well, you know," he began in the same conversational tone, "this is a pretty busy time of year for me. I probably couldn't get to Mr. Thompson much before Monday afternoon. Yeah, I'm pretty sure that's when I'll see him." He held out a hand to help the boy to his feet.

Penley's grip was warm, strong and sincere. "Thanks, Mr. L. Thanks very much." A quick smile. "But I bet I'll beat you to the headmaster."

Gil nodded. "Now you better go chase down those other two clowns before they do something rash. How you want to handle them is up to you. And oh, yeah, best of luck this weekend."

Penley nodded back. "Thanks, Mr. L, thanks again." A final smile and he was gone.

*Soft old fool*, Gilles Letourneau reprimanded himself.

Claxton Hall survived the preliminary and quarterfinal rounds in the CPSAA annual basketball tournament but lost to McEnroe Academy, 49-45, in the semis. In his final high school game, Don Penley scored eighteen points, had four rebounds, two blocks and three assists.

On Monday morning following the tournament, he presented himself at the headmaster's office shortly before eight o'clock, planning to absent himself from first period Chem if necessary. Marshall Thompson arrived at his office at 8:04, whereupon Donald Penley turned himself in for illegal smoking. He was placed on disciplinary probation and was given a two-day in-house suspension, which he served at the pots-and-pans sink in the kitchen. A letter was sent to his parents informing them of the affair and a copy was sent to Emory University and DePaul, informing them of the disciplinary action. Upon learning of Penley's action, Michaels and Whittier also turned themselves in shortly before noon.

On a sunny Monday morning in early May, Gilles was checking some inventory for the final time when Don Penley poked his head through the open door. The Weizmann kid was with him and they both looked as if they might have been up to something Gilles would rather not know about.

"Hey, Mr. L. I wanted to see if you were coming to the senior dinner tonight."

The senior dinner was nominally the last full-class function before Baccalaureate, shortly before graduation. At this moment awards were bestowed by the faculty upon deserving seniors, usually book prizes of some sort, but sometimes small scholarships as well. The Senior Class President made a speech—usually a humorous one—and there was some good-natured jesting between the seniors and faculty, the former bragging about what they had gotten away with, the latter group revealing just how many embarrassing details they knew about the graduating class. Gilles was puzzled as to why he was asked to attend.

"Well, Mr. L, there's a lot of teachers retiring this year, and, seeing as you are too, I thought you should come. It'll be a lot of fun."

Gilles nodded. "Well, maybe." After all, he did like a lot of the boys, and he might be seeing them for the last time. Maybe he should go.

"Great. See you then." Penley slapped the door jamb in a sort of gesture of farewell. Gilles went back to his inventory.

At seven o'clock, after the underclassmen had been fed and shooed away (except for the fortunate few who had been chosen to serve as waiters and would therefore be allowed to hear the stories and inside jokes of this year's senior class), the $6^{th}$ formers and about half of the faculty assembled in the dining hall. The tables had been set with linen cloths (a rare occasion) and for once, the tableware would be spot-free.

Somehow, enough ration points had been collected to allow everyone to have a small steak, tough, but nevertheless real beef. There were baked potatoes and asparagus and small paper cups filled with nuts and mints. Ashtrays were placed on all of the tables, not just the head table, for this was the only occasion during the year when those boys who wished to smoke—cigars were the usual fare—would be permitted to do so outside of the designated area.

The head table was occupied by the Headmaster, of course, a few of the senior faculty and those retiring: Mr. Edwards, Latin; Mr. Brentwood, History; Mr. Tuckwell, Music; Mrs. Mapleton, typing, spelling and penmanship. There didn't seem to be a place for Gilles, but he hadn't really expected one. He didn't know if the Headmaster had expected him to be here, either. The rest of the attending faculty, along with Gilles Letourneau, seated themselves here and there with the boys.

The speeches began after the dishes had been cleared. The Head's address was a little long, Gilles believed, and far too optimistic. Some of the class officers were evidently humorous, but most of the references went over Gilles' head. He nodded approvingly and applauded when the prizes were announced. The air became somewhat heavy with smoke.

As a finale to the evening, the Editor of the yearbook and the yearbook advisor came forward to announce the dedication of the 1943 *Herald*. Gilles only half-listened. It was going to a dedicated member of the community, who had served the school long and well, going far beyond…earning the respect of…would be sorely missed…many contributions, and so forth. Fairly standard stuff.

There was a slight pause before the name of the honoree was announced:

"Mr. Gilles Letourneau."

Dazed, he was prodded to his feet as the room stood, applauding and cheering loudly. He only had time to see the wide grin on Dan Penley's face before tears blurred his vision.

## THE GRANBY *REGISTER*, February 17, 1949

### Fire guts local landmark
### Original Claxton Hall building to be razed

*By Mark Stafford*

UPPER GRANBY LAKE—Fire destroyed one of the area's oldest buildings this morning. Firefighters responded to an alarm at about 2:30 and arrived at Claxton Hall to find the interior of the building of the same name completely ablaze. Fire chief Stephen Rand said it was too early to tell, but that it appeared the fire might be electrical in origin. No one was in the building at the time, though Headmaster Marshall Thompson said "the records housed in that building can never be replaced. We've lost a good piece of history here tonight."

The brick exterior of the building still stands as a shell, but the fire has so weakened it that Chief Rand said "it will have to come down." The building was used primarily as office space.

Thompson said there were no immediate plans to replace the building. "We'll build something there," he said, "but it's too early to say what. There will be a plaque to mark the spot. After all, this is where Claxton started."

Headmaster Thompson said that all classes would meet as scheduled and that school life would continue "in as normal a fashion as possible."

# ROGER S. NIELSEN (1951)

**Transcription of notes of the emergency meeting of the Board of Trustees, Wednesday, August 8, 1951.**

**Chairman Emmons:** Mrs. Liebermann, gentlemen, thank you for coming at such short notice. I appreciate the fact that many of you had to come a considerable distance and that all of you left important business unfinished.

We face perhaps the greatest challenge in the history of the school. We have narrowly averted one crisis only to find ourselves faced with a larger one. Those of you who attended our May meeting recall that our financial situation was grave at best, and it was only through the willingness of Roger Nielson to accept such a task that Claxton was able to remain open. Unfortunately, he never got a chance to put his plans into action. His heart attack and premature death may signal an early demise of the school itself, for it appears we lack the means to continue, having no backing and no leadership. It is with deep and profound regret that I must propose that the school be closed, at least until and unless someone is willing to step forward and take up the reins of what I feel may be a hopeless cause.

**Mr. Carter**: Bill, we can't just turn these students and teachers out in the street with no warning. How long will our available funds last? Maybe one of us, or one of the senior administrators could fill in as head.

**Chairman Emmons**: Stu?

**Mr. Livermore**: Well, we can probably meet expenses and pay salaries through December, if we tap into some endowment. But there's going to be a helluva lot of tuition to reimburse if we close, to say nothing of outstanding contracts we'd still have to honor.

**Chairman Emmons**: Such as…?

**Mr. Livermore**: Well, Rector Hall isn't paid for yet, we'd still owe the architects for Cater Hall for the blueprints, even if the building never got built… Let's see, vehicle payments, insurance through December…and

I think the dining hall contracts for a lot of food on a yearly basis. There's stuff that's already been ordered that'd have to be paid for.

**Mr. Stearns**: Excuse me, Bill, but I don't think we can anticipate all of the possible problems and scenarios at this meeting. I think maybe we just ought to decide whether or not we can keep the school open, and if so, how and for how long. Then we can tackle the problems as they arise.

**Mr. Dube**: I have to go with Bill on this one, I'd like to call for a vote on the matter, so at least we know where we all stand.

**Mr. Record**: Wait a minute. Let's not commit ourselves before we've explored all of the options, at least. Stu, how much money would we need to keep operating until the end of the year?

**Mr. Livermore**: Wow, Ev, that's kind of hard to say without some more study. Maybe as much as a hundred thousand, maybe less. That would meet our current obligations, anyway, and we wouldn't default on any loans. But that's more than our current endowment, and I can't see the alumni rushing forward with gifts that size.

**Mr. Record**: Suppose I told you I could get you a low-interest loan for any amount up to a hundred thousand, with a twenty-year term?

**Mrs. Liebermann**: Everett, no bank would advance us that kind of money. Our financial situation is too well known.

**Mr. Record**: Not a bank, Flo. A group of businessmen who believe in Claxton Hall and private education. They think it's worth the risk.

**Mr. Livermore**: Who…?

**Mr. Record**: Sorry, Stu. I'm not at liberty to say. You understand: some of their shareholders might not be happy if they knew funds were being invested in what some of them might consider a risky venture. But they needn't worry: there's enough capital to cover it. Most of it will be private money, anyway. From the individuals themselves, I mean.

**Mr. Emmons**: I take it you've already been in contact with these people, Ev?

**Mr. Record**: Yes.

**Mr. Stearns**: They must want some guarantees. I mean, they must have some conditions.

**Mr. Record**: They do. In order to assure themselves that their monies are being used in the best possible way, they want to name the next headmaster—at least until the school can get back on its feet.

**Mr. Dube**: Wow.

**Mr. Livermore**: As generous as their offer is, I'm not sure we could accept those terms.

**Mrs. Liebermann**: I'm not sure we have a choice, Stuart.

**Mr. Record**: Look, I can tell you this much: one of the people I'm talking about is a Claxton alum, and he credits a lot of the success he's enjoying today to Claxton. They're not out to run the school like a company, if that's what you're concerned about. But it *is* a business decision, after all. Interim, to be sure, but a business decision.

Let's look at the larger picture. Closing Claxton isn't just a matter of sending the students home and throwing a bunch of people out of work. This school's been around for almost 160 years. Doesn't that mean something? We're part of the community here, not just an isolated little institution. What might happen to the town if we closed? I mean, sure, it'd still be there, but what part of its economy are we?

We've also got to think about tradition, and about the alumni. I think this may be a good chance to rally some of them. A good PR effort at this point could double donations. Sure, we're facing a crisis, but I also think it's a real opportunity, not one we should pass up.

**Chairman Emmons**: Maybe we're ready for that vote now.

# EVERETT RECORD
# JOHN SINGLETON
# (1952)

"So, Jack, give it to me straight. Just how bad off are we?"

John Singleton fiddled with the cuff of his right pants leg, the one he had crossed over the left. It seemed to be absorbing at lot of his attention. Finally he looked up. His face showed a small smile.

"Do you want the four-letter version, Ev, or what I might say to the Board of Trustees?"

"What I *don't* want, Jack, is any bullshit. Not now, not ever."

Singleton's respect for the man increased a bit. Not that Everett Record was a complete stranger. He'd seen him at Board meetings, taken pledges from him over the phone, met him at cocktail parties. Even so, the new headmaster would be a hard man to dislike. Record was sixty-ish, looked fifty-ish, fairly fit. Gray hair, fading to white. Serious face, fatherly, but not severe. It couldn't be, not with one blue eye and one brown. Nose a bit too big, mouth firm, chin solid. Suit, expensive; tie ditto; everything in good taste; understated wealth. Everett Record came from a long line of people you'd find listed in *Who's Who*, had invested his share of the family money in the market, had doubled and tripled it. He was a quiet philanthropist, probably gave more to charity in a month than John Singleton made in a year.

Singleton considered how to begin. "Well, to start with, Ev, the fact that you're the fourth Head in two years doesn't really inspire confidence in the stability of the institution. Inquiries and enrollment are down—we're going to open with about a hundred and twelve—financial aid is hard to come by, our endowment is laughable, the buildings and grounds are in poor shape, the faculty underpaid and overworked, and…the food's terrible."

This got a brief laugh.

"You've heard most of this at the Board meetings, but the trustees tend to be a bit…ivory tower, Ev. I know you're aware that each year for the last four, the Board's considered might be our last. All budgets are cut to the bone, and nobody wants to send his son to a school that looks shabby and can't offer what others can. Each year they manage to scrape enough together for another nine months, but…" Jack shrugged, and the gesture spoke volumes. "…but I really feel this may be it for the School. There are too many schools in this area that can offer more. We just can't cut it in this market, Ev. Alumni giving is somewhere eleven percent. It's just not enough. I think the fact that you're here—a recognizable name in the business, financial and social world—is their last attempt to make someone sit up and take notice."

Record puffed out his cheeks, as if he might have been holding his breath. "So it's because they see me as some sort of celebrity—a guest artist if you will?"

Singleton nodded. To his surprise, Record laughed again.

"Well, Jack, I *did* tell you 'no bullshit'. So I guess I'm grateful for that analysis." He appeared to consider something for a minute before he looked up at Singleton again. "I guess we're just going to have to prove them wrong, Jack."

After Singleton had left the office, Record stared at his phone for a moment before picking up the receiver and dialing for an outside line.

"Robert Rath Associates," the voice on the other end said.

"Bob, this is Ev. What's doing well?"

Record listened, then said. "Okay, sell one hundred shares. Get a cashier's check—keep it anonymous—and send it to the financial officer at Claxton Hall." He gave an address. "Earmark it for…oh, the chem. lab. No, wait, on second thought, mark it 'unrestricted gift'. Let's see what they'll do with it. Best to Kathy, Bob. Talk to you later."

Everett Record hung up and permitted himself a small smile of satisfaction. Then he got to his feet and left the office. *Okay, Everett, let's see what you just bought yourself.*

He left Bassett House and turned to look at it. It was in fair shape, considering there'd probably been no serious maintenance performed there for forty years. The paint was peeling on the window frames and ivy was attacking the brickwork in several places. The massive wooden front door with its large panes of glass in the upper half was slightly warped and stuck in its frame when the humidity was even slightly high. And in the winter, he'd been told, the wind and snow blew in at the cracks. *Well, at least we have electricity. And the toilet doesn't get plugged up that often.*

Across the road sat Rector Hall, only a couple years old and in good repair. The dining hall occupied most of the main floor, with the kitchen in the basement (*damn poor design*). The rest of the main floor was given over to what they called "function rooms" (*whatever the hell that is*). Upstairs was the infirmary (*why in hell do we make sick or injured kids walk up a flight of stairs?*) and the school's small library (*that sure sends a lot of noisy traffic right by the infirmary*).

To the left of Rector was the Cottage, undergoing renovations. Record and his wife Corinne would move in when they were complete. He turned right and began to follow the sidewalk toward the dorms. The sidewalk itself certainly wasn't anything you'd feature in a catalog: cracked and heaved, with grass growing through it here and there (*must be dangerous in the winter*).

Harper Hall was only slightly older than Rector, but five years' worth of hyperactive adolescents can age a building quickly. The exterior was in pretty good shape. The scribblings on the brick walls could probably be washed off. Inside, the linoleum floors showed signs of wear (*at least they had the good sense to use tiles—we can replace those individually*), but the halls were dim and smelled musty. The room doors showed battle scars of tape, screws and thumbtacks, as well as penciled messages and a few that had been scratched into the surface. "Nuggy's Room" was especially deeply incised; Record didn't think a simple sanding would remove it.

The rooms themselves were sparse—even calling them "Spartan" might have been giving them an overtone of luxury completely lacking: metal-framed cot (*sagging or missing springs*), desk and chair (*might have to take knives away from these boys. How can anyone write on that surface?*), small dresser, equally scarred, tiny curtained-off closet, battered wastebasket. No curtains, but one bent rod. Dirt in corners, unidentified substances on windowsill (*and I certainly don't want to look under the desk!*). The second floor was much the same. Record didn't know if the Master's apartment was occupied or not, so he decided to visit one of those later.

Preble Hall was in worse shape: old, peeling radiators, which had evidently been leaking some sort of corrosive liquid for the better part of a quarter-century, eating away the worn linoleum down to the blackened wood beneath. The furniture was the same standard-issue as in Harper, Early Wobbly. Two of the stalls in the downstairs bathroom were missing doors, apparently wrenched off, and one shower dripped continuously. The tile-work was badly stained, the grout crumbling. The grass outside was long and hid soda bottles, sardine cans, cookie wrappers, among other things. The window frames were rotting, screens missing or ripped, some hinges hanging to life by only one screw.

Record turned and headed south, passing the tennis courts (no longer level; asphalt cracked, cyclone fence sagging) and the outdoor hockey rink (walls leaning either in or out, in spite of bracing; weeds and what appeared to be a small maple tree growing inside.

The date engraved on the cornerstone of the gym read 1924, so that meant it and the Bascomb Building had been erected the same year. The gym, at least, appeared to be higher on the maintenance list than some other buildings. The floor of the basketball court smelled of new varnish and the cement floors of the locker room and corridors had been painted, but the walls of some areas were missing paint and plaster. Several locker doors had evidently been used as tackling dummies. The trophies in the case were dusty and, if one could believe the series of pictures hung chronologically on the wall, Claxton had not fielded any teams since 1939.

Record left the gym, crossed the football field where a couple of lawn mowers were at work and walked to the maintenance area at the southern end of the campus. The former stables, now reinforced, served at present as workshops and garage. Here, at least, were signs of purposeful action. Record introduced himself to several men in blue coveralls and said he'd be receptive to requests for new tools and so forth. This seemed to surprise them. Not wishing to hold up their work, he smiled, waved and left. He was afraid that, had he asked for a list of what needed doing, or a progress report on recent repairs, he'd be there all day. One of the axioms he lived by seemed appropriate here: *Never offer suggestions to a man who knows what he's doing.* He added another mental note: *See if we can add more staff.*

He walked back up the road toward Rector Hall again, passing the old Covenant Church that served both the School and the community, past a private home, and arrived at the classroom buildings, Bascomb and the lower, wooden structure that grew awkwardly out of its side. Bascomb was brick, to match the rest of the buildings; The Addition, dating from 1949, seemed out of place alongside it. It had probably been built as a "temporary" structure, and so had never been named.

He used his master key to let himself into Bascomb. *Do all school buildings smell the same?* he wondered. He started with the science classrooms and labs in the basement. They were typical, he thought of labs twenty-five years ago. *When was the last time they'd added any equipment?* Everything looked neat here, just old. Two windows in the chem lab were cracked and the wall displayed discolored rectangles where posters had apparently once hung. The chemistry smell hung lightly in the air; he doubted that it ever fully dissipated.

A window had been left open in the biology lab/classroom, and the wind had scattered papers. He picked them up and put them in an untidy pile on the worn wooden teacher's desk. He shut the window and departed, avoiding looking at the pickled specimens in jars occupying shelves and countertops. He had never liked biology.

He supposed the next room was physics: he saw weights, inclined planes, rulers in inches and centimeters, and a lot of equipment he couldn't name. The room was hot, almost stifling. He lowered one blind; the other was broken.

The classrooms upstairs were…well, shabby. He wondered when the material on some of the bulletin boards had last been changed. Books on sagging shelves, student desks etched with initials of several generations (along with the usual obscene suggestions, as well as observations on various teachers), a thin coating of chalk dust over everything. *Can we be ready to open in two months?*

He returned thoughtfully to his office where he consulted his watch and his Rolodex. Then he asked Beverly to get him a west-coast number. When the light on his phone flashed, he picked up the receiver and identified himself to the pert voice who informed him he had reached "Masters and Hines Publishing." He asked to speak to his college roommate, Sanford ("Sandy") Masters. He wasted little time on preliminaries, but asked the question at the first pause in the conversation: "Sandy, how'd you like a chemistry lab named after you?"

***

John Singleton had gone into teaching after the War—the World War, that is, not this "police action" thing currently going on in Korea. This would be his fourth headmaster. There was a sort of "tweedy" sameness about most of them: pipe smokers, "old school" morality and resistance to change. But most of them had known all of the boys' names and their hometowns. They spoke in chapel at least twice a month and expected all members of the school community—faculty and students alike—to mold themselves in the image of the headmaster. Mostly they had failed. They maintained contact with alumni, but were generally unsuccessful in squeezing any money from them. Money wasn't something a gentleman asked for.

During his six years at the school, Singleton had worn any number of hats, as teachers and administrators were fond of saying, but had he been asked for a job description or even a job title, Singleton doubted he could have complied. First and foremost, he supposed, he was advisor to the headmaster, but he did some college counseling on the side, attempted some fund-raising, organized reunions, acted as intermediary between faculty and the Head, and so forth. If one cared to check the yearbook, one would see

John Singleton listed as "Asst. Headmaster," but Singleton thought of himself rather as "Chief Gopher."

For all of that, he'd never seen a list like the one he now held in his hands. The words "Headmaster's Office" appeared at the top of the stationery, but the Head's name was given as Roger Nielsen, two administrations gone. Singleton read the list a second time, more carefully, wondering just how much of this he could get done before school opened.

1. Add $100 to all teaching faculty salaries, effective immediately. Check attached. This is CONFIDENTIAL!!!

2. Set up board meeting for earliest. I don't want to wait until sched. mtg. in Oct.

3. Get locker-room walls in gym fixed soonest. Unhealthy conditions. Hire outside if you have to.

4. Sched. mtg. w/ maint. staff—see what they need & let's find a way to give it to them.

5. Get small, tasteful brass plaque made: "Sanford Masters Chemistry Lab." Have engraver order supply of plaques for future use.

6. There's a private house bet. the church & Addition. See if owners might sell. Want it for infirmary.

7. Get list of local alums & send out invitations for big bash (catered—I pick up tab) for Oct. 12 (boys away for long wkend, so we'll hold it in Rector). Prepare presentation & plea for money for Alumni Fund .

8. New light fixtures (bright!) in Harper. Have walls repainted light color. Replace doors I have chalk-marked w/ X. Hire outside.

9. Call Tyner Furniture in Hartford—I have set up acct. there. Order new wooden furn. for all dorm rooms, incl. beds. Replace rods & get curtains!

Singleton shook his head slowly, but permitted himself a little smile. This agenda was more ambitious that the previous three administrations' combined. And he suspected it was only the beginning. He was wondering where to begin when he decided he'd better check his appointment calendar.

It was a good thing he did. He had an interview in fifteen minutes with Alvin Freitag—a teacher seeking a position teaching biology, if he remembered correctly. He rummaged through the confusion on his desk until he found the proper folder. He glanced at his watch. Just enough time to scan the contents again before Freitag arrived.

It was one of those standard résumé forms sent out by an organization that specialized in finding a position for a teacher. They did a thorough, professional job and had more contacts than would be possible for any one teacher. Of course, there was a price for the service. Something like five percent of your first year's salary. Ouch.

Alvin Charles Freitag had graduated from Bowdoin earlier this year, Mu Sigma Something, majored in biology, minored in journalism, graduated with honors—the usual stuff. Singleton glanced at the transcript; Freitag seemed to be a good student, at any rate. Lowest grade in four years was a "C", and that wasn't in his major field, anyway. Science courses were all A's and B's. The attached recommendations got only the briefest of looks, because Singleton didn't believe in them. They were always uniformly enthusiastic. Why would someone ask for a recommendation from a teacher who wouldn't give him a good one, anyway? Singleton was more interested in summer employment, and that was positive: Freitag had worked at a zoo, spent a summer at Woods Hole, and had been a TA his last year at college.

Single, liked basketball (*check and see if we need a coach there*) and baseball (*could use him with the younger boys*), could fill a needed slot for a single master in Harper. The minor in journalism would make him an excellent candidate for yearbook or school newspaper advisor. *Let's see, we could put him on Dorm Council and...well, let's just see what the interview brings up. I wonder how many people realize just how many areas a prep school teacher must be competent in...*

# ALVIN CHARLES FREITAG (1952)

Al Freitag wiped his palms on his chinos again and again told himself to stop doing that. Pretty soon he'd start leaving dirty streaks down the sides. *That could make a difference,* he told himself. *Maybe they look for little things like that. I wonder how many people are trying out for this job? God, I have to pee.*

He checked his shoes again; no scuff marks. He couldn't see his tie (*maybe I shouldn't have worn the one with the school seal*), but he straightened it anyway. No lint on the blue blazer. *I hope they don't invite me to take it off and be comfortable. I think I've sweat through my shirt.* He found he was bouncing his leg again and berated himself for losing control.

Suddenly the office door opened and a head and shoulders emerged: thin individual, but fit. Balding, maybe forty-five. No gray in the brown hair that remained. Small mustache of the same color. Yellow button-down shirt, sleeves rolled up, red-and-silver striped tie, definitely didn't match the shirt. Ballpoint pen in shirt pocket.

"Al?" asked the voice that went with the face. "I'm Jack Singleton. C'mon in." Freitag jumped to his feet a bit faster than he'd intended and entered.

The office was small, cluttered and warm. Singleton waved him to a chair and was just seating himself when the phone rang. Freitag was glad of the interruption. While Singleton spoke, he had a chance to settle himself and look around. Everything bespoke too much work in too little space. There was no available space on the desk or the bookcase; in fact, file folders had been stacked on the floor in small, neat piles. On top of each was a small scrap of legal paper with a cryptic code: SPAN, ENG, MATH, BIO, ART. Freitag realized with a start that these were teacher candidate files. *How many in the bio stack?* he wondered. *Have I even got a chance at this job? God, I'm too young. There must be lots of better-qualified, more experienced teachers who would kill for a job here.*

On top of the file cabinet, a small electric fan tried ineffectually to stir enough air to give an illusion, at least, that it was doing something to cool the room. A curtain encouraged it by stirring gently from time to time.

Jack Singleton was, from long experience, an excellent interviewer. He sized up Freitag immediately: *This kid hasn't had many interviews and this is undoubtedly his first 'real' job. He doesn't realize that he's got a better-than-even chance. Of the eight applicants, three are married with families, and we've no housing for them. Two are in their sixties—maybe of limited use as coaches—and probably looking to finish their careers here. They may be burned out or less than enthusiastic. One's a woman. Well-qualified, beyond a doubt, but again, no housing, no coaching. One comes from a college. He's got a master's and is working on a Ph.D. We couldn't afford him.*

Singleton's first question was designed to put a candidate at ease: "So, Al, have you had a chance to look around?"

"Uh…no. To tell you the truth, Mr. Singleton, I got lost and I only got here about a half-hour ago. So I just waited."

Singleton nodded. "Fine. No problem. We'll take a walk when we're through here.

"Now, what would you say were your greatest strengths as a teacher?"

Although that question, too, was unexpected, Freitag found he could answer it. Actually, things went more smoothly as the interview progressed, and he found himself working up quite a bit of enthusiasm for his chosen profession. An hour had passed without his being aware of time.

The apartment Singleton showed him in Harper would have sent an experienced teacher running for cover. Basically, it was a couple of student rooms joined together, with a tiny bathroom squeezed in. There was a kitchenette of sorts; a real stove, anyway, not the two-burner hotplate in an alcove they'd shown him at Crenshaw. But it had a bedroom and a living/dining area. Freitag couldn't imagine needing or wanting any more.

Singleton talked about faculty duties and planned facilities as they toured the campus. They got a sandwich in the kitchen where the one cook on duty made lunch for the maintenance staff and whoever happened to be on campus that day. They made a five-minute stop in the Headmaster's office. Record put Freitag completely at ease. They asked Freitag to wait in the outer office for a moment before they left.

On returning to Singleton's office, the assistant head was suddenly very business-like. He spoke about salary and benefits. "We could offer you twenty-two—no, twenty-three hundred, Al." He remembered in time Record's memo about increasing salaries. "It may not sound like much, but you've got to remember that you also get housing, utilities, Blue Cross,…and, oh, yes, all you can eat." He smiled.

For the second time, Freitag was caught a bit flat-footed. He hadn't expected an offer to be made right away. Crenshaw had offered him a bit more, but it was only a junior high, and Freitag had his mind set on high school. And the apartment they'd shown him at Crenshaw had been awful, even to his mind. "Don't worry about the lack of kitchen facilities," they'd told him, "you'll be taking all of your meals in the dining room, anyway." He'd hadn't told them "no," but he didn't think much of the place.

He looked at Singleton. "Yes, thanks…I'll have to think about it." *Is that the right thing to say?*

Singleton smiled again. "Of course. I know you have other schools to consider." But he heard Record's words: "*I'll trust your judgment, Jack, but I'd go with this kid, if you like him. You say he's the best fit thus far, and we probably won't get too many more applicants this late in the year.*"

Freitag was actually halfway back to his car when he realized he'd made a mistake. Claxton looked like it was ideally suited to his needs—well, better than Crenshaw in any case. And he'd only planned to stop at one other school to look it over; he didn't even have an interview scheduled. *A bird in the hand…*

Hoping he wouldn't appear too stupid, he walked back to Jack Singleton's office.

For the first term of his first year, they'd gone easy on him: no coaching and only two preparations: two sections of freshman biology, and two sections of General Science. He'd determined—catalog listing notwithstanding—that this was where most of the scientifically disadvantaged ended up. A student needed two lab sciences for a Claxton diploma, one of which had to be Bio. Normally, a student then took Chem or Physics and was done with the requirement. But physics had too much math for some, and chemistry seemed to be beyond the reach of the weaker students. Hence, General Science. One term of "natural science," one of "laboratory science" (a watered-down chem and physics introductory thing—its main purpose seemed to be to get the kids familiar with some basic lab equipment) and then astronomy. *Thank God it's in the spring. I'll have to do a lot of reading and playing with the telescope before I can fake my way through this one.* He also had a floor in a dormitory to supervise (or the whole dorm, when he was officially on duty), a yearbook to advise and a table in the dining hall for which he was responsible every noon and four dinners a week, plus rotating breakfast and weekend coverage. Although he wasn't coaching, he might be called upon to drive a team in one of the school station wagons. Several times a term, he would pull the weekend shift, more or less responsible for everything that happened on campus. He was also in charge of entertainment for those weekends.

*I'm sure glad I have a light load this term…*

His head was still spinning from the new faculty orientation. He wondered how long it would be before he knew everyone's name, before he had the schedule memorized, before he knew all of the boys' names, before he didn't have to ask stupid questions every day. ("Is there a bathroom in this building?" "Where's the bursar's office?" "What should I do if a kid gets sick on a trip?")

He was appreciative of bits of advice from the older, more experienced faculty. "No, Al, I guess it doesn't *really* matter if they like you as a person. But if they don't, it's going to be harder to get their respect. Without respect, it's hard to communicate. Without communication, it's damn tough to teach."

"Start out a little tough. Then ease up a bit if you can. Then they'll think you're a good guy and that they're getting away with something. But you can't start out easy and then try to be strict. It doesn't work."

"If a student comes to you with a problem you can't solve or a question you can't answer, be honest and tell him so. You can't fool these kids for long. They'll respect you a lot more if you just admit you don't know and then suggest someone who might help them."

"Don't venture opinions on their music or clothes—at least not in front of them. Kids this age are very sensitive. I know most of them play that God-awful rock-and-roll stuff, but they're going to, whether we like it or not."

"Never reprimand a student in front of his peers."

"Don't eat the tuna salad."

He read the green pages in his teacher's editions very carefully. They contained hints and tips and strategies as well as suggested lesson plans for 10- and 12-week semesters, lists of projects, materials needed for labs and even a couple of sample tests. He read it all twice before he sat down and wrote out his lesson plans for the first week. He wouldn't go in unprepared.

The first day's classes would be short, following an all-school meeting. The purpose was mainly organizational, twenty-five minutes to introduce yourself, make sure the kids had the proper textbooks, give out assignments, and so forth. *Twenty-five minutes? Piece of cake.*

He had bought a couple of stenographer's notebooks, one for each subject. He could flip the pages easily to the day's lesson; very professional. He wrote out the first day's plan in some detail, noting in the margin how much time each activity would take:

Introduce self, 2 mins.;

course expectations, 8 mins.;
quizzes, tests & labs & class mngmt., 10 mins.;
stu. questions, 2 mins.;
give & explain assign., 3 mins.

Then he added "check atten." and deducted a minute from "Introduce self" and another from "course expectations" to allow for that.

On the first day of classes he waited in front of his freshly-washed board for his General Science students. The class roster said he could expect thirteen, mostly sophomores and juniors. Beyond their names, he didn't know what to expect. They arrived more or less on time (*well, some might be new and unsure of where the classroom is*) and found seats. Some carried books, some didn't. They all wore the requisite "uniform": coat-and-tie, slacks or chinos, socks, leather shoes. Most of them wore the name badges required for the first week. The theory was that after that, you'd know everyone's name. Freitag didn't think it was possible to learn to associate over two hundred names with faces in a week, especially if you had no contact with the kid.

He greeted them, announced his name and turned and wrote "Mr. Freitag" on the board. *That was stupid*, he realized as he turned back. *The damn thing's on my jacket and on their course schedules as well.* He noticed that, in spite of this, two or three students had laboriously copied his name into their brand-new notebooks, referring to the board several times during the operation. He almost added "It's German," but caught himself in time. *Maybe some of these kids lost a brother or father or uncle in the war.*

His notebook was open on the desk, and he launched into his lesson plan. It seemed to go very smoothly. When he had finished, he looked at the classroom clock. He was shocked. He'd used thirteen minutes of the twenty-five. *Now what?*

Desperation supplied an idea: "Uh…I'd like to go into a little more detail about the course. Please take out your textbooks and open to…uh…the table of contents, page…" *Why did they have to use Roman numerals?* "…uh, four. That's 'iv'."

Four textbooks surfaced. Explanations and protests were forthcoming.

"This is supposed t' be an introduction class."

"Yeah, nobody said 'bring books'."

"The bookstore ran out, sir."

"I haven't been able to get to the bookstore yet."

"Yeah, an' nobody gives homework the first night."

"How come they changed books this year? What am I supposed t' do with this one I bought off a kid last year?"

"Sir? Sir?"

A count revealed that ten of the thirteen had books and would bring them tomorrow. Freitag promised he'd check with the bookstore. And he intended to give homework every night, even if other teachers didn't.

"But what am I supposed to do with this old book I bought? Can't I use it? Will the school buy it back?"

Freitag had a thought about what the student might do with it, but suppressed it quickly.

He discovered that he was sweating slightly. "Now," he began, "you'll notice that the first chapter's called 'Scientific nomenclature'. Here's what that means..."

He had no memory of the rest of that short eternity. He couldn't even have told you what he was saying when the bell finally rang, releasing him.

*How in hell does anyone ever plan for forty-two minutes? How can you fill up that much time?*

When he returned to his cramped quarters, he carefully tore the first day's lesson plans out of the notebooks and set about revising those for the rest of the week, a total of twelve classes needing rewriting. It took him three hours.

He was on duty in the dorm that first weekend. Since the boys had been there only a week, the weekend was "closed," that is, there were no weekend permissions. The dorm would be full. Mostly, he was just supposed to keep his door ajar, though he was also expected to walk through the dorm at irregular intervals. He put some soda in the icebox and made some popcorn, just in case some kid might want to stop in and talk.

He made his first pass at 7:43 pm. He could hear loud talking and the click of a ping-pong ball from the basement. There would probably be five or six kids down there most of the evening, or at least until the last of the balls was broken. He asked one room to turn down the volume of the record player, found four students playing cards in another; one room contained one student, asleep; in another, a student quickly stuffed something under a mattress as he opened the door and pretended to be sitting idly on the edge of the bed. Freitag suspected it was a "girlie" magazine of some sort and decided not to press the issue. The other rooms were empty and dark. He supposed—hoped—that their occupants were at the movie being shown in a large classroom in Bascomb, provided that they'd gotten that cranky 16 mm projector from the gym working.

At 9:15, the basement was quiet, but some Coke bottles and candy wrappers lay around. Freitag cleaned up a bit. The card players had switched to *Clue*. The record player was quiet and the room empty, but all of the lights had been left on. Freitag switched them off. The sleeping boy's roommate had returned and was seated at his desk, reading a novel. The senior proctors had returned from wherever senior proctors go and interrupted their discussion long enough to greet him. In the next room, a boy lay stretched full-length on the floor, his head under the bed.

"Lose something?" Freitag asked conversationally.

No response.

A bit alarmed, Freitag stepped into the room. "Hey, are you OK?"

No response.

*Oh, shit.* Freitag crossed to the bed quickly, squatted and shook the boy's leg, repeating his last question. The boy neither moved nor answered.

*Omigod.* Grasping the boy's belt, Freitag hauled him out.

It was Kevin…Kevin something. Oh, right, Kevin Clarke. Freitag shook him, calling his name. No response.

*A pulse. Feel for a pulse. Is he breathing?* Freitag found a pulse—he thought, unless it was his own heart pounding, and the kid was definitely breathing. But he wouldn't wake up.

*Seizure? Diabetic coma? Heart attack?—no, that was ridiculous. Does he have a health problem I should know about?*

Freitag got up and ran for his own quarters, pausing just long enough at the proctors' door to gasp, "Kevin's sick. Watch him. I'm gonna call…"

He reached his desk and with a trembling finger, found the infirmary number on a list thumbtacked to his bulletin board and dialed the number. It rang three times.

"Infirmary. Mrs. Warren speaking."

"Yeah, Betty. This is Al Freitag. Over in Harper. Got a kid we can't wake up. He's sick or something." *God, that sounded lame.*

She advised him to see if Hal Emhart, the senior master, was in, telling him she'd be right over.

Freitag ran to Hal's apartment on the ground floor. He'd just returned with his wife. Freitag filled him in quickly and they ran back to Clarke's room where a small crowd had already gathered. The speed of a tornado was tortoise-like compared to how news spread in a closed community.

Hal bent to examine a still-comatose Clarke. At almost the same moment, Betty Warren came in wearing her nurse whites, black bag in hand. It took her only a moment.

"Mr. Emhart, Mr. Freitag, I think the students can leave now. Kevin's in no real danger."

Freitag shooed the curious out and shut the door. He looked questioningly at the nurse.

"No need to worry, Al. The kid's just dead drunk."

Freitag was a bit stunned. *Drunk? That's it, drunk? I couldn't spot that? How the hell am I going to make it here? It's only been a week, and I feel like I've been through the friggin' wringer. Is this what I can expect every week until June? I'll never last. You have to be super-human to make it in this job.*

In fact, it did get a bit easier. By mid-November, he was only spending a couple of hours a week preparing lesson plans. He never looked at the green pages again. But now, he was correcting papers or lab reports for one section or another almost every evening, or making up tests or quizzes. It seemed that there was a faculty meeting or department meeting or yearbook meeting or something of the sort almost every night of the week.

He began to look forward to classes. He'd come up with a "science trick of the week" to keep the General Science kids amused and interested: really old stuff like using air pressure to suck a hard-boiled egg into a bottle or using a piece of thread to pick up an ice cube, stuff he'd learned as a student. But it was all new to this generation. Now students were dropping in at night when he left his door open. At first, it had been his own students, to ask a question, but then other teachers' students had come, too, and not always about science. One wanted a paragraph proofread. Another wanted to know how to prove a geometric theorem; Freitag had sent him elsewhere for an answer. Once in a while a kid was even asking for advice on something that had nothing to do with school. They had stopped testing him and were accepting him.

He even had time to notice the girl working in the alumni office…

*Mr. and Mrs. Aubrey H. Wellington III*

*request the honor of your presence*

*at the wedding of their daughter*

*Tracy Elizabeth*

*to*

*Mr. Alvin Charles Freitag*

*Friday, the tenth of July, nineteen fifty-three*

*at 2 o'clock in the afternoon*

*Covenant Church*

*Upper Granby Lake, Connecticut*

*RSVP*

# BRYCE REGIS
# PIETER VAN DEVOORT (1958)

## Bryce Regis

*Are they getting anything out of this?*
*Am I getting through to any of them?*
*Do they even care?*

Bryce Regis shook his head slowly as he looked over his gradebook. He tried to refrain from asking himself the same question that seemed to pose itself every day: *What's the matter with kids today? Why are they so damned apathetic about almost everything? Maybe it's that rock and roll.*

*Still, you'd think they'd have* some *curiosity about* something.

He'd tried just about everything he could think of. True, he'd only been a teacher at Claxton for five years—his entire teaching career, come to think of it—and there must be lots of ways he hadn't thought of to get these kids motivated. But…

The department syllabus called for *The Forsyte Saga* for senior English. Regis had never been a great fan of John Galsworthy, thinking him too dry for kids at this age, but the alternative suggested by the department head was Henry James, not much better, in Regis's opinion. This was the same head who'd put generations of students to sleep with his reading list drawing heavily on Joyce, Tennyson and Blake. Regis thought his superior to be completely out of touch with today's youth and their reading preferences.

But then, Regis couldn't pin down their preferences, either. If you looked in their rooms, you could turn up copies of Captain Marvel comic books and the occasional dog-eared, heavily underlined paperback edition of *Lady Chatterly's Lover*, passed surreptitiously from boy to boy until it fell apart. It was literature of a sort, but of course they never read the whole work. Regis had lobbied for a relatively new work, *The Catcher in the Rye*, thinking its subject might well appeal to a bunch of disaffected sixth-formers, but his suggestion had been vetoed by the department head. "Bad language, bad thinking," Ned Cowles had told him. "Stick with the classics, Bryce. That's what education is all about. None of this modern nonsense. That isn't what these boys' parents are paying for. They won't get into college reading such tripe as…as that baseball book, or whatever it is."

Regis tried to make himself believe that the old ways, the curriculum, the semi-standardized tests, and so forth, were really the way to go. After all, the methods were tried-and-true, and thousands of kids had used them over the years. He looked at the stack beside his gradebook: on top of the thick tome of *The Forsyte Saga* rested Westerley's *Grammar Review for Effective Writing*, Poore's *Speed Reading and Self-Tests*, Shakespeare's *Merchant of Venice*, Barber's *Vocabulary for Success*, and Masterson's *Stylistic Elements of Essays.* Wow. And this was without counting the enthralling *Poetry of the Romantic Era* by Reynolds and Browning, which happened to be in his briefcase at the moment. Maybe it wasn't surprising that today's kids couldn't "get into" any of this stuff. Regis wondered if any of the books had a copyright date after 1920.

He began idly tapping his teeth with a pencil. *What can I do to get them involved without departing from the curriculum?* He looked at the short rank of books lining the front of his desk, a rather ragged row prevented from escaping by a brick at each end, serving as bookends.

## Pieter van Devoort

Pieter thought he'd rather read science fiction. Well, almost anything would be better than this stuff for English. It wasn't that Mr. Regis was a bad teacher, or anything like that. He could almost make you like poetry, the way he read it aloud. Almost. But nothing could save *The Forsyte Saga*, he suspected, not even if they made it into a movie. And who ever heard of anybody named 'Soames', anyway?

His father had introduced him to science fiction...well, he couldn't remember how long ago. The book was on the nightstand on his father's side of the bed. It was the cover that attracted him: the guy in the spacesuit standing on the wing of his spaceship looking up at the stars. Really neat. He'd asked his dad if he could read it, and his father had said, "Sure. Let me know what you think."

Then he couldn't get enough. His favorites were the Ace Double Novels. Today, they'd probably be classified as the junk food of literature, but the extended novella format was just right for an adolescent. He went through Asimov, Bester, Clarke—the whole alphabet. He got hooked on reading, to the point where his father had to threaten him with bodily harm, if he didn't put down the book and go outdoors "on a beautiful day like today."

Looking back, Pieter thought those had been really great days, golden days. Then Jan van Devoort had remarried, and that was the end of the family, as far as Pieter and his sister were concerned. Mildred Standish had been all honey-and-cream before the marriage, but once the ceremony was over, she lost no time in letting the children know that she would rather not have them around. Not openly, of course. But there were the accusations—completely unfounded—the twisted half-truths, the insinuations, the innuendoes of wrongdoing on Pieter's or his sister's part. It took a couple of years, but their stepmother ("You must call me mother now, because that's what I am.") finally managed to convince their father that they'd be far better off out of the house, at a boarding school somewhere. Not together, of course. If they were together, they'd be plotting against her.

So, suddenly sundered from his family, Pieter had little left except reading. His tastes in literature were quite a bit broader now, but there was a limit… The stuff they'd read in junior English was better: *Julius Caesar, Moby Dick* (well, it *was* a bit long-winded at times), Willa Cather… "The Enchanted Bluff" had really moved him, although the rest of the class didn't seem to get it.

Pieter had taken to writing short stories to fill in the void he felt. He'd tried writing once before, when he was quite a bit younger, and had at one point declared he wanted to make his living as a free-lance writer, or perhaps a novelist, until a teacher had told him that he couldn't make a living that way. He told Pieter that he could write for his own amusement, if it pleased him, but he shouldn't take the idea seriously. Pieter had stopped writing.

Now he felt the need again. He wrote a four-page story about a submarine captain faced with the choice of allowing one crew member to die in order to save the ship or trying to rescue that sailor and risking many lives. Pieter had never been on a submarine of course, but he figured he'd read enough books and seen enough movies to make it believable. He wrote stories about serving in the Roman legions, about deep-sea diving, about dog fights in fragile biplanes, about stopping a runaway locomotive. What the stories lacked in detail and character development, they made up for in action. The best of them might have been called mediocre, if one were inclined to be generous.

In his sophomore year, he'd had a roommate, Ben, who convinced him that he'd had a story published in a "men's magazine." He recounted the story in exquisite detail, then went on to read aloud another he'd written, but not submitted. Pieter listened, fascinated by the stories, but disturbed by words like "breast," "nipple" and "panties." Surely one didn't have to descend to such immoral depths to write a good story.

So Pieter composed one about a race car driver faced with an awful choice. Either he had to swerve to save his buddy and risk hitting the wall (crippled for life at the very least, if not immediately immolated in a ball of flame) or cut his buddy off and risk sending his friend spinning off the track and probably crashing, doomed to suffer one of the fates just avoided by his uncaring former friend. Pieter had been to a stock car race once, so he was pretty sure he had all of the background necessary for a real thriller.

He carefully transcribed the address from his roommate's copy of the men's magazine onto a brown manila envelope and send it forth into the literary world.

The inevitable rejection letter seemed to him to be firm but reassuring: "We regret that your story does not fit our needs at the present time…" They didn't reject it for all time, anyway. Just "at the present time." Pieter was sure the moment would come when they'd write, asking him to submit his story again. They never did, and Pieter set aside his literary ambitions for a second time.

## Bryce Regis

It had worked.

Well, at least it had *seemed* to work. They were quiet and politely attentive, at least. And he thought he'd detected real interest on the faces of some of the boys.

He'd hurried through the grammar lesson that morning, paying scant attention to past participles used adjectivally and contenting himself with a summary of today's reading from *The Forsyte Saga.* Usually, he'd ask several of his students to read aloud, just to get them involved, but he decided to forgo that trial and ignore vocabulary completely so he could start what he was already thinking of as The Great Experiment.

The book he'd chosen to read from was Tarkington's *Penrod.* Penrod was a bit younger than his charges, which meant that most of the boys should be familiar with that period of growing up, at least. Penrod didn't like school, resisted authority, but was still naïve enough to believe many of the things students would recognize as mere childhood fantasies. He hoped this would allow them to feel a bit superior to Tarkington's hero, while still interested enough to see if some of Penrod's grand schemes would really work.

The second reason he'd chosen this particular work was for the vocabulary. Tarkington wrote for a college level audience, but Regis didn't plan to stop and explain any of the words. If they were interested enough, they might look up words like "inscrutable" and "loathsome." He suspected that some of their vocabularies didn't reach much beyond the "pow" and "bang" and "rat-tat-tat" they read in those comic books.

He remembered that in his first year of teaching there had been one kid—Bosworth—who had shown a spark of interest and a bit of talent. But Bosworth was always looking for the easy way out. Maybe he could kindle another spark in one of his current charges.

## Pieter van Devoort

Pieter listened, enthralled. He couldn't remember the last time a teacher had read aloud to the class. Certainly not since first or second grade. Mr. Regis hadn't given any introduction or told them why he was doing this. Evan Worcester had raised his hand, and without waiting to be called on, had asked, "Are we responsible for this? Do we have to know this for a test?" Mr. Regis had merely looked at him for a couple of moments and then resumed reading without answering the question. The idea of reading for pleasure, it seemed to Pieter, was simply beyond the grasp of many of his classmates. Pleasure reading for many of them seemed to be the backs of record jackets and magazines featuring singers and song lyrics.

It was the second chapter that made the difference. Penrod had abandoned taking notes and instead had devoted the remaining pages of his composition book to the adventures of Harold Ramorez, a road agent and rascal of some notoriety. The description was minimal and the plot weak. Most of the narrative seemed to be given over to dialogue, unencumbered by any sort of punctuation or regard for conventional spelling, if one could believe Mr. Regis' pronunciation. And much of the dialogue, as repeated by the teacher was something on the order of "Why you blank blank blank. You are no better than a blank blank." But it was enough. Pieter's imagination filled in the missing words.

He knew he could write better than Penrod.

He returned to his room and pulled from his desk a new, spiral-bound notebook with a yellow cover, one he'd initially reserved for English, a course in which he actually took few notes. He wrote a story about a Soviet scientist who had spent his life researching where life might actually have begun on Earth. He'd even used banned books, like the Bible, to narrow the search area to a section of mountain range in Russia, coincidentally. The scientist was able to convince the Russian Air Force (details of how he did this were unimportant) to fly an Ilyushin bomber over the site. Pieter had seen the aircraft in question as a plastic model in a shop in town, and he felt that using the name added a touch of real authenticity to the story.

At any rate, the bomber was to use all of its radar, cameras and other high-tech gear to photograph the site in question. When the photos were enlarged and studied, it would turn out that they had photographed Noah's ark, entombed in ice at a mountain summit. Pieter was sure it was by far the best thing he'd ever written. He showed it to Mr. Regis.

## Bryce Regis

Well, maybe it wasn't much, as stories go. There was little development, either in plot or character, but it was original, he had to give the kid that. Besides, it was quite a bit better than anything else his other students had submitted, in class or out. And any student who wanted to do creative writing outside of class should certainly be encouraged. Regis reached for a cigarette from the pack on his desk, but he merely tapped its end on the desk, never putting it into his mouth or lighting it.

*Could we start a Writing Club or a creative writing group? Would that be a good option for kids who aren't terribly athletic but who need a creative outlet and perhaps another way to succeed? Come to think of it, maybe we could start a literary magazine, published once or twice a year. Poetry, short stories, essays...*

*Do I really need another responsibility?*

## Pieter van Devoort

It was really great, having a story published in the school paper. And Mr. Regis says he's planning to start a literary magazine, too. Well, maybe it's not like the Pulitzer Prize, or whatever award they give for writing, but it's a start.

He also says the best way to develop your style and vocabulary is to read a lot. Read everything. I guess that's why we're supposed to trudge our way through some of the junk they're giving us.

Today he read a couple of our essays in class—without giving any names, of course, but you could tell by the look on Evan's face that one of them was his. Anyway, we were then supposed to say one good thing about it and then either ask a question about something that wasn't clear or make a suggestion about another way to do something. It's kind of hard to do that without being critical, but it does help you think in a certain way. And so I think maybe I'll be looking at some of the stuff we're reading a little differently.

I think I'll like English more now.

Maybe I can do some extra reading for extra credit. Mr. Regis says he has this really good book by J.D. somebody.

# FROM THE CLAXTON HALL STUDENT HANDBOOK, 1967

## Dress Code

Claxton Hall students will present a neat and clean appearance at all times, on campus and off. At no time will boys wear clothing which has holes or is in obvious need of repair.

Athletic clothing, including footwear, is to be worn in the gymnasium and during athletic contests. It is not to be worn in the dining room or to classes, unless a special dispensation is given by the Headmaster (e.g., for pep rallies or Spirit Days).

## School Dress

School dress is to be worn during the class day, to include the classroom, and all formal meals. It always includes coat and tie. Trousers may be flannel, wool or linen, or those popularly known as "chinos". Dungarees and shorts (of any material) are not acceptable. Coats (or jackets) shall be those designed to be worn with formal outfits, i.e., sport coats or suit coats, with lapels.

Neckties shall be in good taste, neither overly wide nor in garish colors or patterns. The wearing of the school tie is encouraged, and it is suggested that each boy have at least one. Certain school functions (e.g., Chorus) may require one. The same guidelines apply to bow ties, which may be clip-on, if the wearer desires.

Shirts shall be cotton, of the type designed to be worn with a tie. Muted colors or patterns are acceptable (except on Sundays). Shirts without collars are not acceptable. Shirts must be tucked into trousers at all times.

Belts (when worn) may be leather or canvas, solid colors only. Suspenders (narrow, solid color) are also acceptable.

Matching socks shall always be worn.

Shoes shall be leather or suede, never canvas. Sandals (even leather) are not to be worn with school dress. Shoes will be shined and in good repair (no loose soles or missing heels). Two-color shoes (i.e., "saddle" shoes) are allowed, providing they are not excessively scuffed. Shoes may be laced or loafers, though "penny" loafers do not have a place at Claxton.

V-neck sweaters may be worn in appropriate weather, but always under the jacket, never in place of it. The tie must always be visible; therefore, crew-neck sweaters are unacceptable.

## Informal dress.

"Informal" dress is exactly the same as school dress, but coat and tie need not be worn. This dress is also permissible during evening study and Saturday supper and Sunday breakfast.

## Sunday and formal dress

This is the same as school dress, with the following differences: suits of a conservative color and cut are worn in place of slacks and a sports jacket. Shirts must be solid color only: either white or pastel; no patterns or "loud" colors permitted. This is the proper dress for Sunday Church services (morning worship and Vespers), Sunday dinner, Sunday Tea, and any school dances, whether at Claxton or away.

## Casual dress

Permissible after sports until dinner, Sundays except for the functions specified above and Sunday study hall, if a student studies in his dormitory. Students attending any supervised evening study may wear informal dress.

Permitted during hours of informal dress: Solid-color T-shirts, dungarees, footwear of any sort, with or without socks, "sweat" shirts, "polo" shirts, etc. No clothing may portray or advertise any products or services. As stated above, clothing must be in good repair and without holes. "Bermuda" shorts may be worn in warm weather, although students wearing them should also wear knee socks.

Violation of the dress code shall result in a warning for a first offense, and the student must immediately come into compliance with the code. A second offense shall result in a demerit, a third in disciplinary action.

# THE *HORNET* (1969)

*Editor's note: The* Hornet *was a short-lived "student" newspaper in the late '60s. In the course of writing this book, we contacted numerous alumni, in the hopes of getting some period documents: yearbooks, letters, newspaper clippings, admissions brochures, etc. We had heard of an underground publication dating from the era of student protests and general dissatisfaction with any type of expressed authority, but had always come up empty-handed until we asked a certain alumnus (who wished to remain anonymous).*

**Alumnus** *(with a chuckle): Yes, I've heard of it. As a matter of fact, you might say I was one of the founding fathers.*
**Editor:** *Could you tell us anything about the publication?*
**Al.:** *I guess it started innocently enough. The kids weren't satisfied with a lot of what they called "Mickey Mouse" rules. Of course, the official school newspaper—the* Trumpet, *it was—wouldn't print anything remotely critical of the school or its policies, so we started our own.*

*It was supposed to be funny—gentle satire. But by the second issue, the satire had turned biting and then kids started turning in articles that were really vicious personal attacks, usually against teachers they didn't like. Oh, the names were changed of course, but everyone knew who they were. At that point, I disassociated myself from the paper—I thought things were getting out of hand, and if we got caught...well, I feared for my college chances.*
**Ed.:** *So how was the newspaper produced?*
**Al.:** *Well, I guess after all these years, it doesn't matter. I won't name any names, anyway.*

*The students had quite a few school keys. I mean, faculty members would leave a key ring unattended, and the kids would swipe a key or two. Anyway, someone had a key to the kitchen. In the kitchen office there was a mimeograph machine—I think they used it to print menus. I also think some kids tried to get high sniffing the fluid. We typed the newspaper—it was usually a single sheet, sometimes two—in our rooms, onto a ditto master swiped from the office, then one or two of us would go in late at night and run off fifty or a hundred copies.*
**Ed.:** *Didn't the school try to shut you down?*

***Al.:*** *Not until after the second issue. I guess they figured the first wasn't too bad—it wasn't overly critical, anyway—and the kids had to have some way to blow off steam. But they made a concerted effort after the second. Still, there were several more issues before they caught the kids. And it was their own fault—they got overconfident and made a dumb mistake.*
***Ed.:*** *Did the newspaper serve its purpose? I mean, did any of the rules get changed?*
***Al.:*** *Not that I recall. It might have worked, if the thing hadn't turned so quickly into a gripe sheet.*
***Ed.:*** *How did it get its name?*
***Al.*** *(chuckles): Well, that I can take credit for. It was supposed to be satiric, remember. And since the official newspaper was the* Trumpet, *we called ours the* Horn. *But we wanted something with a little sting, so it was the* Hornet.
***Ed.:*** *I don't suppose you'd still have a copy around, would you?*
***Al.:*** *Well, now, I just might.*

*Ed. Note: No attempt has been made to correct spelling, grammar or errors of syntax in what follows.*

A MODERN FAIRY TALE

Once upon a time in a far away land, a king ruled over a backward kingdom. This kingdom operated under the futile system, where the king had all of the power, but his subjects had none. The kingdom had no contact with the outside world, so no body knew what was going on and King Klax didn't care. He told them what uniform to wear and how they should cut their hair, forbidden to wear it to long.

Now one of the guys went away for a vacation and he saw how things were in the outside world and he went back and told the king "Your majesty, he said, "everything is really modern and people can decide what to wear and how to cut their hair and there aren't so many really stupid rules and people are much happier."

"I don't care", said the King. "I'm not going to change anything. I like things the way they are. You are not going to decide what is best because this is the way its always been done and its not goin to change." He said.

"Then there might be a revolution," the man said. "You better watch out."
The end

MATTRESS TESTING ?

One of our on the spot reporters noticed some interesting activity in a dormitory last Thursday nite. We won t say which dorm was involved, but it wasnt Preble or Harper. Our investigative reporter was patrolling the hall about midnight when he saw a certain faculty member escorting an unknown female into his apartment. Now we all no that it is forbitten to bring girls into the dorm, but in a little wile he heard noises like mones coming out of the room and squeaking like someone was jumping up and down on a bed and he didn t know what was going on, but was just reporting the facts. Maybe they were testing the mattress, he said. Certain faculty members should remember that the walls in some of these dorms are like cardboard but thanks for the show we all enjoyed it. Ha ha.

FOR SALE: Ethics tests and exams for last 2 years See an ed. Of this paper.

Which senior proctor was giving "French lessons" in his room after lights last week?

Why isn't there any student representation on the Headmaster's council? This is supposed to be a school for the students, so we should have some say in the decisions which are being made. Not only are a lot of the decisions poor, but they really don't benefit anybody. Its ridiculous to think that standards which might have been OK when some of these teachers went to school still apply today. They don't seem to get the message that we really don't want to look like them or act like them. It just seems to me that if their going to make decisions which effect our lives that we should have some say as to what is going on. The student council is worthless, because it doesn't represent the students but the faculty won't

let anybody on who doesn't think like them. Let's get real, Claxton faculty and open your eyes to the real world.
--the Editor.

# THE GRANBY *REGISTER*

Wednesday, October 14, 1970

## Headmaster Announces Co-Education

UPPER GRANBY LAKE — Following the annual fall meeting of the Board of Trustees of Claxton Hall, Headmaster Everett Record announced that the school would begin accepting applications from qualified young women for the 1971–1972 school year.

"This is a sound decision based on several factors," Record said. "We no longer live in a male-dominated society, and we feel strongly that all students have the right to equal educational opportunities. Many of the schools which have been traditionally all-male have already made the decision to accept girls, or will shortly do so." Record said the School was not "trying to keep up with the Joneses," but rather "keep up with the times."

"It's also a sound economic decision," he continued. "There's a large pool of qualified applicants, and, in these difficult financial times, we'd be foolish to ignore it. Obviously, more students mean more revenue, and more revenue means better services, better faculty, a better education."

Asked if he expected any opposition to the move, the Head said that the Board's decision was unanimous. "But there might be some of the 'old boys' who object," he admitted. "Some may wish to remember the school as it was when they attended. And while traditions and conventions are all very well, perhaps it's time for some new ones. This can't help but make Claxton Hall a better school, from all points of view."

Prospective students may request more information from the Admissions Office, PO Box 235, Upper Granby Lake, CT, 06319.

**Shawmut & Noyes, C.P.A**
**114 Parker St.**
**Hartford, CT 06100**

October 20, 1970

Mr. Everett Record
Claxton Hall
PO Box 235
Upper Granby Lake, CT 06319

Dear Mr. Record:

Your announcement of the 14th has caused me to think back on my own experiences at Claxton. I am a member of the class of 1954 and I, like my classmates, have always considered our time there to have been of critical importance in molding our characters and shaping our destinies. It would not be going too far to say that my two years at Claxton were a turning point for me: I learned discipline, respect, and a great deal from all of my teachers. I attribute much of my success to Claxton.

However, I believe that this success was mainly due to the fact that Claxton was an all-boys school, free from many of the distractions that plague today's adolescents, but rich in male role models. I cannot believe that the addition of girls to such an institution, rich in tradition and history, could benefit it in any way. I believe that such a move would so fundamentally change the school we love and revere that it would no longer be recognizable as one of New England's premier institutions of learning. This saddens me a great deal.

Given the circumstances, I regret that I can no longer support Claxton as I have been proud to do in the past. I must therefore withdraw pledges of financial support and ask that you remove me from all future mailings.

Mr. Headmaster, I urge you and the Board to reconsider a hasty decision, one which will alter our school beyond recognition.

Respectfully yours,
*Arthur M. Holt*
Arthur M. Holt

# CAROLYN MEACHER (1971)

*(Carolyn Meacher, 18, will be a senior in Claxton Hall's first co-educational class, the class of 1972. She will be writing a year-long series of articles for the* Register, *detailing her experiences in a previously all-male school. We will follow her progress from registration this month to graduation next May, covering all aspects of prep school life. —Ed.)*

**Sept. 8th, 1971.** I am one of twenty girls who arrived on campus today. Not all of us are boarders, but we're all here for orientation. It's exciting, but kind of scary, too. Since there are 231 boys here, the odds are over 11–1, which is great for us! Most of us are seniors (PGs), but there are a few from each class, also.

There are 12 of us who will be boarders. The school has built a brand-new dormitory, Cooper House, just for us. The bottom floor is a faculty apartment for Miss Kane (more about her later), and there are three rooms on each of the other two floors. Each room is for two girls. It's like a big family, which is great, but the person who planned the dorm obviously didn't have 12 daughters, or he would have put in more bathrooms! Also the closets are a bit smaller than mine at home, but since there is also a storage room on each floor for suitcases and stuff, we can put extra things in there.

Today was just a day for all new students to move in and get acquainted, both boys and girls. We had campus tours (though most of us had already seen the campus on admissions visits) and the boys got assigned lockers in the gym, but we'll have to change in the dorm for the time being.

Because there are only twenty of us, we won't have any choices for sports this first year. In the fall, we'll be the girls' soccer team, basketball in the winter (though maybe some can ski) and softball in the spring. I'd rather do track (I was a hurdler in public high school), and maybe they'll let me, but there isn't any girl's team yet.

Tomorrow we get our class schedules and books and take language tests, so that they can put us in the correct classes (unless you already have three credits, like I do). First day of classes is Friday!

**Sept. 17th, 1971**

We are at the end of the first week of classes. The work hasn't been too difficult so far, but maybe the teachers are just taking it easy on us right now!

We have seven periods in the day, each one 45 minutes long. So Monday looks like this:

Period 1: 8:00–8:45
Period 2: 8:50–9:35
Period 3: 9:40–10:25
Period 4: 10:30–11:15
Period 5: 11:20–12:05
Lunch: 12:15– 1:00
Period 6: 1:15–2:00
Period 7: 2:05-2:50

On Tuesdays, the periods run 2, 3, 4, 5, 6, 7, 1
Wednesday is a half-day: 3, 4, 5, 6 (40 minutes each)
Thursdays: 7, 1, 2, 3, 4, 5, 6
Fridays: 4, 5, 6, 7, 1, 2, 3
Saturdays (also a half-day): 2, 1, 7 (40 minutes each)

It sounds very complicated, but you get used to it really fast. I wasn't really used to having classes on Saturday, but since we only have a half-day on Wednesday, I guess you have to get them in sometime!

Sports generally start about 3:15 on days when classes end at 2:50. Most of our games will be on Wednesdays and Saturdays, which is why those are shorter class days. We have our first soccer game against Hale next Saturday.

Claxton Hall has a formal dress code, like many prep schools. For the guys, it's easy, and they don't even think about what they have to wear: slacks, dress shirt, tie, jacket. For girls, it's much more complicated. Dresses and skirts are acceptable, of course, as long as they are no shorter than one inch above the knee. With a skirt, you can wear a blouse and blazer or sweater set. No denim. You can also wear dress slacks, a dress blouse and blazer, but if the slacks have pockets, they can only have pockets in the front, and nobody's really sure what a "dress" blouse is. Some faculty say it has to have buttons, but others are satisfied if it just looks good.

In my next article, I'll talk about how our arrival has changed things on campus and tell you about Miss Kane.

**Sept. 30, 1971**

Katie Johnson and I were elected captains of the first-ever Claxton Girls' Varsity Soccer team, but we lost our first game ever to Hale, 3–1. Well, they've been a team a lot longer than we have!

Most of the boys and the faculty seem glad to have us on campus (there are even a few romances blossoming), but a few of them are not. I heard one boy mutter "We're gonna be such a wimpy school now." And another complained, "They say we gotta clean up our !@#$ language." Another comment made me laugh: "Well, there goes the grade curve." Don't they realize that they have to live with females the rest of their lives?

The school has done a pretty good job getting ready for us, but there are some things they didn't think of or didn't have time to do. I mean, what girl really wants to go into a restroom marked "WOMEN" and see urinals on the wall?

Most of us wish that we had equivalent athletic facilities. Maybe we should have our own trainer.

I interviewed a couple of male faculty members and asked them what changes they'd seen in the school. One said it was too early to tell and didn't want to say any more. Another said it was "nice to have girls around," and a third said it presented "exciting new challenges." I think the school is gradually getting used to us.

Miss Kane is one of only two women on the faculty, and she has to work incredibly hard. She teaches Spanish, is the dorm parent, and has to coach all three seasons, because the only other woman, Mrs. Federowicz, can't coach sports. Mrs. F. teaches Algebra and Geometry.

I think we're very fortunate to have Miss Kane. She's a great listener, and you can go to her any time with a problem. But I think the school really needs to get some more women on the faculty.

**October 18, 1971**

Parents' Weekend is over and we have won our first soccer game, defeating Miss Fremont's 2–1! On Saturday morning, we took our parents around to "mini-classes" so they could meet our teachers and ask questions. I think most of them would have preferred to meet the teachers one-on-one and ask questions about us. We have a couple of days off now while the teachers write up grades and reports. I think I'm doing OK; I got a B+ on our first major English paper.

When we return to classes, the seniors will be meeting with the College Counselor to start what they call "The Process." Our teachers are already talking about SAT's. I think it's going to get a lot harder in the next few weeks!

**November 6, 1971**

The pressure is increasing. First of all, I've been "asked" to serve on the Student Government Board, because there weren't any girls there. I really didn't think I could refuse, even though Miss Kane also wants me to act as proctor in the dorm, along with Michelle Sanchez. Then I found out that each dorm and team organizes a skit for "Pep Night." Because I'm soccer captain, it's up to me to come up with an idea, but I asked Miss Kane if she could ask Michelle to do the one for the dorm.

BIG paper for Current Events: "How the War Will Shape American Foreign Policy in the Next 10 Years." How will I get that done? Physics lab report due the same day. My lab partner doesn't really do his share, so I've got most of that to do, also.

By next Tuesday, I'm supposed to have a "pretty firm" list of colleges I'm planning to apply to, and have all of the catalogs, forms, financial aid stuff, and so forth. I haven't even started that! Then there's the senior portrait sittings. What am I going to wear? No idea. To top it all off, we're supposed to hand in the first draft of our college essay on Monday. Normally I try to sleep in on Sunday, but that's not going to happen tomorrow.

Lost to Bishop's today, 6–1. Ugh. I didn't play particularly well. Our record is 2–8. Last game is next week. We won't qualify for the playoffs. I don't know if that's good or bad. Right now I really feel I can use the time.

**November 9, 1971**

They've asked me to do a piece for the school newspaper on how our arrival has changed things here. This forces me to think about it. But when I think about it, I realize that I'm maybe not the best one to answer the question. I mean, how do we know how things were before there were girls on campus? And if we don't know that, then we can't know how things have changed.

But I'll try, so here goes:

First of all, almost everyone has been pretty nice. The teachers aren't really all that different from the teachers at my old school. There are some really good ones. The big difference is that you see them a lot more often. I mean, they may be at your table at lunch or dinner or you might see them coaching or at an activity. Mostly, they seem to have more time for the students, and there's never really a problem about getting extra help.

The attitude among the students has been mostly positive, too, though I have heard some grumbling, as I said before. There are some groups of boys that don't want any girls to join them at a table and a few seem to feel that we're detracting from the athletic program, because now they can't get transportation to a game because the girls' team has to use the van. Maybe this is another form of prejudice.

Then there are the boys who are really glad to have girls in the school. I really appreciate when I have company walking into town or coming back to the dorm from the libe at 10 at night. This is a pretty safe place, but I still appreciate the gesture. There are even a couple who will hold doors open for you! And some are always asking for help, as though they think we're much smarter than they are (in some things, anyway. No boy has ever asked me for help in math!).

OK, here is my preliminary college list. Some are "reaches" and there are a couple of back-ups, but since this is going to be published, I decided to list them in alphabetical order, so I don't offend anyone:

Boston College
Bryn Mawr
Columbia
University of Connecticut
Drew
Emory University
University of Mass.
Ithaca
New Hope College
Rutgers
Syracuse
Vanderbilt

Wish me luck! Now I have to start on a college essay which is also my English assignment! Mr. Dixon says we can expect to do at least four drafts! Ugh!

Carolyn Meacher
Eng. IVA (Mr. Dixon)
College Essay no. 1
Nov. 19, 1971

LEARNING IN THE COMMUNITY

Not all learning takes place in the classroom. If we consider that learning is a life-long process, then very little of it actually does. If we're six when we begin school and twenty-one when we graduate from college, then we've spent only about fifteen years in school. Yet most of us can count of living to age seventy, or even beyond. What about the other 55 years?

What we learn outside of the classroom must therefore be as important (if not more so) than what we learn inside. Everyone we meet is therefore a potential teacher. But how many of us are prepared to accept what we do outside of school as important as what we learned in the classroom? How many times do we hear someone say "Well, I certainly learned my lesson that day!" or "Let this be a lesson to you" or "That'll teach you!" We're always learning, but we don't think of it in the same way.

This topic really made me think about how I learn and what I learn when I'm not in school. Since I'm supposed to be learning all of the time, I tried to pick an area where I'd learned the most in a community. That wasn't hard to do.

During the longer school vacations, I sometimes volunteer in a nursing home. It's a type of work that really interests me, although I don't get paid. But it's like going to school tuition-free!

Just think! The youngest resident there is at least three times as old as I am! That means he or she has lived three lifetimes! Just think what I can learn from people like that. I think to myself "Wow, this is like living history!"

Many of these people are alone. Either their other family members are dead, or they live so far away that the resident sees them only once in a while. A lot of them don't have anyone to talk to. I find it difficult to talk to them, because we don't have much in common. I can't talk to them about their youth, because I wasn't around. It's hard to talk to them about my life today, because, although some are interested, we don't have much in common. Our tastes in music and clothes are certainly different, as are our views of movies, TV, and so forth.

So how do I make this a learning experience?

I listen. Most of them will talk freely, if you just ask the right questions, like "Where did you live when you were young?" "Did you travel by train a lot?" What kind of games did you play when you were young?"

Their stories are fascinating. It just occurred to me that I should have been writing them down, because when they're gone, they're gone. "They're history," as kids say today.

I'm sure it's possible to learn in any community. But not like this. This is surely one of the best learning experiences available, and I'm going to take advantage of it, because I'll never get another chance.

***

*(For whatever reason, the following piece was never published in the* Register. *It may never have been submitted, or perhaps was suppressed by either the School or the newspaper. Since the events described are now thirty years in the past, however, it was felt that the article, in its original form, could be included in the present work. —Ed.)*

**December 4, 1971**

Well, I have a single room now. Michelle Sanchez was dismissed yesterday for smoking violations (she had been caught twice) and for other things I guess I didn't know about. I really liked her and I wonder if the school did the right thing. It's not just because it will be a bit more of a burden on me (I'm the only proctor now, so I won't get any nights "off" from checking in the rest of the dorm), but because I'm not sure she deserved it.

It's not like the school has an Honor Code or anything. I'm not sure it would work here, anyway. Kids don't always agree with the school rules and so think it's all right to break them. I'm not sure I agree with that, either. After all, the fact that you're here means that you agreed to live by their rules, doesn't it? We're all going to be living in societies that have rules we don't care for.

At the same time I'm not sure that a couple of smoking incidents should really change a person's whole life. Is Michelle going to be able to get into another school? She's going to have that "dismissed" on her record, isn't she?

I guess what makes me angry and sad at the same time is the fact that I really don't know *why* she was dismissed. No one will talk about those "other incidents" and ultimately her fate just depended on one person: the Headmaster.

On the other hand, I guess I realize this can't be like a democracy here. I mean, if we had to wait until everyone talked and decided and voted, we'd never get anything done. Can you imagine trying to decide what to have for lunch tomorrow if we had to have a school meeting? No, there has to be one person in charge. I guess it can't be easy having to make those decisions.

Well, just a couple of weeks before Christmas vacation! Then we have two weeks of glorious freedom! (Of course, Mr. Dixon has given us an assignment. I have to research Joseph Conrad. He says we shouldn't let our minds get idle. Maybe there's a movie about him I could see.)

**January 26, 1972**

Did you know that even though Conrad wrote in English, it's not his native language? He was born in Poland, but he's considered one of the great novelists. That's just incredible. I took three years of French, but I don't think I could put together two sentences without making a lot of errors. But Mr. Dixon says that Conrad has written over a dozen novels.

Speaking of writing, the final draft of my college essay is done! I'm almost finished filling out college applications, too. I'll be glad when this is behind me, but then I can look forward to all of those acceptances (or rejections). I don't think adults can really appreciate all of the stresses we have in our lives at this point.

Another girl was dismissed yesterday. She had been hiding liquor in perfume bottles which she kept on her dresser. Now there are just eighteen of us girls left. I wonder how many will still be here at the end of May.

We weren't able to put together a girls' ski team for several reasons, so fifteen of us are playing basketball. That's not really enough for two complete teams, plus subs, so we're just sort of making do. Our record to this point is 6 and 5, not too bad for our first year. I play a forward, though I should be taller to be effective at that position.

**February 15, 1972**

We had our "Winter Formal" in the gym last weekend. Claxton Hall doesn't have a Senior Prom, so this is supposed to substitute for it and include all of the school. I think this is maybe an issue that needs to be brought up at the next Student Council meeting. I think that there are some privileges that should be extended to seniors alone to make their last year in high school special and meaningful. We're supposed to be adults now (or almost) and we should have adult responsibilities as well as privileges. This is a tough issue, but it needs to be addressed.

There are some seniors who feel the same way, but too many—at least to my way of thinking—who want the privileges without the responsibilities. I guess these people aren't mature enough yet to see that you can't have one without the other. One of the problems is that the adult community doesn't always set good examples for us.

For example, this happened before I came to Claxton, so I don't know if it's true or not, but it's the best example I can find. Two years ago, as everyone remembers, they started up the military draft again because they needed more troops in Vietnam. This time, though, it was a sort of lottery, so that if your number was drawn early, it meant that you had a good chance of being drafted. Apparently, there was a young teacher here whose number was the second one drawn. The next morning, he didn't come to breakfast, and the talk was that he'd packed his car and was headed for Canada. He left a dormitory and classes uncovered and didn't even leave a note. That was about as irresponsible as you can get and certainly wouldn't serve to inspire anyone in my generation.

I guess this turned out to be more of an editorial than an article about school life, but maybe the paper will print it anyway.

**March 8, 1972**

Winter term examinations are over and we'll be leaving on spring break tomorrow. Two glorious weeks! Some kids are going to Florida, but I don't have the money, so I'll work at the nursing home and maybe get away for a weekend to go skiing in New Hampshire. College acceptances will start coming in, so the suspense and tensions are building.

The girls' basketball team made it to the first round of the tournament! We lost to Carter Prep by a score of 37–34, so we finish our first season at .500.

Two senior boys were caught breaking into the Ledgeview Country Club two nights ago. Only about ten weeks until graduation, and they threw it all away. How do they expect our generation to earn any respect when they do things like that?

Another senior boy was rejected at the only college he'd applied to, and that was Early Decision. His parents pulled him out of here and sent him somewhere else. I guess they figured that the school wasn't doing its job if it couldn't get him into the college his parents wanted him to go to. I guess they didn't ask him if that was his choice, too. Maybe they're worried that he'll get drafted if he isn't in college.

**April 4, 1972**

I guess I can relax a little bit now. I'm into college! Here's how my final college list looks:

Boston College (turned out to be my first choice) ACCEPTED!
University of Connecticut – accepted
Drew - rejected
University of Mass. –accepted
Hamilton – wait list
New Hope College - accepted
Rutgers - rejected

Syracuse – wait list
Xavier – rejected

So I will be in Boston next year! I really liked the city on my visit there, so I know I'll like BC. Can you imagine going to a Pops Concert and seeing Arthur Fiedler in person?

I know that I'll still have to keep my grades up (my letter of acceptance said my final acceptance was contingent on that) and that I still have one more set of exams to get through, but I feel that the pressure's less now and that I'll be able to complete the year OK. There were moments when I worried about that.

I guess on balance that this year has been a positive one. I've seen some changes (we seem to be more a part of the school now), but I think Claxton still has a way to go to make girls equal to boys. The opportunities aren't the same yet, and not everyone is ready to accept us.

But someday they'll have to.

# ROBERT BOSWORTH (1974)

Robert Leroy Bosworth's was one of nineteen applications the Board of Trustees considered. On the surface, his was certainly not the most impressive. One was from the current Headmaster at St. Thomas Rectory School in Rhode Island. Several were from high-placed administrators at other well-known eastern schools. A handful came from the business world, CEOs and other executives looking for a new career. Two were from high-school principals with a combined fifty-four years of leadership experience. One was from an "educational consultant" in Chicago. His credentials were impressive, but one of the Board had promised to look more closely into those before the candidate would be asked to come for an interview.

But they selected Robert Bosworth. At 39, he was the youngest of the candidates, by almost twenty years. His experience in education administration was nil, though he had taught for one year. He'd attended Lovitt Prep in Maine for one year (standard student joke: "Lovitt or leave it"). He had a BA from Pitt and an MA in business administration from Miami. But what some people might consider shortcomings were outweighed by what the Board considered to be ideal qualities: he was an alumnus, he fit the "tweedy" image they were looking for, and he had spent twelve years in advertising. He had the perfect American family: an attractive wife, Deidre (DeeDee), and eighteen year-old daughter who would be attending Mt. Holyoke next year, and a bright, active twelve year-old son, Herbie, who would certainly be an asset to Claxton Hall in a year or so. Bosworth would remake the school according to the Trustees' vision.

On July 1, 1974, his first day as Headmaster, Robert Bosworth, class of 1954, surveyed his surroundings with some little satisfaction. The weather was typical for a Connecticut summer: hot, hazy, humid. Through the office windows, he watched the grounds crew cutting grass, perspiring freely. But the pleasant hum of the air-conditioning unit in his window drowned out the angry drone of the mowers and kept the outside air at bay. The school buildings weren't air-conditioned, of course, nor were the dormitories. But it certainly wouldn't do to have prospective students, families here for an interview, alumni or visiting Trustees sit around in an uncomfortable building.

Packaging: that's what he'd learned in his years in advertising. In order to market a product, it had to be packaged well, had to be attractively presented to prospective consumers. Impression was everything, substance counted for less. His predecessor had let the place run down; it was frayed at the cuffs and seams, looking generally seedy. It reeked of "deferred maintenance." There had been no new buildings in twenty years. *What parent, seeing Claxton Hall in its present state, would want to send their child here?* he asked himself.

Packaging: Robert Bosworth was going to change that. It was for his vision that he'd been hired. As an alum, he could get money from the "old guard," those who remembered the School from its pre-coeducation days. And his relative youth would help him establish a rapport with the younger parents. The parents liked the dress code: if you made the kids look good, the parents would assume that the School was well-disciplined and well-run. They appreciated the "old" values: not a few of them had attended prep schools themselves, in conditions not terribly dissimilar from those already in place—or which he'd shortly institute—at Claxton Hall today. Pack the old values in bright new paper; that's the ticket.

Bosworth reminded himself that his predecessor hadn't been a bad Head. He'd admired Record and had respected what the man had done, bringing the school out of financial chaos and obscurity to the status of a respected institution once again. But Record had stayed too long. Upon his departure, the School had been just as fossilized as Record was. What was needed now was a plan for the future, a breadth of vision that had escaped Everett Record, at least in his later years.

Bosworth was about to change all of that.

Record had coddled the faculty too much, in Bosworth's mind. He'd raised salaries to the detriment of everything else. Focus on education. *Well, that's all very well, but parents don't see education* per se. *They see their sons and daughters going to the best colleges. That's what counted. Getting them into college. They see the buildings and grounds. They give money for winning football teams and high SAT scores.*

*Well, by God, that's what they're paying for and that's what they'll get.*

Bosworth caught himself humming the opening notes of *Hail to the Chief.* He smiled and sat at his new desk. He was ready for his first Administrative Council meeting. *My cabinet.* In front of him were a new legal tablet, two number 2 pencils sharpened to a fine point, a Dartmouth College mug filled with more pencils and a couple of ball-point pens. Except for these items and his appointment calendar, his desk was uncluttered.

He greeted them warmly as they came in. It was important to make them feel a part of the team, the driving force of the school. At the same time, they had to know that he was the CEO; they were only board members.

John Grayson, Business Manager. *He holds the purse strings of the school, and I get the feeling that he thinks he holds the reins, too. I think one of my first jobs will be to appoint an Assistant Head, just to keep Grayson in his place. At the same time, I've got to get him working with me. Alienate him, and I won't get anything done until I replace him.*

Celia Roberson, Dean of Academics. *I suppose I have to have a token woman. This* is *a co-ed school, after all. Equal rights and all that. I hear she's sharp as a tack, and a holdover from Record's time. She'll have her own agenda. I'll have to make her a believer, but let her think the ideas are her own.*

Al Freitag, Director of Admissions. *Going to have to increase his staff. We've got to get more money into this school, and more students will help. It may crowd us a bit, but that can't be helped. Besides, it'll only be temporary. One thing we've got to do is look at the amount of money we're giving away in scholarships. We can't continue to do that. We've got to find new markets, students who can pay full fare.*

Mike Kraft, Dean of Students. *A fancy name for the discipline guy. I think he'll go along with new ideas. He's young; this is his first real job. He won't want to rock the boat. Maybe he shouldn't even be on the committee.*

Dick Pendergast, Dean of Faculty. *This could be a tough one. The old man's ready for retirement, but keeps coming back for one more year. I think he came the same year Record did. He undoubtedly thinks he's got the best interests of the faculty at heart. Maybe he did earlier, but now he's gonna have to have the best interests of the school at heart, and that's not always the same thing.*

Randall "Bucky" Carstens, Director of Development. *Stupid name. I hope he's not listed in the catalog like that. We're going to have to get along real well, Bucko. I'm gonna load you with work like you wouldn't believe, but I'm also cutting you the biggest share of the budget pie. We're going places, Bucky. The ride might be bumpy at times, but the view'll be worth it.*

He gave them a moment to get settled in the chairs, those high-backed, pseudo-leather affairs that made you sit up straight and which became increasingly uncomfortable minute by minute. Then he looked at each one in turn.

"This is not only the first day of the new fiscal year, ladies and gentlemen; it's also the first day of a new year for Claxton Hall." He talked to them for the next hour, sketching in broad strokes his vision for the school: increased enrollment, increased endowment, new buildings, new facilities, additional administrative staff to sell the school and to handle what would undoubtedly be a flood of applications. "More parent involvement, increased faculty commitment to the school. We've got to build a sense of pride. I realize we can't become an Exeter or a Hotchkiss, and maybe that's not our market. Not yet, anyway. But we've got to make a greater effort to find those markets."

They took a short break at about 10:30 for the coffee and pastries which had mysteriously appeared in Jean's office. "I'll be in touch with each of you individually as I get settled," he told them when they reassembled, mouths full. "But I know I'm going to enjoy working with all of you." He beamed at them. "You'll be a great team."

His first one-on-one meeting was with John Grayson the following day. In one sense, the Business Manager would be the key to much of what he wanted to accomplish. *Well, might as well find out right from the get-go if this guy's gonna come on board or not. If not...*

Bosworth sat across from Grayson in one of the straight-backed chairs. Face to face this time, no desk between them. Bosworth kept his tone chatty, neutral.

"So, John, I take it the Board approved the budget OK?"

Grayson nodded. "There was some of the usual *pro forma* grumbling and questions, but, yes, they accepted it."

Bosworth leaned forward, clasping his hands on his knees. "John, I know we can't alter the amount, and I wouldn't try. But some of the available funds could be... reallocated if need be, couldn't they?"

"I'm not sure I follow you, Bob," Grayson answered carefully. His tone said he didn't like this tack.

Bosworth abruptly sat back and opened his hands, palms up, a gesture of innocence. "I mean, if needed, we could take funds from one area and use them for something else. If needed."

Grayson's eyes narrowed ever so slightly. "In principle, yes. You have...a certain latitude. What did you have in mind?"

"Well..." Bosworth appeared to consider. In reality, it was already all mapped out in his mind. "Well...have the department chairs been informed of their budgets, for example?"

"Well, no. They'll mostly get about 75 percent of what they asked for, unless they were really outrageous. But we don't usually finalize the amounts and notify them until October."

"Ah. So if I needed, say…five thousand for, say, a long-range study, we could find it."

"Yes, but…"

"Thanks, John. Could you get me a copy of that budget as soon as it's convenient?"

That same afternoon, Bosworth sent for Randall Carstens.

"Randy, does the School have an architect we normally use?" *I'll be damned if I'm going to call him 'Bucky'.*

"Yes, Slater and Sons."

"Anything on the drawing board?"

Carstens looked slightly uncomfortable. "If you mean 'do we have any building projects currently under consideration,' I suppose there are always a few blueprints kicking around, mostly pipe-dreams left over…" He almost said 'from previous administrations,' but stopped himself in time.

Bosworth pretended interest. "Mmm. Randy, what would you say was our greatest need, facility-wise?"

Carstens blew out his cheeks. "Wow. Take your pick, I guess. Dorms, more classroom space…"

"Yeah, but what do families *see* when they visit?"

Carstens made a face as though he'd eaten something sour. "The gym. It's one of the oldest buildings on campus, too small for spectators, locker rooms stink—literally—no pool. I know that turns a lot of them off."

Bosworth made a show of considering this. "Mmm. What would it cost to do a study, get an architect to draw up plans…?"

Carstens shrugged. "I'm not sure. Maybe five, ten thousand."

Bosworth nodded decisively. "Get someone on board. This is a priority."

Al Freitag was perched on the edge of Dick Pendergast's desk. The older man was searching for a pipe misplaced somewhere under several unruly stacks of papers. Ordinarily, Freitag wouldn't consult the Dean of Faculty on a matter such as this. But there wasn't much that went on around campus that Pendergast didn't know about. He didn't usually volunteer an opinion, but would speak his mind if he trusted that his views wouldn't leave the room.

"So what's his game, Dick? What do you think he's trying to do?"

Pendergast suspended his search for a moment and looked at the Director of Admissions. "I think he's looking to make his mark on Claxton as fast as possible." He shrugged. "I dunno, it's too early to tell. I think appearance is very important to him: if the campus looks good, it must be a good school."

"Have you had your own personal *tête-à-tête* with him yet?"

Pendergast nodded slowly. "Yep. And the faculty won't like it."

Freitag's eyebrows moved up. "Oh?"

Pendergast's resumed search was finally successful. He dug a battered leather pouch from the pocket of the jacket that hung over the back of his chair and began to stuff the pipe thoughtfully. Freitag noted that he got about as much tobacco on the floor and his clothes as went into the bowl of the briar. It took him another minute to locate a book of matches and set fire to the whole mess. He blew out smoke.

"He's looking to save money," Pendergast said around the pipestem.

"Aren't we all."

"I hear he's going to lay off at least one maintenance person, or put two or three on a part-time basis. Maybe eliminate a night watchman position. He's also told John that he'd like some cheaper health plan alternatives."

Freitag sighed. This was an old story, with a new chapter every fall. "So we'd pay more for less coverage?"

Pendergast nodded. "Essentially, yes."

"Who picks up the maintenance slack?"

The Dean fidgeted a bit in his chair. The older he got, the more uncomfortable the damned things were. "The student work program. That's to say that we'll need additional faculty coverage for the students. The kids don't show up, the faculty has to do the job."

Freitag shifted his position on the desk. The more work the faculty was asked to do, the worse the administrators looked to them. The administrators didn't usually pull weekend coverage, dorm duties or work squad supervision. This didn't make them popular with the teaching staff, who was generally paid less to do more. "You protested, of course."

Pendergast nodded again, spilling ash. "Of course. He said that not everyone was suited to be a teacher in a prep school environment, that it was a calling, not a job, and that we must all be prepared to make sacrifices in a time of diminished revenue and fewer students. For the good of the School."

"Son of a bitch." Freitag made a face. "The way he's headed, he's going to drive any number of good teachers right out of here." He paused, then added, "You know he's planning to put more people on my staff."

Pendergast stared morosely at his pipe, which had gone out. "Yep. He needed money to pay their salaries."

Freitag chewed his lower lip. Although an administrator, he had come up through the ranks, beginning as a science teacher before deciding to leaving the classroom—temporarily—for a stint in the admissions office. Morale was going to take a plunge among the older faculty. Well, he'd bring up that point when he had his own meeting with the new Head.

That happened two days later. Bosworth was all shirtsleeves, smiles and bustling efficiency when Freitag arrived. There were still some unpacked cardboard boxes in the corners of the Head's office, but the normally ultra-neat desk was cluttered. The majority of the items littering the surface seemed to be paint chip samples, Freitag noted. He also saw the two framed diplomas hung prominently on the wall. *Oh, brother...*

"Al!" Bosworth looked delighted to see the Director of Admissions. "Glad you could stop by."

*Did I have a choice?*

"How's the admissions picture?"

Freitag settled himself into the indicated chair. It seemed to have been placed where the sun would shine directly into his eyes. "We're at 84 percent right now," he told the Head, "but, as you know, we'll be accepting right up to opening day, sometimes even after that."

"Mmm. I'd really like to see us reach a hundred percent by, say mid-August. What's our usual acceptance-to-enrollment rate?"

Freitag wondered briefly why Bosworth didn't know that. He'd asked the same question during his interview a couple of months ago. *Does he expect our numbers have changed that much?* "About four to one," he said aloud.

Bosworth pretended to consider this, steepling his fingers and swiveling in his chair. He appeared to reach a decision. "Al, let's try to make it three, or even two, to one."

"You're suggesting...?"

"Right. Let's accept some kids we might otherwise consider borderline, some whom we might help. You know, we could make a name for ourselves that way."

Freitag tried not to show his displeasure. "Well, first off, we might get some problems we're not equipped to handle, academic or otherwise. You know that the school doesn't have a qualified counselor, and we can't ask the faculty to advise kids in areas they know nothing about. Hell, we might spend more time disciplining them or making up individual programs of study than we'd devote to our usual student. Then again, what would we do if we accepted beyond our capacity? Where would we put them?"

Bosworth waved off the objection. "Every school accepts 'beyond its capacity', Al. Besides, we could triple up in some of the larger rooms, if we had to."

"Without increasing the size of the staff?" Freitag asked cautiously.

Another wave of the hand. "Oh, I don't believe another one or two per class would strain anyone overly. Some teachers are only carrying a student load of twenty or even less."

"That's because they're teaching upper-level or AP courses. Fewer kids sign up for those."

"Well, maybe we could increase their class load. More sections."

Freitag fought to check his temper. "Bob, I know that some of them already have four preps."

Bosworth was ready to dismiss the subject. "Well, that's not our concern anyway, Al. That's a problem for the Director of Studies, isn't it? Our problem right now is admissions."

*I'm beginning to wonder if that'll be our biggest problem.*

Bosworth suddenly stopped his side-to-side rocking and became earnest "Al, what percentage of our kids are getting financial aid?"

*Another question he should know the answer to. Or is he testing me?*

"About eighty-five percent, I should think, in one form or another. In some cases, it's just a token amount, a couple of hundred, from some scholarship fund that somebody's grateful relative established fifty or sixty years ago. We've got two on full scholarship. We're about on a par with other schools of our size and endowment."

Bosworth played his *I'm-thinking-and-about-to-come-up-with-a-brilliant-idea* game again for a moment before looking at Freitag once again. "How much lost tuition does that represent each year?"

The question caught Freitag off-guard. It wasn't one anyone asked. It wasn't one he was prepared to answer.

"I…I'm not sure, Bob, I'd have to do…"

Bosworth's right hand made a circling motion in the air. "In round numbers, Al. Make a guesstimate."

"Well, gee, I don't know." Freitag felt uncomfortable. He didn't know the total of all of the scholarships Claxton offered. It varied from year to year, anyway. Some were tied to the market and the interest generated by a certain fund. "Maybe…maybe fifty, seventy-five thousand."

"That's two, maybe three teachers, Al. Enough to pay the salaries of a couple of new admissions staff for you. Enough for a down-payment on a new facility…"

Freitag started to protest. "Bob, we can't just…"

Bosworth waved him to silence. He was very good at that.

"I know, Al, of course not. No one's suggesting we cut our scholarship program. What I *am* suggesting…" He paused for dramatic effect. "…is that we tap new markets. Find kids who can pay full freight."

*Can't he say 'students'?*

Bosworth forged ahead, not given Freitag time to reply. "I know that some of our traditional markets are drying up. That's my business, Al, markets and marketing. In the late 60s, it used to be Iran. Now it's Cambodia and Japan. We're getting some from South America. But there are other markets out there, Al. Where are they?"

"I…"

But Bosworth swiveled away from him, throwing up his hands as though the problem were insoluble. Then he answered his own question. "We don't know. China? Korea?" He swung back. "But we could find out. Really market ourselves there. Bring in twenty, thirty kids who can pay full freight. Charge them extra for extra English instruction. We could make a name for ourselves there, too."

Freitag licked dry lips. "Is that what we want? To become a school catering to rich foreigners?"

Bosworth dropped his hands to his desk. "I don't know Al. Not yet. That's why I've got a guy like you on my team. Let's not rule anything out."

When Al Freitag left a couple of minutes later, his head swimming, he wasn't surprised to note that his shirt was plastered to his body with his own sweat.

Celia Roberson was dressed in a blue-and-white print blouse and a sheath-like gray skirt that almost covered her ankles. Bosworth had read her file but couldn't remember how old she was. Her face didn't give anything away: there were some tiny wrinkles, but maybe not due to age. Her hair, pulled severely back into a tight bun, had several streaks of gray; again, nothing definite there. As far as the Head could tell, she wore no make-up, unless you counted the no-nonsense, you-don't-want-to-mess-with-me look on her face. She was wiry and had no figure to speak of. Bosworth would not have been surprised to learn she climbed mountains without rope or gear of any kind and wouldn't hesitate to go one-on-one with a grizzly bear if it got in her way.

He decided to start off on a positive note. "Academic schedule pretty well set?"

She looked at him as if he'd just asked if the law of gravity were still in effect, then decided he might be serious.

"Not hardly. We haven't even finished our hiring, and admissions can't tell me how many we can expect in each class. It won't be set until the second or third week of classes, once things have shaken themselves out and the kids have decided where they want to be and the teachers have decided where they *should* be. The greatest work of fiction in the English language isn't *Huckleberry Finn* or *Ivanhoe* or *Gone with the Wind.* It's the class schedules we issue on opening day."

Bosworth thought he might have just come upon a coiled rattlesnake. He forced a smile.

"Sorry, of course not. What I meant was, do you have everything you need? Are there any problems I should be aware of or can help you with?" *That ought to smooth her ruffled feathers. God help me if I have to deal with this during my tenure.*

She seemed to soften somewhat. "Yes, Bob. I have to know if you have an agenda. We're severely strained in some departments. Because of the number of courses we offer, we need additional staffing if we're to continue as we have in the past or even look to expand in the future. We may have to, if we wish to remain competitive." She ticked off points on her fingers. "We need another Spanish teacher, or we're looking at sections of over twenty kids. Our language lab is so obsolete, the parts couldn't even be sold for scrap. History needs a film library, but there hasn't been enough money in the budget for three years. Chem facilities are woefully inadequate. We've got several teachers who are planning to retire at the end of the year, and we've got to start planning now if we're going to replace them or just let their programs die: Latin, Scripture, drama." She fixed him with an unwavering stare.

Bosworth found himself on the defensive, a position he was hardly used to. "Uh…well, Celia, it's too early to say on some of those things, of course. What I need you to do," he continued, on surer ground now, "is to make a list of those points we've just discussed. Prioritize them and I promise they'll be right at the top of the list at the next Board meeting."

She was unconvinced. She'd been in this business too long to be taken in by a Johnny-come-lately like Bosworth. *He'd make a better used-car salesman that a headmaster*, she decided. *He's got an agenda, all right, and if half the things I've heard are true, and if he carries it out, God help Claxton Hall.*

As Bosworth watched her leave at the end of their talk, his thoughts turned to some necessary housecleaning at the end of the year, or maybe earlier. *She just can't understand that the first priority of education isn't academics any more.*

In the fall of 1974, Claxton Hall opened with an enrollment of 258 students, just two more than what Al Freitag called the "break-even" point, but eighteen under capacity and thirty fewer than Robert Bosworth would have liked. There would be virtually no money for anything not already in the budget, and should heating costs rise again, or the winter be especially cold, or something break down irreparably, they would operate in the red. Gifts, especially to the Alumni Fund, had been down for the past couple of years, and there was every indication that this trend would continue.

Of the 258 students, one hundred twenty-eight were boarders and the remainder commuters. The graduating class of 1975 numbered eighty-three; there were seventy-five juniors, sixty-two sophomores and thirty-eight freshman. Sixteen students were officially listed as "international." In this third year of co-education, only thirty-one students were female. One of the three proposed girls' dorms, Cooper House, had been completed and was ready for occupancy. The other two were under construction and should be ready for the opening of school next year. It was felt that the girls would prefer living in smaller, more intimate, "family"-style dwellings. In the meantime, the Cottage, the former Headmaster's residence, had undergone renovations and was now pressed into service as a "temporary" girls' dorm, housing six students and one unmarried female faculty member. Robert Bosworth had decided that his family would reside in a slightly more upscale, trim suburban house close to—but not actually on—campus. Some of the "old boys" had grumbled a bit, believing that a Head's place was right in the center of things, but they had to recognize that space was at a premium, and that the Cottage might have been a bit small for a Head's family at this point. The fact that seven people would now occupy a space thought crowded for four had escaped their attention.

Farnsworth Infirmary had undergone some renovation also, to bring it up to state codes, and some of the classrooms in Bascomb had been painted. There was new (and, it was hoped, indestructible) furniture in the Student Union, and new carpeting in Rector Hall. However, proposed renovations in the two boys' dorms, Preble and Harper, had been deferred once again; there had been time only to give them a more-or-less thorough cleaning and repair or replace some of the bathroom fixtures.

The opening faculty get-together had been a bit more somber than in years past. Everett Record had always had the affair catered; he could afford it, and he wanted everyone, faculty *and* staff to be there. Even those who were normally out-of-sight behind the scenes were there: the kitchen staff, the secretaries, the nurses, the maintenance personnel. This year, Bosworth had the kitchen prepare and serve the meal. No lobsters. The old faculty members were careful not to grumble in his presence, but the feeling was general that the "good old days" were over and the waters ahead looked a bit choppy. For his part, Robert Bosworth had never attended one of these affairs, so he had nothing to compare it to. If he were aware that some of the decisions he had made—or was reputed to have made—did not meet with general approval, his demeanor didn't show it.

The first week of school was the usual organized chaos common to all schools of this type. True to her word, Celia Roberson adjusted forty-two schedules that first week. She even forgot to make her normal joke: that revolving doors should be installed on some of the classrooms. Non-varsity students signed up for sports and missed their first practices; nineteen medical permissions were delinquent, one boy left because of severe homesickness, two students were caught smoking, the bookstore came up one hundred and twelve books short, an ancient copier expired and the dining room served cheese in some form six times (macaroni and cheese, stale grilled cheese sandwiches, cheese omelets, ham and cheese, and so forth).

The fall trustees' meeting went very well. Bosworth made an impassioned plea for a newer, modern campus, something to take Claxton Hall into the twenty-first century, something to set it apart from other second-tier college preparatory schools and make it the first choice of more prospects. He was used to speaking persuasively before groups, especially those who controlled purse strings. The trustees—most of them—nodded and agreed. They approved a tuition increase for next year, passed a motion allowing a reallocation of certain funds, and were duly impressed with the "architect's rendering" of a proposed new gymnasium. They were served a fine catered lunch in the "parlor" of Rector Hall.

On Homecoming Day in October, Claxton Hall defeated St. Peter's 28-18. That evening, alerted faculty members broke up one student party in the woods, but missed two others. SAT prep courses were offered.

In November, one member of the graduating class was dismissed for having accumulated no fewer than thirty-two demerits. The girls' soccer team—only in its third year of existence—completed a 13-2 season as Prep School State Champions.

In December, the students took exams just before the holiday break. Not a few of the faculty thought it was a horrible time to give exams—the kids just had their minds elsewhere. Celia Roberson did some statistical work that confirmed what Dick Pendergast had heard from several teachers: the students generally did their poorest work on the first (not prepared enough) and last (just before bus departure) exams. One teacher announced she would not be returning after the Christmas break.

The mindset in January was that the first two months of the year were the toughest: kids were bored, and the weather kept them inside, where the only things they could find to do were not exactly constructive. Personally, Mike Kraft believed that this notion was brought on by everyone's saying that the winter blahs were something to be expected and survived. Being a skier, he loved the winter.

In January and February, the boys' varsity basketball team won their first seven games and lost their next eight. A promising music student made it into the All-State Band. The First Annual Community Volunteer Day was held. There would never be a second. There was a rash of thefts in one of the boys' dorms. The articles were never recovered, nor the culprit apprehended. The sun was out only nineteen days during that period, according to a local radio station. Music got louder. Hair got longer.

March brought rain, mud, championship games and more exams. One senior received an early acceptance at Princeton; another was rejected at Central Connecticut State. Two girls were discovered in bed together in Cooper House. One withdrew immediately. The other announced her intention to stay. She lasted another two days before student cruelty drove her out. One international student did not return from March break.

April brought a freak snowstorm and more college acceptances and rejections. First prize at the Science Fair was won by a freshman and his demonstration of a computer. The Claxton Hall Thespian Society presented *Our Town* at the end of the month.

May was hot. The boys' tennis team made it to the state finals. A fire in Preble Hall was traced to a student smoking in his room. Smoke damage was limited to that room. The student received a sharp reprimand and suspension for the remainder of the year. A senior girl was caught shoplifting in town. After some wrangling, the shopkeeper was persuaded not to press charges. She was suspended until graduation. On a humid May 25th, eighty-one diplomas were awarded. One senior had failed English and did not, therefore, meet graduation requirements. He would take a summer course and the diploma would be mailed to him upon receipt of a transcript indicating a passing grade. He didn't really give a damn. He was already into college.

August 2, 1976

Dear Herb,

Today you stand upon the threshold of the rest of your life. It is perhaps fitting that in this, the 200th anniversary or our country's independence, you take your own first steps towards independence. In a very few days you will become a freshman at Claxton, a place which, if you give it the chance, will nurture you and let you grow to your full potential. In a very real sense, it is the door to your future; it offers you a key to the best colleges in the country and a chance to realize the leadership qualities that are within you.

Do not think that, just because you are the headmaster's son, these doors will swing wide at your approach. On the contrary, many will expect more of you just because of who you are. You won't receive special treatment, nor extra consideration, but your goals may have to be higher. I know that you will strive to reach them.

It goes without saying that your mother and I are very proud of you. You have within you the capacity to excel in many areas. You are a better-than-average student and have a degree of intellectual curiosity which will help you in many of your courses. In addition, your athletic skills will help you to become a leader outside of the classroom, also.

Be yourself, but don't forget that you must always be a model, too. Everywhere you go, from now on, people will be watching to see what you do, because they will want to emulate you. I know that you will be worthy of that trust.

I won't give you any more advice, because I know that you want to get out on your own and make your own decisions. Do remember though, that as well as being the Headmaster, I am also your father, so feel free to come to me at any time with any problem.

Good luck, son.

As ever,
*Dad*

# EXTRACTS FROM THE CLAXTON *TRUMPET*, 1977-1978

**Vol. XII, no. 1** **October, 1977**

## Miss Spencer Interviewed

This year, the *Trumpet* will offer a series of interviews with new teachers, to discover what brought them to Claxton Hall and what they hope to accomplish here. Our first interview is with Miss Elaine Spencer, English teacher and faculty resident of Tremaine House.

**Trumpet:** Miss Spencer, what are your first impressions of Claxton Hall?

**Miss Spencer:** I really like it. Everyone's so friendly and helpful. I'm looking forward to a great year.

**T:** What will you be teaching?

**S:** I'm teaching two sections of freshman English, one section of sophomores and Freshman Honors.

**T**: Please tell our readers something about yourself.

**S:** Well, I'm twenty-one and I graduated last spring from Bowdoin. That's in Maine, you know. I'm originally from Oklahoma, but I like Connecticut a lot. I'm living in the faculty apartment in Tremaine House

**T:** What will you be doing besides teaching English?

**S:** In the fall, I'll be doing field hockey, and swimming in the winter. I don't know about the spring. Tennis, maybe.

**T:** All of the faculty members here have other duties, too. Are there other areas you'll be working in?

**S:** Oh, yes. I'll be helping out with the Decoration Committee and Spirit.

**T:** Do you have any other interests?

**S:** Yes, I love to read and I like horseback riding. I like all sports, I guess.

**T:** What's your favorite book?

**S:** Wow, there are so many. I guess I'd have to say *Tom Sawyer,* but that's a really tough call.

**T:** I hear that you want to make some changes at Tremaine House. Can you tell us about them?

**S:** Well, not changes really. But I'd like to build some dorm spirit, maybe challenge other dorms to games or contests. Be a leader on the campus. You know, that sort of thing.

**T:** Sounds exciting. What's your teaching philosophy?

**S:** I want to involve all of the students. Do more projects, make them responsible for their own education. Make them proud of what they can accomplish.

**T:** Well, Miss Spencer, it sounds like you've got a great year planned. Good luck.

**S:** Thanks. I'm really looking forward to it.

**Vol. XII, no. 2** **November, 1977**

## Trustees Announce Plans

*by Russ Worth*

At a school meeting on October 29th, Headmaster Bosworth announced that the Board of Trustees have approved a study to look into the construction of a new athletic facility. It is well known that our present gym is no longer adequate for the number of sports and students we now have, especially given the fact that there are some rumors that we may be starting wrestling next year.

The Headmaster said that no timetable for construction has been established and that a source of funds must be found before serious consideration is given to the proposal.

The *Trumpet* also learned that tuition would be increased again next year, but Headmaster Bosworth told us that "this just brings us into line with other schools our size. We need to adjust costs to meet inflation each year."

This reporter also asked about plans for an Art Center, but Mr. Bosworth said there were none at this time. "I'll let you know if anything develops," he said.

## Vietnam War Speaker Gives Interesting Talk

*by Alison Court*

On October 4th, Staff Sergeant Raymond Tardiff spoke to the students at a school assembly. He served in Vietnam from 1970 to 1973. Rather than focus on the actual war, he told us about the US presence there, and why it was necessary. He showed some very interesting slides of the Vietnamese and their villages. He said the country was poor and backward and needed our help to move into the 20th century. He wore his uniform, which was very impressive.

There had apparently been some talk about a student protest, but there was no evidence of it that this reporter could see. A question and answer period followed the lecture and slides.

Students who were interviewed after the sergeant's speech said they now had a better understanding of the situation in southeast Asia.

## Dungeons and Dragons Club Forming

*by Russell Worth*

Anyone interested in playing D & D should attend a meeting in Mr. Baine's classroom on December 9th at 5:45 p.m.. No experience is necessary.

**Vol. XII, no. 3** **December, 1977**

## Claxton Choristers to Perform

*by Melanie Hart*

The Christmas Concert will be presented by the Claxton Choristers in the church at 7:45 p.m. on December 18. The program will include some sacred music as well as old favorite Christmas songs. There will be works by Bach and Anonymous. Following the program a Carol sing-along will be held.

All are welcome to attend.

**Vol. XII, no. 4** **February, 1978**

## JV Boys Basketball News

*by Colin Miller*

This year the Boys JV Basketball team is surprising everyone, including Coach Davis. We have a lot of talent and a deep bench. Captain Jim Petrowski leads the team in points and rebounds and has consistently scored in double figures in all of our games. Other team members include Mike Potter, Herb Bosworth and Dave Wence, guards, Pete Piers, Hiro Nakamura, Colin Miller and Les Tyron, forwards, and our center Ferris Longman.

Last week the team defeated Lehigh 30-22 and Hamilton 40-29. Our record stands at 10-1 and we could easily go undefeated!

Come out and see us play! Our games are very exciting. Come cheer the team!

## Carnival Weekend a Big Success

*by Russ C. Worth*

Last weekend was the First Annual Claxton Winter Carnival. In spite of a lack of snow, most events went off as scheduled and everyone had a good time. Here are the results of the events:

Short track sledding: cancelled due to no snow
Free-throw shooting: Jim Petrowski
Costume winner: Jenny Tannenbaum
Dance contest: Herb Bosworth and Lyn Baker
Slalom (changed to bike slalom): Larry diStephano
Best Dorm Decorations: Tremaine House

Everyone enjoyed a great meal of steak and baked potatoes on Saturday night right before the dance in the gym. The dance wasn't as well attended as the organizers had hoped, but everyone there showed a lot of spirit.

**College Applications on Track**
*by Mr. Metzger, College Counselor*

This year's senior class has set its sights high. Ninety-two seniors have sent four hundred twelve applications to sixty-eight colleges and universities. One senior has submitted eighteen applications, while two have submitted only one. Two of the graduating class have indicated that they plan to take a year off and one is joining the military.

Tops on the seniors' lists are St. Lawrence, Wesleyan, St. Michael's, SUNY and UMass. Twelve seniors have applied for early decision, but none have heard at this point.

Seniors are reminded that all applications, except for those schools which have a rolling admissions program, should be complete by this time. Check with your teachers to make sure that all of your recommendations have been submitted.

When you receive an acceptance (or rejection) notice from a college, be sure to let the College Counselor know. And when you make your decision to attend a certain school, it's up to you to inform other colleges who have sent you acceptance notices that you won't be attending.

**Vol. XII, no. 6** **May, 1978**

**Headmaster Announces Capital Campaign**
*by R.C. Worth*

At his address to the parents during the Spring Weekend luncheon, Headmaster Bosworth announced that the Board of Trustees has approved plans for a capital campaign to begin in July with the new fiscal year. The school hopes to raise $6.8 million to pay for new facilities, and to upgrade those in need of attention.

Mr. Bosworth also announced that a donor has been located for a new, Tartan-surface, all-weather track. This track would be built around the football field. For the moment, the donor wishes to remain anonymous, until the school can secure the rest of the necessary funds.

"This is the start of a very energetic building campaign," the Headmaster told the parents, "one which will make Claxton Hall stand out from among its peers and will ensure top-notch facilities and a beautiful campus right into the next century."

The news was warmly received by all present.

### Thespians Present "She Stoops to Conquer"

*by Katie Rugg*

The Claxton Thespians, under the direction of Mr. Robert Carlisle, English teacher, presented Oliver Goldsmith's "She Stoops to Conquer" on May 1, 2 and 3. This is an eighteenth-century comedy with many funny mix-ups. The players were as follows:

Sir Charles Marlow.............................................Franklin Lord
His Son ........................................................ Herbert Bosworth
Richard Hardcastle .............................................Stephen Colis
George Hastings ..........................................................Ben Yari
Tony Lumpkin .................................................Harold Upshaw
Mrs. Hardcastle...................................................... Alison Court
Kate Hardcastle...............................................Regina Sommers
Constance Neville................................................ Crystal Myers
Maid.........................................................................Katie Rugg

**Vol. XII, no. 7 ........................................................ June, 1978**

### Commencement Ceremonies Celebrate Class of 1978

*by Ron Martin*

The last Saturday in May was a memorable one for the ninety members of the class of 1978, their families and friends. In all, more than four hundred and fifty were present to say farewell to the graduating class and wish them "Godspeed."

The commencement speaker's subject was "Putting Your Strengths To Work." It was humorous and inspirational. Following the awarding of prizes, the seniors approached the podium one by one to receive their diplomas and the good wishes of Headmaster Bosworth and Carl Owens, President of the Board of Trustees.

A picnic on the lawn was served following the ceremonies. After the clean-up, the underclassmen looked forward to final exams prior to departing for the summer.

Prizes awarded included: The Claxton Plaque, Lawrence McElroy; the Alumni Student-Athlete Award, Jennifer Corelli, Harvard Book Prize, Avery Cutter, Headmaster's Prize, Carolyn Masters. Have a great summer!

# PIETER VAN DEVOORT (1978)

Dedication page from Pieter van Devoort's *Moving Mountains*, Minneapolis: Red Valley Press, 1978. 265 pp.

*To Josie, my wife of eleven wonderful years, whose love, support and patience kept me going through long months of research and writing*

*And to Bryce Regis of the Claxton Hall school, for fanning a flame neither of us knew was there*

## MICHAEL KRAFT (1980)

Monday morning was always the busiest period of the week, unless the Discipline Committee was going into what Mike Kraft thought of as "extra innings." But that usually happened only in the spring, in the last few weeks before graduation, when certain students—usually seniors—simply couldn't hold it together any longer. The usual scenario was a motel party somewhere: girls, liquor, the whole bit. There were always one or two who wouldn't graduate because of that. So near and yet so far. Some would be awarded diplomas later, some had already been accepted to a college that didn't care about the high school diploma, some…

Well, this was only an ordinary Monday—at least up until this point. There were thirty-eight weekend discipline reports to be sifted through: nineteen for students who had absented themselves from some commitment, two for "disturbances" of one kind or another, four smoking offenses, one for possession of alcohol, ten for missing curfew, one for being in a dorm of the opposite sex; again, nothing really unusual.

Kraft wondered what it was like at other schools. Did Claxton's location, in a fairly affluent suburb of Hartford, contribute to the "crime rate"? Were forbidden substances easier to come by, temptations more numerous? What was it like in a rural school? Did the School's policy of a second or third chance for every student (depending on their economic situation?) encourage kids to break the rules once or twice?

He caught himself staring into space when the phone rang. He answered crisply.

"Good morning. Dean of Students. Mike Kraft speaking."

"Mike? This is Lenny, down at maintenance."

*Some kid's broken something somewhere,* Kraft thought, *or there's been more vandalism at the Union.* But he asked, "Yeah, Lenny, what's up?"

"Uh…we were cleaning out the vans. Always do it Monday morning, you know. They sorta get trashed over the weekend. Athletic trips Saturday and then other stuff Sunday: you know, bowling, movies…"

"Okay…," Kraft said slowly. He didn't like the sound of this.

"Yeah. Anyway there was some…stuff in one of the vans. I'm not sure, but I think you ought to see it."

"What sort of stuff, Lenny?"

"Well, like I say, I'm not sure. But I think it's drugs."

Kraft took a deep breath. "Okay, Lenny. Want me to come down?"

"Uh…no. Too many people. Are you busy right now?"

"No more'n usual."

"Okay, I'll be right up."

Kraft hung up the phone slowly. Drugs were always such a tricky business. Sometimes the toughest thing was determining what you were dealing with. Smoking was easy. You could smell the smoke in the room, on the kid's clothes… It was amazing how they tried to deny it, even if there were a butt still smoldering under the bed. Unfortunately, Kraft had seen enough of the stuff to be fairly sure.

Lenny was there in ten minutes, clutching a small, much-used paper sack. *Probably what he brings his lunch in*, Kraft thought. He waved the balding maintenance man to a hard wooden chair and pushed aside some of the clutter on his desk to make room for the bag. From it, Lenny produced a small, re-sealable plastic bag and one of those tiny plastic spoons you get at a fast-food place to stir your coffee. Kraft opened the bag and took a small, tentative sniff. Then he re-sealed it and looked at Lenny.

"It was in van 6," Lenny began, "stuffed down where the seat back meets the seat."

"Any ideas?" Kraft prodded.

"Six and four went to a lacrosse scrimmage Saturday. Got back too late to go on any activities that night. Six didn't go out Sunday 'cause it was low on gas."

"What about Wednesday or any other time last week?"

Lenny shook his head. "Unh-unh. Was in the shop all week for brake work. Also the inspection sticker had expired, so we didn't put it on the road."

Kraft puffed out his cheeks. "Okay, Lenny, I'll take it from here. Thanks a lot."

Lenny nodded, got up and left quietly.

Kraft massaged his temples. *It wasn't shaping up as an ordinary Monday, after all. Lacrosse. That would be Bruce and Tim. He'd check with them at lunch. In the meantime, he'd better get over to the police station and get someone to positively ID the substance. No sense in alerting the Headmaster until they knew for sure.*

He found Tim Giordino in the faculty room after lunch. Tim had been driving van 6 that day, but it was dark when they returned to campus and he didn't remember who'd been sitting in the seat behind him seat.

"But I remember that Tyler Brooks was riding shotgun, and he kept turning around to talk to the kids in that seat. I'll ask him."

By two o'clock, Mike Kraft had his answer. There had been three students in that seat: Bob Dennis, Pete Patterson, and Herb Bosworth, the headmaster's son. About the same time, he got a call from Sergeant Sayers of the Granby sheriff's office.

"'Fraid you were right, Mike. It's cocaine. Not real good stuff; it's been cut quite a bit. Got a name for me?"

"Uh…no. Not yet, anyway. Those vans are used by quite a few people, as you know. We can't be sure how long it's been there or who's used the van."

"Mmm. Yeah, that'd be tough. Well, give us a call if you need help or if you come up with any leads we can chase down."

"Will do. Thanks."

Kraft's palms were sweating as he put the receiver down. He had an awful suspicion. Dennis and Peterson were "good" kids, never really into trouble, though they'd pick up an occasional DP (discipline point) for tardiness or something minor. But Herbert Bosworth was another story.

In his sophomore year, Herb had become something of a natural leader, though not always, Kraft suspected, for the right reasons. He was captain of several JV teams during his sophomore and junior years, then class vice-president this year, his last at Claxton. More than once his name had been linked with various unsanctioned activities at the School, but nothing was ever proven. Personally, Kraft suspected young Bosworth of acting as a supplier of certain illicit goods for some of the boarding students and of being present at (if not the actual instigator of) several off-campus parties.

Some of Herb's behavior could probably be written off as youthful peccadilloes, with one or two other incidents (possible plagiarism, using his car to furnish transportation for a student leaving campus on a weekend) which were never conclusively resolved. Kraft understood, though he couldn't prove, the subtle pressures emanating from the top downwards. After all, Herb was going to Princeton next year, and we wouldn't want anything to jeopardize his chances, would we?

Kraft sighed and tried to push the thing from his mind. *Even if we accused him, Bosworth would deny everything. We can't prove anything.* In cases like these, nothing would ever happen unless some student decided to squeal or you got very, very lucky.

***

Two weeks later, he got very, very lucky.

It was another Saturday night. The last of the teams had returned and dinner was over. The students remaining on campus were preparing for weekend activities: a pizza trip, movies in the Union…or other activities, not mentioned in the catalog.

Mike Kraft was checking the gym, making sure showers and lights were turned off, doors secured. The lights were still on in the boys' locker room, and Mike was about to walk in and switch them off when he heard voices. Something made him stop and listen.

"…find that shit in the dorm, we're all screwed."

There was the sound of something, probably a shoe, being thrown against a locker.

A second voice said, "They won't find it. Who the hell's going to look in Asher's room for anything? The little ass-kissing wimp. He's scared shitless of everything. He's not gonna say anything."

Mike recognized the first voice as Todd…something. He didn't know who the second boy was.

Todd said, "Yeah, but what if they pull a dorm search or something?"

A snort of derision. "We always hear about it, at least a few minutes in advance. They haven't figured out that you can't pull a search in one dorm without the whole friggin' school knowin' about it even before they're finished."

"Asher could say somethin'," Todd insisted.

"It'd be the last thing he does. That's what Bos told him."

"Yeah, maybe. By why has he got to hide the shit in our dorm?"

The second voice sounded a bit patronizing. "Use your head, Einstein. No sneakin' around campus, no bein' where you shouldn't. Who's gonna stop a kid walkin' into a dorm with an athletic bag?"

There was a silence. Todd's voice was resigned when he spoke again. "Yeah, maybe." Another pause. "I don't see why Bos doesn't get his ass thrown outta here. He weasels outta every fuckin' thing...."

The second boy made a sound like air escaping from a suddenly punctured tire. "The faculty doesn't know their ass from a hole in the ground. A lotta kids think that they know an' they're just ignorin' to save their jobs. They don't know shit. Remember when they made that phony toke outta pencil shavings an' toilet paper an' left it on Reeves' chalktray?" They both laughed. "He went friggin' ballistic!"

There was more laughter, then the sound of two locker doors slamming. Kraft stepped back into the shadows, but the two left by the other door. They didn't turn the lights off.

*I've got to act on this now. Monday will be too late. Chances are whatever they've got hidden in Asher's room will be spread all over campus by tomorrow. I'd like to find Ethan somewhere other than his room. It can't be confrontational. He's too fragile. His parents would probably disown him, at the very least, even if he is an unwitting pawn. The very suggestion of drugs...*

His luck got a little thin then. He couldn't find Asher, not in the dorm, not in the Union. Of course, he could be in town at a movie, or visiting another student in his dorm, though the latter scenario wasn't as likely. Ethan Asher was the smallest, youngest freshman on campus. He'd been homesick from day one, not able to keep up in any sport and almost universally disliked, as far as Kraft could determine. Some kids tolerated him, but otherwise he was the target for quite a bit of abuse. Not in front of faculty, of course. Claxton Hall policy didn't allow bullying of any sort, but plenty of it went on, anyway. Kraft had often wondered what there was in the adolescent psyche that demanded that someone smaller and weaker suffer. Imagining what the kid must be going through, especially if the Head's son was hiding contraband in his room, made Kraft's blood boil. He left word with Virgil Sweeney, the master on duty in Burroughs Hall, to be vigilant, especially if there seemed to be a lot of action around Asher's room. He was intentionally vague.

At about 9:30, during his fourth pass through the Union, he saw Asher feeding coins into the Coke machine. Kraft decided he needed a candy bar from the neighboring machine.

"Hey, Ethan, how's it going?"

Asher glanced up briefly. "Okay, I guess." The soda clumped into the chute.

Kraft retrieved the candy bar which he had no intention of eating. "How about we go into my office for a chat?" He tried to keep his tone light, casual.

Asher shrugged. "Okay, if you want to." Then his serious face sobered even more. "I'm not in trouble, am I?"

"I don't think so. Are you?"

Asher looked a little surprised but didn't answer. He followed Kraft into his office and perched on the edge of the wooden chair near the desk. He didn't open his drink.

Kraft sat down in his own chair after tossing the candy bar on his desk. *How am I going to go about this? If I lead up to it gradually, the kid may freeze up. Better not give him time to think.*

He leaned toward the student in the manner of someone about to impart a secret. He looked directly into Asher's eyes. They looked worried.

"Ethan, is there something in your room you're not supposed to tell us about?"

He hadn't known quite what to expect: shock, astonishment, denial, hesitation, a long, drawn-out confession, a hint that maybe something wasn't right. But Asher went directly to tears, great wracking sobs, rivulets of water coursing down his face. Kraft found a box of tissues in a top drawer and pushed it across at Asher. He let the crying run its course, but it was a full minute before Asher, tissues wadded in his hand, could recover enough voice to speak, but his words were still punctuated with sobs.

"You're...you're going to...to kick me out, aren't...aren't you? Call m...my parents and...and tell them. Oh my God." The crying took hold again and Asher stuffed the heels of his hands into his eyes, trying to staunch the flow.

Kraft spoke very slowly and calmly. "Actually, Ethan, I was going to try to keep you out of it. But I'll need your help. Ethan, if it wasn't you, who is hiding things in your room?"

Ethan merely shook his head and tried to speak. It came out in short gasps. "He...he'll k...kill me if I tell."

"No, I promise he won't. But let's do it this way. I'll give you a name; you just nod or shake your head. Okay?"

Nod.

"Herbert Bosworth."

Asher moaned, then nodded and dropped his head onto his crossed arms on the desk. His shoulders convulsed with silent sobs. He muttered something Kraft couldn't hear, but which sounded like it might be a plea.

Kraft reached for his phone and punched a two-digit school number. It was answered on the second ring.

"Claxton Hall infirmary. Miss McCloskey speaking."

"Sue? Mike Kraft here. I have a student that needs to spend the night in the infirmary."

Susan McCloskey's voice was immediately concerned. "Anything serious? Will he need to see the doctor in the morning?"

"No, it's Ethan Asher and he's not sick. He just shouldn't be in the dorm tonight." *Sue had been in the business a long time. She wouldn't pry.*

"Bring him right over. I've got extra toothbrushes and everything he'll need. Once he's here, I'll phone his dorm and tell them he's been admitted."

"Thanks, Sue. I'll fill you in when I can." He hung up.

Asher was staring at him. His eyes still glistened. "I...I don't have to go back?"

"Nope. I'm going. Where do I look?"

"Footlocker. Under my bed. I…I don't have a key. Bos took it."

"Not to worry. I've collected quite a few keys over the years. Let's get you settled for the night."

After dropping Asher off, Kraft walked slowly back to his office. He was glad the night air had turned chilly. He needed a clear head for what would undoubtedly be a long night. On reaching his headquarters, he flopped again into his desk chair. When, after several minutes reflection, he reached for the phone again, he wondered if it might be the last call he'd make as a Claxton Hall employee. He consulted a phone list and dialed an off-campus number.

The phone was answered on the fourth ring. Kraft could hear music and conversation in the background. The woman's voice was tentative.

"Hello?"

"Mrs. Bosworth? This is Mike Kraft at the school. Is Mr. Bosworth available?"

A hesitation. Then: "Well, if it's very important…." Her voice said it damned well better be.

"Yes, I'm afraid it is."

"Just a moment." The receiver was sent gently down. Kraft waited for a minute, a minute and a half.

"Hello, Mike? What's up?"

Kraft found his mouth was suddenly dry. He licked his lips. "Bob? We've got a developing situation here I think you should know about."

Bosworth's voice was muffled for a second, as though he'd turned aside to speak to someone. Then it was clear again. "Mike, this really isn't a good time. We have dinner guests. Whatever it is, I'm sure you can handle it."

"Uh…I think…that is, Herb might be involved."

"Impossible. He's right here with us."

"Well, perhaps I should speak with both of you."

"I'm sure it'll wait till Monday, Mike. I trust your judgment. I'll back whatever decision you make. Good night."

Click.

Mike stared at the receiver. *Like hell you will. Now what am I going to do?*

He was sweating. He decided to take a walk to cool off again, to think. This wasn't going well.

One of the first things he saw, upon stepping out into the late April night once more, were the flashing blue lights from the two squad cars parked in front of Burroughs Hall.

*Oh shit.* He quickened his steps.

The door to Ethan Asher's room stood open, as did the lid of the cheap metal trunk in the center of the floor. Seated on Asher's bed were two boys, but Kraft couldn't see them; his view was blocked by the two policemen standing in front of them.

Virgil Sweeney, the dorm master, was leaning against the door frame, watching the proceedings. He turned to look at Kraft.

"Hey, Mike, thanks for the tip. It was right on." He gave Kraft a thumbs-up sign. Virgil was an ex-marine—Vietnam—and still looked like a recruiting advertisement for the Corps. He wore a regulation blond buzz-cut and a Marine T-shirt. His muscles strained at the fabric.

One of the cops—Kraft saw now that it was Sayers—moved a bit and Kraft got a better look at the boys on the bed. They weren't Claxton students. *Town kids maybe?*

Sweeney talked around his gum. He often affected a semi-literate drawl when he was in a story-telling mood. In reality, Kraft thought he'd heard Sweeney was a member of Mensa. "These two jokers show up about ten. My door's open, an' I see 'em, but they're too busy workin' the combination on Asher's door to notice me. Now, I'm wonderin' just how two townies know Asher's combination. I'm waitin' right outside the door when they come out, an' I just invited them t' stop by my apartment for a minute. Just t' get acquainted, y'understand. They didn't resist a whole lot."

Kraft was beginning to enjoy this. "I'll bet they didn't."

"No, well, their feet weren't really touchin' the floor, you see. Anyway, when we get to my place, I just ask them nicely to empty their pockets. Hell, they might have been stealin' Asher's stuff."

"And you found…?" Kraft prodded.

"I b'lieve the word's 'paraphernalia'. Well, anyway, they're not our kids, so I call the cops." He nodded at two frightened looking boys. "I b'lieve they're bein' most cooperative with the sergeant."

Kraft stayed until the two were led away. He suddenly felt very tired.

"Good night, Virgil."

"Night, Mike. Hey, thanks for taking care of Ethan."

"No problem."

*No problem at all. Just your typical Saturday night.*

There were Xeroxed notices all over campus very early Monday morning. Kraft read the one taped to the dining room door:

THERE WILL BE A
SPECIAL SCHOOL ASSEMBLY
MONDAY 8 A.M. IN WILSON
ATTENDANCE IS MANDATORY

For once, nobody seemed to know what was going on. Usually the kids knew before the faculty, but this time, no one had a clue.

Mike Kraft sat in the auditorium between Virgil and Al Freitag. He recognized the two men in suits as trustees. The place quieted down as soon as one of them—Kraft couldn't remember his name—stood up.

The trustee cleared his throat. "Uh…can everyone hear me?" He took the silence as an affirmative. He straightened his glasses and read from a sheet. "We regret to inform you that, during the course of the weekend, Herbert Bosworth, whom you all know, was diagnosed with a rather severe illness."

This produced a buzz. The trustee lowered the paper and let it die away.

Kraft looked at other faculty members looking at each other. *What the hell…?*

The trustee rattled the paper for attention. "Now, while this illness is not life-threatening, it is protracted, and Herbert has already left for New York for treatment. It was thought best that he begin it right away."

*I wonder what prisons they have in New York?*

"The…uh…headmaster thought it best that he and his family accompany Herbert. You can understand their concern. We don't know how long the treatment might take. Therefore…" He cleared his throat again, as though the words might be sticking there. "…therefore, it is with great regret that we accept his resignation, effective immediately."

*Well, I'll be damned. How the hell did they find out so quickly? I've never known the Board to act so fast.*

The buzzing swelled immediately into excited chatter. It was some moments before the trustee, palms upraised, could restore enough order to continue.

"Now, in the interim, Mr. Freitag has agreed to take on some of the duties and responsibilities of the Head, but I'm sure we'll all want to give him a helping hand. And now, Mr. Freitag would like to address you."

Kraft glanced at Freitag as he rose, buttoning his coat. But Kraft's mind was already seeking the answer to another question.

He stopped by Jean's office on the way to his own. The headmaster's door stood open. That office was empty.

"Jean, just curious. Do you happen to know who the headmaster was entertaining on Saturday night?"

"It's probably in his appointment book. Just a second." She found the little leather-bound book in question and quickly located the proper page. "Why, yes." She looked up at Kraft. "He had a couple of the trustees over for dinner."

# FROM THE FACULTY HANDBOOK, 1982

Weekend duties.

Each teaching faculty member can expect to perform weekend duty three to five times during the course of the year. Those faculty who coach three seasons will be on weekend duty three times, while those who do not coach may expect up to five weekends.

Weekend duties commence directly after classes on Saturday (or after breakfast, if there are no classes) and end at approximately 8 a.m. the following Monday. Even though all faculty members on duty (FMOD) do not have to be physically present in the duty office during this period, they must consider themselves "on call", and should be easily reachable by telephone and never more than five minutes away from campus, unless on another assignment.

A FMOD must be prepared to carry out any task necessary to make sure the weekend runs smoothly.

Specific duties.

1. The telephone in the Duty Office must never be left unattended. It is turned on by the switchboard operator on Saturday and switched to the answering machine by the faculty member on duty when he/she leaves at the beginning of study hall Sunday evening. A student may not be used to answer the telephone.

The FMOD must be sure to have an accurate and up-to-date telephone list. This must include, but is not limited to:

Numbers of the pay phones on each dormitory floor

Numbers of all faculty, staff and maintenance personnel

Numbers for police, ambulance and fire services

Numbers for the infirmary, local hospitals, poison control centers and suicide hot lines.

Numbers for all schools where teams may be participating in away games

Numbers of local movie theaters

Answer the telephone using the following formula: "Claxton Hall. This is (your name), duty officer."

2. Keys. Before going on duty, the FMOD should make sure he/she has keys to all of the school vehicles remaining on campus. Coaches who return late should turn their vehicle keys into the FMOD so transportation will be available for evening activities.

3. Activities. Weekend activities (dances, movies, concerts, etc.) must always have a faculty member present. For this reason, there will always be at least four faculty members on duty on Saturday night: one to answer the telephone and deal with immediate problems, one or two to patrol the campus (see below), and one or two to transport students to off-campus activities (see below). Scheduled detentions must also be covered. One FMOD should also be available in case an emergency medical driver is needed.

Scheduled weekend activities. Scheduled off-campus activities will generally be covered by the faculty member who initiated the activity.

Other weekend activities (for example, a "food run" to a pizza restaurant or other fast-food restaurant) should be offered if the students request such, if there is transportation available, and if there is a FMOD available. Students must sign out with the FMOD, and a copy of the list must be left with the telephone FMOD.

4. Campus patrols. The entire campus should be patrolled frequently, but at irregular intervals. Patrolling faculty members are encouraged to do so in pairs, where feasible. Patrols should check all areas of campus, indoors and out. Do not assume that a building which you secured earlier is still secure. Flashlights and extra batteries are available in the office.

If students are found in violation of school rules, their names should be taken and turned into Mr. Wallins at the earliest possible opportunity.

The FMOD should also patrol the village of Upper Granby Lake, particularly those areas which students frequent, e.g., the Granby Cinema, Al-Massir's Pizzeria, etc. Vehicles may be used for this purpose, to cover a large area quickly. If no school vehicle is available, a FMOD should use his/her own.

Buildings should be checked and secured (all lights off, all doors locked) when all activities scheduled for that area are over.

5. Dormitory checks. Although at least one faculty member is assigned to each dormitory, all dormitories must be checked before the FMOD retires Saturday night, to ensure that all are covered. FMODs must remain actively on duty until at least one half-hour after check-in (i.e., normally until 11:30), though they are encouraged to remain until midnight, or later if circumstances warrant. In any case, at least one FMOD must remain in the duty office until all activities are concluded and all away trips have returned.

6. Student detail supervision. The FMOD must ensure that all jobs/details/detentions assigned to students over the weekend are carried out. Weekend jobs are important and are not merely assigned as punishment. If the student fails to show for an assigned job, the FMOD must ensure that the job is done, even if it means doing the job himself/herself. Violations are to be reported to Mr. Wallins. Attendance records should be turned into the Discipline Office before classes Monday morning.

7. Cash box. At the beginning of the weekend, a cash box will be delivered to the FMOD in the Duty Office. The money therein is to be used to make change for students who need it for the laundry center or vending machines. Sums may also be given to drivers who anticipate expenses for tolls or parking or admission. Careful records must be kept, and cash out slips

and return slips must always be used. The FMOD is urged to be very careful in keeping records, as any shortfall may have to be made up by the FMOD.

Have a nice weekend.

# MARCIE TAYLOR (1982)

The summons came at 10:30, or about half-way through one of Caesar's campaigns. It was delivered by Colin Mauer, one of the students on the Headmaster's "approved" list. Headmaster Young had one at his beck and call every period of the day, just for such cases as the present. It was considered an honor to be one of the Head's elect, especially because it meant you didn't have to do additional "community service" tasks.

Marcie knew what it was about, even before she unfolded the piece of beige notepaper that Young preferred. Her initial reaction was one of grim satisfaction. *Good, the school is going to act on this immediately. No discipline hearing, no appeal. Just dismissal.*

Colin didn't speak, but watched Marcie carefully as she scanned the note. Even if he hadn't read the note (unlikely), he would have suspected that it pertained to last night's incident—all over school by now, with several versions already circulating at breakfast time. His eyes said the young teacher was in for a rough ride.

Her stomach agreed. It produced a rush of cold acid and she caught her breath in spite of herself. The note said simply "Please report to my office immediately." Not "when you have a free period" or "when you have a moment" or "when it's convenient." No. Report. Marcie Taylor, a twenty-two year old first-year history teacher was being summoned to the principal's office. When she looked up, Colin was still standing there. She realized, with a bit of a shock, that he had been given instructions to escort her. *Did Young think she was going to try to escape? From what?*

She turned back to her class of Ancient History sophomores. It took her two tries to get the words out; her mouth had gone suddenly dry. "I have…I have to go. Do the next assignment on your sheet for tomorrow." As they shuffled out, she methodically gathered her materials and put them in her book bag, carefully aligning and clipping the homework papers before tucking them into the gradebook. She couldn't have said if she was trying to delay the meeting with Young or trying to show Colin that she couldn't be rushed. Suddenly she felt the need to control this one little facet of her life, at least. She left her bag on the desk, perhaps to reassure herself that she would be returning.

She nodded to Colin. She knew she should have walked ahead of him, or perhaps beside him, but that might have required speaking, and right now she wanted to be alone with her thoughts.

*What am I so worried about? Once I explain the facts, even a petty despot like Young has to believe them. There's no way the kid can wriggle out of this one. That's it, Young just wants to get the facts straight before he kicks the kid out. This isn't the first time he's been in trouble, I know. Young was just in a hurry when he wrote the note. After all, he did say 'please'.*

*So what am I worried about?*

They arrived, a solemn little procession of two, in Jean's office. The door to Young's office was closed. Colin took a seat in the chair next to it and picked up a novel. Marcie recognized it as one Senior Honors English was reading. There was no place for her to sit.

Jean Wiggins was middle-aged, pink and sympathetic. As she picked up the phone, her eyes, compassionate, never left Marcie's.

"Miss Taylor is here."

She set the receiver gently back into its cradle. "You may go in now."

Marcie stiffened her back and opened the door.

Young's desk faced the door. There were four straight-backed, pseudo-leather-upholstered chairs facing it. Three were occupied. Their occupants swiveled to scrutinize the new arrival. One of them was Josh Richards. Marcie presumed the older couple was his parents. *How in the world could they have gotten here so fast?* Then she remembered that they lived in New York.

Young half-rose from his seat, gesturing, "Miss Taylor, you know Mr. and Mrs. Richards?"

"No, we've never met. I *do* know Josh, however."

"But you recognize the name, of course. The Richards track is named for them and their generosity."

*Uh-oh.*

Young finally waved her to the vacant chair. She tried to slow her heart as she sat, crossed her legs and straightened her skirt.

Everything about the Richards bespoke prosperity, old money. Richards' tie was silk, as was his suit, and probably cost as much as Marcie's monthly car payment. A precise half-inch of starched white cuff protruded from the jacket sleeve. There was also a flash of what was undoubtedly a very expensive cufflink when Richards straightened an already perfect trouser crease. *The signet ring must weigh half a pound.*

Mrs. Richards, smartly dressed, wore a scowl and enough jewelry to finance a small war. She looked at Marcie as though the teacher were something she'd scraped off her shoe.

"Mr. Desmond has given me some details of the...misunderstanding," Young began, smiling benignly on the Richards, "but I certainly wish to give Josh and Miss Taylor a chance to explain." He turned to Marcie. "Now, as I understand it, you found Josh in the Cottage at about one o'clock this morning."

"That's correct. He was just leaving Sharon Hoyle's room." *I'll be damned if I let them intimidate me. I caught him and there's no way he can get out of it.*

Richards cleared his throat delicately. "Josh tells us he was never in the young woman's room."

Marcie took a deep breath. *It was obviously four against one. Well, I may be just a first year teacher and scarcely older than some of the students, but I'm damned sure going to maintain my composure and handle this thing professionally.* "I heard a noise about one, or perhaps a little later. I knew someone was walking in the hall. Normally I wouldn't have investigated—the girls are always getting up to go to the bathroom—but I heard whispering. I saw Josh in the hall, leaving Sharon's room. I asked him what he was doing, and he said he was looking for me. To return a key. I took the key and told him to get out. He left, and I called Mr. Desmond. Then I made sure the door was locked and the alarm set and went back to bed."

Young nodded slowly, then turned to the student. "Josh?"

"Sir, I was in the Cottage, just for the reasons I explained. But Miss Taylor wouldn't believe me. So I gave her the key and left."

"Perhaps you'd better start at the beginning."

Josh took a deep breath. His parents smiled encouragingly. "Well, yesterday afternoon I got out of practice late. I stayed to shoot some extra foul shots, 'cause my percentage has been off lately. Anyway, I knew I was gonna be late to dinner. I was passing in front of the Cottage, on my way to the dorm to change, when I saw this key right on the sidewalk. Well, I figured it was Miss Taylor's dorm key, 'cause it was right there, you know."

Young held up his hand for a time-out. "Miss Taylor," he asked mildly, did you...misplace your key?"

"No, Mr. Young. It's right here." She fished a heavy key ring from her skirt pocket, selected the correct one and shook it in front of her jury. The other keys jingled.

"Mmm," Young nodded at Josh. "But it was logical to assume that it was Miss Taylor's. Why didn't you give it to her?"

"Like I said, sir, I was late. I knew she'd already be in the dining room, and I had to change. But I forgot when I changed and left the key in my room and I couldn't give it to her at dinner."

Marcie had had about enough. "Mr. Young, it's well known that the students have keys to many buildings: they take them off faculty key rings they find lying on classroom desks…why, last year one of the tour guides had a duplicate made…"

The hand again. "Thank you, Miss Taylor, but we're not talking about last year. I see no reason at this point to fault Josh's explanation."

The cold bile filled her stomach again. *They're going to find him innocent,* she realized, *and it doesn't matter what I say.*

Young turned back to Josh and gave him an encouraging smile. "Why didn't you return it after dinner?"

Josh, more sure of himself now, crossed his legs in an imitation of his father, leaned back in his chair and folded his hands. His blue school blazer and new chino slacks would have impressed any college interviewer looking for someone to represent the New England prep school image. "I would have, sir, but I realized that this would make Miss Taylor look bad. I mean, if other people saw me giving a key back, why, they'd think she had been irresponsible, losing it and all, so I wanted to wait until I could see her alone. And besides, it was study hall. We're not allowed out of the dorm during study hall."

Marcie had to interrupt. "Sir…." But Young held up the stop sign again.

Josh flashed a brief smile at Young and continued. "At the same time, I knew that if I was caught with the key, well, it's a bad thing. I *really* want to be a proctor next year, and I *certainly* wouldn't want to do anything that would jeopardize that, so I realized that I should just, like, leave the key without anyone seeing me. That way, no one would be embarrassed and there'd be not need for explanations, like."

His father nodded approval. "A very mature and responsible decision, Josh. Your methods might have been…a bit unorthodox, but your heart was in the right place."

Mrs. Richards reached over and patted her son's hand. "He's always been such a good boy," she informed the Headmaster. Marcie nearly gagged.

"But you knew it was wrong to be out of the dorm," Young pointed out.

"Yes, sir. But I figured better that than have Miss Taylor get into trouble."

Marcie tried to swallow, but found it impossible. Her mouth had gone completely dry. Her tongue rasped like sandpaper in her mouth. She licked her lips and finally managed to whisper hoarsely, "How…how did you get into the dorm without setting off the alarm?"

Josh managed to look astonished, as though such a thought were occurring to him for the first time. "That's right! You must have forgotten to set it, Miss Taylor."

She shook her head. "No. I lock the door and set the alarm at 10:30. Then I double-check it before I go to bed at 11:00 or 11:30.

Josh shrugged. "Then maybe it was broken."

"Or perhaps you had arranged with Sharon to have her shut it off after I went to bed." Marcie had difficulty unclenching her teeth enough to allow her to speak clearly.

"Now, really!" These were the first words Mrs. Richards had spoken in Marcie's direction.

Martin Richards' eyes narrowed dangerously. "Miss Taylor, it seems to me that the problem at hand is not Sharon's, but your failure to ensure that the dorm was properly secured. I cannot, perhaps, condone my son's method, but I certainly approve the sentiment behind them. He was trying to save you some embarrassment, and you're accusing him with absolutely no proof!"

Marcie had gone beyond shock. She turned cold eyes upon Josh's father. "That is not true, Mr. Richards. In any case, it does not explain what Josh was doing in Sharon's room."

Young looked at the student. "Josh?" he inquired mildly.

Josh spread his hands in a gesture of innocent surprise, astonishment that he should be asked a question whose answer must already be evident to all present.

"Why, I was looking for Miss Taylor's apartment, of course, so I could be sure to leave the key outside of the right door."

"My apartment's on the ground floor," Marcie said, the steel still in her voice. "You we're on the second floor. I saw you come out of Sharon's room."

Young pounced. "Excuse me, Marcie. You didn't actually *see* Josh in Sharon's room?"

Marcie realized she had just made an error that might prove fatal to her defense. But she couldn't lie. Besides, it didn't make any difference now.

"N…no. I saw him closing Sharon's door. He was already in the hall."

"Yes, Miss Taylor." Josh explained slowly and carefully, so that even someone with a wit as deficient as that of the teacher might understand. "You see, I didn't know where your apartment was. I mean, there wasn't any name on the door, and everybody knows that we're not allowed in the girls' dorms, so I'd never been there before." He was all wide-eyed innocence as he looked around at the adults for confirmation of the truth of his words. "So when I realized that it wasn't your room, I said 'Sorry' and closed the door again. That was what you saw."

*You lying son of a bitch...*

"So...," Young summarized, "Josh gave you the key and left without any trouble?"

Marcie said nothing. *Anything you say can and will be used against you...*

The Headmaster nodded as though Marcie's silence were a satisfactory answer. He looked at Josh. "Josh, I think you can return to class now. Thanks for your help."

Joshua Richards rose, nodded to the Head, smiled sweetly at Marcie and left. The closing door made hardly a click.

"Miss Taylor, please wait in the outer office for a moment."

Marcie rose in her turn and walked woodenly to Jean's office where she waited stiffly, numbly in an uncomfortable chair. For perhaps three minutes she listened dumbly to a low murmur of voices from Young's office before the door opened and Mr. and Mrs. Richards appeared. Richards didn't look at her as they left. Mrs. Richards made a sour face at her.

Young waved goodbye and beckoned Marcie in again. She sat in the same chair and stared unblinking at her employer. She hadn't noted until now how repulsive he was. His skin had yellowish tones, making his short, gray hair—or what was left of it above his ears—look like mold growing on a grapefruit gone bad. Even his clothes repulsed her—the light blue jacket, the yellow shirt the color of jaundice and the carefully knotted bow tie. It was always a bow tie. She decided she hated bow ties.

"It's not right...," she murmured, in spite of her resolution to remain silent.

"Perhaps not from your point of view, Marcie. But you must remember that there are other considerations here. Should you decide to remain in the teaching profession," he said pointedly, in the manner of a father correcting a wayward daughter, "you will learn to temper your views with wisdom, to see the big picture."

*I'll tell you what you can do with your 'big picture,' you slug.* But aloud she said, "The door was locked, Mr. Young, and the alarm set. One of the girls must have turned it off."

"If so, then I think you'd better exert a little more discipline at the Cottage, Marcie. Perhaps you're a bit too lax. Perhaps you might consider staying up a bit later, to make sure that all of the girls are asleep. Or you might get up at some point and double-check that door again."

"Mr. Young, I only get about six hours of sleep as it is. Any less, and I won't be able to function in the classroom."

"We all work very hard here, Marcie." Young was earnest now, leaning over his hands clasped on the blotter. "We make a lot of sacrifices for the good of our students and the good of Claxton Hall. If we're not prepared to make those sacrifices, perhaps we're in the wrong profession."

Marcie did not wait to be dismissed. She rose, turned her back and left. She hesitated outside of Jean's door, wondering if she should go to the women's room and be violently sick.

*...perhaps I'm in the wrong profession. I really wanted to be a teacher. All of those education courses at Smith. The practice teaching. The summer studies. For what? I thought I was effective in the classroom. The kids—well, some of them, anyway—seemed to like me. I did the best I could in the dorm. But I can't stay awake twenty-four hours. I'm outnumbered. The girls can sleep in shifts. There could always be someone awake.*

*I can't do this. I can't be a teacher. I'm not even sure I can last the year. They'll know. By lunchtime the entire student body will know how Josh Richards made a fool out of me. The rest of the kids—they'll know they can get away with anything, as long as their parents have money.*

*I wonder what I'll be doing next year.*

## JENNA NDJAI (1990)

Jenna Ndjai was having a good day. It was the fourth in a row, and that always raised her hopes. There didn't seem to be any immediate health problems, nor any side effects from the medications. Perhaps they'd found a combination that worked. For a while anyway.

It had been rough at first. Not the illness as much as the news. The first sign had just been that awful case of the flu. Her father had finally taken her to the doctor. The doctor had given her some pills, but they didn't seem to help much. After the results of the tests had come in, the doctor had suggested that she might get better medical care somewhere else.

Her grandfather, whom she affectionately called Pépé, had offered to send her to America. Jenna wasn't sure she wanted to leave her family and wasn't convinced that the treatment she might get in a foreign country, as big and powerful and rich as it was, would be any better than she might get in her native Senegal. But he doted on her and he had insisted. After a bit, her father had reluctantly agreed, too.

"We'll find you a good school there," Pépé had promised, "and the best medical care, too. There's nothing to worry about. The American doctors can cure anything."

"But," Jenna protested, "perhaps I cannot be accepted at an American school. I mean…"

But Pépé had waved off her objections. "Nonsense. You are an excellent student and athlete. Any school would be proud to have you. And it's not as if you were *contagieuse* or anything like that. We will locate a school which has privacy and confidentiality policies. They cannot refuse to accept you because of a medical condition, Jenna. Not in America, where they have many anti-discrimination laws. I know a doctor in America, in the province of Connecticut. He is *sénégalais* and his discretion can be counted on. I would not be surprised to learn that he knows of several such schools nearby, Jenna. Now you are healthy. But should anything happen, *Docteur* Julien will be right there and will know what to do."

Jenna remained unsure, though she trusted Pépé completely. Since her mother had died, Pépé and Mémère had been even more of a family to her than her own father.

After that, things seemed to move with astonishing speed. David Ndjai wielded quite a bit of influence along with his fortune. A suitable school was found and, one by one, obstacles and objections were overcome, difficulties resolved. The school insisted that student medications be stored at the health center and dispensed by the school nurse. The nurses would know what the medications were for, of course, but they would be forbidden to discuss Jenna's condition with anyone save members of the faculty and administration who might need that knowledge.

The chosen school would prefer a personal interview, of course, but given the press of time and the distance the candidate would have to travel, this could be waived. A telephone interview could be substituted, mostly to check the level of Jenna's English. Her transcripts were certainly satisfactory and her recommendations glowing. Of course, the fact that she would not be requesting any scholarship money was also a plus, as far as the school was concerned.

Gradually, Jenna's doubts dissolved. She had been feeling better, after all, so maybe there was no real objection. Her enthusiasm began to grow. She'd been taking English classes ever since she started school, so she thought she'd have few problems there. She was even able to understand most of the dialog in the American films she'd seen. She practiced her English by sitting through the subtitled films twice. The first time, she kept her eyes closed and tried to follow the action just by the English dialog. The second time, she watched the film and read the subtitles in French and Wolof, to see how much she'd missed.

And so Jenna Ndjai came to Claxton Hall in the fall of 1990: Dakar to Paris, Paris to New York, New York to Bradley Field, located between Hartford, Connecticut and Springfield, Massachusetts. A school van was waiting to take her to Claxton when she had cleared customs.

At first the campus seemed to her to be about as big as her village in Senegal. It *did* seem like a village in itself, she thought. Except for shopping, she could not imagine any reason to leave its confines. There was a large gymnasium, a track, a swimming pool (indoors!), a library, a refectory (which everyone called the dining hall), a whole library of books, including some in French, and even a place to play table tennis and buy food when the kitchen was closed.

She had heard—but not necessarily believed—that America was rife with gangsters and prejudice. She found no evidence of the former, and little of the latter. People didn't seem to care that she was black—if they stared at her, she decided, it was because of her height: one meter ninety-three. Only here they used yards, feet and inches, so that made her "six-four" according to her roommate, who worked it out on a calculator. On her first day on campus, a woman who gave her name as Lisa Carlson introduced herself as the girls' basketball coach. Did Jenna play?

As Jenna grew used to her new surroundings, she was able to forget about her condition for hours, sometimes days at a time. There were periodic check-ups with *docteur* Julien, and her meds were adjusted periodically, but this went smoothly and attracted no attention among the students. She enjoyed all of her classes, especially English, where she wrote her first, tentative poetry in a foreign language. Ms Michaels seemed to like it and got one piece published in the school newspaper, promising to hold the longer one for the Claxton literary magazine in the spring.

She tried out for the cross country team, but, although her long legs enabled her to outrun the other girls over short distances, she found she had little endurance and tired quickly. Her coach put it off to lack of training. Then she'd caught a cold on the weekend. *Docteur* Julien wasn't available and she'd had to go to the Farnsworth Health Center. The nurse, Miss McCloskey, was nice enough, but Jenna thought she was overly concerned.

She was glad when basketball practice started. She had played a bit at home, but never seriously, mostly just chasing balls for her brother when he missed and occasionally taking a few shots for herself. The drills were very tiring, but usually short, allowing Jenna to catch her breath in between. The hardest thing was the vocabulary. She was nominally the team's center, though Ms Carlson always seemed to want her in the "low post," not "at the top of the key."

Now, after four days' of practice, Jenna felt fine and was convinced she was getting stronger. There had been a little bit of nausea when the doctor had changed the dosage of one of her medications, but that was long past.

On Wednesdays, classes ended at noon, reserving the whole afternoon for athletics. If there was no basketball game, practice was early, usually ending before three. This was one of Jenna's favorite times of the week. She'd join eight or nine other students in a Claxton 14-passenger van and they'd be driven into Hartford's inner city, where they'd spend an hour or two tutoring elementary school children.

Her first view of the school took Jenna somewhat aback. She hadn't known exactly what to expect, but it certainly wasn't a stout wire fence protecting an asphalt courtyard in poor repair from a littered street. There was a basketball hoop with no net and a swing set from which hung empty chains. The surface of the play area was a scrawl of chalk marks; Jenna thought she recognized the numbered squares children used for *la marelle.*

She'd have to ask what the name of the game was in English. The bars on the windows weren't very reassuring, either.

"You're really tall," Malcolm told her the when the teacher introduced them. "Are you a giant?" He was a serious second-grader with wide-open, intelligent brown eyes and a grave demeanor. Then, apparently deciding that the question was impolite, or perhaps having lost interest, he continued with a charming *non sequitur*, "I can't read real good. Are you going to help me?"

Jenna chuckled and tried to fold herself onto a small plastic object that purported to be a chair for an eight year-old bottom. There was no question of her trying to get her legs under the miniature desk.

"Well, I've got a secret for you, Malcolm," she began in an earnest, low voice. Malcolm leaned forward, eager to be taken into her confidence. "I'm from Africa, and I didn't speak English until I learned in school. I started to study when I was just about as old as you. I still make lots of mistakes. So I'll help you with your reading if you help me with my talking."

Malcolm nodded solemnly. "I can do that," he declared.

Jenna picked up the book lying on the desk. The drawing on the cover was charming, though the title, *Green Eggs and Ham*, mystified her. "Have you read this? Can you read it to me?"

Malcolm took the book and stared intently at the page. He planted a brown finger firmly under a word. Jenna watched his mouth work. The first few words came out all right, but then the child got stuck. Jenna pronounced the word for him. "Does your mother help you at home?"

Malcolm shook his head slowly. "Don't have a momma. She died when I was born."

Jenna started, wondered if it would be all right to hug the child, but decided against it. Instead, she took his hand.

"Oh, Malcolm. My momma died, too."

Now the child lifted his head. If it were possible, his eyes opened even wider. "Was she sick?"

Jenna opened her mouth, then realized she didn't know how best to reply. *Sick, yes, but it was a sickness she'd brought on herself, one she could have avoided. And now I'm sick, too.*

"Yes," Jenna finally admitted. She didn't elaborate.

The answer seemed to satisfy Malcolm, however. He nodded again. "Okay. So we're the same. We can help each other."

Jenna fumbled in her pocket for a tissue, sniffed, and pretended to be absorbed in the book once again.

By the beginning of January, Malcolm had made great progress. He had started to read at second grade level, though he was still a half-year behind many of his peers. When Jenna mispronounced something—which was increasingly rare as time went on—Malcolm would giggle for a moment uncontrollably, sounding like air being forced from a balloon. Then he'd made his tutor repeat the word correctly—at least to his ears—and they'd continue. Jenna always tried to set aside five minutes or so to get Malcolm to talk about his family.

He was being raised by his grandmother. He'd never known his father, who had apparently walked out just before Malcolm, the last of four children, was born. Jenna shivered when Malcolm told her how his mother had died: "She got stuck by a needle." It was all too familiar. Jenna's disease had been passed from her mother while Jenna was still in the womb. Nobody wanted to name Jenna's disease, but she knew, and she understood why her family was so insistent that it be kept as quiet as possible.

In February, Malcolm started offering Jenna a candy bar whenever she came. After some questioning and some evasive answers, Jenna discovered that Malcolm was using his lunch money to buy her little gifts. Rather than refuse the child's offerings, Jenna started giving him a quarter "for your bank." This was to be another of their little secrets.

The basketball team hadn't played particularly well against St. Stephen's, and Coach had held a rather lengthy meeting in the locker room afterward. There wasn't any shouting or anything like that, nor any blame affixed to anyone; that wasn't Ms Carlson's style. She asked each girl what she might do better and then what they had to work on as a team. Jenna liked that, because it felt as though everyone was contributing.

When the Claxton girls' basketball team left the gym, it was greeted by some fairly typical Connecticut winter weather: sleet mixing with freezing rain, with an occasional snowflake apparently visiting from some other storm. The door closed behind the team with a decisive thump just as they realized that, except for a couple of cars sporting an inch or so of winter weather, the parking lot was empty.

"Where's the bus?" Ashley Connor asked.

"Get back inside out of the cold," Lisa Carlson instructed. "Maybe it's parked around the corner. I'll go look."

"The door's locked, Ms. Carlson." Brittany tugged on it a couple more times, just to make sure."

"All right. We've got to find somewhere dry first." Lisa looked around, then pointed. "I think that's the Student Union or something. Doesn't matter. There're lights on, and that means somebody's there."

"But Ms Carlson," Tammy protested, "if the bus comes, they won't know where to find us."

Lisa debated a moment. "Okay. Wait here. I'll make a quick circuit of the building. If the bus isn't there, we'll all head to the Union, and I'll make a call."

There were murmurs of assent, but some of the girls where already jumping up and down to keep warm, and at least one was shivering. They were already quite damp, having come dressed in their uniforms and warm-ups, not figuring they'd be spending a lot of time outdoors. At most, some had light jackets.

The gym was a sizable building, the largest on campus, so it took Lisa a full six minutes to walk around it. By the time she returned, all were thoroughly wet and cold.

"No bus," she told them. "Let's get inside." The ice was beginning to cake in her hair.

Walking was difficult in the freezing slush and their feet were soon soaked. The Union was warm, at least, and there were hot drinks available, but the girls had nothing to change into. They took turns crouching near the dryers in the restroom and trying to dry themselves with paper towels. Lisa Carlson had found a pay phone and had called Claxton. It took her nearly thirty minutes to resolve the situation.

The team was huddled around a plastic table when she returned. "Driver apparently went to get the bus serviced, but had an accident coming back. Slippery roads. They're sending another. About forty-five minutes."

It was nearly two hours. After fifteen minutes Lisa had asked a St. Stephen's student to locate their Athletic Director. He'd arrived twenty minutes later, and within another thirty, blankets were brought to the Claxton team. The St. Stephen's trainer looked them over quickly, but couldn't detect any hypothermia or other ill effects. The kitchen sent a large thermos of soup.

Jenna was not feeling well.

*Docteur* Julien listened once more with his stethoscope, then nodded, apparently satisfied, but his mouth was a tight line. He motioned to Jenna that she could button her shirt and wrote something on his clipboard. Then he considered his patient again.

"Your lungs are clearing, thank God. It's not pneumonia, just a bad cold and congestion. Jenna, you must realize that more people in your condition die from pneumonia than from any other cause. We were lucky this time, but you simply can't take risks like that. Life's awfully fragile, *ma chère*."

"I know. But it wasn't my fault. There wasn't anything anyone could do."

He nodded. "I could write you a medical excuse," he suggested. "Get you excused from athletics. Then there'd be less danger."

"No." Jenna was emphatic. "I don't want any special treatment. I want my life to be as normal as possible. Besides, I really like the girls on the team."

The physician ran a hand through his graying hair and blew out a noisy breath, a sigh of resignation, perhaps. "Very well, young woman, but please don't take any unnecessary risks." Then he smiled. "Or I'll have to write *Pépère*."

Jenna slid off the table and smiled back. "Okay. I promise."

Jenna usually checked her mailbox after her ten o'clock French class because the mail was normally put out about nine thirty, and she didn't have an eleven o'clock class. She dropped the advertisement inviting her to subscribe to a magazine she didn't want into the trash and unfolded the note on yellow paper. Mrs. Austin, the school counselor, was also her advisor. The note was terse and gave no hint of why she might want to see Jenna before lunch.

The counselor had an office in Rector; Jenna made her way slowly there, turning over possibilities in her mind. She wondered briefly if *docteur* Julien had said anything about Jenna's recent visit, but dismissed that idea. The doctor was a close family friend and certainly wouldn't have gone behind Jenna's back—or her grandfather's, for that matter. Her grades were good, and she wasn't in any sort of trouble that she knew of.

The day was bright, but crisp. The brown lawns were bare, but there were hardened ridges of old snow lining the walks and streets, where the plows and shovels had pushed it. Jenna stepped over a couple of these carefully.

Mrs. Austin's office, by contrast, was warm—almost too much so. At her advisor's invitation, Jenna sat in an arm chair by the door.

"Jenna, are you still tutoring in Hartford on Wednesday afternoons?"

“Yes,” she answered slowly, wondering where this was leading. Were they going to tell her she couldn’t go any more? Were they suddenly afraid she might infect someone?

Mrs. Austin glanced at a pad on her desk and folded her hands. Jenna became aware of the soft clicking sound as the second hand on the wall clock moved.

“You were tutoring a boy named Malcolm Murden?” The question was tentative, hesitant.

The ticking of the clock suddenly seemed very loud, and Jenna felt cold, in spite of the radiator’s efforts.

“Yes,” she said carefully. Then she held her breath.

“Jenna, I’m so sorry to tell you this, but Malcolm was killed yesterday.”

“No…” The word came out in a long exhalation of disbelief.

But the teacher nodded. “I’m afraid so. It was a gang affair, apparently. A drive-by shooting. Malcolm wasn’t the target. He was just in the way. I’m so sorry, Jenna. They tried…”

Jenna wasn’t listening any more. She’d been cold that evening at St. Stephen’s, but now she was frozen all of the way through. Malcolm? Little Malcolm with his earnest face, his puppy-dog desire to please, that silly giggle… Malcolm?

She didn’t remember getting up or going to her room to stare out the window. She waited for tears that wouldn’t come. They were frozen inside, like the rest of her.

*Life is awfully fragile, and the world’s not a nice place.*

*I wonder if I’ll live to see my own graduation.*

# MIYUKI OTA (1995)

Dear Friend,

In English class today the teacher said for homeworks to write a letter to a friend telling about Claxton School.

How are you? Mostly I am good, but not always. Sometimes I am so homesick that I almost cry because I miss my family so much and it is difficult to talk to them on telephone because it is so much difference of time. Also the food is not good, but there are some things that are good. Like rice. But we do not have it every day and it does not taste well as what I have at home. I like pizza and French frys and they do not give enough fish and the veggys are not good either. Because are many Korean people here, some times they make dim-sum (I do not know if I spell right) which is kind of noodle, very spicy. I eat it once, but it was too spicy. Sometimes they have fish (OK) and a lot of chicken (BBQ) (I do not know what that means.)

I have roommate from Brasil. She is very big and strong and good in sports. The boys like her. She tries to explain some hard things to me, like Biology. Very difficult words and it takes me 1 hour and 40 minutes to read 8 pages but I also have other 4 courses, so no time to do everything. Algebra is easy, but the teacher talks very fast and makes jokes which I do not understand so all other students except Japanese and Koreans laugh, but some Koreans laugh too. Art is my funnest class and the teacher says I am good in painting. History and Culture is a class just for international students. There are too many facts to learn. How can country so young like USA have so many history? Capitals and presidents and too many states.

My Engrish teacher is Miss Cummings. She is very nice (I have to say that, because she is reading letter!) But now I am serious. She is very patient and explains goodly most of the time. But she does not always say the same as dictionary, so I do not know to believe her or book. I will tell a example. We have to find story in newspaper in library and tell same story using different words. She calls it "parafraz" (am not sure of spelling). So I tell story of car driver who wins the race and afterwards he licks himself in victory. She writes that this is not the correct word. But I found in dictionary that lap means to use the tongue to eat or clean. So who is right?

In afternoons we must have sports. They are field hockey (game with sticks and ball and coaches with whistles. It is very complicated). There is also cross-country where you run 5 or 8 or 10 km each day. That is not fun too. So I do soccer. That is fun.

In evening we have studyhall. We must be in our room and quiet and study. My roommate does not always study. Sometimes she listens to music with headphone and reads magazine. I work and work but it still is not enough time. Sometime I study after lights (I am not sure why they call it that) to get my homeworks complete. Then I go to bed.

Please to write soon. If you can send food, that is good.

Your friend,
Miyuki

# RAYMOND THOMLINSON (1995)

In the door of Ray Thomlinson's office was cut a small, rectangular opening about the size of a mail slot. On the other side was a box meant to catch whatever was pushed through. Ray Thomlinson called it the "Confessional": whatever notes students pushed through the slot would remain confidential, unless, as he told them, "somebody might get hurt."

Usually the notes were on the order of "Mr. T—I've got to see you G period. Liz M." More rarely: "I know who broke the phone in Tremaine. I don't think the whole dorm should be assessed for the damage. Ask Audrey." Even more rarely: "Mr. T: I think I got my girlfriend pregnant. Tell me when we can meet—*really* confidential. Mark C." Occasionally there'd be a joke: "Mr. T, I love you madly," signed with the forged name of a female teacher. But this one had stopped him cold. He read it three times before it began to sink in.

*I dont think I can take any more. I know my parents dont love me because they sent me to this stupid school. The kids all hate me, even my roomate. I don't think there's any thing else I can do. I am going to kill myself. Dont try to stop me.*

There was no signature, no name. To all appearances, had been printed on a laser printer on plain white paper. Just those three lines.

Ray Thomlinson had majored in psychology and graduated from UConn in 1976. He also had several summers' worth of counseling courses under his belt, but not enough for a master's yet. He'd worked at two other schools before Claxton, always looking for greener pastures. In his three years here, he'd thought he'd seen and heard it all. But the kids could still surprise him.

He sat down at his desk. No classes until C period, and this was A, the first of the day. No appointments until 9, though his door was theoretically "always open." Well, it was closed now, and, just in case the students had forgotten the rule, he'd retrieved the sign from the back of the door and Scotch-taped it to the front: IF DOOR IS CLOSED, I'M NOT HERE OR IN CONFERENCE. PLEASE DO NOT KNOCK.

*Should I take this to Thatcher? No, not yet. I don't want this to be the subject of an emergency faculty meeting. That might spook whoever wrote this, if it's genuine. I'll maintain confidentiality as long as I can.*

*OK, what do we have?* The paper was plain white bond, done on an ordinary printer. Standard font, Times or Palatino, or one of those that come with every printer and which are normally the default font. *No help there.*

*Undoubtedly done at school. The kid talks about a roommate, and not many kids have laser printers at home, and why would a kid with family and friends within easy reach send this to a counselor? No, it's definitely a boarder.*

There were laser printers in every dorm, in the computer lab and in the library. *Hell, it could have been printed at the town library. No, unlikely. Why go that far if you have all of the necessary equipment right here?*

*OK, first step: get the sign-in sheet from the computer lab for last night. Maybe it wasn't last night. Maybe the kid's been carrying it around for a week. No, paper's new and crisp; only one set of creases. Gotta start somewhere. Let's say he or she went to the lab, because someone could be hanging over your shoulder in the dorm, or waiting by the printer for a page to come out. Too risky. Not too many kids go to the lab any more; lots have their own computers. Safer in the lab: if it's crowded, you come back in fifteen minutes.*

There wasn't a class in the computer lab at this time, but Marlon Hartmann was there, attached to the wall by a static strip, poking around the innards of a computer. Thomlinson didn't think any of the words Hartmann was muttering were part of any computer language he'd ever studied. Hartmann straightened when he saw the school counselor, apparently grateful for any interruption.

"Last night?" he repeated, rubbing the back of his screwdriver hand along his jaw. "I think Mitchell was on duty. Wanna check the sign-in list?" He passed a clipboard to Thomlinson.

Thomlinson scanned the list. There were just eight names on it; but didn't see the names of any of the kids he was concerned about. *Doesn't mean anything. Maybe the kid was here, maybe not. I don't think Morgan is particularly stringent when it comes to rules. Guess he's my next stop.*

But Mitchell Morgan was in class and wouldn't be free until just before lunch. Thomlinson decided to spend the rest of the period going through the student directory.

Claxton had 378 students enrolled this year. One hundred seventy-two of those were commuters, so they could be eliminated. Thomlinson thought he could also eliminate the "popular" kids, those who wouldn't have any reason to say everyone hated them. He crossed out another twenty-two names. Only 184 to go. On inspiration, he took out a thick notebook and dug out the rooming charts for the dorms. There were six singles—no roommate. His list was pared down to a mere 178. *This won't work. I've got to go about this another way.*

The next list Thomlinson got out was the teaching schedule, which showed who taught what and when. But by then it was nine o'clock and Thomlinson was out of time.

*How much more time does that kid who wrote the note have?*

Mitch Morgan was a second-year teacher at Claxton, and the general consensus was that this one would be his last. Many teachers thought that he'd already stayed too long. Morgan was a chronic complainer, and lived just on the fringes of Claxton's rules. He applied those rules that suited him and disregarded the rest. He was tolerant of almost any sort of behavior. Thomlinson didn't expect much help from him and wasn't disappointed in this regard.

"Yeah, I was on duty in the computer room last night. Pretty quiet. I didn't even hafta go out and help some kid who'd screwed up. Just read a magazine in the office the whole time."

Thomlinson tried to be patient. "Did everyone who came in sign the sheet?"

Shrug. "I dunno. I guess so."

"You had to sign their passes when they left, didn't you?"

"Naw, I don't usually bother with that. They sign out at the dorm and in at the lab and then check in when they get back to the dorm. So what's the point?"

"The point is, Mitch," Thomlinson explained slowly, "that we could lose a kid for an hour or so that way."

"Anybody reported missing?"

"No, but…"

"Well, there ya go."

Thomlinson sighed and turned away. *Ok, we'll have to do this the hard way. Let's hope the dorm masters still have last night's sign-out sheets. Oh, and I'd better stop at the infirmary and see who was there last night. And...maybe they'll have a record of any kid who's been treated for depression...*

Thomlinson had two classes, Ethics and Introductory Psychology—a senior elective—right after lunch, so it wasn't until later that he was able to resume his search. By dinner time, he'd recovered sign-out lists from four of the seven dorms, but suspected the others had been thrown away. Those lists had a total of forty-two names, nineteen of which had signed out for the computer lab. Obviously the sign-in sheet in the lab wasn't going to help.

Besides that, some kids might sign out for extra-help, then decide to stop at the libe on the way back to the dorm, or maybe just a quick look in their mailbox…

He'd spoken in confidence to Lisa Cummings, an English teacher, but she couldn't immediately come up with a student who didn't use apostrophes in "dont", was apt to misspell "roomate" and break "anything" into two words. That left another six English teachers to check.

Normally, Ray Thomlinson was careful about assigning papers to his classes, spacing them so he didn't have two classes' worth of papers to grade at the same time. But he'd slipped up this time, giving one class an extension because of an extra-long assembly that had effectively eliminated a class. So now there were eighteen on his desk awaiting his attention, ten on "Is Cheating Ever Ethical?" and eight dealing with "Who Defines Normalcy?" He decided they'd just have to sit there. Tonight he had other things to do.

He started in Harper. Since it was study hall, the proctors should all be in. Mark Friedman was prone on his bed, a history book propped up on his pillow. Tony Giordino was at his desk, a copy of *The Stranger* held open by his left hand, while the right hand wrote in a spiral-bound notebook. About two thirds of the page was full.

"Hey, Mr. T," Mark greeted him.

Tony turned from his work. "What's up?"

"Hi, guys. Got a minute?"

"Sure." Tony waved Thomlinson toward his unoccupied bed.

Thomlinson sat and leaned against the wall. "I'm just trying to make sure we haven't let any kids slip through the cracks," he told them. "Anyone in trouble or particularly unhappy in the dorm?"

By ten, he'd covered five of the seven dorms and started his own list. There were twelve names on it. Four were kids he was already seeing. None of the names matched any of the nineteen who'd signed out for the computer room the night before.

No proctors were in Stoneham or Whitman at this hour; they were probably at the Student Union. Thomlinson had an incipient headache and didn't feel like pursuing the matter further tonight. After all, the kids needed their rest, too. But he stopped on his way home and checked The Confessional. There were no further messages.

He saw Lisa Cummings at breakfast the next morning.

"Hi, Ray. I thought I had a brilliant idea, but it didn't pan out."

Thomlinson was stirring a cup of what the kitchen served as coffee. He was convinced that someone in there thought coffee grounds had a half-life of at least a week, and could be reused during that period.

"What was that?"

She gave a sort of apologetic smile and sat down next to him. She took a sip of her steaming tea before answering.

"I gave my English I class a 'quick-write' after I spoke to you. 'Do's and Don't's for Roommates'. I dictated the title, though. Didn't want them copying spellings from the board. Thought it might turn up a match to your misspeller. There were some mistakes, but nothing consistent. Sorry."

He smiled back. "Hey, thanks for trying. It was a great idea." He returned to his coffee, but then was struck by a thought. "Wait a sec. Have you got a copy of your class list?"

She fished around in her book bag, found her gradebook, opened it to the proper page and put it on the table. He took out his own list. One name was the same. One "red-flag" kid did not have a spelling problem. One name could probably be eliminated.

"Thanks, Lisa. That's really been a big help."

She looked pleased. "Should I try it with my other classes?"

"Probably not ESL. But the others, yes, if you wouldn't mind."

"Not at all. And I'll ask some of the other teachers, too."

By the end of that evening he'd added four more names to his primary list, supplied by the proctors at Whitman and Stoneham. He went through the student directory again, just to make sure he hadn't missed anyone, and added a few more names, just to be on the safe side. Now he had eighteen possibilities. Eighteen unhappy kids. And he couldn't even be sure the one he wanted was on that list.

He repeated his mini-interviews with dorm faculty the following day, speaking to each one, in confidence, alone. He got a couple of breaks. Terry Archer had been unhappy about a situation at home—his folks had just told him they were getting a divorce—but was actually happy at school. He was a loner, true, but he and his roommate tolerated each other, even if they weren't the best of friends. Thomlinson crossed him off the list.

Martha Foxx had just broken up with her boyfriend and had spent a couple of nights just crying in her room, refusing to talk with anyone except the dorm parent. She was ordinarily a very positive girl, just going through a bit of depression right now. Her roommate had been very supportive. *One less to worry about. Sixteen to go.*

Thomlinson forced himself to shove the problem from his mind for a couple of hours as he got a belated start on the Ethics and Psychology papers. He worked well into the night, fortified by frequent cups of coffee. But the note with the suicide threat was also open on his desk. He glanced at it every now and then, waiting for inspiration.

His eyes got blurry somewhere around midnight. He reached for his cup, nearly empty and long cold, without taking his eyes from the theme. His aim was poor, of course, and he knocked it over.

He cursed, righted the cup and looked for something to mop up the small quantity of liquid that had spilled. Luckily, most of it had ended up on the desk, with only a couple of drops each on the suicide threat and Colin Fortin's ethics paper. He wiped them off with a paper towel.

The ink on the note smeared.

Thomlinson stared at the two pieces of paper for a minute, trying to figure out why this was important. He wiped both sheets again, staining Colin's work a bit more, but smearing the ink further on the note.

He reached for the phone, gritting his teeth. He knew he shouldn't call the computer center head at this time of night, but…a life might be at stake. Marlon Hartmann answered on the second ring with a crisp "Yep?"

"Marlon? Ray Thomlinson. I'm *really* sorry to call you at this hour, but…"

"Hey, Ray, no problem. I fell asleep watching an old movie on TV. Would've slept all night in that damn chair and woken up stiff as a board. Thanks. What's up?"

"I'm not sure this is important, but it might be." Thomlinson explained what had happened, then asked, "Why would those two pages be so different?"

"Easy. The kid's theme was done on a laser printer. Toner doesn't smear. The other paper—the note—was done on an inkjet. Different kind of ink, water-based. But they look just about the same."

Thomlinson thanked Hartmann and hung up. But for several moments he just stared into space, thinking.

But he was in Hartmann's office early the following morning. The computer center director had just arrived with his insulated cup of coffee. Thomlinson didn't even give him a chance to sit down.

"Marl, do you have an inventory of all of the computer equipment on campus?"

Hartmann thought a moment. "No, probably not all. If it's a purchase from capital funds, then yes, probably. But some departments buy stuff from their own budgets and never bother to tell us about it. That's too bad, 'cause they can't be covered under the school's insurance that way."

"Do you know who's got inkjet printers?"

"Are you planning to tell me what this is all about?"

Thomlinson considered this. "No, Marl, not right now. It's something I have to keep confidential in my role as counselor. But it *is* important."

Hartmann frowned a bit in concentration. "Lessee. Probably some faculty members have them in their apartments..."

"No, this'd be where a kid might get at it."

Hartmann put his head back and looked at the ceiling, as if maybe he kept a list there. "OK. There's one in the math office, the history office, the library, the Health Center... oh, yes, College Counseling has one...Alumni...no, they use the laser in the business office..." He looked at Thomlinson again. "That's about all I can come up with, Ray."

Thomlinson started for the door. "That's great, Marl, thanks, You've been an enormous help."

Hartmann saluted him with the coffee cup. "No problem. I'll let you know if I think of any more."

*OK, we can eliminate the math and history offices. There'd be someone in there all day, and if not, they'd be locked. Locked at night, too. Same goes for College Counseling. Health Center? Very unlikely. It'd be in the nurses' office, and there's always someone on duty there, or close by. I can't see the nurses allowing someone to sit at their desk and use a computer that probably has a lot of medical records on it.*

He looked at his watch: five before eight. Time for class.

At 9:06 he was in the library talking to Ruth Ord, the librarian.

"Well, no, not ordinarily, Ray. Once in a while we do make an exception, if it seems to be an emergency. Normally, the kids use the laser printer in the reading room, but sometimes it's not working, or there's a long line, or the kid just has a page or two and doesn't want to wait. But no, I can't recall anyone using it three nights ago." She gave him a brief smile. "Sorry."

He sighed inwardly. *Damn. This had been the best lead yet.* "That's okay," he assured her, "thanks anyway." He turned to go.

"Oh, wait..."

He turned back Ruth appeared to be considering something.

"You know…" she began slowly, using a finger motion to underline her words, "you know, a couple of nights ago, I was trying to print out some stuff and it ran out of ink. Well, I always keep spare cartridges, but I wouldn't dare try to put one in myself, afraid I might break something. Well, anyway, Charlie Borden was in the reading room, and I know he knows a lot about computers. So I asked him if he could change it for me while I took a stack of books upstairs to reshelve them. He was finished when I got back. I thanked him, but he just nodded, then picked up his books and left. Didn't ask me to sign a pass or anything. I…well, that's all, I guess."

Thomlinson had listened very attentively. Charles Borden was on his list.

"Did he seem upset about anything, Ruth?"

"Well, maybe not upset, just very serious. Didn't smile at all. Is he usually like that?"

"Thank you," he told her. "Thank you *very* much."

At 8:10 that evening he went to Borden's room in Burroughs. Charles, a chubby, introverted sophomore, was sitting on his bed, pulling books from his backpack. Thomlinson sat down beside him.

"Hey, Charlie. I got your note."

# ELAINE LUDLOW BROWNSMITH

922 Forest Ave.
Wilcox. MA 02134
Phone: (617) 555-0094
Email: esbrown@crestworld.net

OBJECTIVE: To work with a talented faculty and a forward-looking Board as the Head of a private school.

QUALIFICATIONS

I am, first and foremost, an educator. I have skills in teaching, administrating and organizing. Outside of the classroom, but still within the school environment, I have organized and participated in seminars and fundraising efforts. I have been a speaker at NAIS conferences. I have strong interpersonal skills and am not afraid of a challenge.

EDUCATION

1961-1964 B.A. in History, Columbia University
1964-1968 MA in Sociology, M. Ed., University of Pennsylvania
1971 University of Massachusetts, Ph.D. in History

EMPLOYMENT

1968-1971 Crestview School, Elliot, RI. Teacher of History
1971-1973 Talcott Community College, Talcott, MA. History Dept. Head
1973-1988 Webster College, Lancaster, MA. Professor of History and Sociology, later Social Science Department Head
1990-1994 Crawford University, Sangerville, NH. Director of Development
1994-pres. Linville Academy, Parker, CT. Asst. Headmaster, History Teacher, Alumni Office

PUBLICATIONS

"Educational Dichotomy: TAG in the Inner City." *Modern Education*, July 1978, pp. 22-30.
"Teaching to the Test: Long-term Benefits." *Forman Review*, vol. XII, no. 6, Feb. 1980, pp. 2-8.
*Historical Educational Models.* NJ: Bellows Press, 1989

# CONVOCATION ADDRESS, SEPTEMBER 18, 2000
## Elaine Brownsmith

Distinguished guests, members of the Board and faculty, friends and students:

To say that it is a pleasure to address you today is an understatement. I am excited by what I see around me—the people, the buildings, the campus—and stirred by the energy I feel. Just imagine—we are starting our third century here at Claxton Hall, one of the oldest college preparatory schools in the nation. None of us were here at its inception, and I hope none of us will be here at its demise. Claxton Hall is an institution, not as some of the students might occasionally use the word to describe it, but an institution in the truest and best sense of the word: an icon, if you will, something that has inserted itself into American history and the American mind.

As an institution, we are at the same time a role model. We've been asked many times, "Well, what's Claxton doing? How are they approaching this issue?" Believe me, when Claxton speaks, people listen.

The school is greater and bigger than any of us, even all together. Someone famous said that the world is but a stage, and we are the players on it. (I don't think that William Shakespeare was a Claxton graduate, but I'll have Mrs. Liston check the alumni records and get back to me.) In the same way, we are only actors on the Claxton stage, here but for a brief moment. Yet our influence can be profound, both while we are here and, especially in the case of the students, afterwards.

For it is not only the faculty, but especially the students who have made our institution what it is today. We, as teachers, may be remembered by one generation. But some of our students may be remembered by many. In some respects, then, we are the stage managers, the dressers, the prompters for our students. Their success is our success. They are worthy of our best efforts.

We have many traditions here at Claxton. During my first year as head, I experienced many of them, but I'm sure there are still others waiting to jump out at me. I think Faculty Appreciation Day and Spirit Night are great. I'm not so sure how I feel about "Head for a Day."

But, if you stop and think for a moment, Claxton is even bigger than its traditions. For as we graduated from a mere school to an Institution, so also did we move from tradition to Legacy.

That's what we're building now. Legacy. Our newest buildings are ten years old, our oldest student just nineteen. But we continue to build, every minute, every day. Claxton is a Legacy. You may or may not be able to pass a tradition on to the next generation; many disappear or are overcome by time and taste. But a legacy keeps growing. The campus has grown immensely since its first tentative steps in 1791. Claxton's reputation has grown geometrically along with it. Claxton has suffered hard times and enjoyed good periods.

As we begin our third century of service, I believe that Claxton's best times still lie ahead. It's going to be an exciting trip, and I'm looking forward to taking it with you.

Let's get to work!

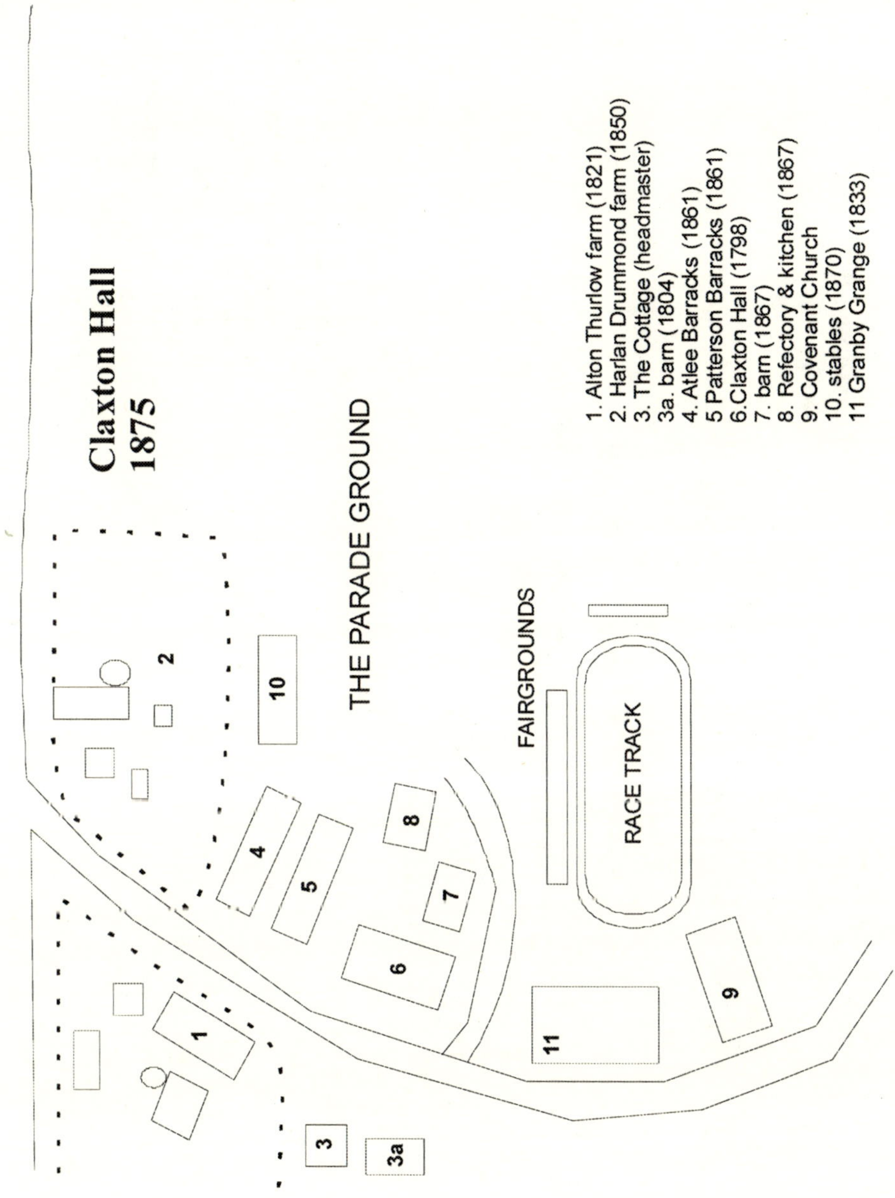
Claxton Hall
1875
THE PARADE GROUND
FAIRGROUNDS
RACE TRACK
1
2
3
3a
4
5
6
7
8
9
10
11
1. Alton Thurlow farm (1821)
2. Harlan Drummond farm (1850)
3. The Cottage (headmaster)
3a. barn (1804)
4. Atlee Barracks (1861)
5 Patterson Barracks (1861)
6.Claxton Hall (1798)
7. barn (1867)
8. Refectory & kitchen (1867)
9. Covenant Church
10. stables (1870)
11 Granby Grange (1833)

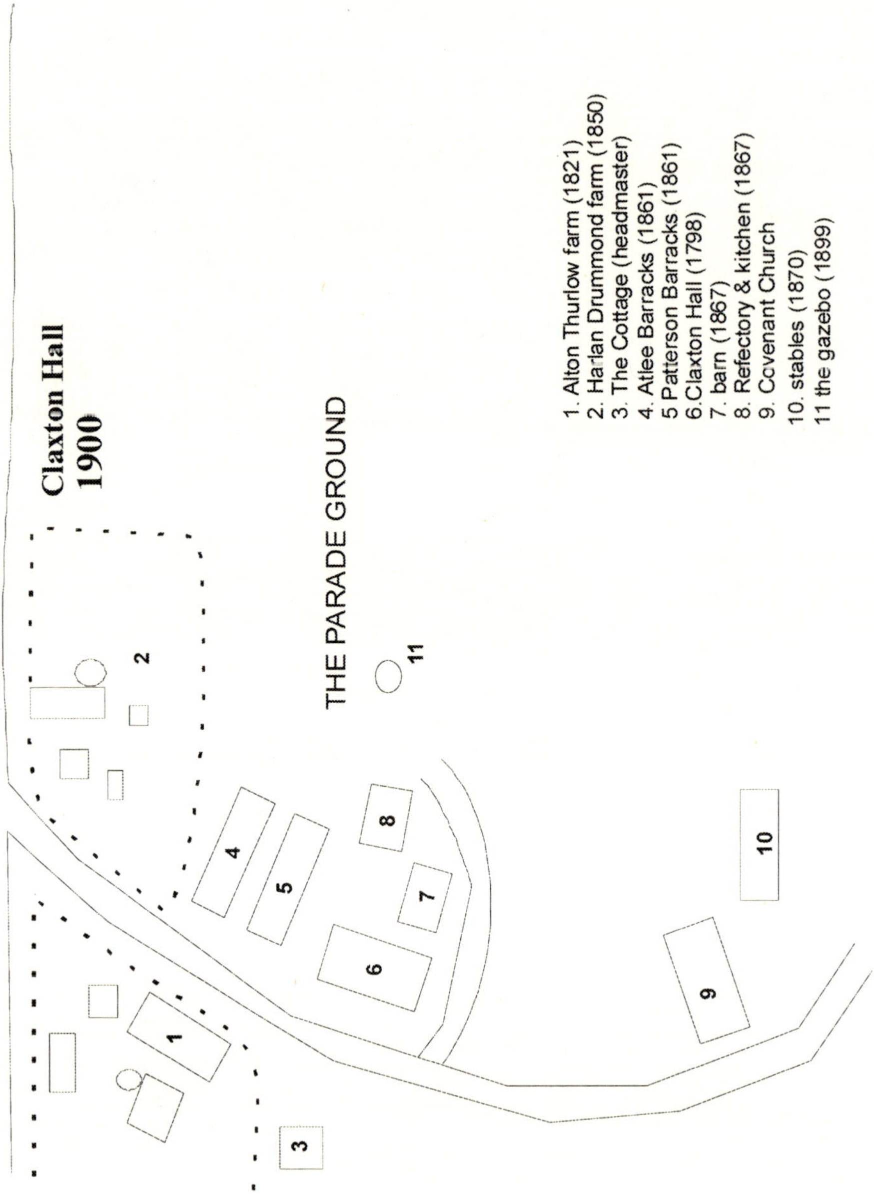
Claxton Hall
1900
THE PARADE GROUND
1. Alton Thurlow farm (1821)
2. Harlan Drummond farm (1850)
3. The Cottage (headmaster)
4. Atlee Barracks (1861)
5 Patterson Barracks (1861)
6.Claxton Hall (1798)
7. barn (1867)
8. Refectory & kitchen (1867)
9. Covenant Church
10. stables (1870)
11 the gazebo (1899)

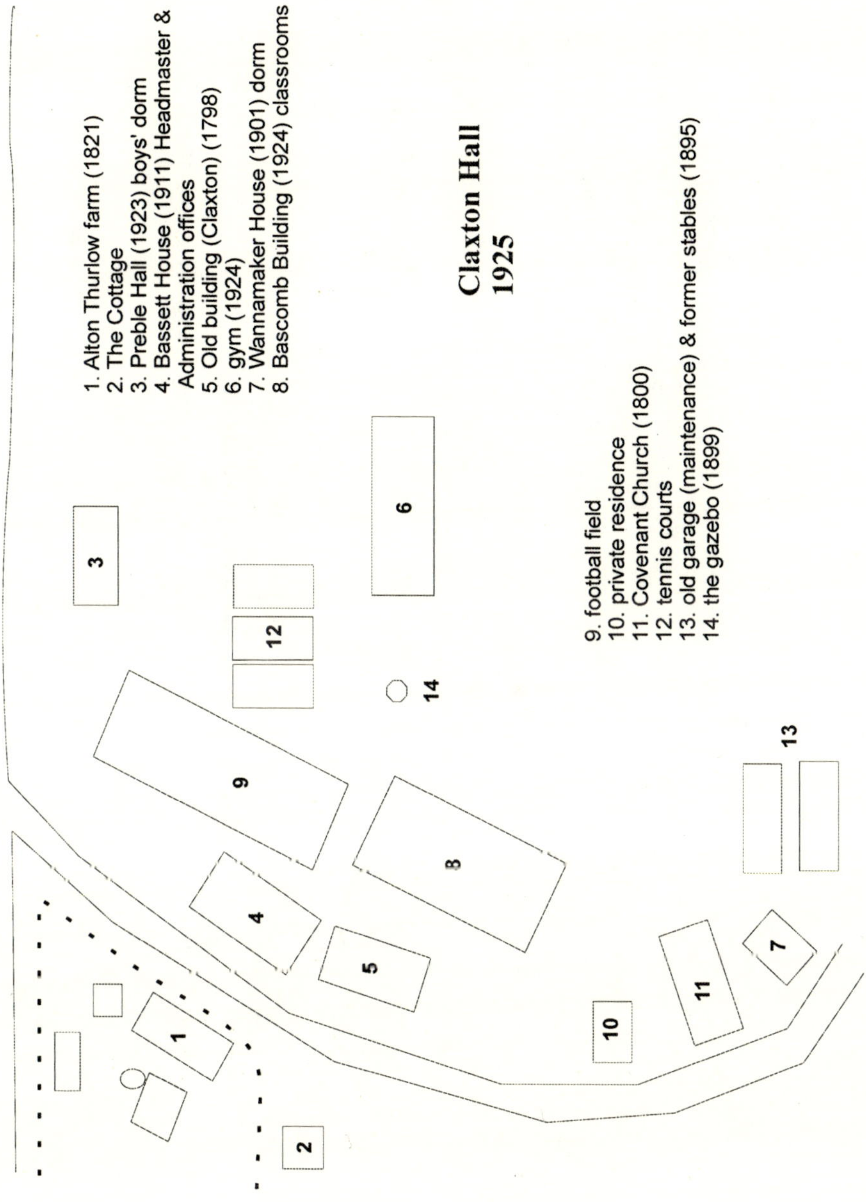
1. Alton Thurlow farm (1821)
2. The Cottage
3. Preble Hall (1923) boys' dorm
4. Bassett House (1911) Headmaster & Administration offices
5. Old building (Claxton) (1798)
6. gym (1924)
7. Wannamaker House (1901) dorm
8. Bascomb Building (1924) classrooms
Claxton Hall
1925
9. football field
10. private residence
11. Covenant Church (1800)
12. tennis courts
13. old garage (maintenance) & former stables (1895)
14. the gazebo (1899)

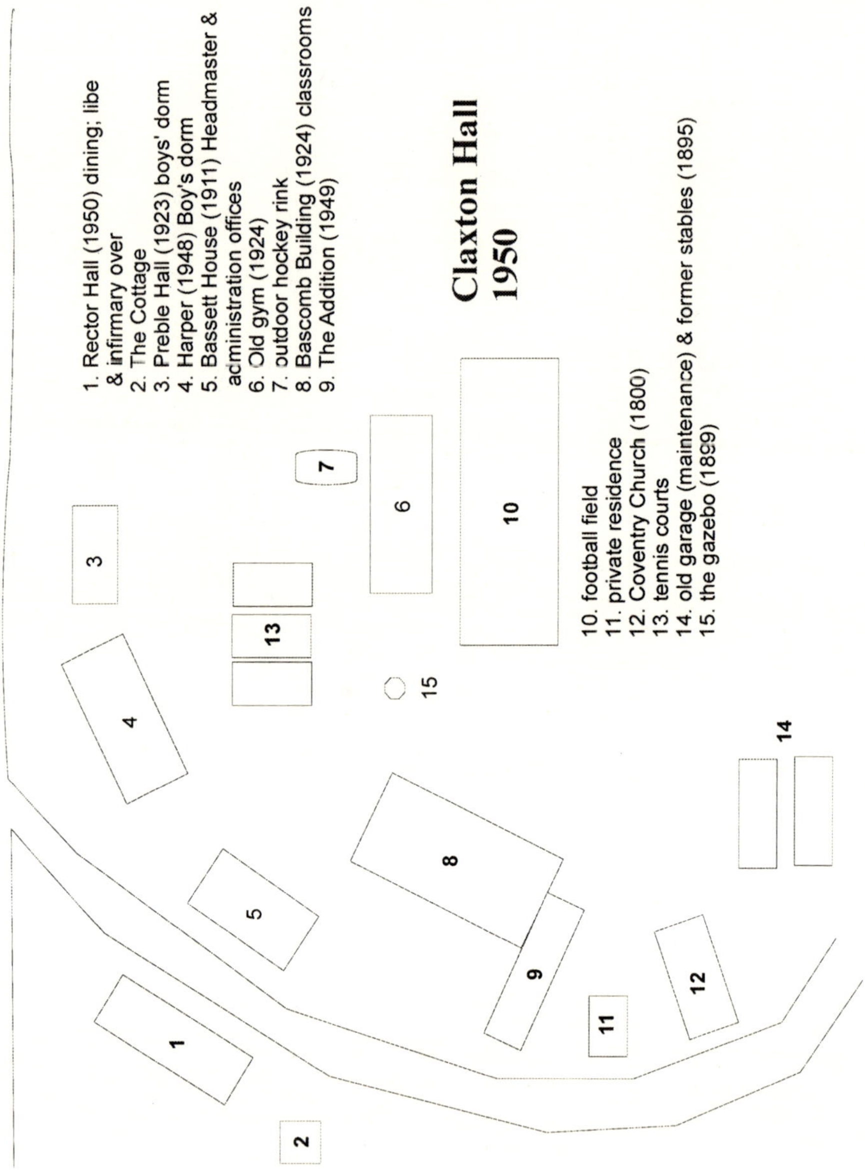

1. Rector Hall (1950) dining; libe
& infirmary over
2. The Cottage
3. Preble Hall (1923) boys' dorm
4. Harper (1948) Boy's dorm
5. Bassett House (1911) Headmaster &
administration offices
6. Old gym (1924)
7. outdoor hockey rink
8. Bascomb Building (1924) classrooms
9. The Addition (1949)
Claxton Hall
1950
10. football field
11. private residence
12. Coventry Church (1800)
13. tennis courts
14. old garage (maintenance) & former stables (1895)
15. the gazebo (1899)
1
2
3
4
5
6
7
8
9
10
11
12
13
14
15

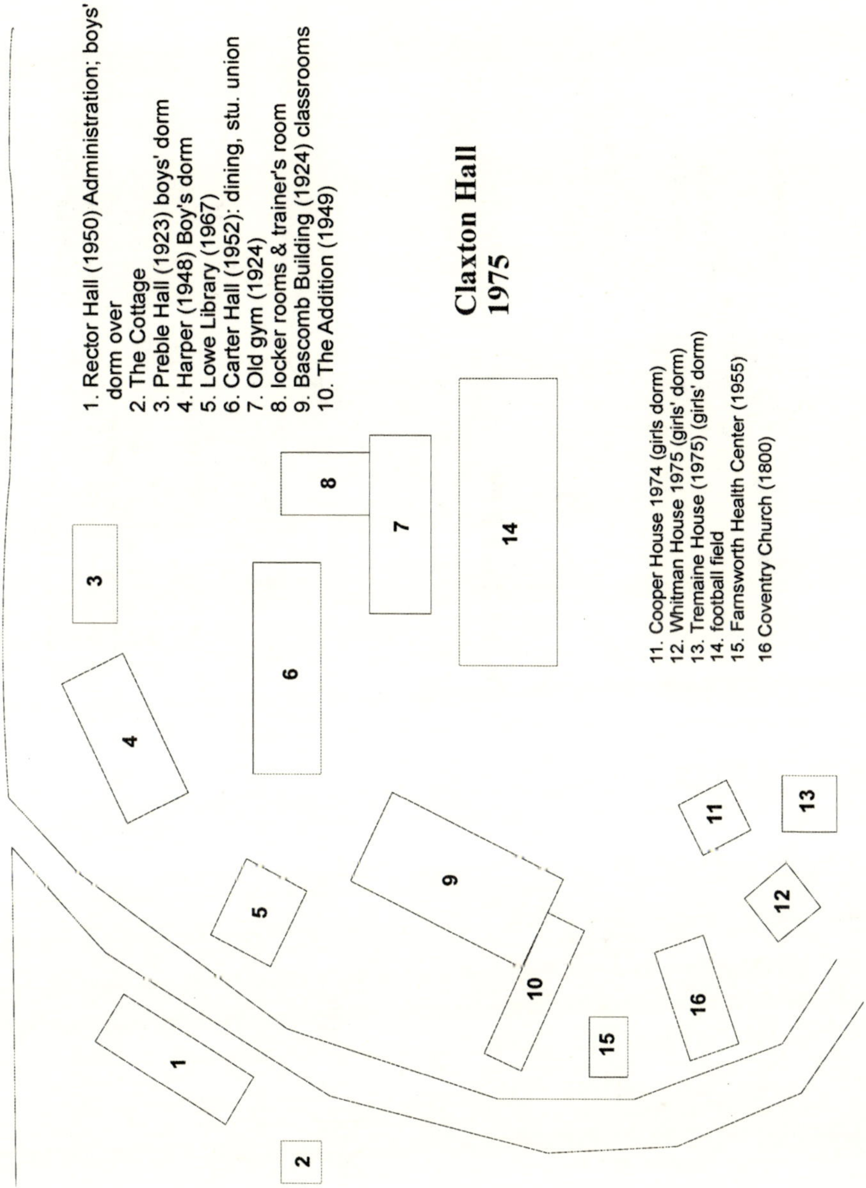
Claxton Hall
1975
1. Rector Hall (1950) Administration; boys' dorm over
2. The Cottage
3. Preble Hall (1923) boys' dorm
4. Harper (1948) Boy's dorm
5. Lowe Library (1967)
6. Carter Hall (1952): dining, stu. union
7. Old gym (1924)
8. locker rooms & trainer's room
9. Bascomb Building (1924) classrooms
10. The Addition (1949)
11. Cooper House 1974 (girls dorm)
12. Whitman House 1975 (girls' dorm)
13. Tremaine House (1975) (girls' dorm)
14. football field
15. Farnsworth Health Center (1955)
16 Coventry Church (1800)
1
2
3
4
5
6
7
8
9
10
11
12
13
14
15
16

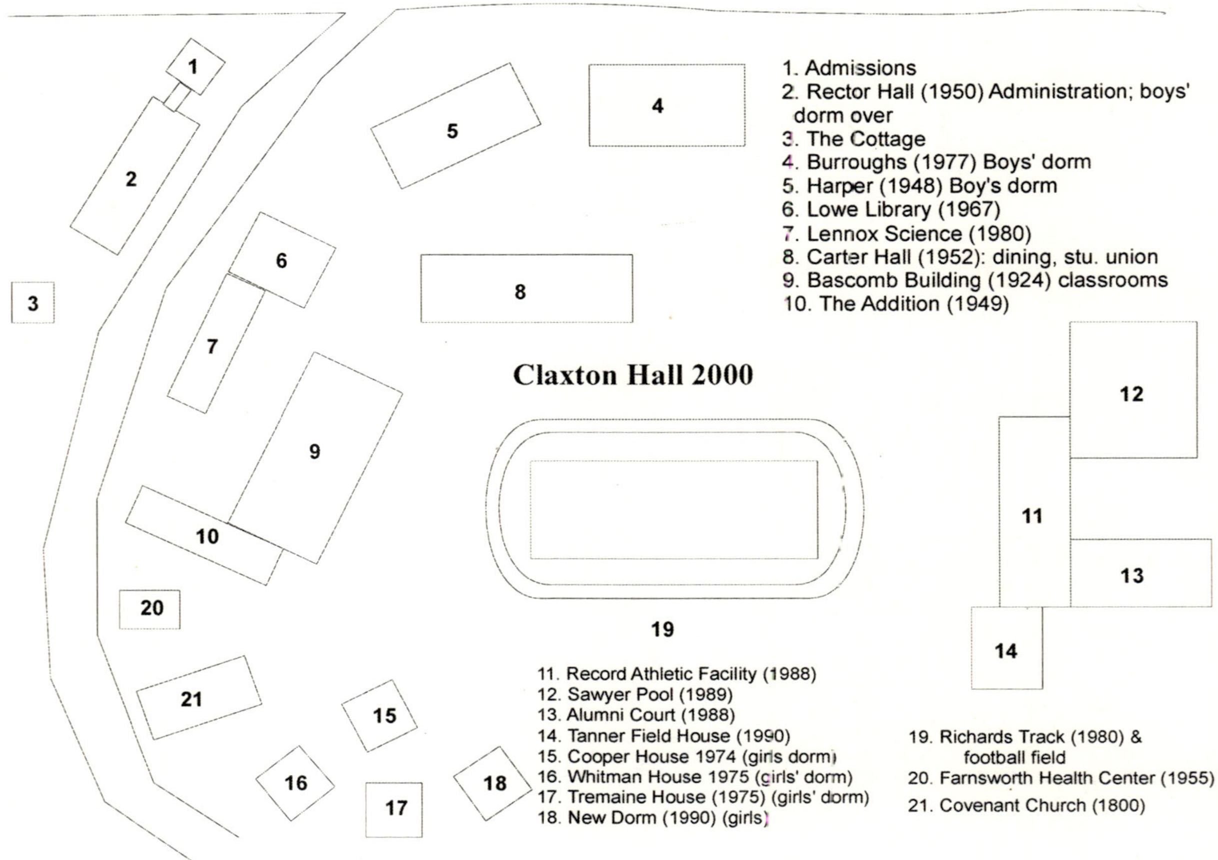
Claxton Hall 2000
1
2
3
4
5
6
7
8
9
10
11
12
13
14
15
16
17
18
19
20
21
1. Admissions
2. Rector Hall (1950) Administration; boys' dorm over
3. The Cottage
4. Burroughs (1977) Boys' dorm
5. Harper (1948) Boy's dorm
6. Lowe Library (1967)
7. Lennox Science (1980)
8. Carter Hall (1952): dining, stu. union
9. Bascomb Building (1924) classrooms
10. The Addition (1949)
11. Record Athletic Facility (1988)
12. Sawyer Pool (1989)
13. Alumni Court (1988)
14. Tanner Field House (1990)
15. Cooper House 1974 (girls dorm)
16. Whitman House 1975 (girls' dorm)
17. Tremaine House (1975) (girls' dorm)
18. New Dorm (1990) (girls)
19. Richards Track (1980) & football field
20. Farnsworth Health Center (1955)
21. Covenant Church (1800)

Printed in the United States
39681LVS00003B/82-105

9 781591 138495